# HERS

# ALONE IN

# ORANGE RAIN

TRACEY ICETON

CinnamonPress

INDEPENDENT INNOVATIVE INTERNATIONAL

Published by Cinnamon Press
Meirion House, Tanygrisiau, Blaenau Ffestiniog
Gwynedd LL41 3SU www.cinnamonpress.com

The right of Tracey Iceton to be identified as author of this work has been asserted by her in accordance with the Copyright, Designs and Patent Act, 1988. © 2017 Tracey Iceton. ISBN 978-1-910836-76-7
British Library Cataloguing in Publication Data. A CIP record for this book can be obtained from the British Library.
Designed and typeset in Garamond by Cinnamon Press. Cover design by Adam Craig © Adam Craig.
Cinnamon Press is represented by Inpress and by the Welsh Books Council in Wales. Printed in Poland.
The publisher gratefully acknowledges the support of the Welsh Books Council.

## Acknowledgements

This book owes its existence to the following people:
Principally to Prof. Michael Green and Dr Fiona Shaw of Northumbria University without whose input this novel would be a pale shadow of the work it became under their expert guidance and insightful feedback. Jan Fortune at Cinnamon, who continues to keep faith with my Celtic Colours trilogy, and who unquestioningly embraced my blending of fact and fiction in this novel, enabling me to tell the story as I felt it had to be told. Danny Morrison who kindly took the time to discuss the premise of this novel with me and who offered suggestions that shaped the plot as well as continuing to support my writing. Jim McIlmurray for welcoming me in to view his unique collection of Troubles memorabilia, for recounting his experiences of the Troubles and for the useful contacts he helped me reach out to.

Maírtín Ó Meachair of Teach an Phiarsaigh (Pearse's Cottage) in Rosmuc, Galway who was kind and generous enough to, again, correct my use of Irish throughout the novel. Hilary Bryans who worked as a journalist in Northern Ireland during the 1980s and kindly shared her memories of life there during that difficult period with me, adding many authentic details to the book.

Fellow PGRs at Northumbria who provided feedback, encouragement and alcohol when needed, in particular Rowan, Jo, Jane, David and Jen. Also, all the staff in the English and Creative Writing department at Northumbria who supported me, helping me make the most of my post grad research opportunity and giving me the chance to develop and share my creative practice for this novel. To all those writers of works creative, critical and socio-political from whose texts I drew both information and inspiration during the research and writing process of the doctorate from which this novel emerged. David Willock who both proof read the novel and generously praised it for its portrayal of the futility of war.

Pen Pearson, poet and author of *Bloomsbury's Late Rose*, who, having read the final draft of the novel, offered what I take to be the highest praise one author can give another when she said it was a book she wished she had written. John Dean, noted crime writer, who found the time to read the novel and who so generously offered a glowing endorsement of my work. Clare Wren who, besides reading the novel, supporting my writing and sharing her memories of the period with me, also made a vital contribution to the accuracy of my depiction of Catholic mass and wedding services. Without her input those scenes would have been woefully erroneous and greatly lacking in significance. Natalie Scott, whose long standing friendship and writer's expertise were both essential to me during the arduous process of writing, redrafting and critiquing this novel for my doctoral thesis.

My family, both Johnsons and Icetons, who continue to unfailingly support my dream of being a writer. Thanks to them I can continue to live the dream. My husband, John, to whom I owe the greatest debt of thanks. For the three years it took me to develop this book he maintained a steady course, encouraging me to do the same, even when it felt like the ship would sink. His unconditional support of my writing is deserving of so much more than I can offer in these lines. Thank you. Thank you. Thank you.

And finally, to all those women and men whose Troubles tragedies are retold in these pages.

# Author's Note

Unlike *Green Dawn at St Enda's*, which was born in the emotive setting of Kilmainham Gaol's execution yard, *Herself Alone* materialised when fellow writer Natalie Scott suggested I devote part two of my Celtic Colours Trilogy to exploring the war from a female combatant's perspective. I wondered if this was possible, plausible. Did women fight for the Republican cause? And if so what was it like to be a woman in the IRA?

Research answered the first question with an emphatic yes. There are twelve women on the IRA Roll of Honour; records of thirty-plus imprisoned for Republican activities. Official numbers are small but unconfirmed accounts report a 50-50 male/female attendance at IRA training camps,

And the second question? How would women volunteers think, act and feel while engaged in actions most cannot comprehend? What would bring them to the armed struggle? Were media portrayals of such women as the dupes of their male counterparts accurate? Some answers can be found in the few non-fiction books exploring the experiences of women freedom-fighters. I drew on these sources to create a character, but my protagonist is a fiction. This novel presents one possible account of what it might have been like to be a woman in the PIRA during the decade that encompassed the shooting of unarmed volunteer, Mairead Farrell, on Gibraltar.

In common with *Green Dawn*, *Herself Alone* also recounts real events, although far more recent, occurring between 1966-1988. Where facts were known I used them as accurately as possible within the scope of a fictional work. Where gaps existed I filled them with what I felt could have happened. Some events are entirely fictional. to greater or lesser degrees, from similar incidents, which did occur. Anything anachronistic is intentional and in response to the constraints of a fictional narrative. Real people feature here, but they are written as I imagined them from what I have learnt of their lives, transforming them into literary characters.

Unlike *Green Dawn*, *Herself Alone* is a telling, not a retelling, for the simple reason that, seemingly, no one has before dared to tell this story. That women do take up arms for their political ideologies is an undeniable truth. I hope in writing this novel I have gone some way towards communicating the lived experience of the women who gave up everything for their beliefs. They have too long been silenced by narratives content to portray them as victims or femme fatales. I offer such portrayals no quarter.

*Tracey Iceton, 2017*

'Every woman gives her life for what she believes…
One life is all we have
and we live it as we believe in living it.
But to sacrifice what you are and to live without belief,
that is a fate more terrible than dying.'
*Joan of Arc*

# HERSELF ALONE
# IN ORANGE RAIN

# Dublin—8<sup>th</sup> March, 1966

## **Explosion Destroys Nelson's Pillar**
## **Mixed Reaction as Imperial Monument Falls**

An explosion on O'Connell Street has destroyed Nelson's Pillar, causing minor damage to surrounding businesses. The incident, thought to be the work of Republicans, reduced the nineteenth century monument to rubble late last night.

No one was injured but falling masonry caused some damage, including crushing a parked taxi. The driver, Steve Maughan (19), escaped injury, having got out of the vehicle prior to the explosion. No group has yet claimed responsibility. The area has been cordoned off and will be inspected later by structural engineers.

The Pillar, erected in 1808 to commemorate the Battle of Trafalgar, has been the source of controversy, with many calling for its removal on practical, aesthetic and nationalist grounds. One local resident, Mr Patrick Finnighan (66), commented, 'It was an insult to 1916.'

There is speculation that the IRA bombed the Pillar to mark the fiftieth anniversary of the Easter Rising, due to be commemorated next month.

The boys called to see me, making sure the ould fella was keeping well and letting me know the scéal\*.

'Mr Finnighan, how are you?'

'Grand. Yourself, Frank?'

'Fine. How's the wee 'un?'

A floorboard behind me creaked. It was herself, coming to investigate and wordlessly answer Frank's question.

'She's such a fair thing,' Frank crooned as she came to me, one soft fist clamped over the ould silver locket I let her wear, the other slipping into my leathery palm, sharp eyes seeing us and quick mind knowing us.

Caught in her gaze, Frank ruffled his hair in that frazzled gesture of his. Bursting to laugh, I watched the pair of 'em battle once again to get the measure of each other, certain

---

\* news or story

9

Frank'd crack first, as always. And so he did, reaching into his pocket for the usual truce token, a lollipop.

She thanked him with the Irish I taught her, 'Go raibh maith agat♣,' put the lolly away for later and went to her room to play.

With her gone Frank set to telling me how they planned to commemorate the fiftieth. I thought it a grand idea. Decided I'd be there to watch and her wee self with me. See, I knew by then she was going soon. I had to pack her off with something more valuable than that useless silver trinket. Sure, she loved it, loathed to take it off, but it was worthless now, engraved with initials that had amounted to nothing. I needed a better bequest. Taking her to watch the boys at work was just the job, chance to show her that life's a struggle, let her see the truth of what I'd been teaching her about fighting what's not fair. I went to wet the tea. When I came back the tray shook in my dothery codger's hands; the boys took it for ould age but 'twas the thrill of my secret plan, making me slop muddy pools onto the doily.

Three nights later I had her ready, muffled in winter boots and red duffle coat; the locket sat against the scarlet like a medal. As we stood in the hall, an odd pair, she clutched my hand, wondering, I bet, at the to-do. We shuffled out into the night as the hall clock chimed twelve.

She held my hand the whole way. As we closed in on the GPO I clung harder to her. I was afraid, in that darkness, of what was there, buried under a heap of time. I saw the bodies, heard the shots, felt the burning end of that unfair fight coming on me again. She musta sensed my fear, kept squeezing my twisted fingers with her mittened hand. I swallowed tears.

We tucked ourselves out of sight in Henry Street. Peering round the corner I saw Nelson, waiting on us, leering down. The eejit thought he'd seen us off in '16. He should've known we'd be back. And so we were, me shivering in the shadows, the boys out there laying the charge. They knew what they

---

♣ Thank you

were about sure enough but I didn't much like the look of them in their Army clobber; heavy boots, blue jeans, dark jackets: balaclavas. I thought of what I'd worn: a kilt and a brat, pinned with a pierced sun brooch; a green uniform topped by a slouch hat; a fedora and trench coat, the length of it hiding a rifle. We'd no need of masks in my day.

The boys by the Pillar were set. I clocked Frank by that daft hair ruffling habit of his; even masked up he couldn't stop hand from patting head. But then they got down to it, Frank pulling a sheet of paper from his pocket and reading it aloud. The night carried the words to me: the Proclamation. But it wasn't the same as when I'd heard it read there before. The speech wasn't his and your man's words were too big for Frank's mouth. Then they held a minute's silence for fallen comrades, praying like the good wee Catholic boys they are. I bowed my head, thinking of poor Mick Collins, how we'd jigged in the street, ducking British bullets as we laid the charge, trying our damnedest to blow ould Nelson to hell. God and I never had any time for each other but Mick and me were solid, until the treaty.

At last one of them produced a lighter, sparked the flame. Rusted joints groaning, I crouched down to the wee 'un, pulling her in close.

'Watch!' I told her as he lit the fuse.

It burst like a star and fled into the blackness. We traced its flight, breath held. There was one almighty bang and one dazzling flash. I felt the sharp snap of shock fired through her, a gun's recoil, but not a peep of fear passed her lips. The street lit up in furious orange; her green eyes shone, eager and alive. Down came the bollocks, in a rocky, rubbly rain. The boys cheered, punching their fists in the air. In our hidey-hole I murmured, 'Éire go bráth*!' before turning us to the long walk home.

It was late when we got in. She'd said hardly a word. I put her to bed, tucking her in tight. One hand closed comfortingly over the locket, she stroked my crinkled cheek with the other.

'Why did those men break that wee man, Daideo?'

---

* Ireland forever

'Sure, it wasn't fair, him being there, so they were doing something about it. Like I've always told you to, Caoilainn.'

'Was he a bad man?'

'He was.'

'Silly Daideo, he wasn't real.'

'I know, love, but you mind what I say: if things aren't fair you fight 'til you make 'em fair. Do you understand?'

She puzzled it out a moment then nodded.

'Good girl. Now to sleep with you.'

She curled up. I reached the door but she wasn't done with me.

'Why was Aidie's daddy wearing a mask tonight, Daideo?'

Jesus, thinks I, she's a smart one, clocking Frank like that.

'Sometimes it's better if people don't know it's you doing the fighting, love.'

'Why?'

'So they don't try to stop you.'

She nodded again. 'Are there lots of bad people?'

'Some, but they won't hurt you as long as you don't let 'em. Remember that.'

I'd said my piece, too much of it maybe, but I couldn't let her go without being sure she understood.

'O.K., Daideo. Can we go to the park again tomorrow and see the ducks?'

'We can, unless it's raining, then we'll get the colouring books out, eh?'

'Can Aidie come?'

'We'll ask his da.'

'Aidie says if you feed them too much bread they explode.'

I cursed myself for letting her play so often with Frank's youngest, little bugger, filling her head with nonsense when I had important lessons for her.

'Does he now?'

'Why do the ducks eat bread if it's bad for them?'

'Because no one's told them they shouldn't.'

'That's not fair, is it, Daideo?'

'I suppose not.'

'Someone should tell them, like you tell me. That's fairer. They'll know not to be eating it. I'm going to tell them. I'll tell the ducks they're not to eat any more bread. I won't let the ducks explode.' She sat up, her wee angel's face screwed down with the fight in her. I saw the past and the future in that look she gave off.

'You do that, a chailín bhig*.' I kissed her goodnight. Left her lying in the darkness, planning a grand wee speech to the ducks. Aye, it was time she went.

Two days later the Free State army were in town to tidy up, demolishing what was left of the Pillar. That was the day the Ryans came to take what was left of me. It was best for her. She drove off with them, wrapped in her red coat, sucking the IRA lolly she'd saved for later.

---

\* little one

# Plymouth—14<sup>th</sup> October, 1980

I step back from the canvas, blinking eyes dry from straining over tiny brushstrokes, stretching shoulders cramped from fighting the whiteness of a painting in progress. Picking up my creased copy of the assignment brief I stare at the Plymouth School of Art and Design logo until it blurs then drag my eyes down to instructions I've read into memory but am still battling:

## Family and Childhood

Explore the themes of family and childhood. The artwork may take any form/style but must be inspired by an artist you have studied on this course. The piece must include some representation (symbolic or literal) of yourself and at least three of the following:
- Siblings, parents or grandparents
- Family home
- Childhood games/activities
- Memorable childhood places
- Childhood playmates
- School
- Birthdays or other family celebrations

This piece is 30% of your second year marks.

I stare at my name, written in spiky pencil letters top left: Kaylynn Ryan. I mouth the four syllables, kay-lin-rye-ann, that tell me who I am and wonder again if what I'm painting is fair, to them or me. I toss the paper down. Fourteen months and four hundred miles between us but I'm still not free of them. I glance around the studio. The others are cracking on; this is no big deal to them and they wouldn't get why it is for me, which is why I haven't bothered telling them.

Col and Rich are doing something with clay. Keith's gone for a collage and Stu for some modern construction using bric-a-brac. Baz's tapping a Warhol vein and Jeff's being ironic with Hopper. Alex hasn't even bothered showing up. Mr Simons wafts into the studio, mug in hand.

'How are we all?'

There's a muttered reply. I glance at him, at Alex's empty place and back at Mr Simons.

'Anyone seen Alex?' he asks, looking at me.

'He's doing field research, for an installation,' Col says.

'In the Field Head,' I correct, 'for a pint.'

Mr Simons nods like he'll do something about that later. He won't. Not as long as Alex's mummy and daddy keep coughing up generous donations to the art department. I shake my head, reminding myself to think tactical. It pisses me off that the system is so easily corrupted but their money buys us better paints, easels that don't collapse, sable hair brushes. It can't buy Alex any talent. Shame. Pity. Tragedy. I'm still smiling as Mr Simons starts his rounds, heading first to Barb, Sandy and Lisa's knot of industry.

Sandy's painting onto a tapestry canvas that she'll embroider over later, her idea of empowerment she says, reclaiming the feminine arts. Yesterday Mr Simons praised her 'modern feminist approach to liberating female expression'. Last night I overheard her telling the other two she's worried her boyfriend'll dump her because her boobs aren't big enough. I considered piping up with the adage 'anything more than a handful's a waste' but they don't get stuff like that. Or people like me.

I pick up my fine brush and go back to the intricate tartan pattern adorning the ducks clustered around the pond in the canvas's bottom left corner. Just because I'd rather not do this doesn't mean I won't.

Mr Simons clacks across the room on slippery brogues. I feel the heat from his body as he takes up position behind me, viewing my work.

Everything is outlined and bits of it painted. It's going to be good, maybe even great, when it's done. I've adopted Dali because surrealist symbolism is the only way to paint my childhood. My brushwork has the Catalan master's accurate touch, the reality that battles hard against the weird in his work and, now, mine. The background is vague mountains that could be Catalonia or Scotland. The foreground's rundown terraced street merges into a well-groomed city park.

Half finished there's enough for Mr Simons to see the whole, disapprove of the aesthetic but grudgingly admire the skill.

'Very vivid. Talk me through this, Kaylynn.'

'I thought art was 'beyond explanation',' I remind him.

'The external moderator will expect you to be able to discuss your work,' he says. 'This is your family home?'

He points to the row of cowering houses that falls off the right hand edge of the canvas. The red brick is soot-blackened, the windows are grey-grimed, the impression that of dereliction and imminent demolition. Only one house is a home, evidenced by an empty milk bottle on the step, the peeling-paint door ajar and three figures on the kerb in front of it.

'Yes.' One of them. The one that provokes the fewest questions about a childhood spent championing causes and fighting for freedoms. I should've let myself off, painted an easy lie, suburban and semi-detached. Or maybe I should've red-lined it and rendered resplendent the dented Transit van whose petrol-fumed interior gave me headaches; the caravan so cold icicles hung inside it, unfestive decorations; the fifteenth floor squat that wasn't worth the climb or the castle commune that sheltered a dozen free-love couples, their placards and their children.

'And these are your parents?'

Standing in front of the house are a man and woman, him in jeans, her in a floral smock. Where their faces should be there are protest posters, his of the Socialist Workers Party, hers of the Women's Lib. movement. Both share the raised fist logo, hers inside the ♀ symbol and his on a red background.

'Yes.'

'Their faces…?'

'Representative. Signifiers.'

'They're activists, are they?' he asks. There's no need for me to reply. He coughs. Continues. 'And this?'

He waves his hand at the third figure, sandwiched between the mother and father. It's constructed from slogans and symbols: a CND badge for a head; arms and legs made of words (free women's bodies, capitalism is slavery, fur is murder, make love not war) and dressed in torn jeans and a T-shirt with the ying-yang Anti-apartheid movement logo on it. The parents have their arms stretched out as though holding the hands of the child that's not a child. There aren't any hands to hold; I'm not there. I've released myself back into captivity.

I loop my fingers through the chain around my neck, winding it up until I reach the locket, and stroke the shallow dent on the back with my thumb. 'It's symbolic.'

'Of?'

'Their child.'

Mr Simons scrats at his goatee and moves on, indicating the image's central portion which shows the flesh-and-blood me, my fair hair cropped, my red duffle-coated back turned to the viewer. I'm three or four. Next to me is a boy not much older. Around us the flock of tartan ducks, waiting for my brush to fledge their check-and-line feathers, clap their wings. On the ground beside us is the stooping shadow of an old man I can't paint any other way because I don't remember him properly. But he was there, once.

'Is this also symbolic?'

I won't tell him it's simpler than that: just a happy memory.

I trudge home to my digs through teatime twilight.

Around the corner a terrace of houses banks up like a cliff-face, four storey Georgian grandeur run down to twentieth century scruff. I stop at no. twenty-five and squint at my attic room. Grey light masks blistered paint, mould-coated rendering and cracked glass. I climb the steps and enter the draughty hallway. Breath held to keep out the familiar stench of boiled cabbage and piss, I traipse upstairs. On the top landing I wrestle my door open, stumble in, dump my rucksack, hang my jacket and flick on the light.

Blue-white fluorescence stabs my eyeballs. Crumb-covered plates and mucky mugs sneer at me from the table. I stride over and grab three cups. As I lift them a misplaced patch of darkness on the table snags my eye. I stare. The dark patch becomes two oblongs, joined at right-angles. My heart crams up against the bottom of my throat. The mugs slip from my pincered grip. I cast off for explanations. My brain dumps everything, smearing images, fusing sounds; colours become blackness and noise silence.

I extend a finger. When I touch it, it will burst and vanish. My finger presses down. Cold hard metal presses back. There is no pop. The gun is real.

Someone flushes my toilet. I spin round to face the bathroom door. A man emerges. His eyes leap to me, drop to the gun, my finger stroking the stubby barrel. The glance forbids, cautions, tempts, suggests: don't walk on the grass; no smoking; don't press that red button. Better in my hand than his. I coil my fingers around the gun. It resists, dragging its weight as I lift it, metal fighting a magnetic draw. I pull it out and point it at him. He raises his arms, hands open, palms facing me, cautioning me like you would a running child.

'Whoa there, go steady. That thing's loaded.'

His words lilt with an accent: 'dat' and 'ting'.

Scanning him from toe to top I note the scuffed boots, raggy jeans, scuffed leather jacket, two days' stubble, blue eyes ringed with tiredness, dark unbrushed hair, tall and thin, scar on his cheek, about twenty.

'Ah, come on, now,' he coaxes.

I can't speak. I'm not breathing. I fight to keep my hand steady, the gun from shaking. It's heavy, solid. Sweat slicks my palm making the handle slippery. We've been like this for seconds, minutes: hours. I've forgotten how it started. I don't know how I'm meant to end it.

'Who are you? What do you want?'

'Do you not remember me?'

I've seen those eyes before, somewhere, somewhen. Mute, I sift back through days, weeks, months, trying to locate him. He blinks twice.

'It's me, Aiden, Aiden O'Neill. Jesus, I thought you'd remember wee Aidie.'

I keep sifting; years fall through my fingers. Two kids run towards a pond. Ducks quack and flap.

'How are ya, Caoilainn?'

He says 'Kee-lun!', not 'Kay-lin'. The syllables buffet me.

'That's not how you say it.'

'Sure, it is. A-o-i is 'ee' in Irish.' His words have a teacher's firmness. It fades. His eyes dart about. 'You used to...'

'I don't... I can't...' I do. I can. Don't want to. Am afraid to. A sing-songy voice chants in my ear: c-a-o i-l-a i-n-n, Caoilainn fair and Caoilainn slender; that's my name, so sweet and tender. Whose voice? Whose rhyme?

'I've something for you. I'm just after reaching into my pocket.' He inches a hand inside his jacket. I tighten my grip on the gun, arm straining against the weight. He withdraws a square of card, pinched between finger and thumb.

I step forward, snatch the card and retreat, keeping the gun pointed at him. Flipping the card over, I see a black and white image of an old man and a young girl. Behind them is the columned entrance of a grand building. To their left squats a mound of rubble topped with an oversized stone head. Fluttering panic settles in my throat. The man wears a shabby suit and macintosh. The girl is wrapped in a dark duffle coat, booties and mittens. I know the coat is crimson. The girl is me. So the man holding my hand must be my time-shadowed grandfather.

When I look up Aiden's closed in on me, has his hand on the gun. He tugs gently; I let go. He pulls out a chair and nudges me onto it. I don't see him put the gun away, it's just gone and he's ruffling his hair. He takes out cigarettes, lighting one and giving it to me because either I smoke or I'm about to start.

'I'll put the kettle on.' He goes to the sink.

Fixed on the photograph, I hear water gushing, a click as he lights the stove. The kettle whistles. He sets down two mugs, fetches the milk. I smell old sweat and wonder when he last showered and changed, slept in a bed: put down his gun.

Why the hell does he have a gun?

He sits opposite. We stare at each other. I study the scar. It's three inches long and curved like a smile. There's a fresh redness to it. Guided by my stare, he rubs a finger along it.

'Sorry for giving you a scare. I'd no business leaving that thing on your table.'

'Why'd you even have it?'

'Just in case.'

'Of what?'

He doesn't reply.

'You should be more careful.'

'Aye, me ma's always saying what a slapdash bugger I am but I never thought you'd go pointing it at me. I thought you'd remember me.' A cough rasps in his throat. 'You shouldn't go aiming guns at people unless you're meaning to shoot them.'

'What makes you think I wasn't?'

He riffles fingers through his hair again. I return to the photo, calculating my age to about four, making it a fourteen year old snap.

'We used to feed the ducks.'

'On the Green.' He grins.

'In Glasgow.'

His grin shrinks. 'Sure, it was Dublin. That's O'Connell Street.' He taps the man in the picture. 'Your...'

At the mention of Dublin a lost word appears.

'Daideo.'

'Aye, your granddaddy.'

My memories aren't where I left them. 'I don't understand.' I tap ash off my cigarette with shaking fingers. 'We lived in Scotland, moved to England when I was nearly four.'

'That's what they've had you thinking?' Aiden asks. He drops his gaze, gulps his tea. 'Do you not remember Ireland at all?'

'I remember the duck pond.' I look at his eyes. 'You.' I take up the photograph. 'Rainy days colouring-in. My name, the way you said it. The rest is hazy, a dream I know I've had but can't recall. Jesus Christ, this isn't happening.' I sit back, close my eyes, reach down through the blackness and see a single point of light, fizzing like a dying firework. It runs off into darkness; there's a loud bang, a white flash. Black turns orange and a small man falls from a great height. A voice rasps, 'If things aren't fair, you fight 'em.' His words. Daideo.

Stroking the photograph, I feel skin, warm, rough and crinkly. 'He died after we moved.'

'He didn't, Caoilainn.'

'Shit.' I lean forward, sick and dizzy. 'I don't understand.'

20

Aiden takes my hand. 'I'm sorry for bringing this to you but we had to. He's not well, not well at all.'

'So they fell out? And now he's dying he wants to make it up?'

Aiden shakes his head. 'He doesn't know I'm here. He won't have doctors so we don't know how bad he is, but it's plain he's ill. We've been worrying about what to do.' A frown creases his forehead.

'We?'

'Me and my ma and da, especially Da. He's been frantic about it, so he has. Feared of your granddaddy being on his own when he...' Aiden withdraws his hand and drags on his cigarette.

Coldness spreads through me. I swirl my mug. A picture develops in the darkroom of my memory, of a few more lads, dressed like Aiden but with balaclavas. I'm not sure it's real. Then one of them moves a hand to his head, trying to ruffle hair covered by a woolly mask. My mouth fills with the sweet sharp tang of a strawberry lollipop.

'Your dad...'

'You remember him?'

'He always had sweets for us.'

'Aye, and you got the strawberry ones. Dead jealous of that, so I was.'

I pick over charred memories, shuffling and sorting until there's something readable.

'So you've taken up the family business.'

He fiddles with his cigarettes.

'The IRA,' I press.

'Why would you be saying a thing like that?'

'You're Irish. You have a gun. It's not the *Times* crossword.' I jab at the photograph. 'That's why they moved, told me he died, isn't it?'

I push the picture away and stand up, knocking over my chair. Aiden grabs my wrist.

'He's a hero, your granddaddy, and he should have his family around him now he's...' Aiden's fingers squeeze.

I pull free. 'How did you even find me?'

'Your granddaddy gets letters, four a year, telling him what you're up to. I swiped a look at the most recent, got your address.'

'Letters? From my parents?'

Aiden shrugs.

'This makes no bloody sense. Why would they write to him about me but have me think he's dead?' I demand.

'Dunno.' He scans the room as though he might find an answer among my clutter. 'Look, I'm just after you coming home with me.'

'No.'

'Jesus, he's your kin.'

'So? I haven't seen him since...' I glance at the photo. 'You're mad to think I'm dropping everything and rushing off with you. Get Mum to go. He's her dad, she can deal with it.'

'Ah, shite.' Aiden backs away from me, worries at his hair.

Fear coats my tongue, the bitter taste of orange pith. 'What?'

He rights my up-tipped chair, drops a hand onto my shoulder and eases me down. 'You don't want to hear this from me.'

And now I have to. I stalemate him. 'I'm doing nothing until you tell me what's going on.'

'Just come.'

'Tell me first.'

'Then you'll come?'

Like hell. Maybe. Depends. I say nothing; the silence forces words from him.

'Da wasn't sure what you'd know, how much you'd remember...' He reaches into his pocket again, pulling out a yellowed piece of paper. He sets it on the table but keeps a hand over it.

I tug at a corner, sliding it free.

It has been quartered, the creases bruised by repeated folding. I open it carefully. At the top is an official crest and the words 'Teastas Beireatais'. Skimming down, I see the remembered Irish spelling of my first name followed by 'Finnighan' and '3$^{rd}$ May, 1962': my birthday. More foreign words follow; máthair, athair, Cathal, contae, Muineachán.

'It's your certificate of birth.' Aiden trails a finger over 'Teastas Beireatais' and translates; mother, father, Charles, county, Monaghan.

I'm not Kaylynn Patty Ryan; I'm Caoilainn Patricia Finnighan. My parents' names aren't Susan and John Ryan; they're Fiona and Cathal, Charles, Finnighan.

'Why did they change their names? Are they... on the run?'

Aiden flinches. 'They're not.'

'So what the hell's going on, Aidie?' I drawl his childhood nickname.

'They didn't change their names. The Ryans aren't your parents.'

'Caoilainn?'

I snap back into the room. 'If they're not my parents who the hell are they? Who are my parents? How can I not have known this?' My voice pitches up with each word. 'Jesus Christ!' I'm too high. I let go. Laughter bubbles up. I hear madness in it. So does Aiden, he edges towards me. I'm scaring him. I stop laughing.

'They're not my parents?'

He nods.

So I'm finally free of them.

But cornered by something worse: the unknown.

I can't fight it blind.

'Tell me what you know.' I rest my hand on Aiden's arm, encouraging him with a be-my-hero squeeze. 'I need the truth.'

He takes my hand in both of his. 'The Ryans, they were friends of friends or something. Your granddaddy had them take you to live with them, 'cos your,' he hugs my hand, 'ma and da had died.'

'How?'

'Your da was a volunteer.'

'A what?'

Aiden looks away. 'He was in the IRA, killed in action I suppose.'

'And my mum?'

'Aye, she was involved too but I dunna what...' He shrugs.

He can't help. I pull my hand from his. 'That's all you know?'

'I know this is who you are.' He strokes the flimsy birth certificate. 'This is your family.' He retrieves the photograph. 'What's left of it.'

I stare at the old man. 'And him?'

'He was after doing the right thing,' Aiden says.

'Getting rid of me.'

'Taking care of you.'

Our sentences criss-cross each other.

'By getting rid of me.'

'It wasn't like that.'

'How was it then?'

'He's old, sick.'

'He didn't want to be bothered with me so he sent me packing.'

'He's a hero.'

'What kind of a hero does that?'

Aiden bangs a fist on the table. Our mugs leap up.

'No! He fought in the GPO with Pearse in '16. Survived the War of Independence and the Civil War. He was protecting you. You've no idea what he musta been through.'

'Whose fault is that? I don't know any of this. Who's Pearse? What Civil War?' Aiden opens his mouth, eager explanations on his tongue. I stop him before they surface. 'Don't. Bloody hell, you've just dropped an atomic bomb on me, I couldn't give a toss about Irish history.' I push up from the table and stagger to the door, the world brightly blurred.

'Where're you going?'

'I need to walk.' I bang out.

Scaly autumn leaves crackle under my boots. Burying numb hands in my pockets, I stride through the city to the sea front. Fading light turns the waves graphite grey. White foam curls up like pencil shavings. I stand at the seawall, watching the water blacken. The rhythm of roll and retreat grinds me to dust. The sea doesn't care about what's happened. Nor does the man who nods goodnight as he walks by. Nor does his Labrador who sniffs me and trots on. Nor do the parents who aren't parents, who will care only about their exposed lie, not its victim. Nor does the old man in the photograph, the one who should care because he settled me on shale, left me to this landslide. I lean over the wall, straining towards rushing waves, wishing it was as simple as dropping into them, letting the tide scatter me into oblivion.

It's not fair. My fucking life and I'm the one that didn't fucking know.

What now? Hide? Walk away from it? Run towards it?

Child-me, gambolling through the painting in the college studio, what would she do?

The answer is easy for her. She knows what she's running towards.

When I open the door Aiden rushes at me.

'Jesus, I was worried. You've been gone ages.'

'I was thinking.'

'And?'

'I still am.'

We sit at the table again. Aiden makes more tea.

'I'm sorry it's like this,' he says, handing me a mug.

I finger the brittle yellow paper. 'How'd you get this?'

'Lifted it from your granddaddy's. He'd kept it, and the photo. Sure, doesn't that tell you all you need to know?'

'It doesn't tell me why he thought it was OK. to dump me on a couple of hippy crusaders who always had something more important than me to take care of.'

'What?'

I shake my head. Explaining the past can't justify it. I go to the bed-settee and curl up. Aiden stays at the table. The hum of the refrigerator and the clanging of water pipes masks our silence. Saggy springs creak as I shuffle into the cushions. There's a metallic click from the table. I look over but he's only lighting a cigarette. I lean back again, closing my eyes, letting myself drift. A car drones along the road. The picture of my past dissolves and reforms, the sliding coloured beads inside a kaleidoscope.

Still that question: what now?

Face it. Understand it. Fight it.

That's what I was taught to do when something isn't fair.

We catch the last train to Bristol and hitch across the channel in a lorry. The driver shoots curious glances at us. Aiden avoids speaking and keeps checking the wing-mirror. We're dropped off in Cardiff to wait for the first train to Pembroke Dock. Aiden goes for tea. I sit on the platform, my coat buttoned against the cold, trying to light a cigarette.

'Here.' Aiden returns with two steaming polystyrene cups.

The tea trembles in my frozen grip. Aiden sits unflinching on the icy bench and when he lights my cigarette his hand is steady.

'Aren't you nithered?'

'I'm used to it,' he says. 'Do you want my jacket?'

I think about what he's been doing to acclimatise himself to long cold hours waiting, a gun in his pocket. I remember us running through the park, scattering ducks, giggling. 'No, but thanks.'

He shuffles closer, his arm pressing mine. 'I know it's been a shock.'

'Will he be glad to see me?'

'Aye, course.' Aiden clears his throat. 'I'll come with you, don't worry.'

But I am worried. I'm not sure I'll be glad to see him.

# Dublin—15<sup>th</sup> October, 1980

The bus ride from Rosslare Harbour takes two hours. I sit by the window, reading bilingual road signs showing off their double-tongue. Aiden chain-smokes, says little. When a sign proclaims 5 miles to Dublin, he lights his last cigarette. His leg starts a jig and his hand goes to his hair half a dozen times. I keep still, afraid movement will splinter me.

Weeds grow through the broken slabs of a drive leading to a child-drawn bungalow.

Aiden calls out as we enter, 'Mr Finnighan, it's me.'

A voice croaks, 'Away in, lad.'

We creep along a narrow passageway. Aiden inches open the door.

'I've brought you a visitor.'

'Who's that, so?'

Aiden beckons to me.

In an armchair, wrapped in a grubby blanket, is a shrunken man. His face is thin and lined, chin speckled with grey stubble, eyes deep-set hollows, nose hooked and twisted, skin sallow. He stoops forward, his crown showing through sparse white hair. Eyes widen, blue glittering. A hand, knuckles gnarled and skin brown-speckled, appears from beneath the blanket, reaching out as though to touch me; I hang back. The hand drops.

'You eejit, what the fuck've you done?' He throws off the blanket, crossing the room on a younger man's legs. 'Ya bloody wee bollocks.'

He smacks Aiden in the mouth. I recoil. Aiden puts a hand to his split lip, drawing it away red-smeared.

'You've no business, so you haven't.'

'We've been worried about you,' Aiden murmurs.

'Haven't yous enough worries?' He swings fierce eyes on me. 'You're leaving. Take her back. Now.'

'Mr Finnighan, it's for the best. Da said…'

He snorts, 'What business is it of his?' Raises his hand again.

I grab the sleeve of his raggy jumper. I want to hate him but the little girl from the photograph wants to hug him. It's the smell; tobacco, talc and pencil shavings. 'It's not him you should be angry at; it's yourself.'

His arm falls. He shakes his head. 'Whatever've you done? Silly ould bastard.' He returns to his chair, sinking down. His eyes settle on mine, searching me. 'What's he said to you?'

'Enough.'

Daideo glowers at Aiden who shuffles on his feet.

'Do you not think she's a right to know, Mr Finnighan?'

'Just 'cos someone's a right to something doesn't mean they deserve it thrown at them,' Daideo bawls. He turns to me. 'Go home.'

He's as afraid of this as me but he doesn't know it yet and I won't tell him.

'No.' I plant myself on the sofa and meet his glare with a neutral expression.

'I'll put the kettle on,' Aiden offers, hurrying from the room.

'Aiden says you're ill.'

'I'm ould, that's all.'

'So you're not ill?'

He doesn't reply.

'You think this is how I deserved to find out?'

'Him and his interfering da. I'll skin Frank, so I will,' he mutters. 'You weren't supposed to know.'

'Well I can't unknow it now. You could at least be sorry.'

He scowls. 'I've nothing to be sorry for.' He unfolds himself, rounded shoulders straightening, and reaches across to the table at his elbow. On it is a sketchpad, three stubby pencils and a tobacco tin. He flips the pad shut and snatches the tin. ''Twas for your own good.'

'Why?'

'Wee 'uns need a proper family, ma and da, caring folks with decent values.'

'Your idea of a proper family's pretty fucked up.' I slap him with the last two words. Wonder if he'll slap back. He doesn't.

'I know they'll've loved you, raised you right.'

I try foul truths instead of foul language. 'I'll tell you how they raised me. Instead of colouring books I had placards to paint. We had our picnics on picket lines. They didn't send me to school because they didn't want me indoctrinated so I did my lessons alone at home which was mostly in some rank doss-house because it didn't matter to them where we lived as long as we were handy for whatever rally was next on the calendar. They didn't care what I got up to because they thought I was a hell of a lot better off than any of the oppressed whose battles they were fighting.'

'Weren't you, so?' he snaps. 'Clothes, food, education, family, freedom: love.' He starts rolling a spindly cigarette. 'You should be glad you'd the chance to learn from them what this world's like and how to set about making it better.' He runs a pale tongue along the cigarette paper, seals it and strikes a match.

'They were too busy marching and protesting to love me.'

'Of course they loved you. Why else would they teach you to stand up and fight for yourself when something's not fair?'

'They didn't want me…'

He interrupts. 'I'd've never given you to them if I thought that.'

'…and neither did you.'

His fierce face fractures. He fights the blow, batting it down, drawing himself together again. 'I did what I thought best. I'm sorry if you're not of the same mind but there's nothing to be done about it now.' He folds his arms.

I'm doing this all wrong.

Aiden returns with tea and biscuits. 'OK. here?'

Neither of us answers. Daideo sinks into the cushions. I settle into the sagged sofa, my feet on the coffee table. He squints at me, studying each feature the way I study things I'm drawing. I wonder what's on the pages of his sketchpad.

'You've still the look of my mother about you,' he says.

'What?'

Aiden sits next to me and pours tea. As he passes my cup he leans in and whispers:

'Give him chance.'

I take the cup, swallow tea and frustration. Wait for the old man in the corner to speak again.

'What are you doing with yourself?'

I came for answers, not questions. At my elbow Aiden lets out a tiny cough. I glance over and he nods, encouraging, guiding me.

'I'm at college.'

'Studying what?'

'Art.'

Daideo stubs out his roll-up. His eyes widen, the blue luminous in the shadows of his sockets.

'I used to do a bit,' he replies. 'Still knock up the odd sketch.' A hand strays towards the sketchpad. He snatches it back. 'But oils were my thing when I was a lad.'

'My favourite too.'

His cheeks flush. Pride? 'A painter, eh? You get that from me.' He shoves a digestive into his mouth. Splutters, 'Are you good?'

'I got a scholarship.' I pause. 'To them it was a sell out of all their years teaching me to denounce The Man, be a free spirit and lobby for liberty.'

'But you went anyway?' He spits biscuit crumbs down his shirtfront.

'They're too lefty for parental dictatorships.'

He peers at me over his teacup. 'So?'

'I packed and walked. That was last year. We've hardly spoken since.' I set down my mug. 'Now I don't see there's anything left between us except mutual disappointment.'

Daideo's mouth quivers. 'A fighter: you'll get that from me, an' all.' He gulps his tea; some dribbles down his grizzled chin. 'I broke with my father when I was sixteen on account of needing to make my own way in the world so I'll say nothing against you on that.'

'Good, because they're nothing to me now.'

He sighs. 'Aye, you're like me, so you are.' He shakes his head. 'And I'm like my father, more than I'd wish to be.' He pauses to snatch at some dark memory. 'Reckon I owe you an answer, lass.'

I look at Aiden. He winks.

*

Daideo starts somewhere in the middle.

'Your ma... Susan,' he corrects, seeing my frown, 'Aye, she's Bethy's daughter. Beth was Charlie's youngest sister.'

'Charlie?'

'School pal of mine. Your da's named after him. Charlie died when he was nothing but a lad.' His sight turns inwards as he peers into the past. 'So when your da was born I give him Charlie's name. He was a grand lad and I kept in touch with his family after, off and on. When your folks...' Daideo presses shaking fingers into his eye sockets, smearing tears. 'I tried, so I did, but it wasn't any good. I couldn't cope. So when I heard Sue was away to England with this fella she'd married we fixed things up for you to go with them. You'd be almost four, young enough to forget. I only asked them to write once in a while, let me know how you got on, and to make sure that you did forget.'

'That's why they changed my name.'

'Aye. They wanted to call you Katherine but you wouldn't have it so they made do with scrubbing the Irish out of Caoilainn.'

His words are only the story's ending.

'What about my real parents?'

'Sure, it was the Troubles killed 'em. A terrible time, so it was.' He falls silent.

Is that it? I sit forward. 'Is that it? What about how? By who? When?'

'You're best off not knowing.'

'That's not your decision.'

'As long as there's breath in me it is.'

'Fine. Don't tell me. I'll find out myself.'

It's a risky sidestep; maybe there'll be no other way of finding out. His mouth twitches. I can't read him so look to Aiden for a translation.

Daideo suddenly pounds his fist off the chair arm. 'You want to hear about how they were killed by a war we've been doomed to fight and lose in every generation? You want to know about brutal enemy attacks; folks afeared to sleep in their beds; spending weeks, months, years, running for safety in our own country; cowering like criminals when all we're after's getting back what was robbed from us; watching our comrades jailed, killed and waiting for the same ourselves?' Words explode from him, slamming me into my seat with a crushing pain. 'You want me telling you 'bout your parents being shot, your ma's chest ripped open by bullets, your da's face such a mess we'd to have the coffin closed? You want me to say how it felt hearing I'd lost two more, my own two, and knowing I was as much to blame as them that fired the guns?' His face throbs with anger. Spit clumps in the corners of his mouth. His breath comes in drowning gasps. His eyes scorch me. He falls back, hand clawing at his collar.

Aiden jumps up, snatches a bottle from the sideboard and tips whiskey into Daideo's teacup, pressing it into dothery hands. Daideo gulps from it, his face cooling, sweat beading on his forehead. Aiden hovers at his side. Daideo pushes him away to stare at me. He gasps one more breath.

'You want to know the agony I felt telling you your mammy and daddy were dead?' He crumples, allowing himself to be swallowed by the chair cushions.

Silence smoothers us. I want to be sucked into a blinding, screaming vortex. I don't, can't, move.

Daideo hands Aiden the emptied cup and twists stiffly to the window. Outside darkness soaks the quiet street. 'It's late. You can stay tonight, then back to that college of yours tomorrow.' He nods to Aiden. 'Make up the spare bed, lad.'

In a voice half a toner higher than usual Aiden asks, 'Shall I see about grub too?'

'Can do,' Daideo says.

Aiden ducks out.

A minute passes, and a second. Daideo doesn't flinch. Sickening shame drains into my stomach. I stand and stagger from the room, following the clang of pans to the kitchen.

Aiden is at the sink.

I kick the door shut, press against it, panic piling on panic.

Aiden comes over, squeezes my shoulder. 'There's a pub round the corner. Fancy a drink?'

*

The Golden Harp is quiet and dim-lit. The landlord welcomes Aiden and starts pulling a pint of Guinness. Aiden calls him Jimmy and introduces me as Caoilainn Finnighan, because that's who I was, am, to him.

When Jimmy learns my name he says, 'Nothing to do with that cantankerous git up the road, are you?'

'Christ, Jim, he's her granddaddy,' Aiden protests.

'Sorry, love. I was kidding.'

A ladylike half of Guinness appear on the bar. Aiden collects the drinks and steers me through to the back room. We sit in a corner. He offers me his cigarettes and I take a tentative sip of Guinness. It's bitter but smooth.

'Sorry about Jimmy,' Aiden says. 'He's had a few run-ins with your granddaddy.'

I shrug it off. Suffocating silence slides over me. I force myself to break the surface of it. 'My parents... is that how they died?'

'It's how too many folk died.' Aiden shakes his head. 'He doesn't talk about them. Hurts too much, I guess. Something we understand.'

'We?'

'Republicans.'

'And me, how do I understand it?'

'You wanting that Irish history lesson now?' he asks.

I study his face, the curling scar. It looks raw, cruel. An accident? A fight? A war wound? I want to feel the pain of it, something to pierce the numbness in my chest. 'How'd you get that scar?'

He glances around the empty room. In a low voice he says, 'Couple of UVF lads jumped me. Gave me this too.' He lifts his sweatshirt, exposing a red, two inch, star-shaped scar in his side. He twists round; the star is mirrored and magnified, wider and redder. I imagine the sharp stabbing of a stitch and know I'm not even close. Alex tried to impress me with a scar once, on his arm. 'Chicks dig scars, don't they?' I rubbed my thumb over the carefully applied oil paint, smearing it. 'Only if they're real.'

Aiden's is real.

'UVF?'

'Ulster Volunteer Force. Loyalists.' He pulls his jumper down.

'Loyalists?'

'Aye, loyal to the Crown. Run everything, so they do. We're after equalling things up but that'll not happen while the Brits are backing them, so it's Brits out then a free democratic, thirty-two county socialist republic for everyone.'

My cheek stings with an imagined slap when he says 'Brits'. I fumble for another cigarette. 'I thought it was about religion.'

'They let on it is but God's nothing to do with it.'

'So what is it about?'

He sparks my cigarette. 'It's about who you are: Irish or British. We're all Irish on this island but when the Brits bullied Collins into signing the Treaty in '21 that meant they kept six of Ulster's counties for themselves they were about saying the people there were British. The Prods kid on it's true 'cos they think it gives them special status but they get called Paddy on the mainland just the same.' He smiles at this. 'Sometimes I wonder the Brits think the Six Counties are worth fighting for but I guess you go hardest over the last crumb, specially when it's all you've left of the mighty British empire. And us, sure, it's for our homeland we're fighting: Ireland wholly Irish.'

A movie flashes onto the screen in my brain: a young woman crumpling to the ground, her chest bubbling with blood; a young man falling backwards, a bullet exploding his head.

'And that's worth dying for?' The words burn my tongue. I rinse with Guinness and swallow.

His eyes are fierce. 'Aye.'

'And killing for?'

'It's not like the papers say. We're at war.'

'But innocent people get hurt.'

'Wise up, that was happening long before we started fighting back. What would you have us do, put up with the discrimination, living in hovels, making do with handouts, being treated like shite? We didn't start this. Sure, we do our best to keep civilians out of it but if the Brits fight dirty…' He shakes his head. 'We've got the worst of it.'

I see him in a ditch, lying in wait, gun in his hand. Crawling under a car, depositing a deadly package. Smashing down a door, dragging a stranger from his bed. But the image is reversible. Him in the ditch facedown, gun in someone else's hand. Him in the car with someone else's package ticking beneath. Him in the bed; someone else breaking in.

I can picture Aiden like that; he's safe: alive. Images of him keep me from seeing the bullet-broken young woman, the skull-shattered young man who aren't.

'You joined because of your dad?'

'I volunteered,' he stresses the word, 'because things aren't right, they need fixing.'

'But he's involved?'

'Everyone in the North's involved, just some folks're good at kidding on they aren't. We're not that daft.' Aiden studies his Guinness. 'We're Republican in our bones. Da's been in the 'Ra, the Officials, since he was sixteen, like his brothers and their da before. It's through the ould man we know your granddaddy. We even had a great aunt in the Cumann na mBan, that's the old women's division. Alongside Pearse in the GPO for Easter week, so she was. When the Troubles kicked off again the Sticks split. The   Provisional IRA came from that. They took over; Da went with them so we moved to Belfast.'

Hearing words familiar from newspapers, I nod.

'Da slipped the first internment swoop in '71, when they grabbed a load of poor buggers who'd nothing against them 'cept they were Catholic, but they got him in '73. We didn't see him for two years. Our house was raided dozens of times, everything wrecked by squaddies. Ma used to serve tea on newspaper 'cos it wasn't worth scrounging new plates just for the Brits to break. We've been beaten up on the streets, hauled in by the peelers, attacked by Loyalists, all for wanting things fairer; the chance of a decent job, nice house, ya know.'

He doesn't shout or bang his fists; these are the simple facts of his life. Cold reality ripples through me. They could have, should have, been the facts of my life too. Why the fuck should I've been spared it? What gave Daideo the right to excuse me?

'D'ya mind my brother Connor?' he continues.

I push down the soured truth, pull faded images towards me: a boy, taller, sharp features, same colouring as Aiden, kicking a football; kicking it towards a smaller boy, fairer, softer, not Aiden.

'Dark hair, older than you?'

'Aye, he's in the Kesh now.' Seeing my frown he adds, 'The jail, call it the Maze, so they do, but it'll always be Long Kesh to us. Danny, born after you left, he's in the Fianna, that's for until you're old enough to be a volunteer.'

'There was another brother, wasn't there?' I see the red-haired boy again, running, cheeks pink, dragging a limp kite.

Aiden draws a shaky breath. 'Fergus.' He looks away. 'Fucking Brits, 'scuse my language, murdered him in Derry two years ago.'

The running boy trips, falls. My memory blacks out. I study the browny snail trails creeping down the inside of my glass. 'Sorry.'

'I'm not after upsetting you,' he adds, 'but you asked.'

'It's just... I don't... What the hell'm I supposed to do? Yesterday this was a news report, a rally to attend, a petition to sign. Now it's...' I go to the window and peer out into the darkness.

'You've to work out what's important to you,' Aiden says gently.

'Oh, that's all.' I stay at the window, trying to focus what little light there is, hoping to break through the blackness.

'You're important to him,' Aiden prompts.

Easy for him to believe that.

'Giving something up's harder than hanging on to it,' he adds, filling the blank of my non-response.

'Why did he send me away?'

'I guess he didn't want you involved.'

'But I am involved. I always was, I just didn't know it.'

'You're best thinking on yourself and your granddaddy.' Aiden has crept up behind me. 'That's why you came back, isn't it: family?'

Is it?

We drift back to the table. Drink slowly. Aiden asks about college, my art. I picture the unfinished painting of my childhood but it's too close to some truth I need to hide, so I'm reduced to scouring a receding horizon of shimmering desert mirages for replies.

Back at the bungalow Aiden cooks egg, beans and chips. I sit in the warm bright kitchen as he chops, stirs and fries. Daideo comes when he's called, lowering himself stiffly into a chair and cramming the food into his slack mouth. I watch as he slops beans down himself. He doesn't look at me, or say anything. He knocks over the salt cellar. I jump up, open a cupboard, get the dustpan, clear the mess, reach into a second cupboard, get the salt and refill the cellar. As I place it on the table, Daideo catches my wrist. His eyes lock into mine and I realise what I've done: I've come home.

After tea we sit in front of the box, the jolly compère on the inane quiz show covering our silence. Daideo is in his armchair. As he reaches for his tobacco tin my eyes are drawn to the table, the sketchpad on it. He notices my stare, lifts the pad and, stretching to the bureau on his other side, locks it in a drawer. I tune out the television, trying to catch windblown thoughts.

There's a life here for me, one that used to be mine. Now it feels like a ring worn on the wrong finger.

Reasons for leaving marshal in my head, overpowering me.

I lie, pinned down by unfamiliar darkness, on the narrow bed that was mine, searching for myself. I can't be who I am because I'm not who I thought I was. I get up and creep into the lounge.

The bureau drawer is locked but I can feel its weakness. I find a sturdy knife, jam it between lock and frame and twist. The catch snaps. I open the drawer. The sketchpad is on top of a junk muddle. I pluck it out and flip the cover.

The pencil lines on the first page are time-faded. The image is me aged four. I flip through the book, watching myself grow-up, a year a page, noting the ragged tears where sheets have been ripped out, him getting it wrong and starting afresh. There are thirteen 'me' in the pad and one blank page. I return to the bedroom, sit at the dressing table and, using his pencils and the dusty mirror, bring the sequence up to date.

The face that stares out from her white-bordered world is an inverted version of me. I hold the pad up to the mirror. See myself.

I can't be the copy-me now I've glimpsed the original. I can't go back as though there's nothing here for me when I know there is. Even if that something bloody terrifies me.

I put the pad in the drawer before dawn and head into town. I find the library and make inquiries. The librarian gives me leaflets. Armed with glossy fliers, I catch the return bus, walking in on a one-sided row.

'It's your fault, ya bollocks. What the hell were you playing at, getting the lad to fetch her?... Shite, Frank, there's nothing the matter with me... He's out looking.'

I clap the door shut. Daideo turns, the phone clamped to his ear.

'Caoilainn, Jesus sake, where've you been? What?... Aye, she's just walked in. If you've an ounce of sense, Frank, you'll not be showing yourself here for a while.' Daideo bangs the phone down and faces me. 'Well?'

I fan the leaflets and hold them like a shield.

'I can go to college in town, stay with you.'

'I've told you what you're doing.' He folds scrawny arms over his chest. 'You'll away back where you came from.'

'Why?'

'I'll have no part in you throwing away your future.'

'How's me staying here doing that?'

He shuffles into the lounge. I follow.

'Well?'

He pinches his lips together.

'This course is just as good. The facilities look excellent.' I thrust the leaflet under his nose.

He swipes my hand aside.

'There's nothing good for you here.'

'Except you.'

'Including me.'

'I'm over eighteen. You can't make me leave.'

'But I can tell you you're not living here.' He drops into his lazyboy and bangs the chair arm. A cloud of grey dust mushrooms up.

'Fine. I'll get digs.' I walk out, slowly enough for him to call me back. He doesn't. Shit.

Aiden is hovering in the hall, hair lank with rainwater. I shake my head at him, dart into the bedroom and repack the bag that was only half unpacked last night.

'What're you doing?' he asks, sticking his head through the doorway.

'Staying.' I push past him, down the hall and outside.

'Wait.'

I keep going, up the path, through the gate and along the street. He jogs alongside me a few seconds later.

'Jesus, Caoilainn,' he puffs, pressing a hand to his side where the star-shaped scar lurks, catching me with his other hand, trying to slow me down. 'You can't...'

'I can.' I double my pace. Don't hesitate. Don't look back. 'Know anywhere I can sleep tonight?'

'Bloody hell. Come on, we'll ring my da.'

We huddle into the phone box, rain rattling the glass. Aiden explains, listens, says, 'aye,' a few times. He holds the receiver to me.

'Hello?'

'Caoilainn.' There's a gulp or a sob, the drawing of a breath. 'Aid says you've a spot of bother with Pat but don't worry. We'll see you OK. 'til the ould fella comes round. It's grand you came for him. He needs his family.'

His words douse me in doubt. What do I need? What the hell am I doing? Either way it'll be wrong. 'Mr O'Neill, I'm not sure I...'

'It's Frank, love, and I know it's a lot you've had dropped on you but you being here's best all round.'

'Daideo said my parents were killed, shot. That's more than 'a lot'.'

A heavy breath in.

'Sure, 'twas a terrible thing for yous. We were worried it would finish the ould fella.' His voice is hollow. It brightens again, black and white flicked to colour. 'But now you're back things are coming right.' He hurries on. 'Sorry, love, there's someone here. Don't fret. We'll look after you.'

With a click he's gone. I don't know what it was I hoped he'd say.

We head for the Golden Harp. It's not 10:30 but Jimmy lets us in. Aiden explains his dad's plan for Jimmy to put me up at the pub in exchange for me working there. Jimmy and I study each other. From the way he looks at me I see he doesn't think he has much choice. Neither do I. Or rather, I've already made my choice.

Jimmy leads me to a poky room upstairs, brown damp mottling the ceiling, wardrobe with one door hanging off and bed with a mushy mattress. I dump my stuff and head into the bar where Jimmy teaches me to pull a pint. The first two fizz uncontrollably but the third is drinkable. I'm serving on that lunchtime, thankful for the frantic pace that keeps me from thinking about anything other than staying afloat.

After closing I call the landlord of my Plymouth digs, tell him there's a family crisis; I'm not coming back. He agrees to send my things if I post a month's rent in lieu of notice. I agree, hoping I can scrounge the money. I hang up the payphone. Is that it? One life ended; another begun? It feels like I should be calling people, making an announcement: Kaylynn Ryan has left herself. But there's only a handful of familiar faces I nod to in corridors, pitch my easel next to. They wouldn't care. Nor would the 'let's pretend' parents I don't want. Nor does the grandfather who doesn't want me. I slump against the glass door, drained and dizzy. I can't even cry because there's no milk spilt.

Later I write to PSAD, withdrawing myself. As the buff envelope slithers into the green letterbox a salty wave drenches me with determination. This needs doing so I'll bloody well do it.

I muddle through a fortnight, Guinness fumes saturating my clothes, my hands chapped from washing glasses, smile warping into a grimace as yet another punter comments on my accent, cracking jokes about immigrants. I'm a curiosity; the usual form is Irish barmaids leaving for English pubs.

Aiden updates me. His dad keeps phoning Daideo but when he finally walks into the bar, sketchpad under his arm, I know what's brought him round.

Jimmy nudges me. 'Catch this,' he mutters, nodding to where Daideo stands, filling the doorway, glaring at cowering drinkers who avoid the challenge. He faces Daideo. 'You're barred.'

'Fuck off with you,' Daideo barks, striding over, 'or I'll have your bollocks for earrings.'

Jimmy winks at me and wanders away to serve.

'You're as stubborn as me, so?' Daideo says.

'Apparently.'

'Lad said you've had your things shipped over, given up your college place?'

'Do you want to see the letter they sent?'

'I do not.' Daideo sniffs. 'Have you found a course here?'

'Yes, but there're no scholarships until next year so I'll be doing this until then.' I gesture to the beer taps with my dishcloth.

He throws the sketchpad down, open to the last page. 'I told you I'd have no part in you throwing away your future.'

I scrub a sticky beer ring. 'Is that you changing your mind?' I glance from my drawing to him.

He drags a hand over his mouth. 'I'll not pretend to like it but you've bested me. Jesus, you're a one,' he admits. 'My fault, I know. Now, while you're under my roof, you'll live by my rules.'

'Which are?'

'Stick in at college, keep out of trouble. No playing nurse for me.'

He is dying, cancer, I guess.

'Anything else?'

'No smoking in bed, keep out of my locked drawers and I've said my all about the past.' He holds out a hand so we can shake on the deal. His grip is fierce. I wring his hand like a dishrag.

'I'll be round after closing.'

# Dublin—18th December, 1980

## Maze Seven End Death Fast
## Prisoners Ask for Food on 53rd Day
## of Hunger Strike

The seven Republican prisoners on hunger strike in the Maze Prison have this morning ended their strike. The decision was made after negotiations between Republicans and British officials. A statement released by the governor of HMP Maze, Mr Stanley Hillditch, announced that the strikers are accepting food and medical treatment. Downing Street has yet to comment on concessions made to Republicans but a Sinn Fein spokesman confirmed that an agreement has been reached in line with the prisoners' five demands.

The strike began on 27th October after a four year stalemate between IRA prisoners and authorities over demands for political status including; the right to wear their own clothes, have free association, access to recreational and educational facilities and not to do prison work. Similar rights were granted to prisoners under the Special Category status introduced in 1972 for those convicted of political crimes in Northern Ireland. Special Category status was withdrawn in 1976 as part of government counter-insurgency strategies.

The strike was led by Brendan Hughes (32), Officer Commanding (OC) of the Republican prisoners. The other strikers were; Tom McFeeley, Leo Greene, Tommy McKearney, Raymond McCartney, Sean McKenna and John Nixon of the Irish National Liberation Army. They were joined on 1st December by three women Republicans in HMP Armagh; Mairead Farrell (OC), Mairead Nugent and Mary Doyle. They are expected to end their strike today.

Unconfirmed reports yesterday suggested that Mr McKenna had lapsed into a coma. It is believed he is being treated by medical staff at the prison.

We hear of the strike's collapse on the radio in Daideo's pokey kitchen as I'm making breakfast. The word, caught on twin currents of steam from the kettle and vapours from the frying pan, splits, the parts drifting away from each other:

break         fast

break                    fast

break                                    fast.

'You know why they did it?' Daideo asks.

'For political status.' I recite what I've learnt so far and spear a sausage. Fat spurts out and drips onto the stove as I lift it to a waiting plate.

'That's what they're doing it for,' he says. 'I mean why they do that.'

I put a plate of sausage and egg down. He pushes it away and grips my arm.

'Sit, Caoilainn, so's I can tell you.'

'Tell me after you eat.' I slide the plate back. His clothes are baggy, his skin ill-fitting. During my two months here he's wizened. I'm worried. Just as I'm getting better at loving him he's leaving, vanishing. Soon all that'll be left will be the granite kernel at his core. It must have filled him once but decades of erosion have left the flesh hanging off him like he's too big to support himself. A sudden blow will reduce him to ash. Only when I sit does he let go.

'It's an ancient Irish practice, from Gaelic law. Troscadh\*. If somebody wronged you, you fasted on their doorstep 'til they saw you right.'

'What if they didn't?'

'You'd die there for everyone to see. The fella that let you die'd be shamed, an outcast.'

'What if you change your mind, go home and stick a fry on?'

'You don't.' His eyes burn through me.

He's teaching me; a folk song, a superstition, Gaelic words: Irish essence. Energy blazes in the watery blue, shining against bloodshot whites as he tutors. He's read me the *Táin* so many times I dream the Cúchulainn legends. I like the stories of Queen Medb and Scáthach best, women of power and knowledge, women with control: women who fight. They get on well with George, the fierce little girl from the *Famous Five* adventures who is the solitary hero from my real childhood. Her cry, 'I'm as good as any boy,' could have come from their lips.

---

\* Fasting

43

But not all his lessons slot comfortably into the past I've grown up with. The bedraggled British Tommy, floundering in the Flanders' trenches becomes Black and Tan butcher hunting Irish Volunteers through the Cork countryside once I've learnt my Irish history. At least, Daideo's version of it, which ends in 1937 with the renaming of the Irish Free State as Eire in de Valera's 32-county constitution, Dev's way of writing partition out of Ireland's story. 1937 was also the year Cathal Finnighan was born, according to my birth certificate, a wound I daren't touch, no matter how much I might want to, for fear of making it haemorrhage again, fatally this time. Of Daideo's history I have only Aiden's IRA legend: the boy who fought for Pearse, then Collins, then Dev, then whoever was left. Time is rubbing my chance of hearing it from the hero's mouth into smaller and smaller grains.

'Finish your breakfast, Daideo. I've a class.'

He lifts a fork. 'When am I going to see your work?'

'You've seen plenty.'

'Those wee sketches! I'd done half a dozen grand oils before I was your age.'

'And I've not seen one of them,' I remark, shrugging on my coat.

'You can thank the Auxies for that, razing the land from Wicklow to Galway,' he mumbles.


When I return from college, a small canvas of the Wicklow mountains in my bag, he's in the hall, wearing his hat and coat.

'We're off out.'

'Where to?'

'The past, if it's still there,' he chunters, taking his stick from the hall stand.

We catch a bus towards Rathfarnham and get off in a quiet street. Neat houses line the pavement and bare-limbed trees stretch overhead. Daideo strides out. I jog to catch up.

'Where're we going?' I repeat. He's said nothing since we set off, keeping his lips pressed into a hard line, his eyes on the scrolling view through the bus window.

'You'll see.'

We round a bend in the road and track along a high stone wall. A few yards on the wall is broken by two sets of wrought iron gates, the first wide enough for vehicles, the second person-sized. The smaller gate is set into a stone entrance, arched around the gate, squared off above and topped with a reclining beast that could be a lion or something more mythical. Gold letters proclaim it the 'Pearse Museum'.

'Didn't say that in my day,' he mutters, passing under the arch. 'Keep up, lass.'

I trot after him.

He slows down further along the sweeping drive, stopping to peer into the undergrowth or across the lawns, seeing things invisible to me. We reach a blind corner. He halts, looking back the way we've come, removing his hat as for a funeral procession. His hand trembles.

'What's wrong, Daideo?'

'It's been too long and not long enough.' He replaces his hat and presses on.

A building, so large and grey it could have been hewed from solid rock, rises in front of us. Steps lead to a columned entrance and three rows of windows reflect the day's dull sky. Above the entrance are the words 'Músaem na Ó Píarsach'. Daideo points.

'What's that say?'

'The Pearse Museum.'

'Are you guessing or did you read it?'

'A bit of both?'

He sighs. 'Do you know where we are?'

'Yes.' I point to the engraving. 'The-Pearse-Museum. Patrick Pearse.'

'Aye, and his brother Willie. He doesn't get forgotten by me.' Daideo shakes his head. 'A bloody museum! There should be boys playing on these fields, sitting behind those windows, learning and laughing.'

'What do you mean?'

'This is, was, St Enda's. The Pearses' school.'

'Aiden said you knew him.'

Knowing Pearse, being with him in '16, fighting at the General Post Office during Easter week, it's Republican grail.

'He didn't hear that from me.'

'It's not true?'

Daideo faces me. 'I knew them all; the Pearse clan, Sean MacDermott, Joe Plunkett, Con Colbert, Tom MacDonagh, James Connolly, Madam Markievicz, Tom Clarke, Mrs Clarke, Eamonn Kent, Mick Collins, The O'Reilly.' He recites their names reverently then climbs the steps, looks through the window, tries the door.

I notice a sign.

'The entrance is round the side, Daideo.' I wave him down from the portico but he sits on the top step, beckoning me. I perch beside him, worrying he'll catch a chill from the stone's radiating cold.

'It's more than sixty-five years since I was here, nearer seventy since I first came up that drive. I was twelve years old, miles from home and bloody terrified. Now I'm a canny bit older, two miles from home and...' He presses his fingers into his eye sockets. 'Jesus, it's still too soon for me to come back. Give me a cigarette for Christ sake.'

I fish in my pocket. 'You shouldn't at your age.'

He snorts. 'It's you that shouldn't.'

We sit smoking, our arses numbing, then head for the entrance. Daideo counts the money for two concessions and remarks on the price being cheaper than when he came as a boarder. The curator asks was he a St Enda's boy?

'I was.'

The entry fee is waived.

Guided by the curator, we meander through the refurbished Edwardian interior, along passageways with tan-polished parquet floors and high white ceilings. Light fittings with shades fluted like lilies hang in the rooms. Mahogany dressers line the corridors, displaying books and teaching resources. We enter the study hall, politely admiring its raised stage, leaf-green walls and recessed chapel. The curator crosses himself as we draw towards the altar. Daideo scowls and mutters curses. We trespass into family rooms filled with personal items; a sideboard draped with a lace doily, a kneeling statuette, an elegantly carved harp, two over-sized teacups displayed like trophies in a glass cabinet. It's the teacups that

Daideo pauses reverently before. The curator leads us to classrooms, now housing information boards instead of blackboards and display cases, not desks. He asks Daideo for memories; which rooms for which lessons, which masters taught there in his day? We stroll between two rows of beds, complete with counterpanes and crisp pillowcases, in a remade dorm. Does sir recall which bed was his, who he bunked with? He's fishing, but daren't ask: was sir there before Easter 1916? Daideo doesn't bite.

We come to the headmaster's office, Pearse's sanctum, and crowd behind the rope protecting this hallowed ground; only the worthy may enter. I try picturing Daideo as a boy, here getting a bollocking from Pearse, but it's too much an Enid Blyton children's story to be real for me.

Daideo listens to the curator's patter about Pearse's books, the family portraits, the seat in which he sat, they say, to pen the proclamation.

'And a few drafts it took him. There was paper strewn all over the night he was finishing it.' Daideo gestures round the room.

The curator fluffs his next line and before he recovers, Daideo has unhooked the rope and crossed the office to where a framed photograph hangs above a bureau.

'Sir, you mustn't...'

Daideo ignores him. 'Caoilainn, come here.'

With a shrug to the curator I join him beneath the photo. It shows the school turned inside out; building, masters and pupils assembled on the drive in front. Daideo presses a finger to the glass.

'There's your man, Pearse.' He moves his finger along. 'Willie.' Up to the rows behind. 'Mr Plunkett, Mr Colbert, Mr Slattery.' He draws the finger sideways, to the face of a boy, about fifteen, fair curls that look pinkish in the sepia-tinted print. 'And me.' He rounds on the curator. 'What happened to the paintings that were here, 'Íosagán'?' Daideo lurches at him. I lay a hand on his arm.

The curator's nostrils flare. 'There wasn't room,' he stutters. 'They're in storage.'

'Show me.' The words are barked.

The curator takes us to the basement. Stale air escapes as the heavy door creaks open. Leaking pipes drip-drip. A misshapen mountain rises, dustsheet-draped, corners jutting, suggestive of boxes.

'That's all of it,' he mumbles, shuffling off.

Daideo rips the sheets aside and begins flinging boxes with mythical strength.

'Are you not going to help?'

In twenty minutes we've moved the mountain, unearthing canvasses tied into an oversized package. With his pocket knife Daideo snaps the twine. We shake off the covering and he squats in front of the first painting.

'No.' He slides it to me. 'Take it, lass.' Studies the next while I move it.

I've shifted five when he gives a stunted cry.

'What's wrong?' I dart to his side.

He's frozen, one hand clutching a painting, a four by three of the building we're in, the other crammed into his mouth. He pulls the canvas free and props it against the wall, face to the chalky brickwork.

'We'll take that.'

'We can't.'

'We can. It's mine.' He starts in on the stack again but stops abruptly. 'And this one.' He takes the second painting over to wait with the first before riffling through the remainder. 'But where's 'Íosagán'?'

'What are you looking for?'

'The painting that hung in the entrance.' He reaches the second but last of the stored pieces. 'Jesus, it's here.'

It's of a boy standing between two trees, fair-haired, bare-chested, a cloth wrapped around his waist, falling to his naked feet. A golden halo encircles his head. His arms are outstretched, making a cross of his lithe body. Daideo hands the canvas to me and I wait while he rewraps the two he's claimed as his own.

We lug all three up to where the curator is waiting near the entrance/exit.

'This,' Daideo points at the one I'm holding, 'needs to be hung in the entrance hall.' He nods to me and I press it onto the curator. 'These others are mine. I'll be taking them, so I will.'

'You will not,' the curator splutters.

'You gonna stop me, wee fella?' Daideo draws himself up, sagging muscles tensing, bloodshot eyes blazing.

The curator withers. 'I'll be telephoning the police.'

'Grand. Been a good while since I walloped a rozzer,' Daideo says as he humps the parcel onto his shoulders.

Back · home, barricaded inside, I make tea while Daideo unwraps the paintings in the front room. When I enter with the tray he has them propped by the fire. I put the tray down and study them.

The painting of the school is impressive in its detail, the brickwork, the window frames, and captivating in the unusual colour scheme. The sky is dawning gold, white and green; the grounds burn redly. A cluster of lilies are planted bottom left.

In the other painting I recognise the boy-warrior, Cúchulainn. The young hero waits, spear raised, among vast hills, under tumultuous cloud banks, hordes of enemy soldiers gushing down the valley towards him.

I drop onto my knees, admiring the fat brush-swirls of sky and earth, the fine lines and tiny dots that make up men and masonry.

'What do you think?' Daideo demands.

His artist's pride is the key to his past.

'Tell me about boy who painted them, then I'll say.'

I sit on the sofa opposite the paintings, trying to superimpose Daideo onto the young boy who was first William, then Finn Devoy, then Patrick William Finnighan; innocent, hero, outlaw. The rucksack he fetched from the attic is on the seat beside me. I pinch age-stiffened leather, trace the letters 'PWF' scored with a penknife into the brown hide. PWF: Patrick William Finnighan, the name he gave himself when he'd outgrown Finn Devoy, borrowing first and middle from the Pearse brothers who once carried that haversack over Connemara's hills. The surname he made up, salvaging what was left of himself when he took the bag and set out on foot, heading for the future. The three names make a total less than the sum of the parts.

Inside the bag is Daideo's life: a photograph of his junior hurling team; another showing two boys dressed as Gaelic warriors; a battered copy of the *Táin* inscribed with birthday greetings and signed 'Cathleen'; a similarly tattered Bible with a mother's love on the flyleaf and a bullet wound in its chest. There's 'Finn's' long-expired American passport; the bullet dug from his shoulder in 1920; a brittle copy of his wanted poster from '22; a matchstick model made in the Curragh sometime between '31-4; a lock of his son's fair hair; the engagement announcement of Cathal Finnighan and Fiona O'Shea; a tiny wrist tag in the name of Caoilainn Patricia Finnighan.

It bundles me into my own past, the dead parents I've gained and the living ones I've discarded. Two mothers, two fathers, all putting their fights, their causes, before me. I can get the why but the 'how could they?' is still hard to fathom.

A tap on the window drags me into the present. I peek behind the curtain. Aiden's face is pressed against the glass. His visits are irregular, dictated by Army business.

'How are ya?' he whispers as he slips in.

'Fine. You want tea?'

'Aye. He's asleep?'

'Yeah, go through.'

When I return with two mugs Aiden is admiring the paintings.

'When did you do these?'

'I didn't. They're his.'

I confess our art heist. He chuckles when I repeat Daideo's remark about walloping a rozzer, is sombre when I recount Daideo's autobiography.

'So you know all about it now.' He puts his arm around me and we lean against each other, transfixed by the paintings. The suburban Dublin peace drones through my head, building from a hum to a roar. I don't know it all, know less than bloody half, the half that's been, not what is and what's coming.

'Take me to Belfast.'

'You don't want to be going there.'

'I need to see it for myself, not that bullshit in the papers. This is my life, I've a right to it. And a responsibility for it.' I wave my hand towards the paintings. 'I can't ignore something that's still happening.'

'It's not safe.'

'I'll be alright.'

'How's that?'

'Because I'm an art student researching a project.' I think. ' 'Art in a War Zone'.'

'Don't be an eejit.'

'I've got my old PSAD student ID, an English accent and a British passport. If you don't take me, Aiden, I'll go myself.'

'You can't.'

'You know I will.'

'Your granddaddy'll kill me if I let you away up there on your own,' he mutters.

'So you'll take me.'

'All right.'

# Belfast—26<sup>th</sup> December, 1980

The border is fifty miles away. During the drive Aiden makes me re-rehearse our cover. I'm researching when graffiti is art and when it's vandalism, less provocative than 'Art in a War Zone' and it gives us an excuse to cruise Belfast. Aiden, now Kenny because that's the name on the fake Irish driving licence he got from a Dublin contact, is the helpful brother of an Irish girl I met at PSAD. We've loaded the car with enough luggage to suggest I'll be staying a few days, a sketchpad of scribbled Dublin graffiti and a camera.

'And for Jesus sake don't call me Aiden,' he warns as we pass a sign saying 'Dundalk 2 miles'.

'I'm not stupid. I know how to deal with the police. All those pickets I went to growing up…'

'This is nothing like that.'

'Of course not. Our protests were peaceful, mostly. But we were still in conflict with state forces. They made sure I knew the drill if we got arrested, which we did.'

He glances over.

'The first time was a sit-in.'

'You weren't breaking the law.'

'Trespassing and disturbing the peace.'

'What's that get you, bound over? Hardly the same as a ten stretch for weapons possession.'

'I know that. I'm just saying I've some experience of this sort of thing.'

'You'll need a lot more than that.'

'If you're so worried, get out. I'll drive myself,' I snap.

He tightens his grip on the wheel. 'You can't drive.'

'It can't be that hard. I don't need protecting,' I say, recalling the row Daideo and I had about my trip north.

Aiden shakes his head. He's worried. This is a risk for him. For me it's a chance.

'I'll learn fast,' I say, 'because I have to. And not just the driving.'

British-blown craters have closed most of the border roads, funnelling us up the main artery. We're stopped at a checkpoint where the N1 becomes the A1. Metal barriers are drawn across the road. On the verge squats a military bunker, solid, windowless and painted a pea-sick green. A colour-coordinated Land Rover is parked nearby. I blur them into geometric shapes and reach for the camera, picturing a cubist composition in oil pastels. Aiden grabs my hand, jerking his head at the soldiers in combat fatigues, flak jackets and helmets. My chest tightens when I see the guns they carry, like something from a Hollywood action movie but these aren't props. The camera stays in my bag.

Traffic crawls; cars are halted, occupants questioned. We inch forwards. Ahead a car is waved off the road. Two soldiers circle it with hunter strides. A third gestures with his gun. The driver, a man about forty, gets out. He's thin, balding, his clothes those of a clerk. He produces ID. More soldiers surround the car, one has a mirror on a pole which he uses to check the car's underbelly, a dentist inspecting a mouth for rotting molars. An officer joins the soldier questioning the driver. He takes the ID, conflabs with the private.

'Whatever happens stay in the car,' Aiden instructs.

The man has his hands on his head now. The soldiers are shouting; Fenian scum, bog-wog, white nigger. Three soldiers hem him in, weapons raised. The man stands motionless. An order is barked: lie down. The man shakes his head. The soldiers look to their commander. The officer nods and strolls off, is a few feet away when one soldier drives the butt of his gun into the side of the man's face. Red sprays from his nose. The soldier hits him again, in the stomach. The man drops to his knees, tries to stand, is kicked by another soldier and falls facedown. All three close on him, weapons slicing the air. The odds aren't fair.

Instinctively I reach for the door. Aiden grabs my arm.

'I said stay in the car.'

'They'll kill him.' I claw at Aiden's hand. His grip tightens.

'Not with us watching.'

'So we just sit here?'

'Aye. Unless you're wanting to make it worse for him and us.'

Fuck sake!

He's right.

I force myself to do nothing except watch: witness.

Two soldiers drag the man along the tarmac. His face is bloodied and misshapen, his jacket has been ripped off and his jumper rucked up, exposing his white chest. He's lost a shoe. His hands are bound behind his back and his head lolls forwards. They fling him into the waiting Land Rover, slam the doors then straighten their uniforms. One squaddie wipes the butt of his gun; another lights a cigarette. The queue creeps forward.

'You said you wanted to learn. There's your first lesson, Caoilainn: pick your battles.'

Rage ripples through me. I was raised believing inaction is collusion, apathy is culpability. We, they, never stood aside. But this isn't a picket line, it's a battlefield. If I want to survive I have to adapt. I wring my hands into tight fists, driving fingernails into palms. Pain replaces anger. Slowly I relax the grip on myself.

'OK. Fine. Sorry.'

Aiden nods and nudges the car forward.

When it's our turn he hands over our IDs before the soldier asks. My British passport and Aiden's false driving licence are examined.

'Step out.'

Aiden complies. A soldier greets me as I open my door.

'Over here, miss.' He shepherds me away from the car, one hand on his gun, the other on my back.

I sidestep his touch. Resolved to be innocently civil I ask, 'Is something wrong?'

The officer approaches, holding my passport. 'Just routine, Miss Ryan.' The old name jars me, jumbling up who I was and who I am. 'What's the purpose of your visit to Northern Ireland?'

They stand Aiden in the middle of the road, make him strip off his jacket and kick off his shoes. They frisk him. I meet the officer's cold gaze, repeat the story we rehearsed.

'Art student, eh?'

'After this I might specialise in war photography.' I keep my tone neutral and paste on a sad smile.

The officer's moustache quivers. 'We are authorised to carry out random searches.'

I glance at Aiden. He's down to his socks, jeans and t-shirt, not shivering, blanking the soldiers who search our car.

I long to tell Captain 'Dutiful' that 'authorised' isn't the same as 'justified' but know I can't. He hears dissent in my silence anyway.

'We're here to protect the people of Northern Ireland from terrorist attacks. Random stop-and-search is effective in limiting terrorist movements. Civil rights are a peacetime privilege.'

He thinks me an ill-informed do-gooder: Amnesty International, Greenpeace, that lot. My pretend parents would be so proud. I allow myself one small poke, just to test where the nerve ends.

'And a wartime responsibility.'

He thrust my passport onto me. 'Take my advice: get yourself home. Belfast's no place for a young woman.'

Aiden is sitting now, tying his laces. He snatches his jacket and sweatshirt, jumps up and slides into the car. I climb in beside him. The officer's words about going home flash a flick-book of memories; a derelict terraced row, a dilapidated Georgian bedsit, a child-drawn bungalow. Which home? We're waved through the cordon and cross the border lost in our own troubles.

A few miles up the road, Aiden pulls into a lay-by and lights a cigarette. I don't know if it's cold or fear making his hand shake.

'What did you say?' he asks.

'What we'd planned.'

'You're OK., so?'

My galloping heart pulses in my ears. 'Yes.'

'It gets worse, ya know. Are you sure you want to keep going?'

I fix my eyes on the way ahead. It's a one-way system; the only route out is right round and down again.

'The sooner we get there, the sooner we get back,' I tell him.

\*

War-worn West Britain: boarded-up houses; rubble littered streets; barbed-wire topped walls; burnt out cars; weary women pushing prams; children, chapped-lipped, scuffing chilblained feet; men huddling in doorways; grey Land Rovers patrolling. Familiar signs, Woolworths, the Co-op, Boots the Chemist, cut into me and more memories of my discarded life bleed out. I press on the wounds.

We swoop into south Belfast, through the university quarter. Queen's, cloaked in gothic red brick, sprawls, imposing and regal. We pass grand Victorian houses, trim gardens and sparkling windows, so middle class this could be middle England. The war daren't advance on these comfortable cul-de-sacs. Aiden keeps driving.

We loop the city anti-clockwise, watched by the gargantuan Harland and Wolff crane. Initials on gable ends tag territories: IRA, PIRA, INLA, UVF, UDA, UFF. It's a war of vowels, 'I' versus 'U'. The streets narrow, houses closing ranks, watching us darkly. They open out again, at ease, lacy net curtains fluttering at open windows. Aiden names neighbourhoods, Protestant or Catholic, Unionist or Nationalist, rich or poor. Fumbling through the paint-bled pattern, I start mapping the city, a tricoloured triptych; Catholic on one side, Protestant on the other, the neutral zone between. I snap photos from the car, collecting images for the painting that's forming in my head.

Aiden parks up. We walk into the city centre. A metal turnstile, like those at football grounds, bars our way. A uniform mans the barricade. We join the queue. The women ahead open their bags for inspection.

'What's this?' I ask Aiden.

'The usual, they're checking for bombs.'

When it's my turn my face flushes with guilt at what I am and what I'm not but we pass unchallenged and stagger along busy shopping streets, bumping against people bored by the dulled novelty of war zone living. Shoppers browse among flashing neon, 50% OFF signs and tinny muzak, pretending today is normal. Aiden says it's not; there's no bomb scare. I'm dizzied by it, relieved when we leave the madness of northern Irish normality.

Driving away from the centre, Aiden points out a road.

'The Crum's up there.'

'What?'

'Crumlin Road Jail. Not on the tour today.' He drives on. 'Shankill down there. Divis Street. We're coming to the Falls now.'

I peer through the rainy, mid-afternoon drear at houses small and narrow, most with at least one plywood window. Behind them tower blocks are stacked like Lego. Oily puddles shimmer on the tarmac; crisp packets clog the gutters. A woman dashes for the entry to the nearest block of flats. Behind her, patrolling soldiers sweep the scene for targets, walking two forwards, two backwards, either side of a monstrous motorised beast which oozes along, a mechanical slug on wheels.

'What the hell's that?' I point to the armoured arthropod crawling on six heavy-duty tyres, its snout nosing forward, the entry hatch set on top like a pork pie hat.

'Saracen,' Aiden says. 'It's what the BA patrol in. The peelers use Newry ice-cream vans, those grey Land Rovers we've seen.'

The soldiers' faces are hidden by helmets; their guns are raised. I think of telling Aiden to go back but, ashamed of my fear, I don't. People have to live here.

We match our pace to the patrol, lagging behind. At the next junction they turn left. Aiden exhales, slumps in his seat and fumbles for his cigarettes.

'Aye, they're off up the Shankill,' he says. 'They'll not want to be heading into the Falls now it's getting dark.'

There are more concertinaed houses, metal-shuttered shops, bald patches of waste ground. Then the land flattens on our right.

'Belfast cemetery,' Aiden explains. Houses spring up again on his side, fall away on mine. We come to a roundabout. An ornate stone wall, broken by a gothic archway, comes into view. 'And Milltown cemetery.' He parks at the arched entrance. 'Where all good Republicans go.'

'What about the bad ones?' I joke, throat tight and chest thrumming.

'Ditch in South Armagh.'

I asked for that.

It's chucking it down. Aiden climbs out, passes under the arch. I follow, fat raindrops pounding my head.

We walk through a forest of Celtic crosses and holy statues. Aiden makes for a tall grey pillar. At the monument he bows his head and blesses himself. Rain runs off the back of his leather jacket. I drop my gaze and study my trainers, now rimmed with sloppy mud. My wet jeans are clagged to my legs. I tuck soggy hair behind my ears and glance up. Aiden beckons me forward. There are dozens of names and dates, right back to 1866, etched on the stone. It's a memorial to fallen Republicans.

Ignorance burns my cheeks. I'd no idea it had been going on this long. I picture the patrolling Saracen, the soldiers and their guns. These lads died for nothing. My parents too. Anger warms me.

Aiden leads me to a plain headstone, the age-blurred inscription reads: Lt. General. Henry O'Hanlon, West Cork Brigade. Killed on active service for the Irish Republican Army 28th November, 1920, Kilmichael, Co. Cork. Age 20. Originally of Belfast. Proudly Remembered.

'Your granddaddy had me bring him here once.'

I rub my fingers over the shallow words and remember Daideo's photograph of the St Enda's junior hurling team. 'He had a school friend, Hal. Isn't that short for Henry?'

Aiden shrugs.

Another question turns in my head. I force myself to ask it:

'Are my parents here?'

'Don't think so. This is the only grave he visited,' Aiden says.

'Then where?'

'Glasnevin? Ask your granddaddy,' Aiden suggests.

I dodge his gaze. 'I can't, not after what he said, how he was when…'

'Aye, maybe best left,' Aiden mumbles.

'What do you know about them?' I press.

Aiden shakes his head. 'Just what I've said, they were active service volunteers.'

'Someone must know more.'

'Like what?'

'Anything; favourite food, bad habits, jokes they told: anything. Jesus, he doesn't even have photos of them.'

'That'll've been to make it harder for the peelers to identify them,' Aiden explains.

'It's not fair. I should know something. Would your dad be able to help?'

'Maybe. He doesn't like talking about them. They were pretty close, I reckon; he was broken up over what happened.'

I stare him down. Aiden relents.

'I guess we can ask,' he says. 'Come on, I'm drenched. Let's go.'

Melting into the car's upholstery, we pull away from the graveyard. A boxy building with a sodden Irish tricolour dripping from the flagpole, sits on the corner of the first side road to our right. The Celtic-lettered sign says 'The Felons'. Aiden swings into a parking space.

'What's this?'

'Republican club. Gerry A's old man started it, for the lads who've been inside for the cause.'

'Gerry A?'

'Ya know, Gerry Adams. My da's usually here about now.'

Inside a stocky man in his fifties, grey hair cut short, sleeves rolled up showing a harp tattoo, sits squashed behind a plastic table.

He smiles and stands. 'How are ya, Aiden? Looking for your da?'

'Aye, Patsy, is he here?'

'In the bar. Don't bother calling him out; I'll sign yous in.' He looks me over. 'Friend?'

'This is Caoilainn Finnighan. She's up from Dublin. I'm showing her the sights. Caoilainn, Patsy Maguire, club secretary,' Aiden says.

At the mention of my new name I'm offered a hand. 'You'll be Pat Finnighan's wee grandkiddie.' He grins at me.

'Pleased to meet you, love. You should tell your grandda to get himself up more; it's been too long.'

My hand is crushed in a heavy fist. I mumble about Daideo not being well.

'Sorry to hear that. Give him my best.'

He scribbles our names into a book on the table, Aiden drops coins into an old raspberry ripple ice-cream tub and we go into the bar.

The light is dim yet harsh, the result of steel grills over the windows and low watt bulbs that don't penetrate the corners. Apart from the grills, it's any bar; tables and chairs, cushioned benches, a dart board, a snooker table, populated exclusively by men. I falter in the doorway. Men only? Aiden strides ahead. Several lads call his name, wave, one salutes; he waves back, turns to me and beckons. I follow him over to a cluster of three older blokes propped against the bar.

One gets off his stool as we approach. He's a shorter, older Aiden; eyes lined with age, dark hair salted with grey. I don't know if I recognise Frank from memory or the likeness to Aiden.

'How are ya, lad?' He pulls Aiden into a fierce hug.

'I'm alright, Da.'

Frank turns to me. He hesitates a moment then grips my hand in both of his. I feel his fingers trembling.

'Look at you.' The last word is croaked. He swallows. His eyes are too bright. 'Last I saw you, you were knee-high. What'll yous have?' Without waiting for an answer he turns, grinding his eyeballs with finger and thumb, and calls for three large whiskeys.

His drinking companions slope off. Frank pulls up a stool for me. 'How's the ould fella? Better for having you around?'

I sip the whiskey. It burns my throat. 'I suppose.'

'Grand.' He hurries on. 'Have yous somewhere to stay tonight? We'd have you home but for the bloody Brits.'

'It's sorted,' Aiden says. 'Have you heard from Connor?'

'He got a comm out last week. He's coping. Your ma's upset though.' Frank lowers his voice. 'There's talk of a second strike. They got nothing from the last. Connor's put in for it.'

Aiden downs his whiskey and taps the glass on the bar; the barman takes it for refilling. I can't ask Frank about my parents now: present trumps past. Not wanting to intrude on their family crisis I look around, spot the toilets and get up. Crossing the room I pass a framed black and white photograph of five smiling lads: friends, larking about. Hung beneath is a wooden plaque engraved with their names and ages; all dead before they reached twenty-one. Next to it is a poster promoting the New Year's Eve party. Life's relentlessness winds me.

'You alright there, love?' One of Frank's cronies is at my elbow. He smiles.

'Yes, thanks. Just looking around.' I nod to the picture.

The smile snaps into a scowl. 'For what?'

'Nothing, I...'

Aiden appears. 'She's with me, Peadar. We're going.' He grabs my arm.

Peadar's scowl fades. 'Sure, that's fine.' He switches the smile back on. 'You were gave me a scare then,' he chuckles. 'Thought we'd let in a spy.'

'What?'

'Your accent, love. You sound like a bloody Brit.' He's grinning when he says it. The words cut through me.

Aiden mutters, 'Christ sake,' and tows me towards the fire exit. I twist round. Peadar is staring and, behind him, Frank watches us from the bar, his face pinched. Aiden lets go of my arm to smack the door open with both hands. He charges through it. I stumble after him, into an unlit side road, the words 'bloody Brit' chasing me.

Squinting against the darkness, I find the car. Aiden's in the driving seat. I climb in.

'Cheeky sod, did you hear that?'

'Shut up.'

'He said...'

'Wise up. My brother's gonna starve himself to death and you're whingeing about your accent,' Aiden snaps. 'You do sound like a fucking Brit. So just shut the hell up.'

We sit there for a minute, two, three. Furious words rage through my head, flood my mouth. I face Aiden, am about to deluge him with curses when I notice his shoulders shaking. I face front again. On the edge of my vision I see him put a hand up, rub his eyes. He sniffs once. Then starts the car and drives methodically at 30mph up the Falls, across the city, passing the floodlit City Hall, and over the river where he takes a left, parking by a house, the windows boarded and 'Taigs Out' daubed across the door in blood-red paint.

'This is us.' He plucks a torch from the glove box and gets out.

A shudder runs across my back. I wait a second before following, giving us both time to pull ourselves together.

The house reeks of damp. There's no power; Aiden guides us with the torch. In the living room an old sofa is pushed against one wall, the cushions ripped, stuffing oozing out. A sideboard lies up-tipped under the window. I pull my coat tighter.

'Have you seen enough?'

I nod.

'We'll drive back tomorrow,' he says, reaching for my hand. 'Sorry for saying that before, about you sounding… ya know.'

'It's true, though. It's why they didn't have me spread out on the tarmac at the border. It's what I am.'

'You were always Irish, you just didn't know it,' Aiden corrects.

'And knowing's enough, is it?'

He squeezes my hand. 'There's a chippy on the corner. You hungry?'

'Yeah.'

'I'll be five minutes.' He gives me the torch and leaves before I can say I'm sorry too.

While he's gone I roam the house, sweeping each room with the narrow white beam. Floorboards are peeled back like banana skins. In the kitchen there's a broken table and the splintered legs of several chairs. Cupboard doors hang on wrenched hinges. The bathroom sink has been pulled off and dumped inside the bath. Slimy water lurks in the toilet bowl. One bedroom has a stained mattress on the floor, another a smashed wardrobe. A teddy bear lies facedown on the bare floor. I pick it up, stroke an ear, and carry him with me.

Clutching ted I retreat downstairs, and sag into the sofa, sinking down through Kapok and memories. I flick the torch off and stare into blackness, squeezing ted, wondering about the child forced to leave him behind in the chaos of fleeing from neighbours wielding clubs, petrol bombs, maybe even guns?

I was seven, eight? We were squatting, camping I'd been told, in a boarded-up house on a ready-for-the-bulldozers estate...

'Why do we have to stay here, Mummy?'

'We're protecting these people's homes.'

'It smells. I don't want to stay here.'

'If we don't stay, love, who'll stop these homes being destroyed?'

'Can't the police do that, Mummy?'

'What've I said about not trusting the police, love? You mustn't trust anyone with that much power; they always abuse it.'

'What's 'abuse'?'

'They do what's best for themselves and don't care if they hurt others. The police, the armed forces, big corporations, politicians; they're all too powerful for our good so it's up to us to keep ourselves and others safe from them, from all powerful bullies and bad guys. That's why we're here. It's important.'...

It was always bloody important.

But never as important as this.

The police came to evict us. There was a lot of noise; shouting, banging. I was led outside. A policewoman lifted me into a van. I wouldn't tell her my name.

The front door clacks, jarring me out of the remembered nightmare, into the real one. I cram ted into the sofa's guts.

Aiden has brought cod and chips twice. The greasy smell hangs like fog in the cold air. We eat with our fingers. I bolt my food; Aiden rakes through his, eating hardly any. We smoke a while then he fetches a rug from the car and we huddle under it on the sofa, in our jackets. My feet are wet; their icy numbness nags me. I lie listening to Aiden's rapid breathing. My mind flicks to the man being beaten at the checkpoint. I reach into the stuffing, slip ted from his hiding place and cuddle him to my chest. How did things get so bad in the north? How did we let it get this way? I don't even know who 'we' is: British or Irish? I don't know which side I'm on. In Belfast you have to take a side. But you don't pick it; fate does that for you.

I wanted to understand the past but now I don't recognise the present.

Voices shout. Glass breaks. Aiden sits up.

'What's going on?' I ask.

He goes to the window. 'Loyalist attack. Stay here.' He strides to the door.

'What're you doing?'

He's gone before I finish asking.

In the street people are running, men, boys, carrying bricks or bottles. Women watch from their doorsteps. Aiden steps out, waylaying one of the older men. They talk. The man points up the road; Aiden takes off. I run after him, against common sense and the growing mob's current, stumbling as I struggle to keep Aiden in sight. He dashes into a house. I stop at the gate, see him through the open front door, standing in the hall, tucking a gun into the waistband of his jeans. A woman in dressing gown and slippers is with him. She sees me.

'Who the fuck're you?' she bawls.

Aiden turns. 'I told you to stay put. It's alright, Mary, she's with me.' He comes over, grabs my arm. 'Go back to the house.'

'No.'

'Fuck sake.' He sprints into the street.

'Leave it to the men, love, they know what they're doing,' the woman says.

Do they? I want to laugh.

Aiden has vanished. I walk into the running crowd; people rush up behind me, charge into me and spin off, deflected. A few hundred yards down the road is a junction where the crowd crushes itself.

Yellow flashes light the scene. 'Fenian bastards!' 'Taigs!' 'Orange scum!' 'Loyalist bollocks!' Missiles are hurled. Others land around me with cracks and thumps. People retreat and reload, snatching up second-hand rocks, lobbing them back. Next to me a boy touches a match to a rag dangling from the neck of a milk bottle sloshing with murky fluid. The rag ignites. He chucks the bottle and I trace its trajectory, watching it shatter against the opposite kerb, spilling fire.

Waves of people sweep back and forth in the fighting's swell. Something whacks me on the chest and I fall. Feet pound around me, over me. I curl into myself. Boots jab my back, land on my shoulder and lift off again as the runner vaults me. I get onto my knees and up, am shoved about. I wobble, clutching for something to hold onto, push off from. The darkness is lit by flaming puddles; I can't tell friend from foe. Fear overwhelms me. I swing round, searching for Aiden, an exit: a weapon.

A brick crashes at my feet, chips off it spattering my legs. It happens in slow motion; I watch each shard fly free. Thoughts crystallise, step-by-step instructions. I pick it up, weigh it in my palm, arc my arm and throw. The weight leaves my hand and soars.

I try to follow its flight but lose it among others sailing through the air. I elbow to the edge of the mob, watching hunks of masonry curve up, over and smack down across the way. Some shatter, others bed in, scarring the road. A man is hit, his forehead split. He takes one pace and drops. The crowd swallows him. I'm suddenly afraid of myself. I've never fought like this before. I've never had to.

Bullets are spat into the air. There's a second's freeze frame then chaos restarts. A helicopter chatters across the sky, its spotlight piercing the crowd. Sirens scream. Around me the swarm swoops and dives, splitting and reforming. I'm pushed and pulled, dragged with it: part of it. I fight towards the ragged edge and glance back as now familiar grey Land Rovers plough into the churning surge of people.

The Land Rovers spew up policemen in riot gear.

Flames slice the blackness. The air ripples with the shattering of glass and clanging of brick on metal.

I'm grabbed, yanked backwards. It's Aiden, cheek bruised and nose bloody.

'We need to go,' he yells.

He drags me into a running retreat, back to the violated house. We tumble inside, him shoving me, me tripping. He whacks the door shut and leaps over me. There's the scudding screech of wood dragged across wood. He emerges towing the sideboard.

'Gis a hand, will ya?'

I scramble up, take the other end and we wrestle it into place, barricading the front.

'Don't reckon they'll check but in case,' he mutters.

I lean against the wall, panting, shaking. In the darkness I lose Aiden.

The torch flashes on; its white beam inspects me.

'Wise up; you can't go jumping off like that. It was really stupid. You could've been hurt.'

Bruises throb across my back and chest. 'So could you.'

'I'm trained for this. You're not.'

'You reckon I've never been caught up in a riot before? What do you think the '72 miners' strikes were, a teddy bear's picnic?'

'You were a only a wee 'un then. And yous weren't facing peelers with guns. Don't kid on you know what you're doing here. You don't.'

'And you do?'

'Aye, this is what I grew up doing. Knowing. I've been at this since I was ten. So stop believing you can pick it up in an afternoon. You'll get us both lifted. Or killed.'

His words slap sense into me. I push the torch away, getting the beam off my shame-scorched cheeks. My face cools. His breathing slows, quietens.

'You OK?' He puts a hand on my shoulder.

My tongue is dried up, my thoughts a wordless mess. He strokes the torchlight back over me.

'You're bleeding.' He points to my face.

My cheek feels sticky. My fingers come away stained.

'So are you.'

He wipes his nose with the palm of his hand, studies the inky smear.

'I don't want you getting hurt.'

'What about you?'

'That's my choice.' He laughs, rubs his hand on his jeans. 'Some sodding choice. You know what they tell you when you join? That you're heading one of two places: jail or the cemetery. But you join anyway 'cos this way you can defend your family, try to make things fairer, better. That's what this war is, Caoilainn, fighting to make things better than they used to be which is nothing but year after bloody year, decades, centuries, like tonight and worse. How's that for an education?'

It's a start.

## Belfast Man Dies Following Newtownards Riots
## Police Appeal for Witnesses

Six days after street disturbances in East Belfast, police have confirmed the death of William Stephenson, 50, of Newtownards Road.

Mr Stephenson, a Protestant, was injured on Boxing Day night when fighting broke out between locals from the Catholic enclave of Short Strand and Protestant residents in the area. Mr Stephenson was struck on the head by a missile and taken to Belfast City Hospital where he remained in critical condition until his death earlier today.

Police are appealing for information about the attack, which occurred as Mr Stephenson stood outside his house.

Mr Stephenson is not known to have any connections with paramilitary groupings.

# Dublin—1ˢᵗ March, 1981

## Second Maze Hunger Strike Starts Republican Prisoner Bobby Sands Refuses Food

Less than four months after the ending of a hunger strike by Republicans in the Maze Prison a second strike has begun today. The strike, announced by Sinn Fein, is in response to the failure of British officials to concede to demands made by IRA prisoners seeking political status.

A prison spokesman confirmed that Bobby Sands, 27, OC of the Republicans in the H-Blocks, has this morning refused food. It is believed this strike will be staged, with men joining at predetermined intervals.

In a statement issued by the Republican Press Centre, Belfast, Sands said, 'Once again under the duress of the British barbarity and in the ugly face of further British intransigence, we are forced to embark upon a hunger strike. If the British Government cling to the forlorn hope that they can break the men of the H-Blocks they should look at their failures during the last four and half years of our protests. In one way or another, victory will be ours because we have the will to win.'

Downing Street has yet to comment on this second strike.

I give up on the past, focus on muddling through the present.

Daideo gives up on the future. He stops eating.

Every morning before college I cook a fry-up. He slowly chews one mouthful. I potter about the kitchen. He's forced to swallow and start on a second forkful. I tie back my hair, lace up my trainers, pack my sketchpad. He carves off another bite. I collect the post, give Daideo the bills. He sets his fork down.

'You'll be late.'

'I've plenty of time.'

He puts the third bite into his mouth. I butter bread, slice cheese, make sandwiches. One I thrust into my bag, the other I leave on a plate in the fridge.

'See you tonight.'

'Aye, off you go.' He pats my arm with a skeletal hand.

When I get home the plate is on the table, empty; the sandwiches are in the bin. The crusts are curled, the cheese sweaty. If I'm lucky there are a couple of bites missing. I cook tea, eat, watch him cutting his food into ever smaller pieces, not eating. Gravy dregs solidify on my plate. Food petrifies on his. The bin fills up with a collage of rotting meals.

He wants to die like this, cheating the cancer.

One night, as we stare at the telly, he says this is mine when he's gone.

'I've made a will, so I have, and been careful with my money. The house is paid off and there's enough to keep you going a fair while. You can finish your studies, set yourself up with a studio, whatever you want.'

'Don't be daft,' I reply, changing the channel before the news blurts hunger strike updates.

'You've a talent; make better use of it than I did mine,' he instructs. 'Some day your work'll be in one of those galleries on Temple Bar, maybe even the National, eh?'

'And you'll be at the opening with me.'

Another night he produces a brown envelope. He's a plot bought and paid for in Milltown, an old Republican's last home. I think of the graves that aren't there: Cathal and Fiona. I couldn't find them in Glasnevin either. But I still can't bring myself to ask him about them and, apart from Frank, who I'm wary of bothering with this now he has a son readying for the hunger strike, there's no one else I can ask. I shelve my questions.

'Put what you want on my headstone,' Daideo adds, 'as long as it's not religious. The priest'll say his bit, those buggers get you in the end, but I'll not spend eternity beneath their blasted blarney. Sure, He'll not have the last word on me.'

'You've years yet.'

'I have not.' He presses the envelope into my hands. 'It's arranged so see you mark my wishes: no prayers and no tears.'

Other times he tells me to go out, enjoy myself. My lack of friends makes him uneasy; his meant so much to him. He says it as I hand him supper: cocoa and barmbrack. He sips the chocolaty liquid and tucks crumbs of the fruit loaf into his mouth, never enough to finish the whole slice.

I swat away his words. I've never been anywhere long enough to make friends; I'm fine without. He flinches. I try to sooth. Anyway, I'd rather be home with him, recovering the time we've lost, time he robbed me of, time he's stealing again. I get him tale-telling; a legend, a myth. Once I luck out, Daideo forgetting himself, his pain, and dipping into the family annals. He reveals how my ma and da met at a local dance, an ordinary story that didn't deserve such a tragic ending. I lose myself in his memories; they paint over our cracked pasts, paste the present together.

Weeks blur by; Daideo becomes a living corpse. One morning his wasted legs buckle as he's shaving. I hear the clatter above the sizzing of rashers, drop the spatula and run. He's crumpled on the floor, red arced over the white tiles, spray from a cut done as he fell. When I lift him he's hollow like a bird, his heart thrumming fast. I sit him on the toilet and stem the bleeding with a towel that, later, I rinse and re-rinse, crying as watery red streams of my grandfather's life trickle down the plughole. The bacon is burnt; neither of us eats that morning.

I think about getting help, but who from? Aiden's on the run; things are bad in the north since the strike started again. When he calls I lie, say things are fine, because I don't want him worrying about my problems when his are so much bigger. I rule out our neighbours, the busybody Brennans or kill-you-with-kindness Kellys. I won't have anyone from college interfering. I even think about Mum and Dad, Susan and John. But this isn't their problem. Maybe Frank? But it's me, not Daideo, who wants handholding.

We battle on, him for death; me for life. I cook and sit over him until he eats. I'm late for college and have to stay back, catching up. When I get home Daideo is asleep, his eyes closed in a papier-mâché skull.

I break.

'Fuck sake, eat it.' I snatch the plate of mince, mash and peas and hold it under his nose.

He pushes it away. 'I'm not hungry.'

'I know what you're doing. Stop it.'

He crosses his arms.

'Daideo, this is crazy, please.' Tears prick my eyes. 'You're killing yourself.'

'Haven't I that right at my age?' He swipes the plate from my hand. It frisbees across the kitchen and shatters over the cooker. On legs all sharp white bone and shivering skin, he hauls himself up and totters from the room.

I fling my own plate at the sink. Then cry over the mess.

That night I sneak into his bedroom while he's sleeping. The air is hot, thick and dry. He stirs, mutters oaths; I glimpse his bloodless shrunken gums, watch his mottled hand feebly striking long-dead enemies. On the bedside table his yellowed false teeth bob in a glass. A rozzer smashed out his real ones during the War of Independence. He told me that, and how he shot dead the RIC man a week later. To some that makes him a hero, to others a murderer. But I've seen him use two cadaverous hands to get his teacup to his lips and lean on his stick, knotted knuckles flexing, to go from kitchen to living room. To me he's just a frail old man, the grandfather I love, am slowly losing. I slip out.

I want to understand him. In the living room I sit with my sketchpad. If he's the original, I'm a print taken from it but I'm too cowardly to see the image of myself in him. The page stays blank.

Next morning I have toast and cereal, tea. I pour him a cup as he enters the kitchen, holding onto the doorframe, the fridge, the cupboards, on his way to the table.

'Do you need a hand tidying up?' he asks gruffly, nodding to the food-crusted cooker.

'No.' I light a cigarette.

He stretches for the cup I've put beyond easy reach. I don't help. Fingers splayed, he grabs the cup, nearly toppling it.

'I'm the last, so I am.' He sighs.

'Of what?'

'My school pals, St Enda's, class of '16. Did the lad show you Hal's grave?'

'Yes. What happened to the others?'

He rubs the loose skin of his brow; I expect it to tear and bleed but it's already dead leather.

'Charlie,' he sighs, 'your… Susan's uncle, he was killed during the Rising, sixteen he was. Patrick too. And another wee lad; Jesus, I don't remember his name but he was our company piper. Freddie.' He shakes his head. 'Freddie was a Freestater, after the Treaty. We never spoke again. I heard he died from heart trouble in the fifties. And Cathleen.' He smiles now. 'Sure, she was too good for me. That,' he points to the locket around my neck, 'was hers. She returned it to me the day she came to tell me she was marrying someone else. Sick of waiting for me to finish fighting, so she was. They went abroad, America. She's dead now.'

I squeeze the locket in my fist.

'Why did you fight?'

'It was too important not to.'

'And is it still?'

'Aye.'

'So if you were young now you'd be fighting?'

'That'd be my choice to make.'

'Would you?'

'I would.'

'It's why you sent me away, isn't it?' I know the answer is yes but I need him to say it.

'You're too much like me for your own good and mine,' he mutters. 'Sure, I was after you understanding why sometimes you need to fight. I knew Susan and John'd teach you that. But I was never after you doing it, not here. Not like I had to.'

'But if I decide to…'

He clutches my hand. His fingers are brittle, frost-burnt branches. 'I've no right telling you how to live, just as my father didn't telling me, but I'll not lie to you: I don't want a life for you such as I had. I hoped the past would end with me.'

'How's that possible when there are still Brits in the north, when you suffered so much for nothing? You haven't seen what it's like up there now.'

'I don't need to. Jesus, I've seen it all before. It needs tearing down, ripping up, painting over.'

I try to pull my hand free but his fingers bite down on mine.

'Caoilainn, I'm tired,' he sighs. 'Christ, I'm eighty-one, it's enough. My fight's over.'

'What about me?'

His grip slackens. 'You'll do what you want, just like I did but I'll ask you to have the decency to wait 'til I'm buried.'

Inside he's already dead, has been for days, weeks, maybe years. Realising that numbs my fear and ramps up my panic.

'Where are my parents buried?'

His eyes dart away from mine. 'Monaghan.'

'Why?'

'That's where we were living at the time.'

'Why not Milltown, or Glasnevin, the Republican plots?'

'It wasn't right.'

'But if they died fighting...'

He bangs his cup down. Steaming tea splashes onto his hand. He doesn't notice. I jump up to fetch a cloth, ice; he stops me with a scowl. I sink down, cowering from his rage and pain.

'They should never have died the way they did. It wasn't fair. I didn't want it marked; tricolours, berets, graveside gunshots. They deserved peace.' His eyes fill with tears. 'We all deserve peace, Caoilainn.'

'Aye, we do.' My words smoulder.

Daideo rubs his watery eyes, squeezes my hand again, cools my anger with his grief. 'Just think on it before you're doing anything. Le do thoil*. Do what your heart tells you is right.'

'I will.'

He nods. Smiles. 'Aye, that's wise advice given me by a wise woman. Yous would've got on.' He lets go of my hand. 'Now get yourself to college. I'll see you after.'

I stand at my easel, squinting at the Belfast triptych. I've been working on it since term started. It's to be my assessed piece but I can't get the city's hostility into it. I've painted, over-painted, scraped back, darkened; it always turns out anaemic. From across the room Mr Walsh, who's on his rounds,

---

* Please

73

checking and encouraging, catches my eye. He pushes his glasses up his nose, heads over.

'How're you getting on?'

I scowl and smear more black into the clouds.

'If you're not happy with it there's time for you to start something else,' he says.

'No.'

The word booms around the studio. Several students look up. Colleen smirks and leans over to Clare. They giggle.

'Come into my office, let's have a chat,' Mr Walsh suggests.

'What for?'

'I'm worried. You've not been yourself this term.'

He's thinking about the bruise on my cheek, still visible after the Christmas holiday, and the 'chat' he tried to have with me then. He's thinking he's young and cool enough for hearing confidences but old and wise enough for giving advice. I'm thinking he should mind his own fucking business.

'How would you know?'

'I can see it in your work.'

I pick up the Nescafe jar filled with mucky turps and splash the grey liquid over my canvas. The scene bleeds into itself. 'What do you see now?' I kick the easel. It clatters to the floor. I walk.

In the car park I stop to light a cigarette. The wind is wild and my lighter keeps blowing out.

'Try mine; it's windproof.' Mr Walsh offers me his Zippo. The wind has flicked up the collar of his corduroy jacket. With his John Lennon glasses, pudding-bowl haircut and paint-stained fingers he's some leftover beatnik Beatle. 'Am I not allowed to be worried about you?'

'I'm fine.' I turn to go.

'Caoilainn.'

I stop.

'I know it must be hard for you, trying to settle in, make friends. If you ever need to talk I'm…'

I head for St. Stephen's Green.

When I get to the park I find a bench near the pond and sit hunched into my anorak, watching the ducks waddle and squabble. Memories of Daideo, Aiden and me bob on the ruffled water. It feels like this is where I started, because it's the furthest back I can reach. Now I'm here again as though I never left. But I did, and coming back isn't the same as going back. Too much has changed.

I stay in the park all afternoon, wondering what the hell I'm doing: will do.

When I finally get home the house is empty. Daideo is in his chair. He's been dead a while, the doctor says.

# Belfast—7ᵗʰ May, 1981

## Republicans Bury Their Hero
## 100,000 Line the Route of Sands' Funeral

The funeral of Republican hunger striker, Bobby Sands, MP, was held today in West Belfast. An estimated 100,000 mourners lined the route of the cortege from the Sands' family home on the Twinbrook Estate to Milltown cemetery where he was interred in the Republican plot. Following a sixty-six day fast, Sands, 27, lapsed into a coma on 3ʳᵈ May and died in the early hours on the morning of the fifth.

Sinn Fein's Gerry Adams addressed mourners and comforted members of the Sands' family, including Sands' sister, Marcella.

In a statement issued after Sands' death Margaret Thatcher said, 'Mr Sands was a convicted criminal. He chose to take his own life. It was a choice his organisation did not give to many of their victims.'

Three other Republicans remain on hunger strike and there is speculation that more will join if agreement over political status is not reached.

Sands leaves behind an eight year old son, Gerard.

The crowd paces behind the piper. Women sob; men hide tears. Children trail along, dazed by the throng making its painful journey to Milltown. It's my second funeral here in a week.

For Daideo there was only a handful of us: Aiden, Frank, Aiden's ma, Nora, and younger brother, Danny; the Felons' club secretary, Patsy, and half a dozen anonymous men who muttered things like, 'He was a grand ould fella,' and, 'Fought with Pearse, so he did.' Our Dublin neighbours made the journey, the Brennans to gawp, the Kellys to fuss. They left once the priest finished the curt oration that was all Daideo had permitted. As they picked their way between the graves Patsy cocked his head to Aiden.

'Come on, lad, and we can get to the club for a drink.'

Aiden checked over both shoulders, produced a handgun, aimed for the soggy clouds, fired three times and dropped the gun into his mum's handbag. Frank took my elbow.

'It's grand you were with him at the end. Sure, 'tis the best I could've done, getting you back here.'

He stared into Daideo's grave. Two tears dropped from his chin. He shook his head and set off after Patsy, who was making for the Felons where drinks were free in tribute to the passing of the old guard.

I was still in Belfast, staying with Aiden's parents because I couldn't face the empty Dublin house, when Bobby Sands died two days after my nineteenth birthday.

Sands' death is an official tragedy, verso to Daideo's recto in the book of Republican martyrdom.

I stand with Nora and Frank, Danny beside me, head up, jaw clenched. He's begging Aiden to get him into the 'Ra now. He's fourteen, the age Daideo was when he joined the Irish Republican Brotherhood.

Aiden's in the colour party, alongside the tricolour-draped coffin, wearing his Army gear, a warrior in a balaclava knitted by someone's granny.

We mass around the grave. The guns appear, modern-looking rifles.

Frank says, 'They've brought out the Armalites for the wee lad. That's grand.'

I watch Aiden, third from the left, as he raises the weapon and sights along the barrel in formation with the lads beside him. Shots rip the sky.

Nora takes my arm. 'Are you alright, love?'

I watch them put Sands in the ground before nudging through weeping mourners until I reach Daideo's grave. I sit on the mound of loose earth, facing away from the thinning crowd, facing up to myself.

Daideo thought the Ryans would teach me to fight but all I learnt from them was what it's like to be powerless. Words on placards, voices chanting, feet marching; no one gets killed, but nothing changes.

Here it's fingers on triggers, bombs exploding, feet running. People dying. Things have to change.

Protests only have supporters and critics; wars have winners and losers.

I picture Daideo as a young man, standing on a windswept hillside, kitted out as an ancient Gaelic warrior, readying to lead his army into battle. I see the brushstroke clouds, the smooth blending on his windblown cloak, the gleam of his sword's blade done with a streak of zinc white no.45.

But it wasn't like that. I don't know how it was; the things he told me are just pencil lines, without light and shadow. The only colours I can ever apply are crimson red no.16 and lamp black no.07.

A hand touches my shoulder. Aiden stands there, unmasked and in civvies.

He crouches down. 'Caoilainn, I'm needing to go. Are you OK?'

He's leaving again, taking away his patient resilience, his unwavering strength, his gentle love, right when I need them most. We stand.

'Fine. I'm going home tomorrow. Come and see me soon?'

He frowns. 'I don't know what I'll…'

'Just come and see me, for God sake.'

'Alright.'

I pull away, start walking.

'Are you not getting a lift back with my folks?'

'No.'

I wander around inside Milltown, reading headstones, then up through the Falls, passing the graffiti:

*Blessed are those who hunger for justice*
*Give them their rights, not their last rites*
*Political power stems from the barrel of a gun*
*Oppression breeds resistance; Resistance brings freedom*
*Ireland unfree shall never be at peace—P H Pearse*
*Welcome to West Belfast: Provo Land*

When I arrive at the O'Neills' Nora is dishing out.

'Jesus, Caoilainn, we've been worried,' she says, setting down her spoon.

'Sorry.'

I lay the table. The four of us eat in taut silence. His plate still piled with stew, Danny bangs his fork down and runs out. Frank goes after him. Nora gives one big, dry sob.

'How could she let that wee boy die? She's the iron bitch, so she is!' Her words sear the air. 'He was at school with our Connor. A lovely wee lad, he was, so bright.'

'But this'll be the end of it now, won't it?'

Nora sniffs. 'She'll not be happy 'til she's seen them all in their graves.' She pulls something from her pocket. 'This came yesterday.'

She gives me a small hard lump of tightly folded toilet roll: a prison comm. I peel apart the brittle paper. Cramped writing fills the square, words falling off the edges. Reading it hurts my eyes. It's from Connor. He's to be in the next wave to join the strike.

'Mother Mary, haven't we suffered enough?' She shakes her head. 'But what else can we do against those bastards? We've got to keep going. Sure, every day we manage that we've our victory.'

When I return to Dublin it's like none of it happened; I didn't bury Daideo, wasn't at Sands' funeral, never read Connor's comm or felt Nora's agony. Everything is in place; my rucksack by the door, Daideo's hat and coat on the hall stand, his 'Green Dawn' painting on the wall. The only proof of what I've lived through this last fortnight is the cold silence of an empty house.

Numbness and habit make me scoop up the post and flick through it. There's a gas bill, a letter from college warning unless I explain my absence I'll be expelled and a card with a Dublin frank. I open the card.

It's from Mr Walsh. He's found out about Daideo. His phone number is printed with instructions for me to ring him if I need to talk.

I bin everything but the bill.

The days are shapeless. I drift through them, mooching around Dublin, clutching my sketchpad. I want to draw Daideo before I forget his face but the eyes are always sightless. I try other subjects instead; the GPO's columned entrance, the bandstand in St Stephen's Green, the Roto's Remembrance Garden, but I can't bring myself to finish these drawings. They're all wrong. I give up, devote myself full time to mooching.

During the baggy nights that swamp me I sit with Daideo's cracked-leather rucksack beside me, the fragile contents on my lap, breathing in pale traces of him and replaying everything in my head, sometimes working backwards from where I am now, other times working forwards from any of the places I've been. Twice I pick up the phone, dial the past, hang up before it answers: they answer. I'm afraid they'll actually help me. I tell myself they're probably off sitting-in somewhere anyway. Besides, I need to find my own way. That's what I do most, rehearsing the future in my mind, scene by scene, a comic book story with images of Marvel bright violence. The urgency to act is crushing me but I still can't choose.

One teatime there's a knock at the door. I find Mr Walsh on the step, rain plastering his hair to his forehead and spattering against his glasses.

'Hello, Caoilainn, how are you?'

'What are you doing here?'

He blinks. 'Did you get my card?'

'Yes. How did you know?'

He removes his glasses and smears raindrops onto his sleeve. He looks younger without them.

'I was worried by your absence so I got your number from the college registrar but when I couldn't get a reply I called round. One of your neighbours told me about your grandfather. I'm sorry.'

Bloody Mr Brennan. I shrug. 'He was old. He'd had enough.'

There's no reply to that so Mr Walsh hurries on. 'Your neighbour said you were in Belfast. Have you family there?'

'No. It's where Daideo wanted to be buried. Milltown.'

'But your parents came over?'

My fingers grip the door. 'My parents are dead.'

'I thought they lived in England.' He blinks again. 'Your file, from PSAD, said...'

'They're not my parents.'

We don't speak for a minute. The rain continues battering Mr Walsh, his jacket darkening as the downpour soaks it. He glances at the sodden sky.

'May I come in?'

I could say no, shut the door, but that's not dealing with it. I step aside.

As he wipes his loafers on the mat his gaze falls on Daideo's painting.

'That's not yours,' he comments.

'It's Daideo's.'

Mr Walsh goes over, studies the brushstrokes. 'Artistic talent runs in the family,' he muses. 'The colours are very evocative. Does it have a title?'

'"Green Dawn at St Enda's".'

'Your grandfather was at St Enda's?'

'Yes. I think Mr Pearse helped him paint it.'

Mr Walsh jerks round. 'Willie Pearse?'

'Yes. He was there 1911 to 1916.' I make him wait. 'He was in the GPO, Easter week.'

'He fought with Pearse?'

I smile. 'Yes. You want a cuppa?'

I make tea and we sit in the lounge, me in Daideo's armchair, Mr Walsh on the sofa. He's curious; I tell him, glad of the chance to remember. Daideo's stories dance on my tongue; in them he lives again, growing young and becoming a hero.

'That's quite the life, your grandfather had himself,' Mr Walsh says when I've finished. 'But you haven't said anything about yourself, your parents.'

I shrug. 'They died when I was little. Daideo couldn't cope so he found a family to take me. I came back when I learnt he was ill.'

'And will you be staying?'

'Yes.'

Mr Walsh smiles. 'Grand. I'd be sorry to lose a promising student. I'll have a word with the president tomorrow about your absence.'

I reach for my cigarettes. 'I'm not coming back to college.'

Mr Walsh blinks twice, his eyes large behind thick lenses. 'Why not?'

I could lie but I want to test him. And myself.

'It wasn't just the one funeral I was at in Belfast.'

Mr Walsh purses his lips. 'You mustn't let things in the north prey on your mind.'

'Have you even been there? Do you know what it's like?'

'Sure, it's a terrible situation but what good is it, you involving yourself?'

'So we should ignore the injustice, the suffering, hope it'll go away?'

'Of course not. But there are better ways to fight it.'

'Like?'

'Martin Luther King. Ghandi. Peaceful protests.'

'They've tried that. Paisley's yobs bashed their skulls in with cudgels. I've seen it all my life; protests are a waste of time.' I grind my cigarette out in the ashtray.

He pushes his glasses up his nose, stutters, 'Tell me you're not thinking of, of…'

'Right now I'm just thinking, about everything. I don't know what I'm going to do. I do know I'm not going to be a bystander. Art's not the only thing that runs in the family.'

'A lot of folk could say that but it's not a reason.'

I think of Daideo, my dead parents. 'Isn't it?'

'My grandfather and great uncle fought during Easter week too, Mount Street, I think, but that doesn't mean I should do the same now.'

'Don't you think we've a duty to fight what's happening up there?'

'Innocent people get killed.'

'Don't they in every war?'

'Of course, but you don't put a fire out by throwing petrol on it. You've a talent. Why not use your art instead, to protest? You could exhibit internationally one day, let the rest of the world see what's happening in the north.'

'The lads in H-5 don't have that long. No one up there does.' I stand. 'You need to leave.'

'Do you realise what you're risking?' He stands too, reaches out like he would grab and shake me but stops himself.

I go into the hall and open the front door. He follows.

'You're upset now, grieving. Don't do something quickly that you'll regret slowly and for a long time,' he cautions.

I'm not. I won't. So fuck you.

We face off for a minute. Mr Walsh blinks one last time.

'Please, Caoilainn, think about this.'

'I am.'

He ducks back under the downpour. I close the door on him. Do you realise what you're risking? I charge into the living room and snatch up my sketchpad, flicking it over to the latest attempt at Daideo's portrait. Scrabbling for a pencil I drop onto the floor, the pad on the hearth, and draw his eyes. They stare back at me, defiant and alive. I'm risking everything. It's too important not to.

Days pass, enough to make a fortnight. A letter comes from college saying I've been expelled. I put it in the bin and my art stuff in the attic. Pray for Aiden to show up. He doesn't. I get my art stuff down again and go through my scrapbook of ideas, plans, sketches, colour tests and photographs. I fill pages with Celtic symbols, doodles of Belfast graffiti and stickmen figures cramped into coffins carried by other stickmen and one stickwoman.

Four more dead hunger strikers later Aiden appears. His clothes are rumpled and dirty, he's unshaven, the shadows under his eyes are black. He grins.

'How much trouble am I in?'

'By the look of you, a lot.'

'I mean with you.'

'I'd like to slap you six ways to Sunday but what good would that do?'

He runs a bath. I sort his clothes for the machine, find his handgun in the pocket of his sweatshirt. I transfer it to my waistband then do him beans on toast. We sit in the kitchen.

'How's Connor?'

'They've him on the hospital wing with the others. Martin's bad.'

'And you?'

'Knackered.' He swallows the last mouthful and lights a cigarette. 'How 'bout yourself?'

I pull out his gun, clunk it down on the table.

'Shite, did I leave it in my pocket again?'

I nod.

He reaches for it but I hold on. 'I want to do something.'

He rubs a hand through his hair. 'What?'

'I don't know, something to help.'

'Ach, there's marches being organised, down here as well as in the north.'

'I spent my childhood on marches; they never got us anywhere. There must be something else?'

He inches the gun out from under my hand. My heart throbs, my own breath chokes me. Is this the moment I make my choice? Have I made it already?

'Leave it with me, eh?' Aiden says, tucking the gun away.


Two days later Aiden announces there's someone wanting to meet me, a Republican is all he'll say when I ask who.

We stroll through Dublin's suburbs, the first of June's sun warm on our backs, the evening sky a swathe of pink and lilac. A shiver ripples through me.

The house is a semi with a rose garden and a whitewashed step. We're greeted at the door by a tall, slim man, about thirty, square jaw, smooth skin, hazel eyes, wavy fair hair and smartly dressed in slacks and a shirt.

'How are ya, Aiden?' They shake hands. He turns to me. 'So you're wee Caoilainn.' His grip is strong. Power vibrates the air around him, making my nerves spasm. 'That's a grand Irish name you've got.' He smiles, showing even white teeth.

'Thanks.' I expect him to introduce himself. He just steps back to let us pass.

'Are you not going to tell me who you are?' I ask.

He turns and grins. 'If you're after a name call me Martin.'

His charade reveals more than it hides. He might as well've called himself Michael Collins. He's a big man. I feel suddenly sick. What the fuck am I doing?

He shows us into a front room of flower-print cushions and net curtains, offers tea; Aiden accepts. The big man goes to see to it. I'm standing awkwardly on the rug, staring at a picture of the Virgin, cursing myself, when he returns.

'Tea'll be along,' he says, sliding onto the sofa, stretching out long legs and lighting a cigarette.

Aiden and I take up the fireside armchairs. For ten seconds Martin studies me. I stare back, face neutral, heart pulsing.

'I was sorry to hear about your granddaddy.'

'He was ready.'

Martin nods. A young woman carries in a tray of tea things, including a plate of gingersnaps.

'Do yous want anything else?'

'We're fine,' Martin tells her.

'Then I'm away.'

As Martin pours tea the front door clicks closed. He hands me a cup.

'So you're wanting to help, Aiden says.'

Throat half throttled by fear, I nod.

'I've a wee project might suit you. Aiden says you paint.'

I manage to croak, 'Yes.'

'We're after a new mural for the side of the Sinn Fein offices in Belfast. You were at Sands' funeral?'

I nod.

'Can you do something for him, a memorial?'

I glance at Aiden who smiles encouragement. I feel myself drowning, sinking beneath waves of, what? Relief? Disappointment? I flail about for rescue.

'Sure, she could,' Aiden prompts.

I pull myself up, out. 'What were you wanting?'

Martin shrugs. 'You're the artist. This might help though.' He goes to the sideboard, takes something from a drawer and gives me it.

It's a grainy black and white photograph of Sands, his young face full and smiling, his hair falling in long silky waves to his shoulders; the Bobby Sands people need, alive and living, not the one they've got: wasted to death.

As we stroll home I curl my fingers around the photo, now tucked in my pocket.

'Your first mission,' Aiden jokes.

'Commission.'

'What?'

'Artists get 'com'-missions.'

'Oh, right. But you're happy,' he probes. 'You're helping now, so you are.'

'I thought…'

Aiden jolts to a stop. 'What?'

'Nothing. Yes, I'm glad to be doing something.'

Armed with a sketch pad, two pencils (1H for outlines; 2B for shading), the grainy snap of Sands and Daideo's 'Green Dawn' painting I set to work. The face of a smiling young man with everything to die for fills the paper. I rough out shape, perspective, light and shade, add a quote, 'our revenge will be the laughter of our children', then transfer this to a small canvas. Oils breathe life into the dead; chocolate hair, strawberry lips, buttery skin. I keep the paint thin so it dries fast, letting me start on the backdrop: a green, white and orange dawn. When it's ready I take it to Martin for approval. He says he'll send it north for the final OK. and let me know. But he likes it.

A week later I'm summoned to Belfast. The side of the Sinn Fein building has been freshly whitewashed. An army of Fianna cadets are assembled, one of them is Danny, Aiden's younger brother. A supply of paint and brushes arrives on the backseat of a dented Mini. I look up at the enormous space I have to fill and wonder how the hell I'm going to do it. But I already know: stroke by stroke.*

We work in fractured time, rain, raids and rioting stalling progress. The Fianna start off keen but quickly get fed-up. They're used to running important messages, keeping lookout, other things I'm not trusted to know because I'm not one of them. Painting is kiddie stuff. Grateful for their sneering disinterest I pack them off, all but Danny who Nora dispatches to me as soon as he's home from school. I stay with the O'Neills too, on nights when travelling back to Dublin isn't practical: possible. When I am forced to stay I

---

* The real Bobby Sands mural which adorns the side of the Sinn Fein office building on the Falls Road, Belfast, was painted by local artist Danny Devenney.

work from first light to last, eating perched on my scaffold and falling into bed as soon as I'm allowed, dodging family time with them because I can't handle their kindly fussing.

It's early July before the mural is finished, inspected, approved and covered up for the official unveiling in a few weeks. I'm thanked. I leave, afraid of what I'll do if I stay.

# Dublin—13<sup>th</sup> July, 1981

## Sixth Hunger Striker Dies
## Pressure Increases on Irish Government

The death has been announced today of Republican prisoner Martin Hurson. Hurson, the sixth to die on hunger strike in the Maze Prison, began his fast on 29<sup>th</sup> May. A book of condolence will be opened today outside the GPO where a number of peaceful protestors have been mounting a token relay fast for several weeks. Following Hurson's death fresh appeals calling for Irish governmental intervention in the strike have been presented to the Dail.

A demonstration in support of the hunger strike is planned for Saturday. Those wishing to participate should assemble at 2pm at St Stephen's Green.

Six more men remain on death-fast in the H-Blocks.

Posters advertising Saturday's hunger strike demo accost me on the way into the Green on Friday. I stumble to a stop, stunned by the sight of a young couple handing out leaflets about the march. They are frighteningly familiar, a remade version of what I've left behind. The man comes over, offers me a flier.

'Will you join us?' he asks.

'It won't do any good,' I tell him.

'Sure, we've got to try,' he insists.

Is that what it was about for them? The act of trying was their victory.

'Will you not at least sign the book for Martin?' he continues. 'They have it over on O'Connell Street.'

I duck the question and nip through the gates, into the Green, heading for my usual pondside bench, where I wrap myself up in thoughts.

On Saturday afternoon I venture into Daideo's bedroom, throw open the wardrobe, pull out the drawers and start, finally, bagging his things for charity and scrap.

By teatime bin liners crammed with his life surround me; threadbare shirts, holey jumpers, tattered paperbacks,

88

scratched 78s. The only things of value are the mementos stowed in his rucksack, which sits in the living room, by his chair, curled up like a companionable pet. The phone rings. I scramble into the hall to answer it.

'Are you OK?'

It's Aiden.

'Fine. Why?'

'The riots, I thought...'

I'm flummoxed; he knows I'm in Dublin because he's rung me here so how could I be caught up in anything? 'What riots?'

'Outside the British Embassy. The gardai attacked the march. There's people hurt. It's on the news.'

'Wait there.'

I put the phone down, go into the lounge and flick on the telly. RTE have replaced the afternoon's jovial quiz show host with a stern newsreader. Behind him a screen shows a blurred image of policemen in riot gear, batons raised, shields clutched, surrounding a prone figure. I snap the set off and dash back to the phone.

'Caoilainn?'

'I was checking the news. I've seen it.'

'But you're OK?' Aiden presses.

'Yes.' No. I didn't try. I did nothing. Fuck. Muscles tense and nerves twitch, protesting my indecision.

'I'll have to go,' Aiden says. 'Stay safe.'

He rings off before I can tell him to take his own advice.

I throw on my jacket and trainers, sprint to the bus stop. There isn't one for twenty minutes. I start running, am puffing and hot half-way between stops when I hear the engine rumbling behind me. Fury whips me on. I make the next stop as the bus pulls up. Ten minutes later I'm climbing down near the embassy in Ballsbridge, legs still shaking from the run.

Outside the embassy several ambulances are parked askew, doors flung open to gobble up the wounded which are being fed to them on stretchers. There are bodies on the ground, picking themselves up, slowly, painfully. Some of them are gardai, their shields dented and discarded, their uniforms ripped. More of them are middle-aged women, old men, teenagers. They bleed and groan. Torn banners, splintered placards and trampled flags carpet the road. Gobs of rubble lie where they were spat up. Safety barriers lay collapsed in the street, exhausted by their own failure. On the sidelines journalists gabble pieces to camera. One has a bloody bandage round his forehead which he gestures to as he tells the lens everything.

I was eight. It was the American Embassy in London. We, they, were protesting Vietnam, the futile deaths, the bloody suffering. It got violent; we wouldn't move, the Americans didn't want us staying. Dad was hurt. I remember red covering his face like a cartoon character's mask. Mum used her sequined headscarf as a field dressing...

'We should go, John, before Kaylynn gets injured.'

'Don't worry, Susan, she'll be fine. They wouldn't dare.'

'But what if...?'

'No. We need to stay, show we won't be bullied by self-serving bureaucrats and state-paid thugs.' ...

We were always caught in the current, swimming outside the flags.

Today I didn't even go paddling.

I start tiptoeing through the debris, sidestepping bloody puddles.

Ahead an old man struggles to his feet. I think of Daideo, his final frail form, and rush to help.

'Thanks, love,' he says, turning a bruised face to me. 'Are you hurt?'

'I'm fine. Let me get you someone.'

Before I can go for help a reporter charges us, a young woman with a neat bob, wearing a tan mac and court shoes and towing a cameraman.

'Can you tell us what happened?' she asks.

'Aye, them bastards baton charged us. It was Bloody Sunday all over.'

She pounces on his words, thinking she has the scoop. 'Was there shooting?'

'Ach, I don't mean that business in Derry. I'm talking 1913. The Lockout. My grandda was on the strike. He was only thirty-five but he was made an ould man in one afternoon.

90

Walked with a limp the rest of his life after them buggers broke his leg. He made sure us children knew the horror of it. They're not the DMP anymore but they're the same shites they always were.'

She sags with disappointment. 'What about today?'

'They battered us. Thugs they are. Don't give a damn who they're beating so long as they keep the Brits safe.' He spits bloody phlegm onto the pavement. 'I saw a woman kicked to the ground. They kept hitting her even when she was down.'

The reporter scribbles in her notebook. Turns to me. 'Did you see that?'

'I've just come.'

'Oh.' She refocuses on the old man. 'What else can you tell me?'

I drift away.

I don't know how long I've been walking but it's dark when I realise I'm leaning over the railings, staring into the Liffey's dank waters. I ache with cold, am stiff when I straighten up. I turn from the river and head onto O'Connell Street. I'll sign Martin's book. It's nearly nothing but it's the only thing I can think to do.

O'Connell Street is quiet. A candlelit gathering clusters outside the GPO. I trudge towards the makeshift camp of trestle table, deck chairs and sleeping bags. A purposefully gaunt young man, one of the sympathy strikers I guess, greets me.

'How're you?'

'I've come to sign the book.'

'Grand.'

He leads me to the table. Hands me a pen. I've no idea what to write. I scrawl one word: sorry. Put the pen down.

'Did you see the trouble today?' he asks.

I'm fumbling for an answer when a gardai patrol peels into the street, sirens screaming. Dozens of men spring from the vans and charge us, yelling, 'Disperse, disperse.' We're plunged into a seething storm of batons and shields. I'm shoved against the table, hauled off it and tossed aside. The book is snatched up. A garda rips it apart, scatting the pages. The table is overturned.

'Oi, you can't…' The young man steps forward.

The peeler rounds on him, whacks his arm with a sickening crunch that I feel in my bones. The lad yelps, staggers back. The garda hits him again, knocks him over, kicks him. Raises his baton. Brings it down on his leg. The lad howls, an animal cry that suffocates me. The peeler hits him again. The leg snaps with a dry, hard crack. The pain of it paralyses me. I can't move. The peeler winds up for another blow. The mob swells around me. A thick blue line obscures my view. I'm bundled backwards, feet floundering. I right myself, turn. Run.

# Dublin—19th July, 1981

## Violence Erupts Outside British Embassy

Approximately 200 people required hospital treatment after a demonstration supporting the hunger strikes turned violent yesterday following attempts by the Free State gardai to block the route.

The march, organised by the National H-Blocks/Armagh Committee who have a strict policy of peaceful protest, began in an orderly manner in the centre of Dublin. As the 15,000 marchers neared the British Embassy they encountered around 1,000 gardai, assembled to protect the embassy building.

The gardai, armed with batons and shields and dressed in riot gear, prevented protestors from nearing the embassy, forming ranks twelve deep outside the building. Protestors attempting to disperse found roads blocked by barricades. Frustrated, a small minority of demonstrators began throwing stones towards the gardai lines. The gardai responded with a brutal and sustained baton charge, indiscriminately attacking innocent protestors, journalists and foreign visitors. One man described seeing a woman kicked to the ground and others reported unconscious victims being beaten. Taoiseach Garret FitzGerald said, 'What was done was the minimum necessary to protect the situation.'

Later, in an unprovoked attack, around a hundred gardai destroyed the book of condolences for Martin Hurson and viciously beat those who had been keeping a peaceful vigil outside the GPO. One man suffered a broken arm and leg.

Sinn Fein has called for an enquiry into the brutal actions of Free State forces which saw many innocent bystanders seriously wounded.

I sit with Daideo's boyhood passport on my lap, flipping between the cover with its crest of a free, united nation, and the first page where his real name, William Devoy, is written. Renaming is a family tradition.

The procedure is more complicated these days, there's paperwork, signatures are required but a fortnight later I have an Irish passport in the name of Caoilainn Devoy. Kaylynn

Ryan's British one still has nine valid years. Calculating its possible value, I stow it for future use.

My choice is made.

'Ah, Jesus,' Aiden says.

We're in my sitting room, fish and chip papers littering the coffee table, the ashtray filling up with dog-ends. I've just told him I want to join the IRA.

He rubs his scar. 'What about Sinn Fein? If you're wanting to help that's...'

'Not enough. I won't spend time on picket lines when there are battle lines need manning.'

'You can't.'

'Don't the 'Ra take women?'

'Sure, they do but... you don't know what you're getting into.'

'I've a good idea from looking at the state of you,' I snap. His expression darkens. It's reason, not rage, that'll convince him. 'I've been watching and listening: learning. I've asked myself every question, over and over until I'm sure of the answers. But ask me again, now, if you're needing to hear for yourself.'

He hesitates.

'Go on, ask me!'

'Why this, why now?'

I can't tell him I was at the GPO, ran away when I should've fought.

'I don't want to be powerless anymore, like those poor sods clubbed outside the embassy.'

'Jesus, Caoilainn, you shouldn't do this because of that.'

'I'm not. That's just what made me see military action is the only way.'

He shakes his head. 'It's a rough life; on the run, in hiding, half your time bored to death, the other half scared to death. Can you handle that?'

'I won't know until I try but, yes, I think so.'

'What about if you get caught? Jail?'

'I'll survive, just like every other volunteer.'

He bites his lip, chewing on the indigestible question that I know comes next.

'Are you ready to die for this?'

'No one's ready for that. If they think so they're deluded. Yes, it could happen. I accept it. But I'll do my damnedest to prevent it.'

'Jesus, Caoilainn. You can't do this.'

His intransigence shatters all rational arguments. I lash out.

'Aren't my Republican credentials good enough?'

'Is that what this is about? 'Cos that's the wrong reason.'

'It's fine for you to be 'Republican in your bones' but not me?'

'That's different.'

'How?'

'It just is.'

'Because I don't live on the Falls? Because I've not a brother dying in jail? Because I'm a woman?' I turn away, fight for control before it's beyond me.

Silence simmers.

He sighs. 'It'll be harder on you, so it will.'

'I'm not expecting it to be easy. Women always have to work harder than men to draw level with them. That's what makes us better survivors: fighters. Just because someone says you can't do something doesn't mean you shouldn't still try. You should know that; it's why you've been fighting. I'll do whatever it takes.'

He pulls me round to face him, raises his eyes to mine. 'Even if that means pulling the trigger? You need to understand what a hard thing that is, even if they are the enemy. You've to live with it and you can only do that if you believe, absolutely, that it's the only way.'

'I know. I've thought about all this, been thinking for weeks, months.' I hand him my new Irish passport. Aiden opens it, reads the name. 'I've made my choice.'

Aiden arranges for us to call on Martin. This time there's no pounding heart, no panting lungs. I know what I'm here for and I'm ready. There's no tea and biscuits either, this time. Martin sits us in the lounge and opens with a challenge.

'So you're after joining the 'Ra.'

'Yes.'

'Why?'

'Same reason as you.'

'You saw peelers kicking shite out of women and kids marching peacefully for their rights, getting their skulls caved in by a Paisleyite mob with clubs?'

'No, but I saw what the Gardai did in Dublin.'

He raises his eyebrows. 'Oh, aye?'

'It's wrong and I don't see any other way of making it right, here or in the north. If something's not fair you fight it. That's how Daideo taught me to think. And I don't mean fighting with banners and petitions,' I add in case he tries fobbing me off with Sinn Fein.

'Sure, your granddaddy was a tough ould fella, but that raises another question. I've to ask myself if that's what's bringing you here: family history.'

'Is that a problem?'

'If you're fighting a war that's not yours, then, aye.'

'I've as much right to it as anyone, maybe more. I've been involved in this since before I was born. Of course that's what's brought me here. But the past's only half the reason.'

'The other half?'

'There's an occupying army in the north, who've no right being there, supporting a bunch of bigoted overlords who don't care about anything but themselves. If we want what's fair we have to make it happen. I think the way to do that, right now, is to fight. The Brits are the ones who brought out the guns. They started it. I want to help end it. So our reasons are the same,' I add. 'An end to injustice in Ireland.'

'Fair play to you,' Martin says. 'You'll need to believe that if you're to see this through.'

'I do and I understand the dangers. I've already heard the 'Jail or Cemetery' speech.' I look at Aiden who flushes.

Martin grins. 'Alright, but we don't just give you a gun and send you off. You'll have to be vetted, trained.' He takes what looks like a small school exercise book from the sideboard and drops it in my lap. 'Start with that.'

The cover is a dry, plain green, the pages stapled together through the middle. I thumb through. A heading catches my eye: Guerrilla Strategy.

'What's this?'

'*The Green Book*: your new Bible,' Martin replies. 'No one joins 'til they've studied that. Read it then tell me you're still keen.'

*The Green Book* is a mix of political philosophy and 'how to'. Western individualistic capitalism and Eastern state capitalism are criticised equally for their inability to provide for and protect the people. To me it's familiar rhetoric with a new colour-scheme: the green of Irish nationalism. It covers eight hundred years of Irish conflict, justifies military action, explains the IRA are the legitimate representatives of the Irish people and outlines the fivefold strategy for guerrilla warfare. There are two objectives: long term, Democratic Socialist Republic of Ireland; short term, Brits out. The truth is brutal; the understatement blackly humorous: *Volunteers are trained to kill...before any person decides to join the Army he should think seriously about the whole thing.*

She has.

When I've finished reading, I dial the number given me. The next day a girl in a green blazer and white knee socks rings my bell, hands me an envelope and darts away to school. The note states a time, date and a Dublin address. I'm getting Green Booked in three days.

The address is a florist's. I wander in the afternoon before my appointment? interview? induction? and choose a modest spray. Behind the counter is a middle aged woman in an overall. She counts my coins then rings them into the till.

'Do you want a card?'

I test out the accent I've been practising. 'No, thanks. You haven't a loo I can use, though, have you? I've been caught out by a wee visitor.'

She gives me a motherly smile and points to the door behind her.

I dart through, climb the stairs and open each of the four doors on the landing, the excuse poised on my tongue. There's a bathroom, sitting room and two bedrooms, beds neatly made with candlewick bedspreads, one pink, the other blue. A picture of the sacred heart hangs in one. The only way out is down the stairs.

Satisfied, I thank the florist and leave.

I'm there two hours before the stated time. Sitting across the street in a bus stop, I've an inconspicuous view of the shop. One at a time, four men appear and enter. One of them wears a combat jacket, the others are in suits, jeans, jackets. From his graceful stride I identify one of them as Martin.

When it's time, I hitch my rucksack onto my shoulder, cross the road and knock. Martin opens the door.

'How are you?'

'Grand, yourself?'

He nods. 'This way.'

I follow his tall shadow, smiling at the knowledge that I could have led him.

On the landing is the lad in Army gear but with the addition of a balaclava he wasn't wearing when he came along the street. Martin stops.

'We're needing to search you before we go in.'

I hand over my bag and lift my arms. The Army lad looks to Martin, his eyes widening, the whites visible through the eyeholes.

'Come on, sunshine, we've not got all night,' Martin barks.

The lad pats me down with the trembling hands of a good Catholic boy. If I had half a pound of gelignite in my bra he'd never have found it. I make myself stand motionless, aware it's me being tested, not him.

Search over, Martin opens the sitting room door. Three straight-backed chairs form a semi-circle around a fourth. Martin takes the middle seat of the three. Either side of him, the two others sit eyeballing me. One is stocky, a square face, thick brows over brooding eyes, an unsmiling mouth and a dimpled chin. The other is leaner, a beard guarding plump lips and glasses framing eyes that penetrate.

Martin indicates the waiting chair. 'Have yourself a seat.' He clasps his hands on his lap. 'Tell us why you want to join the Republican Movement.'

'It's the only way.'

'What do you mean?'

'I can't see anything else making a difference.'

'You don't believe in politics?' asks the one with the glasses.

Obviously he does.

I was ten. We were racing to London in a Morris Traveller that rattled and squealed. I was reading *The Famous Five: Five Get Into Trouble*. They were planning the protest for freeing the Pentonville Five...

'It's outrageous, John. They've no right jailing people for picketing.'

'But they have, thanks to this bloody new Industrial Relations Act. You see, Susan, what happens when you put faith in politicians. They screw you over for their own ends. It's always the same; give them power and they abuse it.'

'If you can't trust politicians, Daddy, why do you and Mummy vote?'

'To remind the bastards they owe you, Kaylynn.'

'John, don't tell her that. Love, we vote because it's all our responsibilities to exercise the rights we've got. But that doesn't mean we should trust politicians and governments to protect those rights.'...

'I don't believe in politicians,' I reply. Mr Politics frowns. I add, 'I do believe in doing what needs to be done. Right now, to me, that's fighting. When, if, it becomes voting I'll do that too. But I've been to Belfast and it's not there, not yet.'

Martin smiles tightly. 'And that's what you want, to make a difference?'

'Yes.'

'Even if doing so means killing, being killed?' demands Mr Politics.

*All people wishing to join the Army must fully realise that when life is being taken, that very well could mean your own.*

'Yes,' I say hotly, 'and I've read your wee book so I'm clued up.'

Mr Politics tuts. Martin and the other man exchange raised-eyebrow glances. I choke down mushrooming irritation, rinse my words with cooler water.

'I'm totally clear what this course of action entails. I wouldn't dare come if I wasn't.'

There's some nodding. Politics strokes his beard.

The third man takes his turn. 'You're the wee girl who painted the Sands mural.'

'Yes.'

'You did a grand job.'

'Thanks.'

'Why not stick to more like that?'

'It's not enough.'

He rubs a thought across his forehead. 'Sure, there are other ways you can help.'

'I'm good for more than hiding guns under my coat.'

He sighs. 'What is it you think you can do?' He's a physical force man; action's his thing.

'Anything you can teach me.'

'Can you drive?'

'I'll learn.'

'Fire a gun?'

'I'll learn.'

He snorts.

I pull the two passports from my bag and hand them to him.

'What's this?'

'I'm not known; they won't be looking for me. If they do they'll have a job on. Two people are harder to catch than one. Won't that be useful?'

*Your prime duty is to remain unknown to the enemy forces.*

His face relaxes, rock melting. 'It might.'

I prise apart the tiny chink. 'There are plenty of things women can do that men can't but fewer things men can do that women can't. When we're given the opportunity.'

'You needn't be telling us our jobs,' Martin says.

'I'm not, but maybe you'd be interested in how I know there's a picture of the sacred heart in the bedroom next door.'

They look at each other.

'How the…?' Martin asks.

'She's guessing,' Action Man says.

'And a pink candlewick bedspread.' I relish their mystified stares. 'The wifie downstairs was happy let me use her loo but would she if I was a lad? I can do whatever you ask and more.'

'It's not us you're needing to convince,' Politics says more softly. 'Your problem'll be the boys in your unit, some of them, not all. We advocate equality but it's still filtering down.'

'I'll cope.'

Martin nods. 'I'm sure you will. Right lads, let's have the word on this. Give us a minute.'

I go out onto the landing. The young volunteer has his mask rolled up so he can smoke. He leaps to attention and fumbles for the balaclava, trying to pull it down with his fag still between his lips.

'Shite! Ah, Jesus.' He drops the cigarette and stamps it out, pressing a hand to the red welt on his cheek.

'Have one of mine. I won't tell.' I offer him my pack.

He takes one from arm's length. He's a year or two older than me but trying to grow a moustache to add a few more. 'Sorry 'bout before, searching ya, but orders…' He shrugs.

'It's fine. Are we allowed to do names?'

'Are ya joining?'

'Hope so.'

'Good for you.' He offers me his hand. 'Colm.'

'Caoilainn.'

'Maybe's we'll be working together sometime, Caoilainn.'

The door handle turns. Colm and I jump apart; he drops the cigarette and yanks down his mask. Martin beckons me into the room. The chairs have been pushed back and a tricolour pinned on the wall.

'We've had a wee chat,' he says, 'and you've been approved.' He holds up his hand. 'Providing you get through the training, but that's the same for every recruit. Now, anything else?' He checks with the others.

Action Man casts his eyes over me, taking in my long loose hair, jacket, jeans, ending up at my road-greyed trainers. 'Don't cut your hair.'

'Why?'

'In case you need to cut it later to change your appearance,' he explains, 'and get yourself some decent boots, ones you can run in.'

'OK. Fine.'

'Grand. We'll swear you, so. How's your Irish?' Martin says.

'Foirfe*. Céard faoin gceann seo agatsa♣?'

Martin shakes his head. 'This isn't an outlaw posse you're joining; it's an army, with a command structure: discipline. Respect that or you'll not last five minutes.'

He says it flat, a sober statement, not a bawled rebuke or even a threat. I take it impassively, like an exemplary soldier. I will respect that, and them, but they'll have to earn it from me as much as I will from them.

Satisfied by my silence, he proceeds, in Irish, to take my declaration to 'Serve the Republican Movement by means both military and political, promising that my personal conduct shall never bring disgrace to the Cause and offering my unconditional allegiance to Oglaigh na hEireann.'

---

* perfect

♣ How about yours

# Belfast—9th August, 1981

## Sands Mural Unveiled
## Republicans Honour H-Block Martyrs
## as Ninth Hunger Striker Dies

A mural depicting Bobby Sands, MP, and dedicated to the men who have died on hunger strike in the Maze Prison H-Blocks, was unveiled in West Belfast today.

Painted on the side of the Sinn Fein building on the Falls Road, the mural shows a head and shoulders portrait of Sands against a multi-coloured sky and includes the words, 'Our revenge will be the laughter of our children', a quotation from Sands' prison writings.

Amid a heavy police presence a crowd of thousands gathered to see the mural unveiled. Key figures of the Republican movement, including Sinn Fein's northern leadership, were in attendance.

Speaking to reporters after the unveiling, Mr Gerry Adams of Sinn Fein said, 'Our thoughts and prayers are with the families of the nine young men who have made the ultimate sacrifice for a cause they believed in.'

The ninth hunger striker to die was Thomas McIlwee who survived sixty-two days without food. He died on 8th August. Michael Devine, who joined the strike on 21st June as the tenth man, is believed to be close to death. Three others continue the strike and there is speculation that more will refuse food if an agreement is not reached.

During the unveiling cries of the Irish phrase, 'tiocfaidh ár lá' were heard. The phrase, thought to have been coined by Sands, translates as, 'Our day will come'.


I stand among a crowd that doesn't know the mural is my last artist's commission and my first volunteer's job. Around me people sob and cheer as the cry tiocfaidh ár lá goes up. I study my new boots as the men on the platform spout their rhetoric. Their words are blanks fired over my head. *A new recruit's immediate challenge is the removal of his* (her) *ignorance about how to handle weapons, military tactics, security, interrogations etc.* Training starts tomorrow.

*

103

We're driven over the border into wild, anonymous countryside. There are thirty of us. I'm the only woman. The lads alternate between staring and avoiding my gaze. Some know each other and huddle together, sharing cigarettes: speculating about me. I guard everything I do. Twice I stop myself reaching for the tube of lip salve that is the only luxury I've let myself bring. I won't be caught out. I'm afraid of proving them right.

The hills and woodland are our cover and base for the coming fortnight. We bivvy up in tents borrowed from the Fianna and cook over campfires. The training officer runs classes in an old barn lent to us by a Republican farmer. We're shown how to strip, clean and load a rifle, build and arm a bomb. On the third afternoon it's unarmed combat. When it's my turn I go in hard because the TO is 6ft 2 and solid around the middle while I'm 5ft 5 and 8 stone wringing wet; because the last three lads landed on their arses and because my ears are burning just thinking of the jeers I'll get when I go the same way. I crash into him and he buckles too easily, letting me pin him facedown in the mud. Behind me, a single pair of hands applauds. I see a tall, thin lad, jet-black hair and dark eyes, clapping. He winks.

After the demo the TO, Mick Casey, comes across, offers me his hand.

'You gave me a good hiding there, so you did.'

'Only because you let me.'

'Aye, I'll not be making that mistake again,' he grins.

'Good. Don't,' I says. 'It doesn't help me.'

'Fair enough.'

He orders us into pairs to practice. The lad that clapped me comes over, introduces himself: Liam, from Belfast. He shakes my hand and, with a chuckle, says he's glad I'm on his side. I don't let on about Casey's chivalrous cheating and, because it's got Liam thinking I've stepped off the pages of the *Táin*, some modern-day Scáthach, he barrels into me like a charging bull. I land hard, pain ringing up my spine, air slammed from my lungs. Liam drops down beside me.

'Jesus, you alright?'

I nod, fight for breath and struggle up. Liam grabs my arm and hauls me off the ground.

'Sorry, I didn't mean…'

'It's fine.'

'You sure?'

'Yes.'

We go again but Liam backs out, dropping when I've barely got a hand on him.

'What's that?'

'I don't want to hurt you.'

'It's not you I'm worried about; it's the bloody Brits. I need to be able to do this properly.' I shove him. 'Come on.' I grin and shove again. He grabs me.

By teatime I'm bruised and achy but Liam's been on his arse as often as me.

We train in the open, on rainy windswept moors, far from the streets where we'll fight. We squelch through mud, wade across streams and scramble over stone walls, dodging sheep that litter the hillsides. We're drilled, staging mock attacks, sham firing Armalites and handguns, saving precious bullets for real targets. After a week I'm cold in my bones. The muscles in my arms and shoulders scream with pain as I raise the machine gun to sight along the barrel. My legs stiffen, my knees lock out, every crouch cracking rusted joints. I wear the cold and live for small victories: one good night's sleep; forgetting, for five minutes, that my feet are soaked; running two miles on just a cup of tea; not being the last to get my weapon reassembled. Everything is done in the moment. I don't let myself think of what's coming next. If I do I'll sink.

The OC comes to see me.

'We've a journalist arriving tomorrow to observe. He's dead on, trusted, so he is, or we'd not have him here. He'd like a word with you.'

'Why?'

'Wants to know how you're finding things, that's all. He's sent a list of questions. We'll go through them so you're clear what you can say to him.'

I nod, take the paper he's holding out and scan it. Reading the questions I'm glad I'm not hunting alone for the answers.

The next morning a Hiace van pulls up the lane. We're issued with balaclavas as a figure is helped out. Once we're masked his blindfold is removed. Blinking against the sudden brightness, he stumbles through the field towards us. The OC explains who he is. We're not to talk to him without permission. He glances at me. I nod. The journalist draws close, huddling into his raincoat. We're fallen in for inspection, our clothes smeared with muck. A greasy brown slop coats my boots. I'm held together by dirt and sweat. We haven't had breakfast yet. My stomach chews on itself. I fantasise about biting through thick white bread, greasy bacon and creamy egg yolk, then remember Connor and the others still striking in Long Kesh. My hunger cowers from the thought.

The journalist comes along the row towards me, his stride steady. Seeing me, a head shorter than the rest, he stops: stares. I keep my gaze on the horizon. Casey moves him on and we're ordered to begin the day's manoeuvres.

Organised into units and moving in pincer formation, we launch attacks, defend, take cover and counter-attack. From a safe distance the journalist watches. We hope we're impressing; his words could win us fresh support.

Lunch is served in a disused milking shed. The quartermaster stands behind a makeshift table, ladling soup into our mugs. I limp forward, pain snapping up my leg, the result of twisting my ankle vaulting a fence. I find a dry corner, prop my rifle against the wall and sit, the soup steaming to tepid, to inspect my ankle.

The skin is mottled black and purple, the flesh puffed up and squishy when I prod it.

'Are you alright there?' It's the OC.

'Fine.' I retie the boot as tightly as I can.

He crouches down. 'Are you ready for that word with your man there?'

'Yes.'

I struggle off the floor and we head into one of smaller barns. Before we enter the OC says:

'Remember, stick to what we went through.'

The journalist comes towards us, holding out his hand to me. I take it and mumble a greeting through the itchy balaclava. We sit on hay bales. I'm relieved to get the weight off my ankle. The journalist produces a notepad.

'Can I ask how old you are?'

'Old enough.'

He smiles wryly. 'Where are you from?'

'Dublin.'

'Yet you've volunteered to fight in the north. Why?'

'Because that's where the problem is.'

'We can agree on that,' he says, writing in his notepad. 'You're the only woman here.'

It's not a question so I don't answer it, leaving him to break the awkward silence with a nervous cough and an actual question.

'How are you finding it, with the men? Is there any...' he fumbles for a word, 'prejudice?'

'Only what there is anywhere. Maybe not even as much as that.' I think about Casey and Liam's attempts to protect me. 'It's harder for them than me, me being here.' I wave towards the huddle of volunteers. 'They're not my problem but I might be theirs.'

'Are you a feminist?'

'I'm an Irish Republican.'

'What about women's rights?'

'What about Ireland's rights?'

'So you don't think the women's liberation movement has anything to offer?'

'Our problems aren't the same as theirs. It's a class issue. They don't understand us so they can't help.' I itch to tell him some braless suburban housewife with a snazzy slogan jiggling across her unfettered boobs can't offer me anything I don't already have or can't get for myself. But that's not on the agreed script.

He scribbles again.

'How many women are in the Provisionals?'

'There's about thirty in Armagh jail.'

'I know.' He grimaces. 'I went there during the no-wash protest.'

I burn to ask what made him sickest, the inhumanity or the blood on the walls. But that's not on the sodding script either.

'Why have you chosen armed resistance?'

'I wanted to help.'

'You could've done than by joining Sinn Fein,' he presses.

He's slipped up, straying from the precious script. Unable to keep my balance, I fall too.

'You think I should be at home writing to my MP?'

'MP?' He pounces. 'I thought you were from Dublin.'

I curse the error; I should've said TD. The OC takes over.

'She is.'

'But you grew up in England,' the journalist guesses, looking to me for more.

I glance at the OC. He whispers in my ear. I digest his advice, form a cautious reply.

'I'm Irish. Where I grew up's irrelevant. The north is oppressed by a foreign army of occupation. We've a right to fight that.'

'I agree, but why've you chosen to fight like this?' He gestures with his pen.

I take it from his fingers and look once more at the OC. He warns me with raised eyebrows but nods that I can answer.

'You might win the peace with one of these but you need to win the war first. That takes guns, not words. So here I am.'

'And how've you found it so far?' His eyes flick to the open door, at the lads clustered together, smoking and gabbing.

'It's not a boy scout weekend,' I say, 'but we help each other.'

'That's enough,' the OC interrupts. He signals the journalist up. 'I'll show you round.'

They leave. I pull off the mask and light a cigarette with shaking fingers. Hot tears, pain, fatigue and frustration, bubble to the surface.

'Hey.'

I look up, see Liam and rub a hand over my face.

'You OK?'

'I twisted my ankle.'

'Shall I get Casey?'

'It'll be alright.'

'If you're hurt you can say, you know,' he coaxes.

I can't. Because that's what everyone's expecting: me to jack it in.

'I'm fine.'

'You've done better than some would.'

Some what, recruits or women?

'That's not good enough for me. I have to do this.'

He shakes his head: disbelief? admiration? 'I've some painkillers if you want.'

'Thanks.'

We hunch into ourselves, sitting on upturned crates in the damp barn for a lecture on anti-interrogation techniques. Casey chalks words onto the brick wall, the letters made jaggedy by the uneven surface. He scrawls; physical torture, psychological torture, humiliation, bribery and blackmail. Liam nudges me, holding out a cigarette. I shake my head and focus on Casey, who's explaining each point. When he reaches 'humiliation' and describes how prisoners are stripped of their clothing two lads turn and gawp at me.

'What's up with yous?' I hiss.

'Pay attention,' Casey yells and they face front. 'Aye,' he adds, breaking from his lecture notes, 'and yous should know the Brits give no favours to anyone. If anything they're harder on women they pick up so don't be thinking otherwise. You look after each other when you're on active service. If you don't you're sunk.' He clears his throat and resumes the lecture.

The session is two hours of cold reality. The brick wall ends up covered with wobbly chalk words: sleep deprivation; brutal beatings; threats of violence against your family; disorientation and disillusionment: be prepared for the worst. Written largest of all is the mantra 'say nothing'. Casey finishes by advising us that volunteers have found it easiest to survive interrogations by focusing their minds on something else, whatever will keep you from panicking: breaking.

We file out in dark silence.

That night, curled in my sleeping bag, I play out what'll happen if I'm caught, planning what I'll do, how I'll survive:

You're yanked out of the meat-wagon, the door slammed behind you so hard it causes an airquake. Your arms are twisted up your back, pulled so high you're lifted off your feet. Your wrists are bound with a cable tie, the thin band cutting through your flesh. You hope the fear thrumming in your heart doesn't show on your face. A hood is pulled over your head. Before it goes down you close your eyes, hoping if you make the blackness yours it won't be so frightening. Your other senses take over: the feel of hands gripping your arms; the stink of diesel fumes from the van; the rutted ground under your feet; the slosh of water as you stumble through a puddle; the banging of a heavy door; the sweet-sour blend of wafted sweat and aftershave; heat, through the hood, from another face close to yours: silence.

A chair is rammed against your legs. Your knees fold and you jolt down onto it. The hood is snatched off. A branch man leers over you. At the door is his partner. You pick a spot to his left, where the wall is flat and grey, and let your eyes blur it, getting ready to think yourself out of there.

I settle on repainting Daideo's 'Green Dawn' piece as my survival strategy. Rolling onto my back I stare at the barn's beamed ceiling and start projecting it, brushstroke by brushstroke; the verdant sky, the Hermitage's square form, the flaming lawn, finishing with fine strokes and signing my name. I pray it will be enough to keep me from breaking.

Towards the end of the second week we get target practice with live ammunition. I like the gun. It gives me power, makes things fairer. I surprise myself, and the lads, by being a decent shot, keeping the Armalite braced against my shoulder and producing a grouping of hits on the target. Casey is less astounded.

'Women are often good shots,' he tells the boys. 'Something about hand-eye coordination, they reckon.'

There's a ripple of muttering. I aim again. As I click the trigger someone bumps my elbow. The rifle jerks skyward; the shot misses.

I spin round. Three lads are clustered behind me, smirking.

'Aye, great shot,' one says.

I glance at Casey. He's seen but doesn't step in.

'Can I have a fresh target?' I ask.

He raises his eyebrows but walks the fifty yards to the board and replaces the torn paper.

'The next three shots in the bull's eye,' I tell the lad, 'if you don't cheat.'

He smirks and shrugs. I aim, hold my breath and fire: bang, bang, bang.

Casey collects the target. There's a single hole in the central ring.

'Ya only got the one,' the lad mocks.

'Do you not see?' Casey asks him, tracing the tear which is shaped like Mickey Mouse's head. 'She got all three through the same hole. Now it's your go, boyo.'

On the final night we're sent out in pairs with a map, compass and orders to get to Knockatallan, two miles from the Six Counties border into Fermanagh. Liam and I set out at midnight.

We head north, tramping through fields, wading streams and clambering fences, skirting the villages between us and the pickup point. In the distance occasional cars drone; overhead owls screech. We follow the compass which Liam checks by the flicker of his lighter, dark hair falling into his eyes each time he bends to read the bearing. The half-moon glow lets me pretend he's Aiden. I wish he was here, that we were doing this together, sharing the ordeal and looking forward to laughing over it later.

'How far ya reckon we've come?' Liam asks when we've been going a while, the words snatched between breaths as we lean into an incline.

I stop on the hilltop and point east towards a cluster of lights. 'That's gotta be Three Mile House.'

Liam checks the map. 'You're dead on.' He clicks his lighter shut and strides off.

I fall in beside him.

'Heard you're Aiden O'Neill's lass,' he says. 'Is that how you got involved?'

'Yes, but it's not why. I'm here because I don't like the way things are. I believe in fighting for our rights.'

'Fair enough. Me too.'

'And I'm not 'his lass'. We don't belong to yous, you know.'

'Aye, sorry. I didn't mean...' He trails off.

I pull him to a halt. I want the air clear and warm between us. 'I'm not a ball-breaking feminist, I just want...' He recoils from my words. I drive head on at his pink-bows-and-purity picture of womanhood. 'And that's the problem! Don't think I'm so different from you. I swear. I drink beer. I like orgasms.' He drops his gaze. 'I even fart.' His lips twitch into a grin. 'Do you want me to drop one right now to prove it?' His shoulders shake and laughter erupts.

'Jesus, no, I don't,' he splutters between chuckles.

We giggle contagiously until I smother hilarity enough to speak.

'But do you get it? I'm human. Treat me how you want to be treated. We're comrades: equals.'

'Aye. Sure. And friends?'

'Yes, friends.'

He tells me he's a time-served fitter and turner fed up being passed over in favour of unqualified Prods. I realise the total truth of what I told Martin; all our reasons are the same. We're wanting to make things fairer. That's why Daideo gave up everything for this. It's what'll push me on no matter how hard it gets.

For two hours we stumble with uneven strides, the boggy, rutted ground refusing us an easy rhythm.

'Jesus, this is tough going,' Liam puffs as we climb another hill.

I scan the horizon and point to more lights. 'Nearly there.'

'Sure, it's a rough life we're letting ourselves in for. Hope I'm up to it,' he says, lighting a cigarette and offering me one.

Darkness covers the flush that spreads over my cheeks as an image of myself, seen from above, running away down O'Connell Street, torn pages and broken bodies scattered behind me, flits through my head. I won't run again. I bury the memory. I know I can do this. It's in me like the Irish words I'd forgotten I knew. I will do this.

'Sure, you'll be grand,' I say.

'So will you,' he replies. 'If you run out of bullets you can always cock your arse at them.'

'Yeah, gas attack.' I blow a raspberry.

We laugh again.

'Seriously, though,' he adds, 'if I'd to choose someone to fight alongside, it'd be you.'

'Thanks. Let's hope it works out that way.'


'Jesus, you look like hell,' Aiden says, greeting me at the door.

'No worse than you most of the times you've shown up here.'

'I'll run you a bath.' He goes upstairs.

I ease my boots off. My ankle throbs. Overhead water gushes. Aiden comes down. I hobble towards him. He reaches for me.

'You want a hand?'

'Thanks.'

He helps me upstairs then goes for towels and clean clothes. The bath fills, steam fogs the room. I strip off and step into the tub. The hot water cocoons me. I close my eyes and sink down, tension and dirt sliding from me. After blissful minutes of forbidden ease I sit up, reach for the soap and shake my head as I spot Aiden's gun on top of the cistern.

The door opens.

'Can I do your back?' he asks, grinning.

He kneels down beside the bath and takes the soap, rolling it over my shoulder blades. I wince as he presses a bruise.

'You alright?'

'Bit sore.'

'Aye, you're black and blue.'

'What did you expect?'

'What did you expect?' he returns.

'This.'

He sighs, leans against me, resting his forehead on my cheek.

'I should be taking care of you.'

'You are. But I've got to be able to take care of myself too, and that's not about the Brits, the 'Ra. That's about me.'

'You don't have to be tough with me,' he murmurs.

I know but I can't be any other way. It's not make-up to be removed: it's a tattoo, indelible, part of me. The part that keeps me safe.

'You left your gun.' I point at the toilet.

'Ah, shite.' He retrieves it. 'I'll get tea on.'

He slips out. I lie back, water lapping over my chin. All the things that have brought me here bob about in the bath: the hunger strikes, ten dead men; the support, resistance and apathy, mine and everyone else's; the violence, what it destroys and creates; Daideo, his battles; my parents, both sets, their choices: their mistakes.

I submerge myself, water smothering sound, soothing pain. There's a bang, Aiden dropping something downstairs. In my head the bang becomes a gunshot. The jolt of a fired rifle snaps up my arm, jars through my body, its power filling me.

And I'm on the other side, pain shredding me as bullets explode into muscle, tear flesh, shatter bone.

'...your ma's chest ripped open by bullets, your da's face such a mess ...'

I surface, gulping air into hysterical lungs.

Now I've felt the force I can imagine the agony. It's a truth I wish I hadn't been told.

Aiden shouts, 'Tea's ready.'

We sit in the kitchen, eating cheese toasties. I ask about Connor. He ruffles his hair, can't answer, asks about training instead. I tell him, spilling words like water, and feel weirdly exhilarated, as though I've rerun the marathon and beat my best time. But it's not what I've done, it's what I'm doing now, telling him, that's giving me this buzz. It's the first dawning of what we are: of us.

# Belfast—3rd October, 1981

## Maze Hunger Strike Ended
## Families of Remaining Strikers Authorise
## Medical Treatment

Senior IRA figures have announced the collapse of the hunger strike by prisoners in HMP Maze. The statement came after the families of those on strike said they would authorise medical treatment once prisoners lost consciousness.

The six men still on strike are expected to request food and medical treatment today following a visit by the IRA leadership during which they made it clear that attempts to ring concessions from the British government were futile.

As a result of violence fuelled by the strikes sixty-four civilians, soldiers and RUC officers have been killed.

Ten men have so far starved themselves to death in an attempt to win political status for their terrorist crimes. In a statement released earlier, Mrs Thatcher said, 'Crime is crime is crime. It is not political.'

'It's a fu... it's a disgrace,' Kelly jabs his finger at me, 'sending a wee girl to do this. If it was up to me we'd not let yous in.'

We're in his sister-in-law's front room, me, Aiden and Kelly who's a hardboiled Belfast Provo.

'Well, it's not,' I say, 'and I am so...'

Aiden digs me in the ribs. I suppress angry words; they'll only convince Kelly I'm not cool-headed enough for active service ops.

'This for the lads in jail, to show we haven't forgotten them,' Kelly mutters, ice-cold eyes burning me. 'There'd better not be any cock ups.'

'There won't be,' Aiden says.

Kelly flicks his stare to Aiden. 'It's on you to make sure she does what she's supposed to.' He slides a scrap of paper across the coffee table. On it is a north Belfast address and the details of a car, including reg number. 'No mistakes, love,' he says, face stony.

Outside I vent, firing off oaths about Kelly's bigoted bullshit.

'Forget him,' Aiden says. 'You need your mind on this.' He waves the paper at me. 'Are you sure you're ready for it?'

'I've said, haven't I?'

'Just be clear about it: this is a military attack on a legitimate target.'

I shrug Kelly off, think of Daideo instead, his matchstick arms and legs, the tissue paper skin holding him together, old pains flickering behind his eyes. 'I am clear.'

At 2am, driving a commandeered car, we head for the address, bomb in the boot. The air is sleety; white flakes blowing into the headlights make it seem like we're driving into a time travel vortex. I'll wake up in my bed in Dublin last week.

Aiden drives sedately, stopping at red lights even when the junction is clear. Around one corner a cat darts from an entry; Aiden brakes and we're flung forward. I smash my arm on the dashboard and feel the handgun tucked in my belt jab the small of my back as I rebound against the seat.

'Jesus. Did I hit it?'

We both check behind and see the cat scurrying off up the road.

'Christ, you alright?'

'Yes, but I reckon we're all down a life there,' I joke, not letting myself think about the package in the boot being slammed around.

Aiden drives on. A few minutes later we're there.

'You can stay in the car if you want,' he offers.

This bastard was one of them scrubbing the lads down with wire brushes, spreading them over mirrors and beating them up. He's the enemy.

'No. I need to do this.'

'Fine. Don't forget to…'

'I know what I'm doing,' I hiss, getting out of the car but leaving the door open.

The silver Cortina is parked on the drive; I double-check the registration then get the bomb. The house is asleep, no curtains twitching or telly flickering. I open the wrought iron gate; the hinges whine. I freeze but no lights come on so I creep up the drive and wriggle under the car.

It's a small bomb, magnets for attaching it to the car's underbelly, two primer switches, set on a timer. So it shouldn't go off in my face, which is only inches from it in the cramped space beneath the car. Lying on my back the gun digs into my spine so I set it beside me and lift the bomb overhead, arms trembling with the strain. A second before touching it to the chassis the magnets snatch it from my grip, suckering it in place with a resounding clang that rebukes me for snapping at Aiden; he's only wanting to keep me safe. Jesus, I'm a bitch sometimes. Get this done and I can be back with him, get us both safe. I pull a torch from my pocket and illuminate the switches I need to flick, starting the countdown that will end as the screw pulls up outside Long Kesh for another day's grind.

There's a sound, like a book falling flat onto a wooden floor. I click off the torch, turn my head and see a pair of tartan slippers, wrinkled socks rising from them. They point towards the street, back towards the house and back again: towards me.

I have the gun in my hand before I've picked it up. A face joins the slippers, peering under the car: there's a moustache, grey and bushy; baggy, weather-worn skin. Eyes lock into mine, widening in surprise as they see me. The mouth opens to speak. I point and pull the trigger. The only sound is the gun's crack.

Trapped in the narrow space the recoil jerks my hand, the gun smacks me on the nose. Shards of shock pierce my brain. Scrambling static clouds my vision. I blink back the burning pain and dazzling sparks; see the slippers, upended, worn-through soles staring blankly at me. I fumble for the switches, feel the two raised pimples, and press. Then roll out from under the car.

The screw is on his back, a dark hole in his forehead, a blood trickle trailing from the wound and a larger pool of inky blackness saturating the ground beneath his head where the exploding bullet churned tissue, shattered bone, ripped skin. He's dead. And he's not the screw. I see now he's too old, frail, for the Kesh's brutal work.

Aiden flashes the headlights. I run down and throw myself into the car, not getting the door shut before he has his foot through the floor, speeding us away, the gun still in my hand. The stench of cordite fills the car.

'Jesus. What the fuck happened?' Aiden asks.

I can't speak. I'm trying to unload the gun but keep missing the catch that releases the magazine. He snatches the gun from me, tossing it on the back seat, speeds up. We're thrown round corners, swiping traffic bollards and lampposts, running red lights, heading for the Falls, the unlit streets that can hide us. My mouth fills with the salty metallic taste of blood. I feel myself ragged about but all I see is a pair of tartan slippers, the soles worn out.

We've stopped. Aiden's shaking me.

'We've gotta go.'

A door slams, his. I'm dragged out, hauled to my feet. The street comes into focus; shuttered shops, up-tipped bins, piles of rubble. Aiden leans into the car, grabs my gun and tucks it into his belt. His hand grips my arm and he jumps into a run, towing me, my feet stumbling to find a rhythm. Then I'm running on my own, his grip gone. We're side by side, our boots belting over broken pavement slabs. I want to keep running, heart pumping, legs thrusting, lungs burning. I want to stay in my body; out of my head.

We sprint down narrow entries and into the Divis flats complex where the concrete warren of Lego-stacked blocks squats. Aiden turns left, right, bangs through a door, mounts a flight of stairs and races along a walkway to a peeling blue-paint door. He pummels it. A light snaps on. A woman opens the door, clutching a pink dressing gown to her throat. She looks us over, holds back the door, letting us tumble in, then slams and bolts it.

We stand there, panting. Blood drips from my nose, disappearing into the brown lino. I sag against the wall, shaking.

'Sorry to wake you, Cathy,' Aiden says, the words gasped between breaths, 'but we've a spot of bother.'

'Yous better come through.'

She strides down the passage. We follow her into a kitchen, bright with yellow Formica and green cupboards. She's at the sink, filling the kettle. Aiden pulls out a chair, makes me sit, tilts my chin, facing me into the light.

'Jesus, you're hurt.'

I jerk my head away and pinch my bleeding nose.

'Bathroom's next door,' Cathy says.

On trembling legs I stagger into the loo. The mirror above the cracked white sink reveals the result of my self-inflicted make-over; purple bruises shadowing my eyes, nose swollen and pulpy, blood rouging my lips. I wash off the sticky red film that's drying to a crust in my nostrils.

Back in the kitchen Cathy and Aiden are drinking tea, smoking. She pushes her pack across as I sit. The lines around her mouth deepen as she takes a drag; she brushes frazzled brown hair off her forehead. Her roots are grey. She stares at me but doesn't ask my name which I guess means Aiden's already told her.

'Do I want to know?' she asks Aiden.

'You don't.' He taps ash off the end of his cigarette. 'Can you get a message across town for us?'

'Aye, tomorrow.' She sighs. 'I'll get yous some blankets for the sofa.' She shuffles out.

'Are you alright?' he asks, reaching for my hand.

'Fine.'

'What happened?'

'Weren't you watching?'

'Thought I saw something up the road. Next I knew he was by the car and...' He takes my hand again. 'He was going up in a few hours anyway.'

'It wasn't him.'

'What?'

'It was some ould fella. I didn't see until after...'

'Shite. Who then?'

'I don't know. Maybe his da? Is this going to get me disciplined?'

'Ach, no. You had to get away. You're no use in jail.'

'I'm no use out of it if I'm shooting the wrong people.'

'Don't think that. We don't know who he was. You were reacting to a developing situation,' Aiden reassures, gripping my hand.

I rub at the ache in my forehead.

'You want me to see if she's got any pills?' he offers.

I tell him yes, but two Aspirin aren't going to make this better.

We doss down in the living room, me on the sofa, Aiden in an armchair with his feet, still in their boots, on the coffee table: next to the gun. The night plays on a loop in my head. I see the man's face, the eyes reading mine, the mouth open to plead, and the second face, staring sightlessly. The before and after images alternate, faces on a spinning coin. I lose whichever way up it falls.

When grey dawn finally filters through the faded curtains, I get up. Cathy is in the kitchen, wearing a plain brown skirt, flat court shoes with scuffed toes and a bobbly white jumper with a lace collar, her greying hair pulled into a knot. At the table is a boy about ten wearing a school uniform, the tie clumsily knotted and his shirt cuffs threadbare. Limp cornflakes float in a milky sea.

'If you're not eating that away to school,' Cathy says and he puts a spoonful into his mouth with a grimace. 'Tea?' she asks me.

'If there is some.'

'There's always some, even when there's nothing else,' she replies and tips last night's dregs into the sink. 'Was it Kelly sent yous out or McKearney?'

Panic and saliva fill my mouth.

'It's alright, love, I've been there myself,' she says. 'Kelly was it?'

'Yes.'

She nods and snatches away the half-eaten cornflakes.

'I was eating them, Mammy,' the boy says.

'You'll be late. I need you to run to Mr Kelly's on your way. Tell him to call round this morning. You know where I mean, Callum?'

'Yes, Mammy.'

'Go then.'

Callum stands but doesn't leave.

'Well?' Cathy demands.

The kettle starts screeching.

'You've not given me my dinner money,' Callum says, studying the trailing laces of his scabby shoes.

'I'll make you a sandwich.'

'Can't I have the money?' he pleads.

'I can't give you what I've not,' she snaps.

I dig in my pocket for some change.

'Here.' I offer him the coins but Callum looks to his mum for permission.

'There's no need,' she tells me.

'It's only a couple of quid. Let me.'

She sniffs but gives Callum the nod. 'And mind your manners, mister,' she warns.

He stares at me, his eyes large, brown and smiling. 'Thank you.'

'Tá fáilte romhat,' I reply.

He blushes and drops his gaze.

'It's Irish, 'you're welcome'.'

'Oh.' He braves a second glance at me. 'Cool. What else can you say?'

'Never you mind,' Cathy orders, shoving him from the kitchen.

While she's packing him off, I empty the kettle into the tea pot and scrub two mugs. When I turn around with them full of tea Cathy is in the doorway, scowling.

'We don't speak Irish here. It's asking for trouble.'

'Sorry, I didn't…'

She snorts, 'You wouldn't.' She casts her eyes over me, inspecting. 'So you're the Finnighan girl.'

I nod.

'Heard you'd come back,' she says. 'What're you doing messing in this anyways?'

I clatter the mugs down, slopping tea onto the Formica. 'I've the same right to serve as anyone.'

'So I used to think.' She drops into a chair and lights a cigarette. "Til they threw me out for having a baby and no ring on my finger. A disgrace, they said.'

'Who?' I think of Kelly.

'Those stuck up Cumann na mBan bitches,' she retorts. 'With their holy of holiest vows of virginity.'

I sit across from her. 'I'm not in the Cumann na mBan.'

'Good for you. I hope the 'Ra treat you better but don't be expecting it. Equality: they'll talk it plenty but when it comes to acting, hmph! Now I'm stuck at home, doing them favours when there's no one else.' She sighs, expelling rage and regret. 'They're fond of saying how the Six Counties is one big jail that the boys are born into 'til they get sent up the road to the smaller jail. But this,' she gestures to the peeling wallpaper, grubby lino and mismatched chairs, 'is my own wee prison. It's a life sentence I've got myself, so it is, just for being an unholy mother.'

Her fury forces me into a no-comment position. We sit in silence, tea and anger cooling. Cathy's comments about the Cumann na mBan stir up a question.

'Did you know my mum?'

Cathy puts her mug down. Stares at me.

'I wondered, maybe you served together?' I prompt.

She smiles tightly. 'We did more than that. I knew her, aye. She was a solid comrade and an even better friend.' Cathy nods. 'It was terrible what happened to her.'

I don't want to hear that. 'Tell me about her, just something ordinary. What was she like?'

'Great craic,' Cathy says, 'but serious when she had to be.' Her smile grows as she pulls memories to the surface. 'A terrible cook but she could make amazing soda bread. If you played cards with her she'd always cheat unless you played for money. She was a terrible singer but that didn't stop her when she'd had a few whiskeys, which wasn't too often. She was the only person I knew who could put our Nora in her place, formidable so she was, and when she…'

The door inches open. Aiden enters, rubbing sleep from his eyes. 'Is there tea?' He reaches for the pot.

Cathy's face switches back to surly. 'Men, sure, you're all the bloody same,' she barks, standing as Aiden helps himself. 'I'm away to collect this week's handout. I've sent the lad with a message. Someone'll be round for yous later. Clean up after yourselves.' She bangs out.

Aiden shakes his head. 'Sorry. She's like that sometimes but I couldn't think where else to go.'

'It's OK. We were starting to chat before you interrupted.'

'Aye, what about?'

I don't want to share those precious fragments, not even with Aiden.

'Nothing much. Who is she anyway?'

'Mammy's sister. We only see her Christmas and Easter, keeps to herself since she had the wee 'un.'

A car collects us mid-morning. A young lad drives, eyes welded to the road, while Kelly rages at me from beside him.

'That fella you shot was the screw's bleeding father-in-law. And they found the fu… the bomb before it went off.' He faces me. 'You'll not be doing any more ops here. It's alright yous running messages but, catch yourself on, you're useless at proper jobs.'

'That's not fair,' Aiden bleats. 'She…'

'Don't you say fuck all to me, boyo. Letting your lass do your job, you're a fucking shower,' Kelly barks.

His chivalrous sexism, how he curses Aiden instead of me because he won't swear at women, makes me long to call him a cunt just to shut him up, make him wither, but I'm in too much trouble to risk it, even for Aiden. I reach for Aiden's hand. He tears it free. I don't know who he's mad at; Kelly, me or himself.

I fix on the scrolling view, throat tight, eyes stinging. To Kelly the shooting is a chance lost, justification for his macho bigotry. To me it's a line crossed.

'You're away back south,' Kelly grins smugly at me, 'where you can do no more damage.' He rakes mucus up from his lungs. 'So much for ould man Finnighan's kin.'

*

I wash up in Dublin and find myself lost in my own house. I pace the rooms, searching for something to settle on. Seeing Daideo's Cúchulainn painting above the fireplace, I stand in front of it. The angry army pours perpetually into the valley; the boy warrior waits eternally to face them, believing, against sense and reason, that he can defeat them. Slumping onto the sofa, I stand myself in his place, feeling the ford's icy torrent snaking my ankles, the wind whipping my hair, the fear in my heart: the weapon in my hand. But it's not a gae bolga, Cúchulainn's terrible death spear, it's a handgun. I fire until each man's face is bloodied: tattered. They keep coming, despite their wounds. I claw my way out of the daydream, sweating and shaking, the real gun on the couch next to me. Sinking under the fallout I forgot to hand it back and Kelly, too busy bollocking me, forgot to ask for it. Another fuck up, more Kelly's than mine, his responsibility, but he'll blame me, adding it to his 'against' list. I go into Daideo's bedroom and hide it under his bed, a problem buried in shifting sand.

I drift, sleepless and exhausted, drinking through my misery and the savings Daideo left me, tramping the streets, looping back and round, checking off places on a list someone binned long ago; Northumberland Road, Mount Street, St Stephen's Green, Dublin Castle, Phoenix Park, the GPO: places that don't matter anymore to the people here. They got rid of their enemy. The Free State, Eire, the Republic; they don't have a cause to fight for anymore. Their world is nine to five, Croke Park on Saturday, church on Sunday and close their own front door with no worries of it being kicked in by squaddies or burnt down by Loyalists. They stopped being victims long enough ago to forget how much it hurts. I want to slap them, wake them to the reality they're sleeping through. But I can't so I keep walking, to keep myself awake. I'm afraid of the nightmares that'll come with sleep.

On the first day of term I loiter by the bus stop opposite the college, reviewing what I've given up, watching students carrying their shiny new portfolios through the entrance. I try painting myself into the scene but every time I'm carrying an

Armalite, not an art set. Mr Walsh appears on the steps. I leave.

At home I get my sketchpad. Frustration drives my pencil, drawing lines that shape a Belfast house on a rubble-littered street. The house's corner pose shows only part of the front door and windows but all the gable end which tapers away up the street. The gable wall is patriotically painted; a large tricolour daubed high and, beneath it, the comforting greeting 'Welcome to Provo Land'. Suddenly a figure appears in the composition, standing, back to the viewer, facing the graffiti. The figure's clothes are neutral, jeans and a jacket. It's the blonde hair dripped half-way down her back that gives me away. That and the gun drawn in my hand, the one now hidden under Daideo's bed. What do you do when the choice you made has been unmade for you? By you? I slide the pad into a drawer.

After a week of battling the tide, when I'm knackered enough to crave drowning, the phone rings in the middle of the night. It's Aiden.

'How're ya?' he asks.

'OK. You?'

'Aye, ya know.' There's a pause. 'How are you really?'

'Bloody terrible. Are you coming down soon?'

'I can't. They're sending me to Glasgow.'

'What! Why?'

'Ah, they're saying they need me there.'

'But?'

'It's that prick Kelly.' Aiden's voice hardens. 'He's gobbing on that us being together's messing up my head.'

'Is it?'

Aiden grunts. 'It's not being with you that's messing me up. Jesus, I'd skin him if I could get hold of the bollocks.' He sighs. 'I'm sorry, Caoilainn, but there's nothing I can do.'

'When are you going?'

'In the morning. Shite, I'm running outta money.' The phone pips. 'We'll sort this. I love you.' The line dies.

It's the first time he's said that. I didn't have chance to reply. If I had would I've been brave enough to say it back?

*

I buy a canvas, 3ft x 2ft, and transfer the Belfast street sketch onto it, using it profile instead of landscape so my one house reaches from edge to edge but leaves me space above for an oppressive sky. Then I start painting; blue jeans, brown bricks, white words.

Aiden's mother invites me up for Christmas, even though Aiden can't be there. In the last few months I've had half a dozen postcards from him, pictures of men in kilts, the Saltire, thistle covered hillsides. They've held me together, just about. I tell her I'll think it over; I'm not sure I want to be there without Aiden. At least here on my own I can ignore thoughts of him, cravings for him, on good days anyway. Up there I'll be staring at photos of him, hearing his name, sleeping in his old bed, the one he can't use because he's on the Brits' list. She rings twice more, worries at me, tells me I'm family. Uncertain I can refute that, I pretend someone's at the door, hang up and go back to spackling in the rubble littering my new painting's pavement.

Two days later the phone rings at dawn. I dive out of bed and skid into the hall to answer it.

'Hello?'

'How're you?'

It's Aiden. Pain splits my head, tears scald my eyes.

'Are you OK?'

'Aye, grand. I've not long though,' he says, pausing. 'I need you to do me a favour.' He sucks in a breath. 'Go to me ma's for Christmas.'

Nora's been on at him.

'I don't know.'

'Why not?'

'I'm fine on my own.'

'Moping won't help. You need to be with family.'

His words bite; I swipe at the stinging. 'My family's dead.'

'Catch yourself on; we're your family. Jesus, what's wrong with you? You don't have to tough everything out alone.'

'It's what I'm used to.'

'Then start changing 'cos that's no way to live.' He sighs. 'Just go to me ma's, please. I don't want you on your own.'

'Then come home.'

There's a silence, a sniff and a clattering.

'Aiden?'

'Wouldn't I love to?' he says, words broken and raw.

Fuck. I'm hurting him. What the fuck is wrong with me? 'Sorry. I know. I'll go.'

'Grand.' He sniffs again. 'You might even enjoy it.'

I doubt it, with him missing, but I'll try, for his sake. I lean against the wall and find myself staring into the living room at my almost finished painting. We say hurried goodbyes and he's gone again. I go into the front room and open the curtains. Heavy rain clouds are slung across the sky but along the horizon they've torn, letting through a thin line of dawn light that turns the downpour orange in the east. It's the sky I didn't know I was looking for until I saw it. I drag my easel to the window, squeeze red and yellow onto my pallet and blend until the sky's bitter burnt orange is in my palm.

A week later the painting is finished. A fair-haired woman stands on a road in ruined West Belfast, gaping at a graffitied gable end, gun gripped tightly. I leave it on the easel to dry and get packing, cramming Christmas parcels in my bag; whiskey for Frank, chocolates for Nora, soaps for Cathy, Ireland jerseys for Danny and Callum. One box, gift-wrapped with reindeer paper and green ribbon, clunks heavily. Inside it is the gun I shouldn't still have; I have to confront my failures and take the consequences. Before leaving I write the title on the back of the canvas, 'Herself Alone in Orange Rain', and sign off.

# Belfast—23rd December, 1981

Frank meets me at the bus station. Brits in battledress stamp by as he kisses my cheek and takes my bag.

'OK?' he asks as we get into his car.

'Fine. You?'

'Better now Connor's on the mend.'

'He's alright then?'

'Filling out. You look as though you could do with feeding up some.'

'I'm fine.'

We drive through the drizzle in silence, passing grey Land Rovers, a Saracen, more foot patrols. I stare out the window; dreary buildings draped with soggy tinsel bleed into the rain-soaked day like watercolours on soggy paper.

As we park outside the house Frank squeezes my arm.

'You didn't mess up. You did just fine. There was a problem; you handled it. And got away.'

'To do what?' I pull free. 'Sit on my arse in Dublin while things carry on the same up here?'

'See what the new year brings,' he says, winking.

Hope relaxes me. 'What's that mean, Frank?'

'Ah, sure, I've still a wee bit of influence with the boys.'

The O'Neills terrace house fills up with friends, family and festivities. On Christmas Eve I'm crammed into the kitchen with Nora and Cathy, peeling spuds, chopping carrots and mixing sludgy stuffing. In the front room Frank drinks with Patsy and two other cronies from the Felon's. Danny and Callum are upstairs, keeping out of the way.

Nora takes more beer into the front. Cathy tips the contents of her teacup down the drain.

'Sure, I've been gagging for herself to slip out,' she mutters, pulling a hip flask from her pinny pocket and refilling her cup. 'Don't I miss your ma on days like this? She would've played merry hell if Nora so much as tutted over us having a tipple. Would you take a wee drop? It's only firewater but it does the trick.'

I grin at her. 'Thanks.'

She brims my cup then raises her own. 'To Christmas with family and please God may I survive it.' She tips the rest of the hip flask's contents into the stuffing with a chuckle.

Danny, Callum and I drape the spindly tree with the last strand of silvery tinsel. I lift Callum so he can sit the star on top, my arms trembling with the strain as he adjusts and readjusts until the star is perfect. I'm relieved to put him down. We step back. Fairy lights glitter and baubles gleam. Danny throws his arm around Callum's shoulder and they stand admiring our festive installation. Callum wriggles warm fingers in amongst mine. I fight the urge to retreat; I need to be better at this.

Nora comes into the sitting room. The pinny has been replaced by her Sunday best.

'Yous two, away and get dressed.' She shoos them out. Coming to me, she holds up a square of black lace netting, like a veil from a funeral bonnet. 'You can borrow this.'

I take it, rubbing the coarse mesh between my fingers. 'What for?'

'To cover your head, unless you've a hat?'

My hand strays to my hair. 'Why do I need to cover my head?'

Nora tuts. 'I don't know what you've been used to but here we're modest in church.'

The clock chimes 11 P.M.; I click on and return the headscarf. 'Thanks but I'm not going to church.'

The fabric wilts in her stunned hand. 'You can't mean to miss midnight mass? That's awful, so it is.'

'Only if I'm Catholic.'

'Oh.' A single syllable, not even a word, but it sounds out her dismay, disappointment, disapproval.

'Daideo didn't have time for it and my… the Ryans didn't believe in slavishly following dogmatic religious regimes. They were more into the comparative study of spirituality.'

She stands over me, arms folded, eyes narrowed. 'I see.'

I lock my eyes into hers. Nora wads the headscarf in her fist, crosses herself with two sharp swipes of her hand, spins on her heel and strides out. A moment later I hear muttering in the hall; she's telling Frank and Cathy about the wee heathen on the couch. She shouts for Danny and Callum to hurry up. They stampede down the stairs. There's scuffling; shoes donned, coats buttoned. Franks calls:

'We're away, Caoilainn, love. See you in a bit.'

'Fine.'

The front door slams, shaking the Christmas tree. Alone for the first time since I arrived, I go to the bedroom I'm sharing with Cathy and retrieve my gifts, putting them under the twinkling tree, all but the reindeer-wrapped box. That I open myself, tearing off the Rudolph paper. Cleaned and docile, the gun nestles on tissue paper, the almost full magazine beside it. I load it, replace it in the box and slide it under my bed, wondering who to give it to.

On Christmas morning paper is ripped, kisses and thank-yous exchanged. The kettle is on constant boil and a whole loaf is toasted and buttered. Then it's church again. Nora leaves me orders for setting the lunch away, my penance for shunning her God; I baste chicken and boil potatoes while they're on their knees. At two o'clock we eat, drink, pull crackers, don paper hats and tell stupid jokes: why does Santa have a big garden? Because he likes to Ho Ho Ho! Nora carries through the pudding but Frank can't get the brandy to light.

'There's not enough oomph in this cheap piss,' he moans.

'I've heard vodka works better,' I say.

He snorts, 'It's bleeding petrol we're needing.'

'Frank!' Nora snaps.

'Aye, well, wouldn't be doing much for the taste of it,' he admits, passing round bowls, each containing a mountain of pud, snow-capped with thick rum sauce.

After lunch, when, in another life, I'd have been dragged out to picket capitalist commercialism or hand soup to the homeless, Danny is propelled onto the hearth rug. He sings 'The Wearing of the Green' with a choirboy's voice.

As he finishes an assortment of neighbourhood friends cram into the front room, perching on chair arms or leaning against the sideboard, mantelpiece, windowsill. Among them is Liam. His black hair is shorter. He's wearing a shirt and tie. Cleaned up and clean-shaven he's a good looking lad. He waves to me and smiles. A flicker on the edge of my vision makes me turn. Nora is staring at me. Unjustified heat flushes my face. I excuse myself, go into the kitchen and start scraping grease from a roasting pan with a wooden spoon.

'Caoilainn, how are ya?'

Liam's greeting startles me.

'Fine, yourself?'

'Aye.' I hear the door click shut. 'Heard about what happened. Good on ya.'

I face him now. He comes closer.

'What d'ya mean?

He smiles. 'You didn't panic, got yourself away. Spot on.'

'I shot the wrong man.'

'You did what you had to.' He lays his hands on my shoulders. 'It's the way things go sometimes.' He steps back. 'If you're about later there's someone wanting to meet you.'

'Who?'

'My OC.'

I think of the gun. 'Alright. I've something for him.'

Liam raises his eyebrows. 'What's that?'

'Something I've no business having.'

The door swings opens. Cathy sashays into the kitchen, sees us and pulls up.

'What's this, a cosy wee tête-à-tête?'

'We're catching up,' I say.

'See you later,' Liam mumbles, squirming past her.

Cathy closes the door. 'Know him, do you?'

'We went through basic training together.'

She chews her lip. 'Watch yourself; there'll be talk if you're sneaking off with lads.'

I clatter the spoon into the sink. 'Talk?'

'You're an O'Neill now, as good as. You need to mind that. People here have fixed ideas. I know the cost of going against that so take my advice: remember whose house you're in.'

'Did Frank send you to spy on me?'

'Frank?' Cathy snorts his name. 'It's not him you've to bother about. It's the mammy. It's always the mammy with Catholic boys.'

'Especially when the girlfriend's not Virgin Mary white?' I ask.

'Aye, you're catching on,' Cathy replies. 'Your ma'd be proud.'

The neighbours head on somewhere else. We play charades; Danny sings more rebel songs. Frank falls to snoring in front of the box while the boys start a snakes and ladders game. The washing up done, Nora, Cathy and I make tea. I butter bread, Cathy slices cucumber while Nora validates tinned salmon with white pepper and malt vinegar. Our jobs, assigned by Nora, reflect our family ranking.

Liam taps on the window. Nora sets her fork down, wipes her hands, pats her stiff perm, strolls to the door and opens it. Cathy nudges me and, with a flick of her eyes, repeats her warning. I scrape a buttery curl from the yellow brick and spread it unevenly on a white slice, tearing the bread.

'What can I do for you, Liam?' Nora asks.

'Hello, Mrs O'Neill. I'm just after five minutes with Caoilainn.'

Nora scans him. The shirt and tie have been replaced with a sweater and a donkey jacket. He shuffles under her scrutiny.

'Important, is it?' she sniffs.

'Aye, it's,' he lowers his voice, 'Army business.'

'Today?'

Liam glances at me. Cathy hisses in my ear.

I put the knife aside. 'I'll get my coat.'

Upstairs I retrieve the gun, hiding it under my sweatshirt, fastening my coat over it. Danny waylays me in the hall.

'Where're ya going?'

'Never you mind.'

'Can I come?'

'Aren't you playing with Callum?'

'I'm bored.'

'I won't be long. When I get back you can teach me those songs.'

He pulls a face. 'I know where you're going.'

'Then you know why you can't come,' I reply, entering the kitchen to hear Cathy asking Liam if he has a girlfriend.

'Sure, I've no time for that,' he says, his face pinking.

'Let's go.' I cut through them, shove Liam outside, cross the yard and head into the alley.

'What's up with Aiden's ma?' he asks as he leads me along the lane.

'She thinks I'm after sleeping with you.'

'Eh?' He halts, turns a stunned expression on me.

'Seems we can either be good Catholic girls or hoors. As I'm not the first I must be the other.' I walk on, stamping down my anger. After a few paces Liam recovers and catches me up.

We go into a backyard a dozen houses down the alleyway; Liam knocks on the door. It's opened by a short, wiry man in his thirties, his receding hair cropped close. He's wearing a navy jumper with a snowflake pattern.

'Sean.'

'Liam.' He reaches out and slaps Liam's shoulder. 'Away, yous are letting in a draught.'

We go into the front. He takes a bottle of Bushmills and two tumblers from the sideboard.

'Drink?'

'Cheers,' Liam says.

We sit and Sean pours, topping up his own glass first.

'How're things in Dublin?'

'Quiet.'

He nods.

I want this over with. I set the gun on the coffee table.

'I realise I should've handed this in straight away but...' I trail off, rejecting lame excuses that won't save me from the bollocking I'm overdue.

He barely glances at it. 'No harm. Beginner's mistake.'

'Not my only one.'

He leans forward, raps on the table.

'Says who, that gobshite Kelly? Don't listen to that bollocks. He's up to his armpits in the kinda shit that gets us a bad name. If I'd any say he's be out on his elbow for bringing the Movement into disrepute, the racketeering sod. He's only for himself, so he is. Wants to play the big man. We're not all like him.'

133

'So you don't think I should be at home making bread and having babies?'

'Not if you'd rather be shooting Brits, which I'm guessing from what happened with that operation, you would. Took some nerve, that did.'

'It was a fuck up.'

He raises his eyebrows.

'And I'm not apologising for my language.'

He smirks. 'I'm not after you to. Swear like a sailor, if you want. I couldn't give a shite about your vocabulary.' The smirk vanishes. 'It's your actions and your attitude I'm keen on.' He lights a cigarette, pushes his pack towards me. 'So have a word with yourself, calm down and listen.'

I take the cigarette and the advice.

'What happened was regrettable but sometimes missions misfire; it's your fault, some other bugger's fault, God, fate, blame who you want.' He shrugs. 'What matters is how you deal with it. You were right doing what you did.'

'You're making it sound like I knew what I was doing when it was only instinct.'

'Then your instincts are dead on, and so are you from what I've heard.'

'From who?'

'Frank. If he's up for you, that's better than a blessing from the Pope.' Seeing my confusion Sean adds, 'Did you not know he was on the Army Council when we first split from the Sticks? Big man, so he was. Still is.'

'I'm here on his word, then.'

Sean bangs his glass down. 'Frank gives no favours and neither do I. The lives of my volunteers are too important for bullshit like that.' He leans back, swilling his whiskey. 'We've had a lad lifted by the Brits. I'm needing a replacement: you, if you're keen.'

'I am.'

'Grand. I'll need you here as of now, mind.'

'Fine.'

He offers me his hand. 'Frank said you're Pat Finnighan's...'

A noise outside, someone hand-clapping a staccato rhythm, interrupts. Sean leaps to the window and tears aside the curtain.

'Jesus. Liam, go for Rory. Get the Armalites. There's shooting up the road.'

We're both on our feet.

'Where?' Liam asks.

Sean faces me. 'The O'Neills'.'

I grab the gun and dart for the door.

A dark car and a pale van are askew in the street outside Frank and Nora's, doors open, headlights blazing. Gunfire chatters through the air. I run towards it; someone gets out of the van, the dazzling headlights illuminating a tall, stocky, masked figure, arm raised. There's a bang and a flash as he fires at me. I stop and aim, gripping the gun in both hands, drawing a breath and squeezing the trigger. The kickback jolts me. The man stumbles, scrambles for cover inside the van. I fire again. Four more masked men run into the street, lit up by the glittering fairy lights Danny, Callum and I wound around the tree in the bay window yesterday.

Engines roar; the attackers dart to their getaways. Behind me two Armalites spit bullets at the car and van, blowing out a headlight, shattering a windscreen, denting a door. The car speeds off. I start running again. The van swings into a miscalculated three-point turn, ramping over the kerb, ramming a lamppost, bumping down, charging across the road and smacking a parked car. I fire, once at the passenger window, twice into the side of the van. It stalls. I leap forward, am yanked back by Liam. He aims at the van. Another lad, Rory, I guess, falls in beside him and, synchronised, they fire as the van stutters to life, limping beyond range.

I break away from them, running to the smashed front door. The Christmas wreath is pulped on the welcome mat, the air thick with acrid smoke. I plough through it, up the passage.

Cathy is crumpled in the lounge doorway, her head lolling backwards, her legs folded under her. The front of her white, lace-neck jumper is a red, ragged mess.

'Jesus,' Liam says.

135

I smell the cordite from his rifle; he's right behind me. I step forward. He catches my arm.

'Don't.'

I jerk free.

Frank is sprawled on the sofa, his face ashen and contorted by pain, his knees shot away. White fragments of bone gleam and blood pumps down his legs, soaking his trousers, slippers, the carpet. Nora crouches beside him, fumbling with a towel, keening a stream of urgent Latin. Danny stands on the hearth rug, from where, hours earlier, he'd sung to us. His hands are clenched, his eyes fixed on his daddy. The snakes and ladders board is at his feet, Callum sat beside it. His new Ireland jersey is blood-spattered, chunks of pinky flesh are in his hair, on his face. I go to them, putting the gun in my belt, hauling Callum up, snatching at Danny.

'Get off,' he shouts, shoving me away.

I slap his cheek. His face fractures, tears bubbling over. Pretending not to see I lift Callum, balancing him on my hip, and turn so he can't see his murdered mammy in the doorway. Holding him with one hand, I grab Danny's shirt and tow him along. Liam is waiting in the hall, his weapon propped against the stairs. He swings Danny out of the room; I step over Cathy, Callum clinging to me. Sean and Rory are here now, Rory guarding the entrance, facing out. I take in the back of his ginger head, the grey t-shirt, faded jeans, red and green striped socks; he didn't wait to put boots on. Shouts from fretful neighbours, already mourning another death, flutter in to us.

Sean takes Callum from me. My sweatshirt feels wet. I look down, see the damp patch, transferred from Callum's crotch. Sean pulls Danny and Callum together, pointing them down the passage.

'Get yourselves into the kitchen,' he orders.

Danny glances at me.

'Now,' Sean barks and Danny leads Callum away.

'We need to go,' Sean says.

'I can't leave them like this.' I gesture to Cathy: Cathy's corpse.

'It's not up for discussion,' he says. 'Peelers'll be coming. If you want to be useful it's better they don't know you exist so get your stuff now.'

Grasping at torn parts of myself, I take the stairs two at a time, bundle my things into my holdall and race down. Rory moves aside; Sean, Liam and I step out, Liam carrying his gun down by his leg. Rory follows. The crowd closes round us, led by Patsy.

He calls to Sean, 'Ambulance is coming. I'll take care of everything.'

Sean nods. The crowd parts and we head up the street, through a door opened and waiting, into a house, out the back, over the alley, into another house, through that to a waiting car and off across the city, Rory driving, Sean beside him, Liam and me in the back.

'You alright?' Liam asks.

'Have you a cigarette?'

He gives me one, lit, and I gulp at it.

'Fucking bastards,' Sean says, 'on Christmas day.'

'Who were they?' I ask, cigarette shaking in my fingers, gun digging me in the back, the stench of smoke and piss churning my stomach.

'UFF, hit squad for the UDA who're just off-duty UDR pricks, service weapons handed out by the Brits and they don't give a fuck what the fuckers do with 'em as long as they're killing Catholics,' Sean explodes. 'There'll be a payday on this.' His words are black underlined. They rule us off into temporary silence.

Sean twists round. 'You're a canny shot.'

'I missed.'

'Looked to me like you got him in the shoulder.'

'I was aiming for his head.'

'At fifty yards with half the streetlights out? You always this hard on yourself?' he asks.

'It's the only way I can keep up,' I say.

'Well, there's no need for it,' he says, as if he gets what it's like for me. 'Mind, you go charging off again and I'll skin you same as I would the lads. A dead volunteer's no use to anyone. Next time wait for orders.'

Rory drops us at a safe house, leaves with the guns, heading for the nearest weapons dump.

The house belongs to a wifie, sixty-five or more, white hair in rollers. She greets us in her slippers and dressing gown. From behind bifocals her eyes fix on me but all she says is:

'I'm away to bed, Sean, help yourselves to tea.'

'Thanks, Ma,' Sean replies.

Liam takes me into the kitchen. I sit at the table while he brews a pot. Sean joins us, bringing whiskey. He gets mugs and pours three measures.

I push mine away.

He pushes it back. 'Drink. Then tea and bed.'

I down the dram in one and wait for tea, visions of Cathy, her chest ripped apart, her legs buckled, flashing behind my eyes. I curse Aiden for not being here; I need to hold onto him, let go of myself. I sniff back tears. The smell of Callum's piss wafts up from my jumper. I gag and drag it over my head to sit there in my t-shirt, shivering. Sean thrust my top into the washer, goes out, returns with a pink knitted jumper. I take it but don't put it on. Liam pours the tea and Sean tips whiskey into each mug.

'I'll see you're in the guard of honour,' he pauses. 'There's something else you can do too, if you're needing help getting your head right.'

'There's nothing the matter with my head. They attacked; we fought back. If you're talking about reprisals I'm not interested. I volunteered to fight a war.'

'And if reprisals are a legitimate military tactic?' he asks.

'Convince me they are and I'll do what needs doing but I'll not kill out of revenge, that makes us as bad as them.'

He eyeballs me. 'You're a hard one.'

Blinking away fresh tears, more thoughts of Aiden, I drag the pullover on. 'I need to be.'

'Fair enough.'

*

We move twice in the week before Cathy's funeral. Liam and I stay together but Sean disappears after a couple of days, other things to see to. Nora gets in touch. We meet in a café on the outskirts of West Belfast.

She's sat in the corner, sipping coffee, hands clasped, face impassive, when I arrive. She hugs me. We wait until the waitress goes before talking.

'How's Frank?'

'He'll live,' she says, then sighs. 'As for walking…'

'Danny? Callum?'

'Callum's staying with us. There's nowhere else for him to go. Danny…' She shrugs. 'He's after the boys every day about letting him join. I can't stop him but I've told them he's too young yet.' She reaches for my hand. 'You saved our lives. If you hadn't come…'

'I didn't save Cathy.'

'She never would go down without fighting. She thought they were after Callum, charged at them, so she did. Mother's instinct.'

I wonder if it wasn't something else, her years in the Cumann na mBan, maybe a combination.

'You'll be there on Wednesday?' Nora asks.

'Yes.'

She lowers her voice, 'In the colour party?'

I nod.

'She'd have liked that.'

When I return to the safe house Liam greets me at the door.

'You've a visitor.' He nods towards the lounge.

Perched stiff-backed on the sofa, hands resting in her lap, is a woman. She could be twenty, or forty; her face is made up after Joan Collins, her hair set in soft waves lacquered to stiff with Silverkrin, the cut of her wool skirt tailored for a price. She rises stiffly; offers me a limp hand. When I put mine to it, her grip is vague.

'I'm Pauline,' she says. 'I've brought you this for Wednesday.' She points to a parcel.

I unwrap a black skirt, v-neck jumper, white blouse and black beret.

'I assume you've some shoes?' She presses her mouth into a tight line, eyeing my steel-toe capped boots, crusted with mud.

'What's this?'

'Your uniform, for the colour party.'

No it's not. It's a fucking insult, to me and Cathy.

'It's what Cumann na mBan girls wear,' she adds, mistaking my unblinking angry silence for moon-eyed stupidity.

'But I'm IRA.' I remember Aiden, at Sands' funeral, olive green trousers, camouflage jacket, boots shiny, face hidden by a balaclava. That's my uniform.

She sniffs. 'I'm aware but Cathy was Cumann na mBan. I thought as a mark of respect you'd dress appropriately.'

'So she's worthy of your respect now?'

'Of course she is. She was one of us.'

'One of you?' I snap. 'Where was that sisterly camaraderie when Callum was born?'

Pauline's mouth twitches. She'd love to bollock me. But I'm not one of her girls. 'How dare you?'

'How dare you!'

I'm dangerously close to calling her a two-faced bitch and winding up on a charge. I take a breath, drop into the nearest armchair and light a cigarette, a handy show of nonchalance that heads off my trembling thighs before they give way.

'Now we've won ourselves the right to be 'Ra volunteers I'll not be surrendering it.'

'I'll have words with your OC about this insolence.'

Bubbling rage bottled, she gathers the clothes and bangs out.

Liam comes in as soon as she's gone.

'You're a one,' he says.

'Hypocritical cow. After how they treated Cathy!'

He grins but shakes his head. 'Ach, she's alright, served well in her day, so they're saying. You shouldn't judge her by your standards. When we went to the cell structure the Army Council disbanded them, skimmed the cream into new units and the rest left to curdle.'

'What's that, women's lib IRA style?' I joke.

'Sure, I know nothing about that stuff. I'd fight with a one-legged leprechaun as long as he, or she, could aim straight.'

Despite my outraged outburst the Cumann na mBan still parade for Cathy's funeral. A dozen women, black bandannas tied across their noses, eyes hidden behind sunglasses even though the day is concrete-grey, follow the coffin like bridesmaids behind a sacrificial bride.

Aiden's here too, thank God, allowed back from Glasgow because Cathy was family, his and the 'Ra's. Seeing him again I realise I've been holding my breath for three months. Now all I can think about is breathing him. As we line up to take the coffin he winks at me, the only greeting possible thanks to the masks we wear. I think my lungs will burst. If we're lucky we'll get the night together.

The tricolour covering the coffin flutters into my eyes. The wood digs into my shoulder as it tips awkwardly towards me because I'm shorter than the boys who carry it with me. Aiden and Liam are behind with Rory and two other lads on the opposite side. We lower it slowly, my arms trembling under the weight I won't drop, then step back for the brief orations, one by the priest and another by a Sinn Fein member I've not seen before. He speaks of Cathy's dedication to the Republican Cause, how she died protecting her family from a Loyalist murder squad. The words numb like codeine. I see why Daideo didn't want this for my parents' funerals. Aiden bumps against me. I daren't look at him. It would break me.

Armalites are handed out. I haven't fired one since basic training and sneak a glance at Aiden, copying his movements. We aim, fire three times and pass the weapons to waiting hands who disappear them under long coats. The proceedings completed we strip off our Army gear and mingle with the mourners. I lose Aiden in the crowd and, while searching for him, see Frank, wheelchair-bound and swaddled in blankets. Amongst the Republican graves we're safe so I go to him.

He grips my hand with both of his, pressing my palm hard.

'Jesus, Caoilainn, you've no idea,' he says.

'I didn't stop them.'

'You chased them off, so you did. Saved my life.' He lowers his voice, 'You're active again, are you?'

I press my other hand over his. 'I know you spoke up for me. Thanks.'

'They could see for themselves you're a capable volunteer. I'm just an ould fella now.' He presses fingers into his eye sockets, squeezing water from them. 'Talking's all I'm good for. But not you.' He crushes my hands between his. 'All I've wanted was to see you right.'

'Thanks.'

He nods and lets me go.

Aiden appears. I feel his hand on my arm, finally I can breathe again. Air rushes into my lungs.

'How are ya, Da?' He bends to kiss his broken father.

'Grand, son, yourself?'

Aiden smiles, laces his fingers through mine. 'Grand, now.'

We spend the night in Cathy's old flat. The council hasn't reassigned it yet so we're safe. We drink too much whiskey and make love in front of the gas fire, getting toasted on one side and chilled on the other. Later, sobered up, we talk.

'Your OC had a word at the funeral,' Aiden says. 'He tells me they've picked a target, UDR fella they reckon could've been one of the lot that did Cathy. He said I can be in on it.'

'And will you?'

'Won't you?' he challenges.

He's already had the answer from Sean but he's daring me to say it.

'No.'

'She was family.' His voice is hard with anger

'And that's why I won't do it.'

'Jesus, Caoilainn, that makes no sense. If you won't do it for Cathy you should be doing it because he's one of them, just a Brit in a different uniform: the enemy.'

'If I could be sure that's why I was doing it then I would but how can I live with myself if I make it personal?'

'How can you live with yourself if you kid on it isn't?' He starts dressing.

'Where're you going?'

'I've stuff to do.'

He turns his back, pulling his sweatshirt over his head, stuffing his feet into his boots, grabbing his leather jacket. The front door bangs.

It's like the sound of a gunshot but worse.

# Belfast—9<sup>th</sup> January, 1982

## Off-duty UDR Man Murdered in Belfast

Steven Carlton, 24, was killed yesterday in a brutal attack on the Antrim Road in north Belfast.

Mr Carlton, a part-time member of the Ulster Defence Regiment, was working at a petrol station when two masked gunman pulled up in a stolen car and shot him six times at point blank range. The assassins made off in a waiting car.

Mr Carlton, married with a young son, is the first member of the UDR to be shot this year. The IRA later claimed responsibility.

There is speculation that the killing was in retaliation for the shooting, on Christmas day, of a Catholic woman in West Belfast. The RUC believe Miss Keenan, 39, was shot by Loyalists.

Mr Carlton is not known to have any connection with paramilitary groups.

# London—27th April, 1982

## Prime Minster Addresses Parliament on the Recapture of South Georgia

Prime Minister Margaret Thatcher made a full statement yesterday to the Commons about the recapture of South Georgia, announced on Sunday.

Mrs Thatcher told members of the House that, at 4 P.M. London time, British troops were landed on the island by helicopter. They quickly overran the Argentine garrison which surrendered. She confirmed there were no known British casualties and reportedly only one injured Argentine soldier. She praised British troops for using minimal force.

Mrs Thatcher said she would continue to seek a peaceful end to the crisis, which began earlier this month when Argentine forces invaded the Falkland Islands, but she concluded by defending military action, under the sanction of the UN:

'I am standing up for the right of self-determination. I am standing up for all those territories—those small territories and people the world over—who, if someone doesn't stand up and say to an invader, 'Enough, stop,' would be at risk.'

British warships continue sailing for the Falklands for the purposes of engaging the Argentine army.


I fly to Paris on my Irish passport and depart Charles de Gaulle International for London Heathrow on my British one. At immigration the passport control officer on the 'UK Nationals' desk twirls his rubber stamp.

'That's an unusual name, how'd you say that then?'

I pronoun it carefully, old syllables rusty on my tongue, 'Kay-lin.'

He raises his eyebrows, stamp poised.

'My parents were hippies,' I say, ensuring my words come out English, not Irish. It's a challenge after eighteen months away.

He stamps a smudgy black seal, scribbles the date and waves me through.

At the gate I'm met by a man I recognise from a photograph: Brendan. He's taller than I expected, early forties, mousey hair cut tight, dark eyes in a round face, dressed in trousers and a sports jacket. He acknowledges me with a nod and I greet him, letting him kiss my cheek. Swamped by the arrivals crowd nobody notices we don't speak.

He leads me to a beige Ford Escort. I throw my bag in the boot and we join the queue signed for the A4, heading towards south west London.

'So you're Charlie Finnighan's daughter,' he says, inching the car to the traffic lights. His accent is a harsh Ulster drawl.

I pounce on the remark. 'You knew my da?'

'Aye.' He rasps a cough. I wait, hope. He doesn't help me.

'What was he like?'

'A good volunteer in his day.'

That's not what I want. 'What else?'

Brendan shrugs. 'A decent fella.' He turns, stares at me for five searching seconds. 'Grand with the arrows. Saw him do a nine-dart finish more than once.'

A horn swears at us. The lights are green now and a two car gap has opened up ahead.

Brendan jerks us forward. 'You remembered to travel on your British passport?'

I'm not that fucking raw. 'Of course.'

He shoots me another glance. 'Hope you're up to this.'

'Would they've sent me if I wasn't?'

'They sent you 'cos you're a native and a wee girlie that no one'll look twice at but having the right accent and a pair of tits doesn't mean anything if you can't handle operations.'

Bastard chauvinist. I choke down a mouthful of curses, reminding myself that he's my new OC. And he might tell me more about my da, if I ask nicely.

'I can.'

He huffs wordless doubts as we swing through London on the South Circular in muzzled silence, leafy gardens and neo-Georgian houses compacting down as signs swap Richmond for Putney. The safe house is a 1950s terrace on a dreary estate that alternates rows of houses with three-storey maisonettes. A young woman pushes a pram. A toddler, reined to her wrist, jogs beside her on chubby legs. Brendan parks behind a van with 'Stevenson Electrical and Plumbing

Services' on the side. As we get out the woman calls a neighbourly greeting. Brendan waves; she crosses the street to us.

'Lovely day,' she says.

'It is,' Brendan replies. 'This is my cousin, she's staying a while, looking for work.' The words are forced out in taut syllables that could pass for Scottish.

The woman smiles at me. 'I'm Sheila, from over there.' She indicates the nearest block of flats.

'Kaylynn,' I say, the name easier this time.

'What work are you looking for?'

'Anything. I'm saving for college.'

'Good for you. Sorry, I've got to go, it's nearly this one's lunchtime.' She nods to the pram. ''Bye, Brian. Nice to meet you, Kaylynn.'

She strolls away, the toddler bumbling along at her side.

'Brian?'

'To the neighbours, aye,' he says, 'so don't go calling me Brendan in front of them. At least we've got your cover out; that daft cow'll gob it round the estate by teatime.'

I swallow more curses. I have to obey his orders but I'm free to ignore his sexist slaggings. I won't be riled by him. I'm here for the Cause. Nothing's more important than that.

He shows me round the house, introducing me to Joe and Tommy, who make up the four man cell. Now three men and me. They shake my hand and Joe offers me tea. While he's brewing up Tommy fills me in: they're brothers, in their early twenties, an electrician and a plumber with their own business; the van outside is theirs, used for recce jobs and collecting supplies, their emergency call-out service covering late night operations. They actually are brothers and time-served tradesmen. Tommy is also the bomber. Joe does the driving and provides backup. Brendan is in charge of intelligence and logistics.

'What is it you need me for?' I ask Brendan.

'We're planning some big jobs GHQ thought you'd be useful for.' He smirks and adds, 'Like an ashtray on a motorbike.' He goes out as Joe returns with tea and Kit Kats.

He passes me a cup, raking fingers through brown curls he shares with his brother. 'Don't mind him. You were in Belfast?'

'Yeah.'

'What's it like there these days?' Tommy asks.

'Same. How long've yous been here?'

'Too long,' Joe says.

'Six months,' Tommy adds.

'Homesick?'

'Fed up of bottled Guinness,' Joe moans.

I remember the warnings from GHQ when they assigned me to the England department: keep away from Irish ex-pats and out of Irish pubs.

'It's shite being away, feeling like you're doing nothing,' Tommy admits. 'Still, now you're here we can get on.'

I sip my tea, light a cigarette and rake around for frost-thawing conversation.

'Did you hear about the Springfield Road shooting last month?'

They shake their heads.

'That stuff doesn't make the news here. No one gives a toss about what's happening in Belfast,' Joe says.

'Three squaddies on foot patrol got shot up.'

They exchange covert glances.

'You don't need to tell us that,' Joe says. 'We're glad you've joined us.'

'Brendan's not.'

'He'll be grand when we get going,' Tommy replies.

Tommy moves into Joe's room, giving me the box room. I dump my bag in a corner and, still in my boots, drop onto the narrow bed. A plane drones towards Heathrow. Direct it's only an hour's flight to Belfast, back to Liam and Rory, lads who know me, and Sean, an OC who trusts me. But I'm needed here. And going back there wouldn't get me closer to Aiden. I shut my eyes, try not to think.

*

Knocking wakes me. I sit up, chest tight, hands clenched. When I uncoil my fingers blood oozes from four crescent-shaped wounds on each palm.

'Caoilainn, you alright?' Joe calls.

'Fine.'

'Brendan wants a word.'

'I'll be down in a minute.'

I swing my legs off the bed. It was only a dream; Aiden is where he's been for months, somewhere in East Tyrone, probably a crofter's cottage, sitting with his feet up on the range, getting fat on griddle cakes and waiting to join Jim's lads on their missions, helping keep order in 'Ra country. Until I'm told differently this is what I have to believe.

They're waiting for me in the living room.

'Nice wee beauty nap?' Brendan sneers.

Burning to bite back, I take up the armchair opposite and fix him with a blank stare.

'Aye, well,' he mutters, dropping his gaze. 'We'll have a briefing.'

It's a familiar scenario: England's difficulty is Ireland's opportunity. The Argies have trumped us, temporarily, as enemy of the empire. GHQ wants us capitalising on this, hitting military targets on the mainland while the Brits are engaged overseas. Brendan reels off some installations. One is Fylingdales.

'You'll not get near that,' I tell him.

'Why?'

'It's in the middle of nowhere, on the moors, not enough cover for a rabbit, never mind us and a couple of cars.'

'Been on a recce have you?'

'Demo, actually, CND, years ago, but it'll be no different now.'

The muscles along his jaw flex. 'Fine, you suggest something.' He tosses his notepad at my head.

I catch it. 'What about targets in London?'

'Who'd you think ya are, bleeding Guy Fawkes?' Brendan snaps.

'We don't have to break into the Tower of London.'

'What then?'

'There are soldiers on the streets every day,' I say, thinking at 90mph, wishing I'd given myself time: distance. 'Changing of the guard for example.'

Joe and Tommy grin at each other. Brendan drags on his cigarette, massages his creased brow.

'Suppose we could put it on the list,' he mutters.

I spend May, including my twentieth birthday, watching the changing of the guard. I go with Joe, with Tommy and with Brendan. My hair is up, down, straight, curly. We wear hats, sunglasses on bright days. I buy three wigs; short and dark, long and brown, red ringlets. Twice we go in a borrowed orange Cortina. We vary our outfits and choose different vantage points. I carry my camera and, mingling with tourists, we take photos which I get developed at the chemist on Putney High Street. I tell myself it'll be OK. There'll be a warning. We'll be careful; it's busbies not bystanders we're after. But I know it's a soft target, one I suggested in self-defence.

One hot Saturday towards the end of May Tommy and I detour through Regents Park on the walk home. He buys ice-creams and we stroll round the boating lake, holding hands, a cover I instigated.

'Have you a boyfriend back home?' he asks.

I nibble the soggy cone. 'Why?'

'Just wondering what he's thinking about you over here.'

'If he's thinking anything it's that I'm doing my bit.'

'There is one?'

'I don't know.'

'That's a funny answer,' Tommy says.

'We had a row; I haven't seen him since.'

'About you doing this, was it?'

'Sort of. We draw the line differently.'

'Is he not involved?'

'He's Aiden O'Neill.'

Tommy pulls his hand free and strolls to a bin, dumping his half-eaten cone. A cloud of flies buzzes up. He carries on walking, heading for the bandstand with its wrought iron railings and spiked green parasol roof. It's a bit like the one in St Stephen's Green. It draws me forwards, and backwards. I inch towards it, wishing I knew if Aiden's alright, if we'll be alright one day when this is over. My heart throbs in panic, the pounding terrifying me.

Jesus, I'm in love with him.

A notice board is propped against the bandstand. I stare sightlessly at it, Aiden's face blurring, fading. I blink the image and the tears down, and pull myself into now, reading the poster. The Royal Green Jackets regimental band will play songs from the West End musical *Oliver!* in a lunchtime concert in mid-July.

Tommy is at my side. 'They never do the good ones,' he says, pointing. '*Grease, West Side Story*, that craic.'

'Handy of them to advertise, though,' I say.

'You're not thinking we could…?'

'I am.' The sooner this is done, the sooner I can get back to Ireland: to Aiden.


That night, eating fish and chips off the latest Falklands headlines, we tell Brendan. He praises Tommy for suggesting it. Tommy starts protesting but I shush him; we're a team, the operations are what matters. I'm not after winning Brendan's approval. Joe fetches a map and a notepad; we sketch out the details.

The concert, on 20th July, gives us seven weeks to prepare. Brendan suggests, as we know the exact time and date, a bomb on a timer, planted under the bandstand weeks beforehand. For maximum effect we'll hit the changing of the guard the same day. Our best chance there is a car bomb along the route, detonated by radio control. We flip through my photos, marking possibles on the map.

'What's this?' Brendan flaps a picture of Tommy and me, his arm around my shoulders, the Blues and Royals trooping past all swishing tails and gleaming buttons.

'It's just near the…' Tommy says.

'I don't give a shite where it is, I mean this, the two of yous. Who took it?'

'A Japanese tourist. He saw me taking pictures of Tommy and offered.'

'And got himself a good look at yous while he was about it. Jesus, you're not even disguised.' Brendan flicks my face in the image, my fair hair flowing over my shoulders. 'Are ya trying to get us lifted?'

Under the table Tommy grabs my hand. 'He won't remember us.'

'Not now maybes.'

'You really think he'd connect a photo taken in May with a bombing in July?' I retort, fighting to control my fury and crushing the shit out of Tommy's helpful hand in the effort.

'It was stupid,' Brendan says.

'It would've been a hell of a lot stupider to make a fuss, refuse. He'd remember that,' I reason.

'I shouldn't've let them send you,' Brendan rages. 'Yous've got no idea how to be discrete, always making a show of yourselves, coming over hysterical at the slightest wee thing.'

'You're the fucking hysterical one. Jesus, get a grip.'

He thumps the table. 'Wind your neck in, silly bitch.'

I fire heavy calibre words at him. 'I will, if you stop waving your dick in my face.'

He launches across the table. I leap to the side. Tommy gets between us.

'We can't be carrying on like this,' he says.

'Get her outta my fucking sight,' Brendan spits.

Joe takes my arm, coaxing me towards the door.

'Bloody women, yous're nothing but…' Brendan shouts after us.

I spin back but Joe shuts the door on Brendan's insults.

'For Christ sake, cool it,' he tells me, ''less you want sending back to face a court-martial.'

'He's been on at me since I got here and I'm sick of it. I shouldn't have to take this caveman crap.'

'I know and, Christ, you've had it rough but you've managed so far and me and Tom don't want you going, or getting into trouble higher up. We know the score; you're sound with us. Take yourself out for a bit. We'll talk to him.' He nudges me onto the front step and nods encouragingly.

I walk to the pub on the corner, crazy thoughts goading me: I'll be on the first flight to Dublin in the morning; I'll make them send me to Belfast or better, East Tyrone; I'll fix things with Aiden; I'll jack the whole thing in. Fuck the 'Ra. It takes the barman interrupting my private tirade with, 'What can I get you, darling?' to make me realise I'm in the pub.

Whiskey. Double. Fuck it, just pass the bottle.

*Volunteers are warned that drink-induced loose talk is SUICIDE.*

'Hurry up, darling, there's punters waiting.'

'I'm not your fucking 'darling'.'

I stalk out before he can bar me for cursing in the lounge, where there are ladies present.

I'm half-way down the street when I hear my name, turn and see Sheila from across the road chasing me.

'Are you alright?'

I mumble about a row at home.

'Men!' she says. 'Can't live with or without them.'

'Pardon?'

'I've been stood up. Again.' She shakes her head.

'Oh. Yeah. Men!' I copy her head shake.

She links my arm. 'Why don't we have a girls' night? I've already paid the babysitter so I might as well enjoy myself. We can have a proper bitch about them and a damn good drink.'

But I can't trust myself. I'm too angry, with the barman, Brendan, even Aiden. Not that he could contact me here. The cell's security outranks everything. However much he might want to make it up he can't. We can't. Not even a fucking postcard. I take my arm from her comforting touch.

'I best not. I should...' I stare at the house. Should what, apologise? Rage at him? Quit?

'Well, maybe another night,' she suggests with a smile.

I smile back vaguely. She's being kind. I'm grateful. But I can't befriend her. She's a civilian: a British civilian.

I wait until she's closed her door then head off, wandering the streets until dawn, trying to be thankful it's a short, warm summer's night.

When I return the house is empty. Exhausted, I stumble upstairs. A note is stuck to my bedroom door. Brendan's block-capital lettering greets me: 'Wee present for you in the usual place! xxx.' I troop downstairs, through the kitchen and out to the matchbox garden. Digging keys from my pocket I undo the shed's padlock and fall into damp darkness. Clattering a spade, rake and hoe aside, I prise up the two loose boards that cover our hidey-hole. On top of our stash of incriminating bits and bobs is a shocking-white, slightly soggy envelope. I pick it up, tug its innards free; a map, coded notes: the Hyde Park plans. I take them outside, standing in the sun to read them. My stomach contorts. I slump against the shed, the plans screwed up in my fist.

I meet Brendan at the door, not giving him chance to get his jacket off or me chance to change my mind. If I don't confront him hard, now, on something this important, I might as well sign for every one of his sexist putdowns.

'What the fuck is this?' I wave the map.

He snatches it and barges past me, into the front. I follow.

'You can't be serious.'

'Can't I, now?' He plants his boots on the coffee table.

'A nail bomb this size on South Carriage Drive?'

'Aye.'

'And no warning.'

'Aye.'

'What about the spectators, tourists: civilians? There'll be a media lynching if you go through with this.'

'I knew you'd not the stomach for a real job.' He snorts. 'Not the balls either.'

'That's got nothing to do with it. This'll be carnage.'

'What it'll be is a successful attack on an enemy target.'

'A soft target.'

'You suggested it.'

'Not like this I didn't. There should be a warning. Or a smaller bomb.'

He strides over. I don't retreat.

'We're needing to remind these bastards what it's like to be under attack. Have you forgotten why you volunteered, those innocent folk at home who've suffered; internment, raids, Bloody Sunday?'

I picture Cathy, her chest ripped opened by bullets issued to a soldier, fired by a murderer.

'Of course not, but there's no need for this.'

He backs me into the wall.

'Get it straight in your mind, wee girl, this is a fucking war. If you're not prepared to fight fuck off and leave us to it.'

That's why he's doing this.

'I am prepared to fight, to kill. But we don't have to be butchers.'

There's a roar. The side of my face explodes. Pain blinds me. When my vision clears I'm on the floor, Brendan leering over me.

'You'll do this or I'll have you thrown out for disobeying orders.'

I get to my feet, pressure splitting my head. 'Not before you're thrown out for striking another volunteer.'

It's a serious charge: instant dismissal.

Brendan recoils, panicked by what he's done. Blood tickles my cheek. I don't wipe it away. Let him see the evidence that'll get him officially bollocked. His mouth twitches. He's trying out words, rejecting them, scrabbling for excuses, counter-accusations, maybe even apologies: anything to save his own arse.

'Ah, I, er, I lost it there.' He rubs a trembling hand over his mouth. 'Sorry. But, er, you know, heat of the moment. No need to report me, eh?' He recovers himself. 'But you've to remember I'm in charge. You can't speak to me like that.'

Reminded of Martin's warning about the command structure, respecting it, I falter. If I complain will they listen? Act? Even if they do I risk being tarred: that mouthy bitch, she got a good volunteer dismissed. I refocus on what matters, those brutal plans, and change tactics.

'Have you Army Council sanction for doing this no-warning?'

'I'm cleared to do whatever I think needs doing. And you'll do as you're told or go home.'

Home: where he thinks I belong, in the kitchen, and the bedroom.

*All volunteers must obey orders from a superior officer regardless of whether they like the particular officer or not.*

'I'm going nowhere. But when the press're baying for Irish blood, getting Loyalist thugs killing innocent Catholics in Belfast and Derry, you'll wish you'd...'

He shrugs. 'Ach, the boys can take care of things at home. If you're so keen to fight for the Cause, shut up and do what I say.'

I don't have any other fucking choice.

Two days later we're meeting the first courier, bringing funds from Dublin. After doing a recce on the shopping centre Brendan picked for the meet we move into place, watching for her arrival from predetermined vantage points. When she appears, sitting outside WH Smiths as instructed, I see she's about my age, wearing a flowery sundress and sling-backs. She carries a small clutch bag, green patent plastic to match the print on her dress, and a shopping bag. Large sunglasses hide her eyes. Once we're sure she's not been followed Brendan signals me to approach her. I hesitate, feeling in my pocket for the note, folded tight as a prison comm. Not all jails have bars and Belfast doors. I shouldn't be sending it. I still might not. The only permissible contact with Ireland is vital military communications. Anything else is a monumental regulation breech that could get me dismissed but I have to know he's O.K., try to hold onto him. Without that I'll drown. Brendan signals again.

I greet her friend to friend.

'Briege! Jesus, how are you?'

She pushes the tinted lenses onto her head, holding back her sleek, chin-length, auburn hair with them and revealing kohl-rimmed eyes shimmering with purple shadow and surprise. She forces a smile and stands.

'I was expecting...' Her gaze fixes on my black eye, 'I'm grand, thanks. Yourself?'

'Fine. Let's walk,' I tell her, sticking to the approved format.

In a hushed voice she chatters nineteen words a second. This is her first run. She's dead pleased to be helping us. She had an easy trip over. She's never been to London before. Isn't it so hectic, so mad? How do you cope? Her Galway brogue tests my Britishized ears. Frustrated, I ask if she speaks Irish and, when she says yes, suggest we use that. Struggling for words I haven't spoken in a while, I hear Daideo's voice helpfully hushing them.

I fascinate Briege. Under the cover of our alien language she asks me about life as a volunteer. I can't say much, a few vague answers, nothing about the isolation crushing me. I ask why she's chosen to help but to not be a volunteer. The question silences her. Eventually she says:

'It's different, isn't it?'

In the bag she carries is a bundle of well-worn notes, money for buying fertiliser, six inch nails, a radio controlled toy plane we can cull a detonator from, a VCR for the timer.

'What do you mean?'

'Sure, I couldn't. I'm not brave enough.'

'What makes you think I am? I just believe we've the right to use military force. It's the only thing that evens the odds. Once you believe that you do what needs doing. Even if you are crapping yourself.'

She goes quiet again. I've said too much. We stop at a kiosk and buy drinks. She gets a coke. I roll the comm in my pocket, weigh the risks again but it's never going to balance: duty vs. love. Don't. Do. Don't. Fuck.

'Would you do me a favour when you get home?'

'Aye.' Her head wags like a dog's tail.

'Can you get this to the East Tyrone Brigade.' I pass her the note. 'To Aiden O'Neill.'

She glances over her shoulder. 'Have yous a problem?'

'No. It's... personal.'

'Ah, your fella, so?' she guesses with a shy smile.

'I haven't heard from him since I came over. I need to know he's OK.' I rush out excuses, explanations, instructions. 'There's nothing incriminating in it, no names or anything about what we're doing so it should be safe. It's only a couple of lines, letting him know I'm alright.' I nearly tell her about the row, how I'm frantic for that not to be our end, but back away before I get there. 'Even so, make sure you hide it until

156

you're through customs. If there's any chance it'll be found, destroy it. Just in case.'

She nods again.

'Look, don't take it if you'd rather not.' I change my mind for the umpteenth time, reach to take it back from her. 'Forget it, it's too risky.'

'Sure, I will not. It'll be grand. Yous need some comfort from home. How'll I get you the reply?' There's a sudden strength glowing in her. Underneath the flimsy flower-print dress are resilient roots. She wants to help, not just the Movement, but me. There'll be no problem. She won't allow it.

I withdraw my hand. 'He'll manage that himself. If he can.' If he even wants to.

'Will I at least give you my phone number in case you're needing to be in touch?' she suggests.

'I wouldn't be able to ring you. They might trace the call,' I explain.

'Ach, you'd be fine using a phone box. Anyway, my folks run a wee bed and breakfast; what would be suspicious about a call to somewhere like that? If they even could trace it, it'd just look like you were making a booking,' she reasons.

There's sense in it. 'OK.'

Briege smiles. 'Grand.' As she passes over the shopping bag she murmurs the number slowly enough for me to remember it.

We part with a hug, real friends now as well as comrades, then she totters off on her heels. Watching her go, my note in her pocket, her bag straining my arm, I wonder what's coming.

Joe and I start shopping. Tommy puts the Regent's Park bomb together in the kitchen. Chemical smells poison the air and there are no clean pans so we make do with sarnies and takeaways. Joe dismantles the brand new VCR. I watch everything they do, learning frenetically.

While Brendan's doing a final recce of Regent's Park I go to the PO box we have, rented in a postal district on the other side of London to our base. My heart flutters with hope that my brain can't talk it out of. There's one letter, addressed to

'K'. The handwriting is Aiden's. Expressionless, I take it from the clerk. Make myself wait until I'm at the bus stop to open it.

Just three sentences, in Irish:

Tá mé buartha*. Tá mé i ngrá leat♥. An bpósfaidh tú mé?♣

My brain dumps every Irish word I've ever learnt and they pulse through me.

Pósfaidh? Marry?

I have until the next time Briege comes to figure out my answer.

The last Wednesday in June Joe and Tommy plant the bomb under the bandstand, the timer set for 12.30 P.M. on July 20th. Brendan and I wait at home, in separate rooms, protecting our fragile truce. I lie on my bed, thinking about Aiden, knowing what answer I want to give but fearing it's the wrong one. Is a volunteer, like a nun, married to a higher power? I merge the two images; me in a habit, expression piously cynical, hands clasped in prayer, gun holstered at my waist.

The front door bangs. I stare down at the notebook I didn't realise I was holding, the blue biro sketch of Sister Caoilainn I didn't know I was actually drawing. I screw it up and charge downstairs.

'We're set,' Joe says.

A week before the 20th Brendan buys a blue Morris Marina at a car auction in Enfield. He drops it with a contact who parks it in various west London locations, never the same place twice. The next day we have another meeting with a runner. Just in case it's Briege I have my single word answer hidden in my pocket. The meet is the same routine, different location. And it is Briege.

'Did you ever hear back?' she asks in eager Irish.

---

* I'm sorry.

♥ I love you.

♣ Will you marry me?

There was no candlelit dinner. No bended knee. No sealing it with a kiss. There'll be no engagement party or ring. No warm congratulations. Snub that romantic bullshit all you want but don't kid on you're not wishing things were different. Tell her. Share it with her. Make it real.

'He wants to marry me.'

'And?' She squeezes my arm.

I nod and slip my note to her.

'Sure, when they said I'd be running errands for the Movement I didn't think it'd be this romantic,' she says, hugging me.

But I'm not so sure it isn't more tragedy than romance.

The night of the 19th I go to bed early and lie awake, thinking of the people, sleeping in easy ignorance, unaware of tomorrow's coming catastrophe. In our quiet corner of London the war doesn't exist; tomorrow it will be headline news. People will be dead because of it: us. Me. A montage of faces; Daideo, Cathy, Sands, plus a faceless couple, the parents I'll never know, scrolls round in my head. We have to do this. But I wish we didn't.

# London—20<sup>th</sup> July, 1982

Before dawn Joe and Tommy load the bomb into their van, amongst plumbing supplies. Brendan watches, face dour, as I squeeze in next to Tommy.

'Don't bollock this,' he warns me.

I shut the door.

Brendan's contact meets us in a Kensington car park, leaning against the Marina, smoking. Joe reverses the van up to the car's backend.

'Hey, Sean, how're ya?' Tommy greets him.

The contact shakes his hand. 'Grand, but I'm using 'John' these days.'

'Right ya're,' Tommy says.

John glances at me, eyes widening.

'This is Caoilainn,' Tommy replies.

John shrugs and reaches into his pocket. 'Keys,' he says, 'and yous'll need this to get out of the car park.' He holds out a ticket for the barrier machine, offering it to Joe.

I reach for it. He raises an eyebrow.

'Cheers,' Tommy says.

'If yous need anything else, Brendan knows where to find me. I'll be watching the news, shall I?' Before there's any answer he strolls away, whistling, leaping the barrier at the exit.

'Is he alright?' I ask.

'Dead on,' Tommy says. 'Anyway, he knows nothing 'cept he's been minding a mate's car.'

They transfer the bomb to the boot and Tommy primes it; I watch, taking every chance to learn. When he's done I get into the driver's seat. Liam taught me to drive months ago and I've been practising in the van to be ready for today but the pre-mission cocktail of adrenalin and anxiety impairs my co-ordination. I stall at the barrier. Breathing curses, I restart the engine. The clock on the machine says 6:50. I've got to get the car in place before London is awake. I slot the ticket in. The barrier lifts and I'm away.

South Carriage Drive runs south of the Serpentine. Trees line the road's lake side. In a few hours tourists will shelter under them, waiting for the parade. I decide to park across the road, in front of the commercial properties there. It's the only compromise I can make. I climb out, tuck my gloves away because it's a warm morning, and walk to the bus stop without a backward glance.

Brendan and I, posing as Mr and Mrs Ordinary, forgotten before we're noticed, stroll among joggers and city workers criss-crossing Hyde Park. He links his arm through mine. I shudder and wish he'd let Joe or Tommy come with me instead. But he set the exam, now he wants to grade my performance. He carries the camera. I wear the short dark wig. The detonator is in my handbag. He buys tea from a stall and we sit on a bench. A dapper old gent opposite doffs his trilby and smiles a greeting. Brendan nods back. I force a smile and focus on forgetting the man's face, in case later he's one of the dead. Brendan checks his watch. He keeps checking it. At 10.30 he nods to me and I reach into my bag, feeling for the two switches that power up the remote control and transmit the signal.

'Come on,' he hisses.

I flick the switches and pull my hand out, clutching a packet of cigarettes.

In the millisecond between button-press and boom that divides 'before' and 'after' a hand lets go of a balloon and it's lost forever.

A bang echoes through the park.

People stop, look at each other. Some start heading for the sound.

Brendan takes the cigarettes, lights one and stands.

'Let's go.'

We flow with the curious, blown towards the epicentre.

As we get closer, cries and sirens hurry us along. Ahead people are scattered under the trees, some running, others frozen. The smell of burning meat wafts over. I hear the whinnying of horses. Brendan grips my elbow, restraining, not supporting.

A woman is on the ground, her hands pressed to her thigh. Blood seeps between her fingers.

I pull free, go to her, kneeling down, gathering words in my head, making sure they'll sound English when I say them.

'Are you alright? What's happened?'

'I don't know. Oh God.'

'I'll get someone for you.'

I sprint from the park and into a dense cloud of dazed and wounded bystanders. Ambulances are arriving. The Met boys are already here. More pull up as I watch. Across the street the Marina is belly-up, flipped by the blast.

On the tarmac, lying on their sides, are seven beautiful black horses.

'I'm a first-aider. Are you hurt, love?' a man asks.

'No but there's a woman over there.' I point towards the trees.

'Thanks.' He dashes off.

The police set up a cordon, clear the street. Paramedics dart through the swirling crowd. One crouches beside a fallen soldier. A colleague races to help but the first shakes his head.

A car pulls up. A man in a tweed jacket and brown trousers scrambles out and goes to the nearest policeman. They talk for a minute, the copper pointing to the horses. The man fetches a bag from his car and crosses to the injured animals, moving on quickly from the first two but stopping at the third, stroking his hands over the horse's flank. At his touch the horse lifts its head and neighs a feeble plea. The vet keeps stroking, his lips moving, crooning a comfort. One hand caressing the horse's neck, he reaches into his bag with the other.

'What the hell're ya doing?' Brendan spits in my ear. He yanks my arm.

'Get off me,' I reply. 'Unless you're wanting me to 'go hysterical' in front of all these peelers.'

He lets go.

The vet stands. In his hand is a bolt gun. Arms outstretched, he aims for the horse's forehead. There's a shot. People freeze again in the cold-water shock of panic and fear. The vet replaces the gun in his bag and moves to the next horse. I hear more shots as Brendan drags me up the road, his hand crushing my arm.

*

The bombings headline the lunchtime news. The explosion in Regent's Park only went off at 12.30 so reports of that are sketchy. Three Blues and Royals are dead from the Hyde Park blast. A third is on life support. An unspecified number of civilians are injured. Seven horses have been killed. Tommy's chin quivers at this news and Joe mutters, 'Ach, them poor creatures.' Brendan's hand trembles as he reaches for a cigarette but he says nothing. I wish I'd thought about the horses before; maybe he would've listened to that argument. The newsreader continues:

'Reports from Regent's Park are yet to confirm casualties. There is speculation the IRA were behind the attacks.'

Our statement's not been issued yet.

Brendan threatens, again, to have me dismissed, this time with ignominy, for breaking the execute-and-leave protocol to help that woman in the park. He's on stable ground and I'm falling. I stew over an essential apology but before I get it out he starts calling me the usual names. Savaged by his patriarchal bullshit I retaliate, calling him a pathetic prehistoric wanker, telling him I know his barbaric plans were about beating me, not winning the war and countering his attempts to corner me with a threat to report him for that, and for hitting me. Tommy and Joe try reasoning, pleading, shushing. Brendan keeps raging, giving up ground with every bigoted insult. I force down futile arguments, win by regaining control first. Defeated by my silence his threats wither; he'll report my misconduct, have me recalled. When the filtering new reports don't mention either a young woman with short dark hair or a round-faced older man he sulks out. I seethe. I let him bait me and fucked up because of it. But the harder the lesson the more it's worth learning. I apologise to Tommy and Joe for putting us in jeopardy. They forgive me, blame Brendan. But the fault's not all his; I insist on that. They reassure; I've taken an undeserved drubbing from Brendan. Taken it, Tommy points out, survived it. Done my duty despite it. I'm the stronger for it.

Maybe, once I recover.

Joe makes tea. Tommy makes me sit. A marathon runner at race end, I collapse into myself, let them mother me and guiltily enjoy it.

The mission's success is marked soberly that night, each of us cocooned in the memories that led us here. We drink to lost comrades, murdered loved ones and to Martin Hurson, hunger striker number six who died a year and a week ago.

Shockwaves mushroom out, bowl into me, washing over me in a hot plume of energy, hurtling me skyward. I flounder in air, clawing for a hold on nothing. I fall, the ground rushing up to me, the space shrinking, time compressing. In less than a second I will be dead.

I wake with a jolt; sink back onto the sweat-soaked pillow.

I stand over a sleek black horse. It lies in the road, a jagged pink gash startling against the dark flank. It rolls its head back. Warm brown eyes plead for mercy. In my hand is a gun. I pull the trigger but the gun only clicks. I pull again. Another empty click. The horse whinnies. I crouch, put out a hand and stroke the silky neck, soothing pain. Under my touch the horse starts to shrink. There's a moment of relief when I think it will vanish into its own suffering. But as the dark neck becomes shorter it pales, pink skin breaking through the glossy coat. The mane grows in reverse, shortening into a man's dark tousled hair. The front legs become arms clad in a leather sleeves; the back ones wear blue denim. The hooves are hands, feet wearing mud spattered boots. The brown eyes blue. The horse is Aiden. The pink wound is in his chest. He licks bloodless lips, croaks:

'Le do thoil.'

I aim again, pull the trigger again. And again. And again. Click follows click, the hammer striking a cruelly empty chamber. His eyes stay on mine, the blue fading to grey.

When I wake for the second time, shaking and breathless, I vow I'll never do another no-warning bombing. I'll fight as fairly as the enemy will let me.

### IRA Carnage in Royal Parks
### Massacre Kills Eleven Men
### and Seven Horses

In a statement issued yesterday the Provision IRA claimed responsibility for two bomb attacks which took place on 20th July in Hyde Park and Regent's Park.

The first explosion, at 10.30 A.M., killed three members of the Household Cavalry, the Blues and Royals. A fourth man, the regiment's standard bearer, died later in hospital. Seven horses were also killed, some needing to be euthanised at the scene. An eighth horse, Sefton, and his rider, are receiving treatment for their injuries.

The second explosion, in Regent's Park, occurred at 12.30 P.M., as members of the Royal Green Jackets regimental band were performing numbers from the musical Oliver! Seven bandsmen were killed at the scene and witnesses reported seeing one man thrown thirty yards onto an iron fence by the blast.

There were civilian casualties at both locations and police said it was a miracle there were no fatalities among those gathered to watch the changing of the guard or concert.

In their statement, echoing the prime minister's recent words about the Falklands conflict, the IRA said, 'The Irish people have sovereign and national rights which no task or occupation force can put down.'

Visiting injured servicemen, Margaret Thatcher said, 'Our anger at those who did this is total. They're just barbaric and vicious, the people who did this.'


The next courier drop brings much needed money and a letter for me, marked with my initials but not by Aiden's hand. My heart stops.

He's dead. This is from his OC. 'With deepest regret etc.'

All the way back to the safe house the letter smoulders in my pocket while dread corrodes my heart.

Alone in my room, shaking fingers tear raggedly into the envelope. It's a coded instruction for me to ring a number I don't recognise at a precise date and time.

If Aiden was… would they…? The 'no personal contact' rule is theirs to break. But they wouldn't. *The most important thing is security.*

Bollocks. It must be from high up. Who else would contact me like this? They've caught on to me using military channels for personal communications. A flush of panic scorches my face. I'm finished.

It's no more than I deserve.

Two days later I sneak out to make the dreaded call, resigned to my punishment.

Inside the phone box I dial with fear-drunk fingers, listen to the ring and wait for the expected male voice that'll summon me to the court-martial ending my IRA activism.

A woman answers.

'Hello?'

'Caoilainn, is that yourself?'

'Nora?'

'Aye, love it's me. Thank goodness you got my message.'

What the fuck…? Overwhelmed by the reprieve, stunned by the reality, instilled instincts take charge.

'I can't talk to you.' I move the receiver away from my ear. Telephones can be tapped, calls listened to by invisible enemy operators.

'It's grand,' she says quickly. 'I'm in Lisburn. Sure, we're fine here. I'm in this posh hotel on the right side of town.'

She means she's in a Protestant neighbourhood where security forces don't monitor calls because if they don't know about a bombing in a Nationalist area they can't be blamed for not preventing it.

'What?' I hover the phone over my ear.

'Caught the train this morning.'

'How did you know the number for me to call?'

'Came a fortnight ago and found the pay-phone in the lobby.'

Has she gone fucking mad? What the hell's she playing at?

'The note you sent, you shouldn't have done that. I could get into a lot of bother.'

'Ach, you're fine. I went through the proper channels.'

There are no such channels I know of. She must've involved Frank. I'm furious she's taken such a risk but because

166

she has I have to know why. Aiden... I can't finish the thought.

'What is it, Nora?'

'Aiden says you're to wed.'

'Pardon?'

'Yous're getting married.'

'Yes, but...' A gale force wind rags me about.

She sighs. 'Then we've some things need sorting. Yous'll have to get permission.'

I mentally thumb through *The Green Book* for a section on volunteers marrying but don't find anything.

'From who, for what?'

Nora tuts. 'The bishop. He'll have to approve yous marrying, seeing how you're not of our faith. Then we'll need a priest who'll do it, some won't.'

'I thought we'd...'

Nora interrupts. 'Catholics marry in church or not at all.'

It isn't just the bishop's permission I need.

'I've nothing against you, love,' she adds, softening, 'but you've to understand this is important to us, especially for someone in Aiden's line. He needs his faith, even if to you it's nonsense.'

'I've never said that but I'll not apologise for who I am, Nora. I've a right to my own code.'

'But if you're wanting to marry a Catholic you've to abide by ours,' she replies. 'It'd be best if you could be baptised.'

'I can't do that.' Won't fucking do that.

'Didn't I know you'd say that.'

'It'd be hypocritical.'

'Not if you converted.' Her voice hardens.

'I can't make myself believe,' I reason.

She tuts.

If I fight her I'll lose Aiden. 'Will a church wedding do you?' I suggest.

'It's a start,' she agrees. 'I'll see what's to be done. You'll have to...'

The phone starts clicking. 'That's the pips. I've to go. Please don't contact me again like this. It's not appropriate.' I hang up.

167

How dare she? Taking such a stupid risk for such a petty purpose. I thought Aiden was… but he's not. I wouldn't have made the call if I'd known. Furious, I leave the call box shuddering from my slam-door exit and start walking, fast, fleeing from her disapproval. Distance calms me. I ease up but keep going, stretching out the miles until I have a clear enough view to be able to throw and catch her words. An idea forms. Coins jingle temptingly in my pocket. I make myself walk to the next corner, and the next, and the next, arguing for and against, craving and resisting, willing myself not to, talking myself into, walking until I'm so far from the safe house I've run out of breadcrumbs, unwound my ball of string, left no trail between there and here. Finally, somewhere in Islington, I convince myself I'm lost enough to the safe house for telephoning Ireland. I find a box and dial, Briege's words about the innocence of calling her parents' Galway B&B placating my rising panic as I spin memorised numbers.

'Hello?'

'Briege, it's me. I've a problem.'

I explain about Nora, her requirements. Briege says she can help. Her priest, Father O'Brien, is dead on. She'll have a word. It'll be grand. I trudge back, hoping she's right.

# Loughrea, Co. Galway—20th September, 1982

I land in Ireland three days before the wedding. Fr O'Brien has agreed to marry me and Aiden in his tiny Galway church, being flexible over religious regulations, cramming our compulsory pre-nuptial lessons into a single afternoon, his Republican sympathies, our devotion to the Cause and the practicalities of circumstance justifying the irregularities. So I find myself in a doily-festooned parlour, sipping tea from a china cup. Aiden's on the sofa next to me. Last night was clumsy. We fumbled over words, feelings: each other. I feel like I've had a tooth pulled; the bone-deep ache is gone, things are better now, OK., but there's still the soreness of healing.

Fr O'Brien is jovial and the room warmed by midday sun but a chill shudders through me as he explains Catholic doctrine on marriage, 'that sacred union between a man and a woman, symbolising Christ's union with his church and demanding openness to bringing forth new life.' He asks about our relationship, our future plans. I nod, smile, make replies I hope are acceptable and tell calculated lies when necessary.

An hour ticks by. The housekeeper delivers fondant fancies. I nibble one awkwardly. Fr O'Brien talks of sin and salvation, gives me prayer sheets, words printed in the bold type of Sunday school lessons. They are the words of the marriage rite. The second hour is gone.

'There's just the matter of signing.' Fr O'Brien stands, brushing crumbs from his black shirt, collects two sheets of paper from the sideboard and sets them on the coffee table, handing Aiden a pen. He squiggles his name.

I scan the pages. 'What's this?'

'Aiden's pledge to remain true to the Catholic church and your solemn promise not to pervert his faith,' Fr O'Brien explains.

I scowl.

'You also vow that your children will be raised in the church, a sacred duty of both confirmed Catholics and anyone they marry.'

His words thump me with impossible realities: having children and raising them in a faith I don't follow. The pen is heavy in my hand. I tell myself it's X multiplied by zero: nothing, and scribble my name, the letters cramped and uncomfortable.

Fr O'Brien takes the paper. 'Will you want communion, Aiden?'

'I thought we couldn't do that, Father.' Aiden glances at me.

'It's not usual but wouldn't your mammy like it?'

Nora's been on to him.

'She would, Father.'

'Fine, we'll have mass before the wedding, so,' Fr O'Brien nods. 'You'll remember to use the side door?' He looks at me but speaks to Aiden.

'Sure, Father,' Aiden replies, 'and thanks for your help.'

'You're welcome,' the priest replies. 'A thousand blessings on you for a long and fruitful marriage.'

He shakes our hands and we escape into late afternoon sun.

As we walk to the pub where we're billeted I scrutinise the net-draped windows lining the lane.

'What's up?' Aiden asks.

'Are we being watched?'

'Have you seen something?' Aiden scans the street.

'No, but what he said about using the side door. Is he worried there'll be peelers waiting to nab us?'

Aiden stops, runs a hand through his hair, which has grown past his collar in the months we've been apart. 'It's just an old custom. Don't mind it.'

'What d'ya mean?'

He starts walking.

I catch his arm. 'Tell me.'

'You can't go in the front because you're not...'

'Oh, tradesman's entrance for heathens, is it? Jesus, what century is this?'

'Fr O'Brien's been really good about this, Caoilainn. He's letting us have everything else our way.'

'None of this is my way.'

Aiden jerks to a halt. 'You want to forget it?'

'Of course not. I just didn't think I'd be a pariah at my own wedding.'

'You're not. But this is properly irregular. If the bishop knew how much we've had the rules bent Fr O'Brien'd cop it so he doesn't need us making a show of things,' Aiden says. 'Does it matter which bleeding door you use as long as we're married?'

I try convincing myself it doesn't but I'm narked. When we reach the pub I lead Aiden to our room, lock us in, seduce and strip him and get him on the bed. As I push him inside me, anger ebbs away. I love him. The wedding is one day, the marriage for the rest of our lives. I'll play the part like it's a mission. He comes with a moan and a shudder, his body taut then quivering then limp against mine. We lie naked, tangled in sweat-dampened sheets, watching the sun drowning.

'What time is it?' Aiden asks.

I check the clock. 'After six.'

'My folks'll be here soon.'

'Your ma still annoyed?' I ask.

'Ah, she's fine. Just likes things done right, so she does.' He untangles himself and starts packing his stuff.

'What're you doing?'

'Moving my things out.' He ruffles his hair.

'That's what you mean by 'right' is it?'

'There's no point winding her up again now,' he mutters, cramming clothes into his haversack.

I throw a pillow at him. 'Alright, mammy's boy. I'll control myself for thirty-six hours.'

'You'll get me sent straight to hell, you will,' he says, dropping the bag and coming back to bed.

# Loughrea, Co. Galway—23rd September, 1982

Shielded by half-drawn curtains, I watch Aiden, Frank, Nora, Danny and Callum set off for mass an hour before I'm to join them in church. As they head onto the road, Nora leading, Frank hobbling on his sticks, Aiden looks back. I duck away from the window.

Fr O'Brien meets me at the side door. Fatherless, I follow the swish of priestly robes, entering the nave alone. Would he, my da, have been happy giving me away to Aiden, the 'Ra? I don't know. I know hardly anything. Like, was he tall, fair? Did he have Daideo's eyes? I wish there was just one photo of him, or her.

Nora and Frank occupy the front pew. Danny and Callum are beside them. Liam and Rory have driven down from Belfast this morning. They sit on my side in collar and tie, with Briege glowing beside them in a pink and lemon dress. She waves and Liam winks at me. They're sitting where Daideo should be, and my ma. Was she pretty, slim? Would she have worn a big hat and cried? I think of Cathy's too brief stories about her and imagine the row she'd likely have given Nora for insisting on a Catholic wedding, the drunken, off-key singing she might've done at the reception. Jesus, they should all be here.

I join Aiden at the altar for our abbreviated ceremony.

Fr O'Brien begins. I steer raggedly through unfamiliar rituals; Liturgy of the Word, scripture readings, marriage rite. When Fr O'Brien asks will we accept children lovingly from God and bring them up according to Christ's law I say I will because there's no 'don't know' box to tick.

'Since it is your intention to enter into marriage join your right hands and declare your consent before God and his Church,' Fr O'Brien commands.

I repeat the vows, echoes in my head of my other sworn oath: unconditional allegiance to Óglaigh na hEireann.

'Take this ring as a sign of my love and fidelity. In the name of the Father, the Son and the Holy Spirit.' Aiden puts the gold band etched with Celtic scrolls, on my finger. It was his grandmother's but age hasn't mellowed the metal's fierce brilliance; it gleams in the dimness, leaden on my finger.

Fr O'Brien directs us to kneel for the nuptial blessing. I close my eyes and sweep myself off to a wild Gaelic hillside, flying through a turbulent sky of purple-grey clouds broken by a waking sun. It's Daideo's 'Cúchulainn Faces the Hordes' painting. I strain to stay in it but Fr O'Brien's rolling chant rips the canvas:

'Father, by your power you have made everything out of nothing... You gave man the constant help of woman... Give this woman the grace of love and peace. May she always follow the example of the holy women... May her husband recognise that she is his equal... May they live to see their children's children...

Aiden murmurs, 'Amen,' nudges me and I repeat it a beat behind.

Fr O'Brien signs the cross over us. Then he lays his hand on my head and murmurs words too soft for me to hear. His palm warms my skull. His compassion welcomes me; I should be grateful. Instead, when he lifts his hand from my head I'm glad it's over. He collects the waiting chalice and wafer. Aiden opens his mouth. I drop my gaze. When I raise it again he's crossing himself and Fr O'Brien is moving away. With a scuffle everyone stands and the others come forwards for their sip of the cup and bite of the bread. I don't watch. Aiden takes my hands.

'You alright?'

'Fine.'

He leans in to kiss me but I dodge him. I don't want to taste what he's just swallowed.

Frank shuffles over, his sticks tap-tapping on the stone. He shakes Aiden's hand and pecks my cheek.

'Didn't I think I'd never see a day as grand as this?' he says. 'It cheers my heart to have you in the family, Caoilainn.'

He sniffs, scrapes a tear from his eye with his thumbnail. Nora draws up, hugs Aiden, then me.

'I hope yous'll be happy together,' she says, frowning at me.

Before I can reply we're swamped by congratulations, more hands are shaken, more cheeks kissed. We're married.

That night there's a ceilidh in the pub. Friends arrive to celebrate with us. Among them is Sean, my former OC, Casey, the TO and Patsy who promises another party at the Felons as soon as we've chance. I thank him, not letting on that we can't risk it, with Aiden on the Brits' wanted list and the UFF's hit list.

Martin is also here.

People call me Mrs O'Neill. It's the fourth name I've had but my real name'll always be Caoilainn Devoy.

Guinness flows and music plays, the landlord alternating between pulling pints and bowing his fiddle. Patsy produces a guitar and Casey a penny whistle. Nora sits at the piano. Everyone sings except me; I only know the obvious songs, 'The Irish Rover', 'I'll Tell Me Ma' and 'Whiskey in the Jar', which I still get wrong because the traditional timing is different from the Thin Lizzy version I've heard. Aiden, half-cut, mounts a chair and calls for order. When the room settles he nods to Nora. As she starts playing I realise they've rehearsed this. I've not heard him sing before and am surprised by the strong, pure notes.

'Come over the hills my bonny Irish lass,

Come over the hills to your darling.'

The song, 'Red is the Rose', tells of a young man whose heart is broken when his lover leaves him.

As he sings Aiden fixes me with beer-blurred eyes and the sticky heat of embarrassment prickles my face. I'm glad when he reaches the final chorus:

'Red is the rose that by yonder garden grows.

Fair is the lily of the valley.

Clear is the water that flows from the Boyne.

But my love is fairer than any.'

Song finished, Aiden clambers down. Pulling me into his arms he bends his mouth to my ear.

'That's you, my bonny Irish lass but, sure, I hope you're not gonna leave me like that.'

'I won't if you won't.'

'Fair enough. Shall we swear to it?'

'Haven't we done that this morning?'

He laughs. 'Course we have.' He fumbles for my hand, raising it to his bleary eyes, twisting the ring now bedding into my finger. He kisses it then me.

'I don't deserve you,' he mumbles.

His words fill me with dread. I am too happy.

People call for more music; Danny is urged up. I haven't heard him sing since Christmas and that memory taints this one.

He starts softly:

'There is not in this wide world a valley so sweet,

as the vale in whose bosom the bright waters meet.'

Callum's eyes lock into mine as the notes rise up.

'Oh, the last rays of feeling and life must depart.

E'er the bloom of that valley shall fade from my heart.'

I turn away, unable to hold on.

Danny's voice is melodic. The song ends:

'Sweet vale of Avoca how calm I could rest

in thy bosom of shade with the friends I love best.

Where storms that we feel in this cold world should cease,

and our hearts like thy waters be mingled in peace.'

As the notes fade the room falls into a hush, lulled by Danny's graceful singing and the dream of peace.

Aiden squeezes me to him.

'Where's Avoca?'

'Wicklow. Sure, I'll take you there. It's a grand place,' he says.

'Can I borrow you a minute?' Martin materialises at my other side.

'Can it not wait?' Aiden protests.

'I've to be back in Dublin first thing. I'll not keep her long,' he replies.

*The Army enters into every aspect of your private life.*

I disentangle myself and we slip outside. The night is moonless but a million distant stars are embroidered on the blackness.

I light a cigarette.

'Heard you were against the London operation.'

I pull smoke into my lungs. 'I was against unnecessary slaughter.'

'But you saw it through.'

'I did.'

'And now?' Martin presses.

'I'll not do another like that. There should be a warning if there's a chance civilians will be hurt.'

'There's some with you on that.'

'What do you think?'

'Military force is justified but,' he pauses, looking to the sky as if for the approval of an indifferent deity, 'we're pulling Brendan out.'

'Oh.'

'We'll send yous someone else soon.'

'What do we do meantime?'

'That's up to you. You're OC now.'

I gag on the gobful of responsibility he's expecting me to chew and swallow. 'I can't. I've not that much experience.'

'True enough.' He shrugs. 'But you've not wasted what you've had and that counts for a lot. The Council think you're up to it: brains and nerve.'

Fuck ups and failures jeer in my head. I shut them up with the realisation that I'm here because I've learnt from them, not copied off them.

'So the leadership really do believe in equality?'

Light from the pub window shows his Colgate-white smile. 'You best be about proving them right. But we want things quiet for a wee while. We'll be in touch when we're ready.' He goes inside, leaving me standing on my head.

In the morning, after our first legitimate night together, Aiden and I pack for our honeymoon in Rosmuc, near where Daideo stayed with Pearse in his holiday cottage when they were pupil and teacher. We load the borrowed car, Aiden's head banging with stale Guinness and mine with Martin's news. Briege waylays us.

'Have you a minute, Caoilainn?'

She and I wander a little way from the pub; behind us Aiden throws up.

'Did yous have a good night?' she asks.

'Yes, thank you.'

'You're welcome.'

We reach the road, turn ninety degrees and continue.

'I've decided to become a volunteer,' she says.

My foot slips over a loose rock, stumbling me. 'What's brought this on?'

'I always wanted to be properly useful, not just fetching and carrying, but 'til I met you I didn't feel I could. You set me thinking. If you can, I can. Now it's not enough, being a messenger.'

'We need couriers as much as…'

'I know,' she interrupts, 'but this is what I want.'

'Don't do this because I am,' I caution her.

'I'm not. You've just helped me see that wanting to do it's all I need to be able to do it.'

'You're sure?'

'I am.'

'Then good on you.'

We spend three peaceful days walking the lanes, climbing the hills, listening to the silence and gazing at Connemara's wild, barren beauty. The war is a hundred years away. Pearse's cottage is two miles. I search our holiday let for drawing materials, find a small notepad and stubby pencil in a kitchen drawer and sketch the landscape; glassy loughs, jagged peaks, broken coastline and Pearse's cottage. It hugs the hillside, brooding over the shimmering water it guards. I wish for watercolours to capture the buttery thatch yellow, the brilliant whitewashed walls, so vivid against the verdant undergrowth that encroaches on it. It haunts me, a memory I wish was mine, not Daideo's. On our last evening, as we stroll back from the pub in Rosmuc I find myself turning up the track to the cottage, pulled by someone else's past.

'I don't think we're allowed,' Aiden says as we scramble up the steep path.

'I just want to see it. Daideo came here.'

'Sure, I didn't know that,' Aiden pants.

'I think it was shortly before the Rising. I can't remember what he said now, something about it being a decisive moment for Pearse.' I make the top of the bank and stop, breathless, at the cottage's green door.

He was here, Finn Devoy. The boy I can barely imagine, never know. I stroke the cold rough stone, the weather-splintered woodwork; peer through the tiny windows, half-hoping, half-dreading, the sight of ghostly figures, a man and a boy, by the fire. There's only my own reflection. It blurs. I blink down tears, shade the window with my palm and stare in. The cottage's empty interior stares back.

'There's nothing here,' Aiden says. 'Let's go.'

I face him. Over his shoulder the Twelve Pins loom. Yesterday we drove out to them, clambered over their rocky feet, rested in their shadow. Tomorrow Aiden'll be in Tyrone and I'll be in London. Fuck knows when we'll next see each other.

'In a minute.' I reel him towards me, looping my arms around him.

'Aye, in a minute,' he murmurs.

We stay on Pearse's doorstep, drawing out the moment, stretching it to snapping point. When we finally leave the darkness pulls us apart as we stumble through it.

For the next year I head up the London cell. It's easy because GHQ tell us to hibernate; we drift into ordinary life. Tommy and Joe make a living from their trades. Having completed basic training, Briege joins us at Easter, at my request. She's inexperienced but earnest plus another woman is easier to explain to the neighbours. She gets a job waiting tables. With her red hair, fair skin and the melodic softness of her Galway accent she's safe being openly Irish. I take a class at the local college: 'Watercolours for Beginners'. It's me and a load of pensioners but I do a series of Connemara landscapes, washed with summer blue skies and always with a tiny white cottage on a hillside. It's twee compared to the art I used to produce but, soothed by it, I ask myself no hard questions about this shift in my creativity. When term ends I buy a 1973 125cc Honda XL, learn to ride and buzz down to the coast where I sit on various piers doodling more cosy landscapes into a little sketchpad that I now carry everywhere. Some nights we go about as two couples, eating in cheap restaurants and drinking in bars that don't have Guinness on draught. We celebrate my twenty-first in Chinatown. I wear my wedding ring on the chain with my locket. We tell Sheila 'Brian' is working in Scotland.

I go to Ireland four times in twelve months, juggling my two passports so British immigration think I've been in Amsterdam, Paris, Barcelona and Copenhagen. If questions are asked I'm visiting art galleries, which I read up on, some I even actually see thanks to lengthy delays between flights. Aiden and I spend a total of seven weeks, five days and twelve hours together, most of them bunkered down in my house in Dublin which he uses as his whenever he isn't needed in Tyrone or Armagh. Every minute together is time we beg, borrow and steal from the war. I don't know if life will ever be different, normal, for us. This is normal.

We're lying in front of the fire, naked and wrapped in each other, our skin toasted by the glowing turf. We've been married a year and a day.

Aiden nuzzles my neck. His hand rests on my stomach. He traces a petal-pattern with his forefinger around my bellybutton. His lips are hot against my ear.

'When're you gonna stop taking those daft wee pills and give me a chance?'

I close my eyes to avoid seeing the pleading in his.

'Caoilainn?' He strokes my hair. 'Don't you want to have a family?'

The phone rings. I push up. Aiden snatches at me.

'What if it's…'

'I don't give a shite who it is,' he says. 'We're talking. Haven't you thought about it?'

The phone rings out.

'I'm not saying we won't but now's not the time.'

'Plenty of the boys have wee 'uns.'

'The 'Ra give maternity leave, do they?'

'You don't have to keep at it,' he says.

I pull free. 'So you'd have me give up what I believe in to have babies for you? Jesus, Aiden, you know what this means to me.'

'I thought I meant more.'

The phone rings again. I go to answer it.

When I return Aiden's lying on his back, blowing smoke rings.

'Who was it?'

'Martin. We've a situation.'

# County Antrim—25<sup>th</sup> September, 1983

## IRA Gunmen in Maze Break-out
## Dozens of Criminals on the Run
## in Northern Ireland

Thirty-eight Republican prisoners have escaped from the Maze prison near Lisbon. Using guns and knives smuggled into the jail, inmates, all from block H-7, overpowered guards before hijacking a lorry and driving through the prison gates. One officer was stabbed to death during the break-out and another is receiving hospital treatment after being shot.

Police and soldiers have sealed off the area and set up checkpoints in a five mile radius of the prison. Ten of the escapees have been recaptured and an extensive search for the remainder continues.

The prison, twenty miles south of Belfast, houses around 1800 prisoners, most of whom are Republicans. The escape is the largest in the history of Northern Ireland.

It is believed that some of those now on the run were involved in the 1981 hunger strikes which saw ten men starve to death in a failed protest for political status.

Authorities ask the public to remain vigilant but caution against approaching anyone suspected of involvement as the men are armed and dangerous.


We drive north overnight, crossing the border into Tyrone, stopping outside Coalisland where a car waits for Aiden. The driver climbs out to greet us and I realise I know him. Colm grins as he comes over.

'If it isn't herself. How are ya?' He shakes my hand.

'Not too bad. See you finally got that fuzz sorted out,' I say, pointing at the moustache that has grown in, aging him more than the two years that have passed since he tentatively patted me down before my Green Booking with the big men.

He retaliates, teasing, 'Sure, but I'm still waiting for you to stop mickeying about. When're you gonna join a proper brigade, do some real fighting?'

'Oi, watch it. I outrank you these days,' I joke. 'You want me complaining to your OC about the gob on you?'

'Ach, you're all trousers and no mouth,' he laughs, pointing at my jeans. 'Anyway, you've no rank this side of the water,' he reminds me, stealing the advantage in our bantering.

I let him have the win; I'll out-quip him next time. 'Fair enough. How is he, your OC? I've heard he's a hard man, Big Jim.'

Colm shrugs. 'Fearless, so he is. The two of yous'd get on.'

'Maybe when the Christmas campaign's over.'

'Grand, I'll look forward to working with you.'

'For me,' I grin, unable to resist one final craic\*.

He laughs. 'Aye, righto. Ready, Aid?'

'Gis a minute,' Aiden replies.

Colm retreats to a discreet distance.

Aiden loops his arms around me, pulling me close, enveloping me in his leather jacket. I take a deep breath, filling my lungs with the smell of him, feeling our bodies fitted together, a two-piece jigsaw. I kiss him. He kisses back; heat moves between us, then he draws away and cold air creeps over me.

'About before,' he says, 'I was an eejit.'

'It's not that I don't want to but how can we with this going on?' This is why Daideo sent me away.

He strokes my cheek. 'Sure, we've time for wee 'uns when this is over, so we have. I love you.'

'I love you too.'

We kiss once more then he walks to Colm, turns and they both wave.

I watch until they've driven out of sight then point the car northward, heading for Carnlough.

North of Larne the road narrows, tracking the coastline. To my right a flat colour wash of waves, stretching beyond sight, rolls and swells gently beneath the shadowy light of an unborn day. On my left rocky, grass-spackled cliffs climb skyward. The road pitches around knee-scraping bends, unfurls into high-velocity straights. I promise myself a TT

---

\* literally—joke

tuned motorbike and a return here one day, Aiden perched behind me, whooping with exhilaration.

Reaching Carnlough's southerly town boundary I park, shoulder to the sea, get out of the car and step up to the railings. Rust mottles the white-painted metal. I perch on the bottom rail, grip the top one and lean over, stretching for the beach which is sluiced in high tide. Waves slosh against the sea wall. I put out an arm, fingers splayed, and icy salt-spray tingles my skin. Balancing on the bottom rail, I open my arms to the sea, hugging the cold bay, clutching at the headland, scooping up the town that lies scattered to my left, trying to pocket precious predawn peace. On the horizon the sun eases itself out of the sea, replacing greyness with gold. In my sketchpad I outline the coastal scene, studying the colour, light and texture, storing it for painting someday. When sunrise is done and the light blandly blue I put my back to the sea and wait.

I recognise Connor as soon as he slouches into view, moving along the seafront with Aiden's easy-rolling gait, the sea, lit by the risen sun, glittering behind him. I lean against the car, watching. When he gets to within a few feet I see how thin he is; cheekbones cutting through greyed skin, eyes dark holes. When we shake I'm afraid of snapping his fingers. Fear chills me. This could be Aiden in ten, twenty years, when the war has finally spat him out, if he's lucky and his coin lands jail-side up. Connor's been seven years in the Kesh, four sleeping on a piss-soaked mattress, decorating the cell with his own shit, being beaten and humiliated by the war we're told isn't happening, for the freedom we're told we already have. That's Irish luck Republican-style.

'So you're the wee light in Aiden's eyes,' he says.

'And you're the big brother he looks up to,' I reply.

He drops his gaze, studies his trembling hands. I pull out my cigarettes.

'Want one?'

'Aye, thanks.' He drags deeply; coughs violently. 'Jesus, been so long since I smoked anything but roll-ups.' He looks around. 'Are we going?'

'Yes but first give me the gun,' I say, pulling on a pair of gloves and holding up my hand.

He jerks his head round.

'You need to trust me.'

He reaches into the pocket of a jacket that's too large for him and gives me the handgun. I wipe it off thoroughly then sprint across the road and shove it into the post box as instructed.

'What d'ya do that for?' he cries.

'The last thing we need is a collar for possession. One of the local brigade lads is postie on this route. He's collecting it later.'

We get in the car. I slip a brown envelope from the glove box. 'Here.' I drop it onto his lap, start the engine and pull away.

Connor tears the seal. 'What's this?'

He opens an Irish passport that says he's Michael O'Leary. Inside is a black and white photo of Aiden, taken only hours ago, in the Dublin house of his friendly forger.

'Are we leaving the country?' Connor's voice pitches up.

I outline the plan Aiden and I scrambled together under the duress of necessity; cross the border into Donegal, drive for the airport, fly to Amsterdam.

Connor thumbs the passport. 'Are we gonna get away with this?'

'Yes,' I say, strangling worries about the photo. It's been years since Aiden saw Connor. He couldn't have known, wouldn't have wanted to, that now his big brother looks more like their da than him.

'And when we get to Amsterdam?'

'Stay a few days, fly to London when things've settled.'

'London?' The word is croaked.

'Aye, but it's temporary. If we'd've known you were escaping, had some time to prepare…'

'My cellmate chickened out last minute. He only had six months to serve, decided it wasn't worth the risk,' Connor explains. 'I took his place. I don't want to go to London.'

'Don't worry. I've things sorted there. I can hide you.'

'Aye, sure,' he mutters, gazing out to sea.

'It's hardest finding a needle in a pile of other needles,' I say, thinking he's worrying about capture.

He shakes his head. 'I thought I'd be going home. I don't want... I'm not sure... London's so big, so busy.' There's strain in his voice. He's fighting not to cry.

I never thought about how it would be, getting out after being in so long. I assumed being out would fix everything but Connor's so broken that plain-old freedom isn't enough to mend him.

'That's why you'll be safest there,' I say with false certainty.

By rights he should be going for debriefing, then through decontamination before being hidden well away from military activity. But with so many to hide and so few places the Brits don't know to look options were limited. Martin only agreed to us, me, taking Connor to London because he couldn't suggest anything else on so little notice and with resources pulled so taut. It's got 'balls up' stamped all over it.

'You'll be grand. We'll look after you,' I add, hoping Connor won't realise, until he's strong enough to cope with another run, that our safe house can only be a temporary priest-hole for him.

'Promise?'

'Geallaim*.'

A week later we arrive in Putney. I'm annoyed to find myself glad to be home and dismiss it as relief over getting Connor safely here.

Briege has organised a welcome: bottled Guinness, homemade soda bread and barmbrack; paper-chain shamrocks dangle in doorways and a large tricolour is pinned to the lounge wall. That night we are wholly Irish, wholly Gaelic, singing songs, telling folk tales. When it's my turn I think I'm going to recite something from the Ulster Cycle but the words come differently:

Long ago there was a young boy, born across the sea from his homeland. The son of a once great and still powerful

---

* I promise you

185

man, he was sent to live and to learn in the old country, the land of the bog and the little fields. There he studied under a wise master, becoming skilled, clever and strong, living out the master's motto: strength in our hands, truth on our tongues and purity in our hearts.

The others listen in silence to Daideo's story. As the Easter week surrender approaches, I dredge my mind for a point to finish on and decide to leave my young hero free, roaming the Irish countryside. It's the closest I can get to a happy ending.

Connor has learnt Irish in jail so he, Briege and I start speaking it but after a while Tommy and Joe, who only have a few words, start fidgeting and I switch us back to English. We don't go to bed until the sun is red in the sky. It's only then I realise we haven't sorted out who's where. I clear my room, moving in with Briege so Connor can have his own space. Late morning, when I drag myself up, mouth dry and head pounding, the door to his room is open. He isn't there. I fly round the house, banging doors, waking the others. Joe spots him, lying on the unkempt lawn in our postage-stamp garden. His face is peaceful, younger. We leave him to sleep outside.

Connor can't adjust. He panics if we shut doors. He can't sleep inside so Tommy and Joe pitch a tent in the backyard and he sleeps there. He won't leave the house but doesn't like being left in alone. I give up my straggling art class, life drawing this term, to stay with him but being cooped up drives me crazy and too many times I ride off on the Honda, worries pounding my head. We're not a rest home for recuperating Republicans; we're an ASU; without meaning to, Connor could expose us. He nearly does once, sleepwalking outside in his underwear. Sheila sees Tommy and me coaxing him inside at midnight and asks who he is. Using a small truth to camouflage a bigger lie, I tell her he's a relation of mine, just released from prison. She repeats her favourite phrase, 'Men!' and leaves it there.

Briege is the only one who can handle Connor. She's patient when Tommy, Joe and I are irritable. She sits, talking to him in soft Irish, holding his hand. She cooks proper Irish dinners; Connor begins to lose his death-grey pallor. My jeans bite into my waist and I blame Briege's hearty plates of coddle and stew. One day she persuades him to walk to the corner. The next day they make it as far as the bus stop but Connor won't get on. The underground is unthinkable. Gradually she gets him to a nearby park, into a newsagents, the corner pub, into the van so Tommy can drive them to the outer reaches of Connor's universe: Richmond Park. He'll have to leave soon, should be gone already. Every day he's here we're teetering on a precarious outcrop. But I fear sending him away'll cause us to topple and fall; you don't leave a trail for others to track if you're not on the move. I resolve to sit still a bit longer, waiting until I'm as sure as possible that we're not being stalked.

By the end of October two things are confirmed: Harrods will be the target for the Christmas campaign and I'm pregnant. Joe and Tommy take turns recceing Knightsbridge with me, carrying shopping bags, pretending to be bored boyfriends. Tommy gathers supplies for the bomb. Joe buys a second hand banger, a red Triumph, rents a lock-up and leaves it there. Briege baby-sits Connor.

I arrange an abortion, no 'soul searching', 'looking into my heart' or 'sleeping on it'. *The Army claims your total allegiance without reservation...it fragments your family.* I convince myself it's the right thing. This life is my choice but I won't chose it for someone else. That wouldn't be fair.

Not able to shoulder their guilt when I'm buckling under my own I tell Briege and the lads GHQ have called me over to discuss the mission and I'll be gone a few days. Then I check into a shabby hotel in Earl's Court for a three night stay. In the morning I take the tube to the clinic. The doctor is Asian and avuncular. He talks me through the procedure, describing how they will open my cervix, insert a tube into my womb and vacuum out the foetus. I listen, expressionless. He reads my forms and, so he can be confident this is the right decision for me, asks me why I want this. An antagonistic voice in my brain screams, 'Because there's a good chance I'll be spending the rest of my life in jail for terrorist atrocities.' I silence it, saying that I have to; it's a no-choice choice. Maybe it's my unemotional tone, or the blank look in my eyes but all he says is:

'You're on your own?'

'Yes.'

'Today, I mean,' he clarifies. 'You didn't bring a friend?'

'No.'

'But you want to go home today?'

'Yes.'

'We don't let people leave alone after they've had a general anaesthetic.'

'Can't I have a local?'

'That is possible,' he nods, 'but some women find it harder, being awake during the procedure.'

'I'll be fine.'

'If you're sure?'

'Yes.'

There's a pause.

'This won't have any detrimental effect on your future fertility,' he concludes.

I paste on a polite smile.

I lie, legs apart, knees in the stirrups. A well-meaning nurse holds my hand. The doctor rolls over on a wheeled stool, his head disappearing into my crotch. I focus on the ceiling, try projecting Daideo's 'Green Dawn' painting like I practised during training, for resisting interrogations, but the image won't come. Instead, a single line of Celtic-lettered text writes itself on the iceberg-white tiles: our revenge will be the laughter of our children. How can we ever win if there's no one left to live the victory? The suction device is turned on, whirring like a vacuum cleaner. Memories rush at me: the old man I shot, his head blown apart; Cathy in her bloodstained jumper; the maimed horses, lying on their sides; the carnage outside the embassy in Dublin; Daideo's emaciated form, upright and sightless in his armchair. I can't stop them so I feed off them, vowing to make every sacrificed life matter.

By three o'clock, loaded with painkillers, I'm returning to the hotel. On the way I stop at an off-licence, buying a bottle of Jamesons. The cramps start later. I swallow more pills and drink until I'm numb.

The next day I'm weak, drained, and sleep fitfully, waking to a siren, shouting, bins clanging. I drag myself into the grim bathroom a dozen times to change the blood-sodden pads wadded in my knickers. There's more blood on the sheets. I'm too tired to care and lie on the sticky stain as the day darkens to night.

It's still early when someone raps on the door. I stumble up and open it. A swarthy middle-aged woman, grubby apron over her tracksuit, peers through the crack.

'You go now,' she says. 'Check out or Lady be mad.' She means the surly, bottle-brunette manageress who rules reception.

'Isn't checkout 10.30?'

'Yes, but Lady mean, always make people go soon. I tell you so you no get into trouble.'

'Thanks, but I'm not ready yet,' I say. 'I'll go when I'm ready.'

'When you be ready?'

'10.30.'

The elderly cleaner grins. 'You brave girl,' she says and waddles off down the passageway.

I close the door and slide into a crumpled squat on the floor, laughing, crying, my stomach throbbing.

I'm back in Putney by teatime. The bleeding has slowed and the pain eased.

Tommy calls out as I enter and I follow his voice into the front room.

They're waiting for me. Tommy stands. Joe stares. Briege avoids my eyes. Connor fumbles for a cigarette.

'Where the fuck have you been?' Tommy demands.

'What?'

'You heard.' He strides over, slamming the door closed behind me. The bang resounds in my head. ''Cos you haven't been in Dublin.'

I say nothing.

'We rang GHQ. You weren't there. So where the fuck were you?'

His arm twitches. I look down; he's holding a gun. We never have guns in the house. We can get them but only for operations, like when Joe and Tommy were doing the bandstand. I'm trapped between a lie that'll get me shot for a tout and a truth that'll have me crucified as a baby-killer. Another no-choice choice.

'Not that it's any of your fucking business but I've been in Earl's Court, having an abortion.'

Briege yelps then covers her mouth. Tommy steps back. Joe glances away. Connor stares at me.

I snatch the gun off Tommy. 'Gimme that. What the hell were yous gonna do, shoot me in the kitchen, dig me into the garden? Eejits.' I unload it.

'Caoilainn, Christ, why didn't you say?' Joe asks.

'Because of this.' I wave the empty gun over them. 'The looks on your faces. I've enough to deal with without your Catholic guilt. Here,' I toss Joe the gun, 'get this back to the cache now or I'll have the lot of yous on a charge: taking weapons without the cell leader's consent.'

I storm out. Across the road Sheila is struggling the pushchair down the steps while trying to hold onto the wee man. She sees me and waves. I ache to go over, lend a hand, give her chance to ask me so I can confide, cry, be consoled. But I fucking can't because of who we are, not two women fighting our way through a manmade world but one woman and one Irish Republican Army volunteer, fighting in parallel, but very different, worlds. I wave and turn away, walking in the opposite direction to the park Sheila is heading for, where kids go to play. On the corner I look back, see her bending to check inside the pushchair before zipping up the oldest's coat.

When you have the most, you have the most to lose.

I regret nothing.


I return to apologies and awkward glances. Briege hugs me. Tommy mutters something supportive. Joe makes tea. Connor is quiet. He stays up after the others go to bed and I brace for the accusations.

'It was Aiden's?'

I resolve to be calm. There's no need for anything else.

'Yes.'

'Did you tell him?'

'No.'

'Will you?'

'No.'

'He's a right to know.'

'But he deserves not to.'

Connor exhales a cloud of cigarette smoke, screening his face.

'You could've given this up.'

'And Aiden?'

Connor shrugs. 'It's his duty.'

'But not mine? Christ sake, Connor, after what you've put yourself through how can you ask me to quit this?'

The smoke clears. He rubs his eyes. 'Because of what I've been through, that's how.' He sighs. 'If we ever get the Six back there'll not be a man fit for it. Look at the state of me, Caoilainn.'

'Give yourself time, you'll be fine.'

His shoulders shake. He covers his face with his hands. I think of calling Briege, end up cradling him, stroking his hair. He sobs. My shirt is soaked. We don't speak. When he settles I get the Jamesons from my bag. We empty the half-full bottle and Connor falls asleep on the couch. I leave him there, hoping he'll stay indoors tonight. In the morning the sofa is cold and Connor curled up in his tent.

Sitting round the kitchen table, sink full of plates spattered with the remains of one of Briege's stews, we finalise the Harrods plan. We're after maximum chaos but minimum casualties so it's a lunchtime attack with a proper warning, a car bomb on a timer, parked up mid-morning in Knightsbridge. There's a debate about who'll do this. Although we're a team and not ruled by ranks, officially I'm in charge so when there's disagreement the decision's mine. And it's easy. I don't want Briege having the responsibility so soon and it'll be harder for Tommy or Joe to blend into the crowd of shoppers and city workers. I can wear one of the wigs, a sharp suit and park up as though I'm going shopping, slip into the nearest public loo, where Briege will be waiting, change and the two of us can leave inconspicuously on foot together.

'One of you can ring the warning through,' I tell Tommy and Joe.

'I'll do it,' Connor offers.

'You're not here on active duty,' I remind him. 'You're laying low until we can safely move you somewhere secure: suitable.'

'Please, let me be useful,' he begs.

'You're not fit for it.'

'And I won't ever be if I don't start up again.'

His eyes flash with anger but I know it's himself, not me, he's raging against. He needs this.

'O.K., but take one of the lads with you,' I agree.

'I'll go,' Joe says.

'I don't need you to,' Connor argues.

'I've said,' I reply. 'This is important. I'm not having another Hyde Park.'

Connor scowls but I'm right to insist; he's still wobbly in public places.

We agree on the 17th December. We have a month to get ready.

# Coalisland, Co. Tyrone—4th December, 1983

## SAS Ambush IRA Gunmen

British special forces, on covert operations in East Tyrone, have shot dead two IRA men and wounded a third, who escaped. The operation took place near Coalisland, where, last month, three Protestant church elders were killed.

An army spokesman said the SAS, who were patrolling in the vicinity, encountered two armed IRA men who failed to lay down their weapons when ordered. The soldiers opened fire, killing the two men instantly. A third man made off in a car. The SAS believe they shot and wounded the driver. The vehicle was found later with blood stains on the front seat.

It is understood the two dead men, Brian Campbell (19) and Colm McGirr (23), were carrying machine gun-type weapons at the time of their deaths and there is speculation that they were approaching an IRA weapons dump. The Provisional IRA has yet to confirm the two dead men as members.

Local Republicans accused the SAS of operating a 'shoot to kill' policy in Northern Ireland which endangers the lives of civilians. British army regulations give soldiers the authority to open fire without warning if there is a risk of injury to themselves or others.

Police continue to hunt the third man.

# London—13<sup>th</sup> December, 1983

## Public Warned of Possible
## Christmas Bombings in the Capital

The Metropolitan Police have issued a statement warning of a possible IRA pre-Christmas bombing campaign centred on London shopping districts.

In the statement a spokesman for Scotland Yard said, 'While we are not aware of any specific threat by the IRA, intelligence sources suggest there is a strong possibility that this terrorist organisation may target commercial properties in the run up to Christmas. We advise members of the public to remain vigilant and report anything suspicious.'

Addressing the House of Commons shortly after the statement, Prime Minister Margaret Thatcher said, 'We will not bow to terrorists and criminals.'

# London—17th December, 1983

At 10 A.M. Tommy, Joe and I travel to the lock-up in the van. Tommy transfers the bomb to the car, resprayed black, sets the timer and checks everything. I wait in the van, trying not to get my new fawn skirt, cream sweater and red wool coat dirty. Around my neck is a string of costume pearls; matching studs adorn my ears. I wear the curly red wig and have the short dark one, plus another outfit, in a John Lewis bag.

Joe signals to me. I scramble over lengths of pipe and tool boxes. Tommy moves the van while I get into the Triumph. I drive one way, they the other.

I pass Harrods twice, searching for a suitable space. On the third loop a car indicates into traffic. I stop, letting the driver out, then nip into the gap. I put four hours on the meter. The ticket reads 11.23-15.23, enough time to collect the car if something goes wrong.

I walk briskly along the Harrods shop-front, armpits damp, mouth dry, heart thrumming. Gaudy window displays advertise crap nobody needs; people rush to buy it before it sells out. I want to scream, laugh, cry. Now their biggest problem is what to get Aunt Mabel. Later it will be the ultimate 'almost' moment, a story they'll tell over Christmas lunch. But at 1.30 they'll be reminded that life is more than complaining about repeats on telly and checking their share dividends. If they could remember that for longer than five minutes, care about something other than their own needle-in-the-groove lives I wouldn't be planting a bomb.

I'm jolted and look down to see a little girl tumble to the pavement. Stunned by the fall, she stares up at me, eyes large. A woman crouches beside her.

'Darling, are you alright? Let Mummy kiss it better.'

Realising she's supposed to be hurting, the girl bawls. I merge into the crowd, reassuring myself; we've prepped meticulously, there's a proper warning, no one will die.

I drift with the current of laden shoppers heading for the tube. Round the corner, passing Harvey Nichols, head light and stomach heavy, I cross to the Hyde Park Hotel and into the ladies' room which Briege and I recced last week. Inside I enter the last cubicle but one and tap on the dividing wall. Briege taps back, then flushes her toilet. I do the same a beat later and when I emerge, outfit and wig swapped, Briege is at the mirror, powdering her nose. A matronly woman in tweeds, comes through the door. Briege and I greet each other with air kisses, exclamations of surprise and suggestions to take coffee. The woman enters a cubicle. Briege and I leave.

We take the Piccadilly line to Gloucester Road. Briege swaps to the District while I stay put. We arrive at the house a few minutes apart.

'Fecking bus was late,' she chunters as I unlock the door. 'You OK?'

'Dying to get these shoes off.' I throw the door wide, kicking the crippling stilettos up the passage.

She giggles.

Tommy appears in the kitchen doorway. His face is white. The cigarette in his hand quivers.

Briege stops laughing.

'What's up? Has something happened?' I demand.

Tommy nods.

I charge at him. 'Is it Joe and Connor? Aren't they back yet? For God sake, tell me.'

'We're running behind, they've not long since set off.'

I glance at my watch. 'Jesus, Tommy, it's gone half twelve. We said an hour's warning. Was it Connor, did he…?'

Tommy shakes his head. 'Forget about the bloody warning, will ya? This is more important.' He pushes open the kitchen door. Sitting with his back to me is a lad, dark tousled hair, wearing a leather jacket. He puts a hand to his head, rubbing fingers through his hair.

'Aiden?'

He turns. It's Danny. I haven't seen him since the wedding. A light shading of stubble stains his chin. His spindly frame is padded with budding strength. He's smoking. He is the younger Aiden to Conner's older one.

Panicked by his presence here, in the kitchen of a safe house no one's meant to know about, I pitch uncatchable questions at him.

'What're you doing here? How did you find us? What's going on? How did you get here?'

'Steady, Caoilainn,' Tommy cautions. 'We're OK. He's been careful. We're not exposed.'

'Connor wrote to me,' Danny explains, 'said where he was.'

'He'd no right,' I snap, horrified by Connor's breach, the piling calamities.

'I haven't told anyone,' Danny insists.

'Sure, Connor was just wanting some contact with home,' Tommy excuses.

'And we don't?'

'But you can understand,' Briege says, laying her hand on my arm, 'after everything he's been through.'

I shake my head. I can understand. Bollocks. But, fuck sake, secrecy is our only armour-plating. And fuck knows what the fallout of this'll be. I picture the car on Knightsbridge, the bomb quietly ticking time away…

'You've no business coming here, Danny. Whatever's happened at home, you being here makes things worse for all of us.' I go to him, snatch his cigarette. 'And you're too young for these.'

'I'm not a fucking baby; I'm seventeen.'

I slap his face. It crumbles as it did before; he's a child again. He storms to the backdoor and dashes up the garden. A second too late I realise it's Connor I should be caning.

'Caoilainn.' Tommy pats my shoulder. 'You best sit down.'


Aiden collects Colm from the farm. Colm has the two Armalites, both empty, that are for returning to the cache. Wee Brian is with him, their latest recruit. Colm suggests he comes along to see the armoury. There's no harm so Aiden agrees. Colm's ma was making soda bread in the kitchen and heard them so this much is known, reported and reportable.

The cache is a dugout under a hawthorn bush in a field. (The brigade QM confirms this later.) Aiden parks in the lane below. Colm and Brian head for it, each carrying a weapon. The Armalite is heavy in Brian's hands. Maybe he remembers the stuttering kick against his shoulder when he first fired one during training. Maybe Colm hurries them; perhaps his brother is having a few pints in town and he wants to get along.

In the car Aiden probably lights a cigarette and idly watches their progress across the sodden ground. Maybe he thinks about me, will I be home for Christmas? Maybe he tries to remember the smell of my hair, the warmth of my skin, the feel of my lips on his. Maybe he wonders what's for tea.

Soldiers spring up—a fact vague enough to make it admissible in BA records.

Aiden drops his cigarette and scrabbles in the glove box for his handgun which is found later by his OC in the top drawer of the bureau in Mrs Donovan's spare bedroom.

The soldiers shout. Colm half-turns to the sound, the Armalite held loosely by his leg. As the bullets strike his side and back he might just have time to think he won't be joining his brother for that drink later. Does he die looking into Brian's terrified eyes? He falls as the guns sight Brian.

Aiden remembers where he left his gun. Probably he swears. Fuck. Bollocks. Jesus Christ. Colm and Brian are dead. He starts the car, too hurried to close the glove box. The soldiers hear and turn on him, opening fire as he reverses up the lane. Bullets strike the windscreen, shattering it. More strafe the sides. Aiden feels the heat of one in his thigh, another in his shoulder, a third in his belly. Blood pools in his lap. Sweat and pain pour off him. He swings the car round and speeds away, bouncing off the grass verge, the road blurred and shimmering. The physical evidence, skid-marks, bullet holes, blood stains, recount all this.

He knows he has to get help. He heads for Jim's place, over the ridge.

The car crashes against something. Aiden staggers from the wreck, clutching his side, hands slick with his own blood. Jim's wife opens the door, taking on the bloody story. Aiden collapses into her arms, smearing red palm prints onto her pale blue blouse. She drags him inside. Jim is away but she knows what to do. She calls the doctor they use, presses towels to Aiden's wounds, keeps talking to him.

Aiden hears her voice. They say it's the last sense to fade. Maybe he thinks it's me; Jim's wife is blonde too. He raises a hand, feels warm fingers wrapped around his cold ones, squeezing gently. He takes a breath. His chest is loaded with a crushing pressure. Air come slowly, through a straw. It isn't enough. He takes another breath. The pressure doubles. He can't understand why I don't lift the weight from his chest so he can breathe. He looks at the hazy face bending down to his, fair hair falling into my eyes. He wills himself to live for me. He fights for that next breath, gasping, guttering, drowning in a red vortex...

I stop here, afraid of wrongly reconstructing his last thoughts.


Tommy starts at the end. Danny arrived an hour ago after three days hitching down from Stranraer with two quid in his pocket. He's run away. Because Aiden's dead and he didn't know what else to do. Briege utters a prayer and crosses herself. I walk slowly into the garden, to where Danny stands swallowing tears, kicking the straggly perennials that border the lawn. I hug him. He sniffles against my neck. I think about Connor's security breach, scripting the words I'll have with him over it. Doing that is better than scripting the words I'll never be able to have with Aiden.

We're still outside, clinging to each other, when Joe and Connor return. He comes to us and Danny pulls away, wiping his nose on his sleeve.

'Hey, kiddo,' Connor says, and hugs his baby brother.

I go to leave them but Connor catches my arm.

'Where're you off? Come here.' He draws me back and the three of us fall in on each other.


I postpone reprimanding Connor until after tea when I take him into the lounge and shut the door.

He reaches out to hug me. I draw back.

'You told Danny our address.'

His expression morphs into surprise. 'That's what you're wanting to talk about? My brother, your husband, has been murdered by the Brits and you're gonna give me a telling off for writing home.'

'For risking exposing us,' I correct calmly.

'Jesus, what kind of woman are you?'

The bullet goes straight to my heart. I'm afraid of the answer. I give myself five, then five more, seconds, to recover.

'This cell is my responsibility but we depend on each other. Our first, most important, duty is not to family, or home, or even missions; it's to each other. Because over here that's all we have.' My voice volumes up. I stop to turn it down. 'Connor, you can't do stuff like that.'

'And you can't do shite like this,' he rages.

'Yes, I bloody well can. It's my job,' I snap. 'Consider this an official warning. The only one you'll get. And yous are both going home as soon as I can arrange it.'

The door bangs open. Danny is there, face screwed down, hands balled into fists.

'Stop yelling at each other,' he screams. 'Stop it. Stop it!' He turns and runs. Three strides and he makes the front door, bangs through it.

I chase after him. Catch up a few houses down the road and manage to get a hand to his jumper. I claw at it, miss with the first go but get a decent hold with the second, hauling him to a halt. He tries to fight free.

'You'll tear it,' I warn.

The motherly words press some kind of pause button on him and he surrenders. I let go and we stand in the street, gulping down air.

'This is why you shouldn't be smoking,' I say with a wry smile. 'You'll be puffed out and run out.' I throw a sisterly punch at his arm.

He looks down at his trainers, scuffs them over the tarmac.

'Sorry,' he mumbles.

'Me too.' I squeeze his arm. 'Come on, it's cold, let's get in.'

I nudge him towards the house but he doesn't move. He rubs a hand through his hair again; my heart cries.

'Can't I stay here?'

'It's not safe. Anyway, I don't even know if we'll be staying.'

'I want to do something,' he says.

'And you can, when you're eighteen.'

'I don't want to wait.'

'You have to.'

We lock eyes, deer locking antlers. He's thinking it's not fair. He's thinking he hates me. He's thinking of running. He's thinking he'll do anything to get rid of the pain.

If I don't stop him he won't see eighteen.

I grab his arm, crush down through polyester, skin, flesh. Pain flickers across his face. He wriggles but I'm on a familiar nerve and the more he fights the worse it hurts.

'Caoilainn, you're...'

'I know.' My grip tightened on bone, I pull him back to the house.

Connor and Briege are huddled in the doorway, watching for us. I tow Danny through to the lounge.

'Sit.' I shove him into a chair

He surreptitiously rubs his aching bicep.

I flick the television on, looking for what I'm dreading, what I've been shirking.

'You've no idea what it's like, doing what we do.' I find the news. 'See that?' I point at the stuttering images of people, their faces smut-stained and bloodied, fleeing a smoke-filled Harrods. 'We, I, did that. The agony that's been tearing through you since you heard about Aiden, these people, their families, tonight they'll be feeling the same way. How do you live with that?'

'You don't think about it,' he challenges.

'Yes, you do, no matter how hard you fight not to.'

His gaze slides off the screen. I turn the volume up, making us both listen to a bystander telling us we're cowardly murderers.

'That's me he's talking about. And Connor. And Aiden. Every volunteer. You, if that's what you choose.'

Danny snuffles, wipes at his nose. I sit next to him.

'I'm not trying to keep you from joining, but you've got to be doing it for the right reason. If you're not, you'll never survive in here.' I tap his forehead.

He nods.

I glance again at the screen, listing those right reasons in my head. The camera pans along the street, showing the charred building, survivors squatting amongst the ruins. One of them, a man, turns, looks into the unblinking lens, looks

201

straight at me. It's Aiden. I stand. The man rubs his grimy cheek. It's not Aiden. Of course it's not. I fragment, crumbling onto the sofa. I'm ash, scattered by the breeze. Danny sniffs again. The sound draws me together.

'It's got to be justified. And it's not if you're doing it for revenge, for Aiden or anyone else. Promise you won't do anything until you're ready to live with it as well as die for it.'

'OK. I promise.'

The door creaks behind me. Connor is hovering. He's wiping his eyes, smiling a small, meek smile and nodding his head. He's heard the answer to his question, he thinks, about what kind of woman I am; I heard it too, but I can't believe in it.

The only luck the Irish have is bad. Because of Danny turning up today of all bastard days they didn't ring the warning through until 12.50. The bomb went off at 1.30. The media crucify us. The IRA statement counters, saying the warning was adequate. I know it wasn't. I also know it wasn't our fault. Six people are killed, three of them civilians, ninety are injured. I cry for them, locked in the bathroom because it's the only place I can be alone. I cry for their families. I don't cry for myself: for Aiden. If I did, it would kill me.

Running hard trying to outrun it keeping ahead of the shockwave cloud running with feet and thighs arms and hands lungs and heart running in fear panic despair away from the noise the light the heat hoping you can run to safety as brick and rubble somersault through air hit pavement people fall behind fall down fall dead you keep running back to the invisible plume that mushrooms through space through no space spraying glass flying rubble gushing smoke you run over ground that drops away you pass a hand a leg a torso a head flecked with red grey black you see the end flashing blue slices of luminous yellow the finishing line you keep running feeling the resistance of air like a brick wall blast against your chest knowing their waiting arms will grab you pull you in stop you you keep running driven by the cracking crumbling ending of everything.

You stop running.

It is the only dream I've had where I'm on the other side.

I creep downstairs, find Connor on the sofa, smoking his way through a pack. Danny's in Connor's room tucked up, not sleeping. He's been here four days and we've decided he'll have to stay until after Christmas. Connor makes room for me on the couch.

'How're ya?'

I shake my head. He tosses over his cigarettes.

'How did you do it, in the Kesh?'

He sits up. 'Ya mean the strike?'

'All of it. How did you keep going?'

'It's that or be beaten,' he says.

'But weren't you? Aren't we?'

He grabs my hand. 'As long as we're still fighting, they can't win.'

'But we can lose.'

He sighs. 'If you want out of the Movement no-one'll think badly of you for it; you've done your bit, so you have.'

If I quit it'll all have been for nothing. If I go on there might be nothing left. Another no-choice choice. I won't know until the last second of my life if the decisions I've made are right: Aiden, wishing he'd parked somewhere else, not forgotten his gun; the people in Harrods, wishing they hadn't come shopping; my ma and da, wishing they'd picked home with me instead of away on a mission.

'Do ya, want out?' Connor asks.

The question hurtles towards me, transforming midair into some fragile, precious thing. Yes or no? Drop or catch? I stretch my hands out...

'Don't know that I've a choice after this,' I reply, aware the real answer doesn't exist yet.

'Don't be daft,' he says. 'They're just wanting a report from you.'

'They didn't call Brendan back after Hyde Park.'

'Because they were planning on pulling him. This isn't like that,' he tells me.

'What is it like? How'm I gonna explain this?'

'It's not your fault. If those SAS bastards hadn't...'

*The enemy exploits a volunteer's mistakes.*

'Don't, Connor.'

'Why not?'

'Because it's fair enough, isn't it?'

'Jesus, they were unarmed. They didn't have a chance.'

'And if it'd been the other way round, wouldn't we have done the same? Haven't we already, shooting off-duty UDR lads, squaddies, peelers?'

'And what're we supposed to do?'

'Nothing, just what we have. I'm not going against the armed struggle; I'm saying this is what it is: war. Enemy killing enemy. We've to accept that. But when civilians are hurt...'

'That's down to the Brits,' Connor says. 'They're why we're doing this.'

For the next few days unanswerable questions hover in the air above me. I think over everything from my life, Daideo's and beyond, out of memory; I predict, playing out hypotheticals and correcting for a cross-wind. I step back far enough to watch things in slow motion and come in close enough to see every detail. Then I go for the catch: make it. Relief gushes over me; I know it's the right answer.

On Christmas day Briege produces a stash of goodies, bought bit by bit with her miserly pay so she can do a decent dinner. I send Joe to the pub with our last tenner and he returns with bottles of Newcastle Brown and a half bottle of Bells. We pull his leg about it being Scotch instead of Irish, pretending to be poisoned by the first sip. He offers to drink it all himself, leading to more jibing about his imagined inability to hold liquor. We laugh, even Danny, who sneaks a tipple when he thinks I'm not looking. There are no presents or crackers and we don't have a pudding slathered in rum sauce but we have Irish humour and that sees us through until the Queen starts her speech, providing us with thirty minutes of booing and cursing at the telly, releasing anger and pain we can't vent any other way. Briege does the washing up while we're swearing our heads off and when Connor goes too far I send him in to help her. When Liz is done, I get up to fetch the biscuit selection given to Tommy and Joe by a grateful widow as a thank-you for fixing her boiler two days before Christmas. In the kitchen steam rises from the foamy sink; dishes, in various stages of washing, are stacked on the counters. Connor and Briege are locked into a deep kiss. I creep out.

The day after Boxing Day we meet a courier bringing two more fake Irish passports, one for me and one for Danny. They're in the name of O'Leary to match Connor's. The three of us will travel to Ireland as a warped version of ourselves; Mr and Mrs plus kid brother.

Joe drops us at Heathrow and we fly direct to Dublin. Connor's beard and the forged passports coupled with the general lethargy of an immigration officer with a post-Christmas hangover gets us through and I take them straight to Daideo's house.

That's what it's reverted to now it won't be mine and Aiden's. The place is cold. The power's been cut. Three red bills lurk on the mat. I use them to light the fire. Connor goes to the corner shop for crisps and pop. At 3 o'clock I leave for my meeting at the florist's.

The shop is in darkness. A silver Rover is parked outside. As I walk over the front window drops and the driver says:

'Get in.'

He drives through the university quarter and towards Rathfarnham. The modest semi he parks at has Christmas lights twinkling in the window.

The driver stays in the car, watching me walk up the neatly paved path to the freshly painted door, nerves sweating from me despite the December chill.

A man I don't know opens it.

'Caoilainn?'

'Yes.'

'Away in.' He leads me into a front room littered with kiddies' toys, some still in boxes.

'Have a seat.'

I choose an armchair, trying to sit relaxed but alert.

'Trip alright?'

'Fine.'

We study each other for a minute. He's mid-thirties or older, thin with a long face and receding hair slicked back. A white crescent scar gleams on the back of a weathered hand. The house is tellingly quiet, empty apart from us.

I break the silence. 'Is Martin coming?'

He hesitates, I think because he's trying to work out who I mean. 'You'll be dealing with me from now on.' His face is uncarved marble, his hands rest motionless on the knees of his corduroy trousers. His eyes bore through me.

I'm exhausted, running on the dregs of myself. I dredge up a reply.

'Fine. So you're…?'

His eyebrows twitch. 'Kevin.'

The latest 'Michael Collins'?

I slouch down in the chair, wondering how long his wife'll keep the kids out.

'I was sorry to hear about your fella.'

'Thanks.' Not as fucking sorry as me.

The big hand hits the six. He eyes the clock.

'The Brits said the warning wasn't long enough.'

'Yous said it was.'

'I'm interested in what you've to say on it.'

'It should've been longer.'

'Why wasn't it?'

'Circumstances beyond our control.'

'It's down to you to control them.'

'I know that but I'm not superwoman.' I'm too tired, too frustrated, worried, annoyed, upset, too slow to snatch back the retort.

He raises his eyebrows.

'We're doing what we can as best we can.' Half-and-half offence/defence. As far as I dare go.

'We had to make excuses.' He means their statement. His tone, his expression, there's regret but I'm not sure what for so say nothing.

'No apology?' he presses.

'Sorry.' I flatten out the word. I am fucking sorry but letting him know won't help me. 'Am I getting court-martialled over this?'

He leans forward. 'You're not.' He sighs. 'You've been a good volunteer. The question is whether you can carry on after what's happened.'

Does he mean Aiden or Harrods? Is he's asking or telling?

'If you think I'm going to have a break down, the grieving widow…'

He holds up a hand, face snapping from stern to aghast. 'You'll get none of that from me. I know you've encountered some,' he pauses, 'opposition but I'm only concerned with whether you can do what needs be done. And that's about what's in your head, not your 501s.' He sounds earnest.

'My views on the armed struggle haven't changed.'

'I didn't think they would've. Do what you need to in Belfast then clean things up in London. You need time out.'

I sit up, ready to protest.

'It's an order, not a suggestion. One I'd be giving any volunteer who's been through the same thing. When you're done in London come back to Dublin. I'll be in touch.'

That night Connor and I have a massive row. He wants to travel to Belfast with Danny and me, see his folks, visit Aiden's grave in the Republican plot. I say it's fucking suicidal. He argues that as the O'Learys we'll not be suspected. I ask if he wants to see Danny in the Kesh. He threatens to find another way if I don't agree. I picture him wandering around in the dark, unarmed, falling into the crosshairs of an SAS patrol.

We use public transport. Our fake Irish passports are scrutinised at the checkpoint. I explain with a half-truth: Danny had a row with his mammy and ran off to his big brother in Dublin; we're bringing him home. The soldiers wave us through. Connor lights a cigarette with shaking fingers.

'Can I have one?' Danny asks.

His face is white.

Connor glances at me.

'Give him one,' I sigh, checking the timetable for the next bus to Belfast.

We alight at the bus station and, with eyes everywhere, make our way through the city centre's neutral zone to the pub where Rory is meeting us.

He's at the bar, half way down a Guinness. He spots us and orders two more plus a coke for Danny.

'Caoilainn,' Rory hugs me. 'How're ya?'

'OK.'

We drink and make small talk, leave together and separate outside, Rory taking Connor to a safe house while Danny and I take a black taxi up the Falls. The driver recognises Danny.

'I was sorry to hear about your brother.'

Danny doesn't reply.

'Thanks,' I say.

'Did you know him, love?'

'I did.'

'Real shame. He was a grand lad.'

Tears sting my eyes. I fight them down. Danny slips his hand into mine and leaves it there until the cab stops at his parents'.

Nora rushes out, slapping then hugging Danny before ushering us inside.

'Caoilainn, love.'

There's nothing left to hold on to. I break. We cry, mother and wife, scavenging strength from our shared pain.

She takes a hanky from her sleeve and dabs raw eyes. 'I'll put the kettle on.'

She slips into the kitchen; I go into the front. Frank is in his armchair, a blanket over his knees. He beckons me to him. I bend to kiss his cheek. Danny sits on the sofa, eyeing his da's cigarettes. I join him and Nora fetches the tea. Talk stutters; I ask about Callum.

'At a friend's,' Frank replies.

'How's he been?'

'Fine,' Frank says.

'Quiet,' Nora admits. 'He's missed you,' she adds, looking to Danny who bows his head.

I feel like a stranger, intruding.

'We didn't know when you'd be back,' Frank says. 'We couldn't wait.'

He's meaning the funeral.

'It's alright. I'll go up later.'

'I'll have one of the taxi lads run you,' he offers.

'I'll walk.'

Aiden's grave isn't far from Bobby Sands' and it's Sands' I go to first, memories of his funeral bright as the gold lettering that gleams on the black plaque as fiercely as when it was laid two years ago. I stare at it, willing myself to go to Aiden; unable to move.

A loud American voice breaks the silence.

'Son of a gun, Betty, I've found it.'

I find myself flanked by a fat man and his fatter wife. She lays a white rose, not realising roses are English. She should have brought lilies. The man snaps a Polaroid.

'Did you know him, honey?' the man drawls, gesturing to the plaque.

'No.' I walk away.

I crouch at Aiden's grave. There's no headstone yet, just a mound of churned earth. I worm my hands down into the soil. It's cold. I want to cry. I try conjuring memories of him. Still nothing. He's dead; I have to find a new way of living.

Daideo's grave is further down. I amble towards it, detouring by Cathy's on the way. I trace his inscription with a fingertip: Patrick William Finnighan, 'Finn'; 1899-1981; Slowly sets the sun of a Green Dawn.

Liam greets me at the safe house. Sean and Rory are also there, keeping Connor company. When Sean pulls me into a surprise embrace I feel the bulge of a gun under his arm. He breaks out the whiskey and by the time Frank, Nora, Danny and Callum arrive under the cover of darkness and accompanied by a discrete IRA guard, we're already half-cut with toasting Aiden, the Cause and the Republic: Up the 'Ra.

Just before sunrise Nora wakes Callum and they help Frank into the waiting taxi while Connor and I say goodbye to Danny.

'You've promised you'll be patient,' I remind him. 'You've to keep to that.'

'I will.'

'Good man,' Connor says, 'I'm counting on you looking after Ma and Da, kiddo.'

'I will,' Danny promises again.

Then they're gone.


Liam and Rory drop us across the Monaghan border the next night. A local Republican drives us to Dublin; we doze through the journey, waking as the car jolts into potholes.

I stay another few nights in Dublin, getting the gas and leccy back on, stocking the cupboards for Connor, working out how much longer the money Daideo left me will last. Long enough, I hope, because a volunteer's allowance is coppers. When I'm happy Connor is settled I fly to London via Venice.

It takes two months to clean up in London; we can't be seen suddenly leaving. Briege goes first, home to Galway where, I suspect, Connor will join her. Tommy and Joe wind up their business, telling the regulars they've work in Holland. I don't know where they go. Lastly I tell Sheila I'm away to Australia for a year on a working holiday. She wishes me well and waves me off, the little man beside her, the baby balanced on her hip.


When I return to Dublin I find a postcard with a Galway frank on the mat. Written in Irish it's signed 'Love, B & C'. They're well and engaged. I send congratulations. They marry in June, while I'm in Cork, exploring the coast on 250cc Bonneville, staying in B&Bs, riding through Atlantic squalls, sketching swathes of barren ocean, empty beaches, jagged cliffs: looking for Aiden in places he never got to be.

In late July I make my final stop before Dublin: Avoca. I wander the tiny town's streets alone and lonely. A young mother bumps a pram up the kerb. An elderly couple rest on a bench. The man holds his wife's hand. Birds sing. Bees hum. The sky is blue. The sun warm. I take the chain from my neck, put the ring on my finger. It's loose and slides down to my knuckle. I push it into my pocket. There's no way of making it fit now. I wait until the old couple leave then abandon my sketchpad on their bench. It's full of coastal vistas plus one unfinished drawing of Aiden.

Time spent touring Ireland's wild coastline has glued the shattered parts of me together. When I blow into Dublin I don't wait for Kevin to call.

'There are a few places we could use you,' he says.

'Where?'

'Belfast.'

'No.'

'East Tyrone?' Kevin raises an eyebrow.

'Sure, if you want me on the rampage,' I say.

He laughs. I don't.

'Derry?'

I shrug.

'England. We're needing a...' he pauses, '...we're after sending a couple, Mr and Mrs on holiday.'

'What's up?'

'Something big. Maybe not for you.'

'Why?'

'There'll be no warning. It's a kill we're after here.'

I suck in air. 'Who?'

'The Bitch herself.'

'It's been approved?'

'By the Council,' he confirms, 'but you should know there's a chance others will be caught up in it.'

*Tactics are dictated by the existing conditions.*

I balance the equation in my head:

$$\frac{(\text{Thatcher} + X \text{ Tory Ministers}) + X \text{ innocent civilians}}{10, \text{ no } 11 \text{ hunger strikers}}$$
$$x\text{IRA armed struggle} = ?$$

'You've principles and I'll not ask you to compromise them. I can get someone else.'

'You don't need to.'

# Brighton—15th September, 1984

We check into the Grand Hotel on Brighton's seafront under the names of Mr and Mrs Roy Walsh. It's two days since I met my 'husband' in Blackpool. His real name is Pat Magee. Like me he's been working in the England department for a while because, also like me, he grew up on the mainland.

The receptionist hands us a registration card. Pat fills in our details, all false, signing with a small neat script. She gives us the keys to room 629, five floors above the palatial suites that will be booked out by Tory VIPs come October.

Pat tows our suitcase into the lift. I carry an overnight bag. Inside it, packed in a large Tupperware tub, is twenty pounds of gelignite, wired to a VCR timer.

The room is Victorian elegance; carved furniture with claw feet, fleur de lys wallpaper and a syrupy carpet that my court shoes sink into, snagging. I kick them off and go to the window. Along the seafront late-season tourists stroll, licking 99s. Pat takes the bag from my arm. I hear his shoes clicking on the tiled bathroom floor.

I scan the room again, notice the double bed, plump with pillows

Pat emerges from the bathroom.

'Did you pack a screwdriver?'

'Side pocket.'

He sees my gaze, follows it to the bed.

'I'll sleep on the floor.'

'Don't be daft. We'll share.'

He returns to the bathroom and begins removing the bath panel. I open our case and hang clothes in the wardrobe. He reappears.

'I've put it in but I'll not arm it 'til we're ready to leave. Shall we take a walk?'

We find a quiet café and sit skimming information leaflets, planning which attractions we'll visit; the Royal Pavilion, Palace Pier, the aquarium. An old habit from my London days makes me reach for his hand. His fingers stiffen at my touch and he jerks his head up.

'Are you alright?'

'Fine,' I say, letting go.

We dress for dinner, dining in the Grand's restaurant. The food is rich; I manage only a few bites. The chatter of other diners covers our silence. I'm glad when the dessert plates have been cleared and we can retire upstairs.

In the bathroom nothing is out of place. I brush my teeth, take off my make-up and change into the t-shirt and shorts I brought in case we decided to go to the beach. I didn't think to bring a nightie.

Pat is already in bed, the stripy arms of his pyjamas resting on top of the covers. I climb in next to him.

'Are you sure you're OK?' he asks again. 'I'll be fine on the floor.'

'I'm alright,' I mumble.

We lie back to back. I hear the change in his breathing, softer and steadier. I keep my eyes open, hoping to stay awake.

Aiden is in the doorway of a house I don't recognise, beckoning to me. I think, 'So that's where he's been. He didn't die.' I walk towards him. Get no closer. Run. He moves further away. I know then that he will die because that's what he has to do.

I sit up, jarred out of the dream. The room is dark and cold, my skin pimpling in the chill. There's a movement in the bed next to me. It was only a nightmare; everything's fine.

Light floods the room. I turn to the man beside me. It isn't Aiden.

'Caoilainn?'

My heart winters.

Pat sits up. 'What is it?'

'Nothing.'

'Is it the mission? If you're worried...'

I shake my head, dumbed by fresh grief.

He puts out a cautious hand, resting it lightly on my shivering shoulder. 'You're cold.' He fetches a jumper, one of his, draping it over me. 'Would you like tea?' He gestures to the kettle, set out on a table with Queen Ann legs.

'I'd rather a whiskey.'

Pat rings reception, asking the night porter to bring some. When it arrives he fills a tumbler for me. I empty the glass and he fills it a second time, putting the bottle beyond reach on the dressing table.

'Tell me if you think it'll help,' he offers.

'It won't but thanks.'

'You've lost someone,' he says.

'Hasn't everyone?'

'Isn't that why we're here?'

In the morning we wander along West Street, passing a large gothic church. Pat stops. Not by accident, we've arrived at St Paul's in time for the Sunday service: 11 o'clock solemn mass. I draw back.

'What's wrong?' Pat asks.

'I'm not...'

'Oh.' He flushes and glances to where the priest is greeting the faithful in the vestibule. 'Sorry, I didn't... I'll meet you somewhere later.'

The priest spots us; we're blocking the entrance. He smiles, heads over.

I nod at the robed figure gliding forwards. 'It'll look off if I leave now. The last thing we need is a memorable fuss.'

Pat glances around for a solution.

I suck in air. 'It's alright for me to sit at the back, is it?'

'Aye.'

He takes my arm, we enter and slide into a pew. High above the nave hangs an ornate cross, gargantuan, dwarfing the tiny Jesus pinned to it by pierced hands and feet. He sacrificed himself for his beliefs. Like Pearse. And Sands. And... Damned if you don't; dead if you do.

The priestly party advances up the aisle. The priest takes the lectern, addresses the congregation. My breath falls into a hushed rhythm. Stillness fills and empties me. Motionless, I sit through the chanting as priest and congregation call and reply to each other, words with the melodic beating of soft wings. The priest brings two silvery cups to the altar. A bell chimes. He crosses himself and the bell tings again. My stomach knots as a veil I've no business peering behind is lifted. The priest reaches into the first cup, withdrawing a fragment of the wafer. He holds it aloft, saying, 'This is my body which will be given up for you.' The bell chimes a third time, binding and breaking a spell. Now he takes the second goblet, also raising it. 'This is the chalice of my blood which will be poured out for you and for many for the forgiveness of sins.'

A soothing mother's hand caresses me: there, there; anois, anois. Aware of everything but anchored to nothing, I drift. Beside me Pat stands. He reaches the alter, offers himself to the priest. I want to look away but my eyes won't close nor my head turn. I have to watch the intimate moment when the bread is placed on his tongue. Pat returns, slipping into the pew, kneeling and clasping his hands, his private prayer naked in my peripheral vision. I will myself to not see but my rapt state makes sight like hearing: impossible to deny. His lips move silently. What is it he prays for? In two days we'll leave a bomb ticking down the final seconds of our enemies' lives...

Pat sits.

A distant voice intones, 'Go and announce the gospel of the Lord.'

I hear Pat telling me we can leave, feel his hand on my shoulder, but I can't reply or move. I'm behind glass.

'Caoilainn.'

The voice's urgency scatters the haze. Noise and colour rush me as the congregation clatters out. I'm steered down the aisle.

On the street I head for the seafront.

'Where're you going?' Pat calls.

'To see the sea.'

The water is grey; wind whips white spray up from the waves. Dogs chase breakers that lap the shore in foamy clouds. A boy peddles his bicycle over the pebble-crust beach. I stand at the railings, picking at scales of flaking paint, watching the sea's endless in-and-out motion, the world breathing.

I find Pat on a nearby bench and join him.

'What do you get from it?' I ask.

He fixes me with dark eyes. 'Hope.'

*

We normalise ourselves, visiting tourist attractions. Palace Pier is reassuringly kitsch, Victorian bawdiness and childish amusement wrapped in colourful paper. The aquarium is educational; Pat reads each exhibit's information board.

'Where is it?' I ask at one tank, the home of the blue spotted stingray.

'There.' Pat points to a corner.

Two small brown bobbles that I thought were pebbles blink at me. The ray flicks itself off the bottom, darts to the other side and shuggles back into the sand, blending with its surroundings.

'The greatest danger's the one you can't see,' Pat comments.

At the Royal Pavilion we listen to the curator explaining how the former seaside palace of the Prince Regent was transformed into one of the most exotic buildings in the British Isles. Styled on an Indian palace, plump domes crown the roof, lattice-work panels adorn the walkways and minarets spike upwards, piercing the sky. The guide boasts that it's a spectacular legacy of the British Empire. Pat and I swap glances.

'Doesn't something have to be dead to leave a legacy?' I whisper.

The next morning I pack while Pat arms the bomb. As I zip the case closed he emerges from the bathroom.

'Ready?'

'Aye. You?'

'Just the timer to switch on.' He hesitates. 'Do you want to do it?'

I'm culpable either way but if I do we can share the responsibility.

'OK.'

We crouch on the bathroom floor. I press the switch; Pat watches. Then he slides the bomb under the bath, replaces the panel, we collect our bags and check out.

*

216

The flight from Heathrow to Dublin is uneventful. We're met at the airport, driven to a house, not his, where Kevin meets us.

'No problems?' he asks.

I think of my nightmare and going catatonic in church.

'Not a one,' Pat replies.

'Grand. Here's what we're thinking for the statement.' Kevin passes Pat a sheet of paper.

The last line reads, 'Give Ireland peace and there will be no war.'

Pat nods. 'Sure, that's the truth.'

We sip tea. Pat and Kevin chat. I fidget.

Pat excuses himself to use the toilet; I pounce on the opportunity.

'I want you to send me into Belfast.'

'You ready for that?'

'Yes.'

He pouts. 'We could use you up there. Did you hear about Sean? Lifted last week. Liam's heading up things. He'd be glad to have you back.'

'Fine.'

An hour later Pat and I leave on foot, take the bus to town and part in the city centre.

'Take care of yourself,' he tells me.

'You too. Thanks for not saying anything about...'

'We've all got scars.'

He shakes my hand, turns and vanishes in the crowd, lost among lunchtime shoppers, blending with his surroundings.

## Thatcher Cheats IRA Murder Plot in Brighton Cabinet Members Among Those Injured in Barbaric Bombing

Margaret Thatcher has narrowly escaped death when, in the early hours of today, the Grand Hotel in Brighton became the latest target of terrorist atrocities. The huge blast, which ripped the building apart, claimed the lives of five people including the MP, Sir Anthony Berry. A further 34 were injured. Norman Tebbit, the trade and industry secretary, and his wife, were among those who had to be rescued from the rubble. They are being treated for serious injuries. The attack was a ruthless attempt to murder the Prime Minister and members of the Tory government gathered for the Conservative Party conference.

In its statement the IRA admitted planting the massive bomb and threatened they would make further attempts to kill the PM saying, 'Today we were unlucky, but remember, we only have to be lucky once. You have to be lucky always.'

A resilient Mrs Thatcher insisted the conference continue on schedule and, despite nearly losing her life, used her speech to vow that terrorism would not defeat democracy. Calling the attack, 'an inhuman, undiscriminating attempt to massacre innocent, unsuspecting men and women,' she added, 'The fact that we are gathered now... is a sign not only that this attack has failed but that all attempts to destroy democracy by terrorism will fail.'

The explosion, at 2.53 A.M., caused the hotel's five tonne central chimney to collapse, wiping out a large section of the eight storey building. Witnesses described hearing a huge bang and seeing a 'torrent of rubble' tearing through the hotel. John Gummer, Conservative Party Chairman, said the attack was, 'Not military action but a cowardly act of terrorism.'


We move every few days, dossing in various West Belfast homes, staying one step behind the Brits, going where they've just been with the idea that they won't think to come back. The ASU is me, Rory, Ciaran and Danny, now eighteen: old enough to die.

Ciaran's twenty, from Fermanagh, been in the Movement a year, transferred to Belfast as part of the strategy to confuse Brit intelligence by having volunteers operate outside their home ranges. He works in a city centre bar as a cover. At first I'm not sure about him; he's quiet around me, stares a lot. I wait, ready to cut him down the minute he criticises women in the Movement, but he doesn't say anything so I tell Rory who howls with laughter. He's told Ciaran about me; not the specific ops obviously, but generally that I'm dead on. It's wide-eyed awe not narrow-minded chauvinism making him gape. One night, when Rory and Danny are on a recce, I have a chat with Ciaran. He blushes, smiles his shy admiration and says he's chuffed to be working with me. I say, 'And me with you.' After that we're OK.

Danny's a trickier problem. I always knew he'd join but that doesn't stop me wishing he hadn't. Father a Republican internee, one brother an escapee from the Kesh and two others in Milltown; he's a known face. At sixteen the peelers did their usual number, pulling him, prints and photos for their files. His risk is twice ours because our mug shots aren't pinned to the board in Castlereagh: yet. Not that I think he'll get us lifted, we're vigilant, but if that ever happens he'll be the one IDed first; the one who'll cop it for everything, anything, things we haven't even done, because, with his background, he'll be an easy fit up. Rory argues it's better he's with us; we can look out for him. I insist on extra precautions. Danny starts a mechanic's apprenticeship with a fella called Mick, who runs a garage off the Falls. That keeps him busy most days; most nights he sleeps at home, keeping things normal. He doesn't do an op alone. He only carries a gun when it's essential.

Rory and I are the unit's full time volunteers. That means spending hours in other people's kitchens, smoking ourselves to death, our stomachs awash with tea. Officially Rory is cell leader but he often asks my advice and we make decisions democratically. Liam checks in on us when he can but he's running several cells across the city and he knows us too well to worry about us so we only see him sometimes. We've a good network of supporters who give up their beds, cook our teas and wash our clothes. We do whatever is needed. Without noticing, I've become a veteran volunteer, aged twenty-two.

'Mammy says Briege is up next week,' Danny announces.

We're in the kitchen of a two-up off the Falls. The old woman and her hubby are in bed. Rory is trying to fix a handgun that keeps jamming. Ciaran thumbs a copy of *Republican News*. I'm watching the black and white portable in the corner. Thatcher is on. Her lips move. No sound comes out. I keep the volume off, something I've been doing since Brighton, because she can't say anything I'd want to hear but seeing her stiff bouffant, stone eyes and that long sharp beak down which she views us with personal loathing keeps me burning. I don't blame her for hating us: I thank her. If she won't let it be political everything is justified.

'She wants to know if you'll come to tea?'

'What?'

'When Briege is here,' Danny explains.

I reach over the table. 'Let me.' I take the gun off Rory and start stripping it.

'Don't you want to see her?' Danny presses.

'We have to be careful,' I say.

'You'd be alright going for tea,' Rory offers.

I hide a scowl. Briege and I have only met a couple of times since she and Connor married. She's stayed on as a volunteer, leaving Connor at home in Galway; Christ knows how he feels about that but with the peelers still hunting him he can't serve. Her operations have kept her in the Republic so we haven't had many chances to get together. Not that I've tried very hard. Her happiness, and my jealousy, fucking terrify me.

'Jesus, when did you last clean this?' I ask Rory.

'So I'll tell her you'll come, will I?' Danny presses.

I wait until it's dark and use the back lanes to reach Frank and Nora's. On the way I pass a Honda XL 125cc like the one I learnt to ride on in London. Seeing it dumps me back there, on the day I heard about Aiden. I kick down the past and let myself into the O'Neills' yard.

The house reeks of fish; it's Friday. Haddock drowns in boiling milk. Callum sits at the table, hunched over a maths textbook. He glances up as I enter.

'How're you?'

'Busy,' he grunts, scribbling algebraic equations.

'Caoilainn, you made it.' Nora comes into the kitchen and hugs me.

'Aye, but I've eaten already.' I gesture to the pan. 'And I best not stay long.'

'Oh.' Her smile fades. 'Well, come through. Briege is dying to see you. Callum, set the table when you're done.' She nods her head at his spreading schoolwork. He doesn't acknowledge her.

In the front Frank is swaddled in his armchair. Danny leans against the sideboard, smoking. Briege rushes to meet me.

'Caoilainn, how're you?'

'Fine. You?'

'Grand,' she says, smiling and tugging me towards the couch. 'I'm so glad you came. I've something to tell you.' She beams round at us.

Nora takes the other armchair. Danny perches on the arm of his da's seat. We wait. Briege starts giggling in that shy way of hers. I guess what's coming and brace.

'We're having a baby.'

Nora claps her hands and gushes congratulations. Tears glisten in Frank's eyes. Danny kisses Briege's cheek shyly and blushes when she mentions him being an uncle. Then she faces me.

'We thought if it's a wee lad we'd call him Aiden Francis.'

I paste on the smile she deserves and manage a brief hug. Then I stand. 'I should be going.'

'You've hardly been here a minute,' Nora protests.

'I've got something to do.' I go through to the kitchen and am at the backdoor when Danny calls after me.

'Do you need me?'

'No.'

'What's up?'

Callum is staring at me.

'Nothing. I'll see you tomorrow.'

Outside I stand in the alley, lashing at thoughts that ambush me from behind. The Honda is a few yards up. It kick-starts first time.

I scream through Belfast, cutting a jagged line in the teatime traffic, car horns swearing at me as I jump queues and nick into wing-mirror scraping gaps. On the dual carriageway I carve up the middle, a tightrope rider balanced on a broken white line. Brake lights glare at me. I don't look them in the eye. I slit Bangor up the middle, engine revving a warning to pedestrians; they leap away from the kerb as I race past. Turning south down the coast, the A2 quietens. I ease off to a cruise, salt-wind bumping the bike, sea and sky a solid black mass on my left, houses cowering to my right.

Between Millisle and Ballywater the bike splutters to a halt, out of petrol. Lights from both villages punctuate the darkness. Millisle looks closest but not close enough. Too tired to face pushing the bike into the village I wipe it clean of prints and dump it at the roadside; the peelers will just have to add it to their joyriding stats. I walk the exposed coast road in November wearing only an anorak and jeans, fingers, feet and face already frozen by the ride. On the town's outskirts I step off the road, jump the seawall and land, boots sinking unevenly, on sand. I sleep in the shelter of a grassy bank, an unthought thought about the rising tide in my head.

I wake, limbs contracted from a night spent shivering into myself. The sunrise is orange, tingeing the rain from squally clouds with an acid hue. The beat of horse hooves drifts down from the road above. I stand, wrenching cramped muscles, blood burning its way into iced-up veins. A young lad in a raggy jumper and dirty jeans rides a piebald mare towards me. He reins the animal to a halt.

'Ya alright, there?'

I nod.

'Ride to town?' he offers, nodding towards Millisle's tiny urban encampment.

'Cheers.'

He stretches down a hand, hauls me up behind him. The smell of manure and sweat fills my mouth. I hold his shoulders, study the frayed neck of his jumper and fight for my seat, legs dangling heavily. We clip-clap into town, pantomime cowboys from a comedy-western.

He stops half-way along the high street, parking his mount between two cars. I slide down.

'Phone box there.' He points.

'Thanks.'

He grins yellowed teeth at me.

''Twas a cold night for camping. You must be hard as ice.'

'Frozen solid,' I reply.

He grins again, gees the horse and trots off.

It takes three attempts to reach Liam. When he final comes to the phone his voice croaks a sleepy hello.

'It's me.'

There's silence then, 'Where're you?'

'Millisle.'

'What the…? Jesus. Never mind. Can you get into Bangor?'

'Probably.'

'Christ sake, can you or not?'

'Yes.'

'I'll have you picked up at the tourist info centre on the quay. We'll have words when you get back.'

In Bangor I wander down the shopping street towards a seafront guarded by garish hotels. Grey clouds colour a flat sea. The tourist info centre faces the harbour, corning the road. It's a cream-washed building with a mock-medieval stone tower attached. Putting my back to it, I perch on the harbour wall, staring at a forest of masts leaved with rigging, trying not to think about the words Liam wants, the ones I owe him. I guestimate how much boats cost, wonder how difficult sailing is, fantasise about life at sea.

Two hours later a car turns into the car park. A woman in her forties gets out, comes across.

'Caoilainn?'

'Aye.'

223

She jerks her head towards the car. 'I've not got all day.'

I trail her to the motor. She tuts as I shed muck inside her neat wee Chevette and drives back to Belfast without speaking, depositing me at a house on Servia Street. Liam opens the door, waves her a thank you; she returns with a curt nod and leaves.

'Who's that frosty cow?'

'Cumann na mBan.'

'Oh.'

'And you'd be frosty too if you'd to waste the morning rescuing AWOL volunteers. In.'

He leads me into the kitchen. I follow, grim thoughts twisting my stomach, apologies burning my throat.

'So?'

I mutter, 'Sorry.'

'Sorry? Jesus Christ, Caoilainn, that's not good enough.' He kicks a chair leg. 'We were thinking you'd been lifted. Rory and Ciaran've been up all night, mad with worrying.'

'I needed to be alone.'

'And you couldn't have told us?'

'I didn't think.'

'You bloody should have. I can't have volunteers going off like that, not even you.' He shakes his head. 'I'm suspending you pending a disciplinary.'

'You can't.'

'I can. I'm your OC.'

'Can't I explain first?'

He sighs and sags into the kicked chair. 'Go on.'

Briege's announcement cowers in a dark corner of me. I tell him I'm still upset over Aiden, it was a temporary attack of grief. Liam softens, reaching for my hand. I don't deserve sympathy. Shame scalds my face. I dodge his concerned gaze, concentrate on not crying. Say again, sincerely, that I'm sorry and ask for mercy. If I lose the right to fight there's nothing left for me.

'We'll forget the disciplinary but you're still suspended.'

'If you're going to do that you might as well charge me with something, otherwise let me do my job.'

'Your head's not right. You're no use to us in a state.'

'I'm not in a state. I bollocksed up but it won't happen again.'

'I'm worried.'

'There's no need.'

'There is if you're putting yourself and your unit at risk.' He studies me, trying to see through me. 'There's no shame in needing a break, you know. We all get there some times.'

'That's why I took off last night but it's dealt with.'

He leans back. 'Jesus, Caoilainn, you do my head in sometimes. When you're good you're better than most but when you do shite like this it terrifies me.' He taps his fingers on the table, Morse-coded thoughts. I pray silently. 'Fine, get back to your unit. I'll have to tell Rory, but it'll stop between us this time.'

I tell Rory myself, and apologise to Ciaran, saying that it was a family thing. They are too nice about it. We're settling in to watch the six o'clock news when Danny appears.

'Caoilainn, have you a minute?'

I look up. Briege is hovering behind him in the doorway. I go to her without a word, taking her into the kitchen.

'You shouldn't have come here.'

'I wanted to see you,' she says. Her face is pale, making her red hair flame against milky skin. 'I'm not quitting the Movement. They've said they'll put me in the education department. I can run training lectures until the baby comes then take as much time as I need. Afterwards Connor's said he'll take over with the wee 'un and I'll be back to work, maybe intelligence.' She rushes the words out. 'I know it's unusual but Connor said this way we're both helping and he needs that.'

She believes my anger is at her putting something else before the Cause. I can't tell her what it really is: the wrong shade of green.

'I thought you'd be happy for us.'

'I am.'

'It doesn't sound like it.' Tears brim her eyes.

I feel like a proper bitch but it's suddenly very raw and I can't heal it; if I don't amputate it'll kill me.

'There's just a lot going on here. I haven't time for fussing over you having a baby.'

Briege bites her bottom lip. 'Of course. I'm sorry.'

'Get Danny to walk you back.'

Time doesn't ease the pain but practice makes it easier to ignore. I blinker myself to the grief, knowing it's still there.

The days count down through November and into December. Ciaran pins an advent calendar above the fireplace in our latest safe house. Behind the first door is an empty manger, the second reveals a heavenly star, the third is an angel with feathery wings. I dread the fourth.

# Belfast—4th December, 1984

A year ago today I was unaware the end of the world was coming. It's my first thought when I wake up hours before dawn, uncertain I was sleeping. I stay in bed, smoking and staring at the ceiling, trying to conjure Aiden's face in the curls of vapour that drift away from me, wondering if I'll be able to go to his grave later.

The door bangs, Ciaran leaving for his lunchtime shift. Alone now, I struggle up. In the bathroom I stand under a cold shower, numbing myself. It doesn't help.

I sit at the table, tea going cold, suffocating in the silence, eyes flicking from object to object, mind fighting itself to remember and forget.

There's a knock at the door.

One of the Fianna lads is on the step in his St Michael's blazer.

'Mrs Murphy says there's a Brit sniper across the way from her.'

'Shouldn't you be in school?'

'It's break. What'll I tell her, about the sniper?'

'Get to school, Eoin.'

'Aren't you gonna do something?' His freckly face screws into an angry scowl.

His rage is infectious. I see Aiden, crumpled, bloodied: dead.

*The IRA volunteer acts most of the time on his own initiative.*

'Leave it with me.' I slam the door, press up against it and rub at the tight band constricting my forehead.

Minutes later I'm walking up the road, an empty rucksack over my shoulder, heading for the butcher's.

Fred acknowledges me with a nod as I cross the shop, pushing through the door to the back; queuing housewives throw curious glances my way.

I dodge the dangling carcasses in the cold store, moving out to the slaughterhouse in the yard. Fred doesn't do his own slaughtering anymore; the shed is our emergency weapons dump.

Inside the windowless shack fluorescent strip lights judder awake, illuminating the gore-stained floor. The stench of old blood, fishy and rotten, makes me gag. Squatting in a corner, I prise up the floorboards and rake around the hole until a plastic bag rustles in my fingers. Hauling it out, I peel back the polythene keeping the damp from an AR-15 and a half full magazine. Broken down, it'll fit in my rucksack. Fingers shaking, I drag bloody air into my lungs, exhale and recite the drill: check the chamber; shoot the bolt; press the pins through; pull from the other side; click the barrel free. I do the rear take down pin but fumble the front pivot pin, not pulling it through far enough to release the barrel. Jesus, a recruit two days into basic training can do this. I put the gun down, take another breath; get it apart.

'Managing, love?' Fred asks from the doorway.

'Yeah. Any chance of me borrowing your car?'

'I took it round to Mick's yesterday, brakes are knackered. If they've sorted it help yourself.'

The garage is a two minute walk away; the Divis Flats, where Mrs Murphy and the Brit sniper are eyeballing each other, is twenty. Even if Fred's car isn't drivable there'll be another I can borrow. Urgency rakes my chest with jagged claws. I have to get the bastard: for Aiden.

At the garage Fred's Vauxhall is on the forecourt. I poke my head into the workshop.

'Mick?'

He emerges from the loo, fag dangling.

'Hiya, Caoilainn, everything alright?'

'Fine. You sorted Fred's brakes?'

'Aye.'

'Grand. I'm just borrowing it for a wee job. He said it's OK.'

Danny rolls out from beneath a Beetle. 'What's up?'

'Nothing. Go back to work.'

He peels off his overalls.

'I said go back to work.'

'No.'

He charges past. I chase but he's already in the driving seat when I emerge into weak winter sun. Yanking the door open, I seize his sleeve.

'Get out.'

'No.' He grips the steering wheel.

'Jesus, I've not got time for this.'

'So get in.'

'You best do it if you're in a hurry,' Mick advises.

Fuck sake. I get in the passenger side. 'You're to stay in the car or I'll have you bollocked for disobeying an order. Divis Flats.'

Danny nods and starts the engine.

He parks in front of Mrs Murphy's block.

The lift is knackered again; I pound up the stairs. She opens the door as I'm running down the walkway.

'Caoilainn, grand, it's yourself. Away in.'

She's a fierce old Republican. Her husband was anti-treaty during the Civil War and pity help Dev's immortal soul when she gets to heaven. She leads me to the bedroom. Net curtains swish and billow at the open window.

'He's across the way. I saw him moving about and knew something was up; that flat's been empty this past month. Here.' She offers me a pair of field glasses, her Dermot's from his flying column days.

Adjusting the focus, I see the sniper stretched out on a table at the window, squinting through the scope of his rifle.

'Can you get him from here?' she asks.

I gauge the distance: six hundred yards at least.

'Hope so.'

'Good girl.' She pats my arm. 'I'll put the kettle on.' She slips out.

I check the sniper again, making sure he's not about to wrap in and go. He's motionless in his firing position. Calmly, I dig the rifle from the bag and reassemble it without fumbling. In a minute he'll be dead and next 4th December there'll be two of us waking up alone, grief suffocating us.

'There you go.' Mrs Murphy sets a china cup and saucer on the windowsill.

Clicking the magazine into place, I stare at her.

'I'll not put you off, will I? Sure, I'd like to see you hit the so-and-so.'

My cheeks flame at the thought of Mrs Murphy witnessing this killing. I bollock myself. He's an enemy soldier: a legitimate target. She knows it's my duty as a volunteer to shoot him. He knows it too. But the hungry gnawing inside me that wants him dead and someone else aching with emptiness makes me know it's not duty or patriotism or faith with the Cause that will have me pull the trigger today.

'Are you alright, love?'

I can't not do this, for all the right, and the wrong, reasons.

'Fine.'

I crouch at the window, bracing the rifle against my shoulder and resting on the sill. The sight isn't telescopic so I take another look with the binoculars for reference, then aim and fire.

My shot cracks the air, singeing a blackened hole through the net.

'Did you get him?'

I snatch the binoculars but before I raise them there's a reply to my shot. We duck; the bullet crunches into the wall above and to the left of our window.

Shit.

He knows I'm here; he'll be on the radio: 'Shots fired.' Half the BA could be kicking Mrs Murphy's door down in minutes. Protocol says I get out now.

'Shite, Caoilainn, you can do it,' Mrs Murphy encourages.

I sight along the barrel, centring the sniper's window in the standard sight: fire again.

Two shots crack back. The second shatters the window, spraying me with glass.

'Fuck!' I recoil, glance at Mrs Murphy. 'Sorry for the language.'

'Have a drink of tea,' she suggests. 'My Dermot was after saying you need to steady yourself for these things.'

Hand shaking I get the cup to my lips, blistering my tongue on the scalding liquid. I should already be gone. When I set my cup down tea slops into the saucer.

I rub my sweaty palms onto my jeans. Either I get him or he gets me, nothing else is viable now. Mrs Murphy steps up beside me, training the field glasses on the opposite window.

'I'll direct you,' she offers.

I fire.

'It hit the brickwork. Go a smidge lower.'

I fire again. The bullet flies from the muzzle.

I fly with it become it spinning and diving across the space between the flats air rushing past me the velocity making me feel like I'm boring through solid rock the world blurs into blue sky grey concrete the target rises up I close on it details emerge the pale lines of cement between the bricks a green window frame the paint flaked patches of dry dead wood exposed a face smeared with camouflage paint the eyes young straining I strike the forehead between them with a jolt and spin down into the warm moist brain tissue coming to rest against the back of his skull my energy dissipated by the distance and the impact.

'Got the bugger! Maith thú*!' Mrs Murphy whoops, lowering the binoculars.

I sit up, listening for boots thumping towards us, the crunch of a door splintering, voices screaming, 'Hands up!' There's only a post-apocalypse silence. My mouth is dry; I drain the teacup.

'Do you want another, love?'

'I best go.'

Sitting cross-legged below the window I unload and disassemble the gun before wiping off any prints and packing it, crushed by a tightening circle of urgency.

Two minutes later I'm running to the car. Tossing the bag in the boot, I open the driver's door.

'Shove over.'

Danny clambers across.

'Did you get him?'

'Aye.'

'Grand.'

'Yeah. Let's go.'

---

* Well done

I u-turn in the quad between the blocks, pulling onto the main road.

Two Saracens are parked snout to snout across the street. I jam on the brakes.

'Fuck.'

'Are they for us?' Danny's words quiver.

'I didn't get him with the first shot. He must've radioed backup,' I confess.

Two foot patrols flank the car. A soldier, captain's epaulettes, climbs from a Saracen clutching a loud hailer.

'Get out of the vehicle with your hands up.'

'What're we going to do?' Danny whimpers.

'Unless you're wanting to be shot we're gonna get out.'

'But the gun?'

'What gun?'

'In the boot, you...'

'What gun?' I repeat. 'As far as those bastards know we've been visiting a wee ould woman, taking her shopping, in a borrowed car. Whatever's in the boot's nothing to do with us. That's what you tell 'em, Danny. Mrs Murphy'll back us. Apart from that you say nothing, not a fucking thing, OK?'

'Get out of the vehicle now. You have five seconds before we open fire.' The captain's words echo robotically.

'Caoilainn?' Danny bleats my name.

'They can only hold us a week. Get through it with your mouth shut and that'll be the end of it.' I forbid myself to think about what'll happen when they realise he's an O'Neill.

'Get out of the vehicle. This is your final warning.'

'And for Christ sake, keep your hands where they can see them. Don't give them any excuse, Danny.'

Swinging open my door, I throw him a final look. His face is white but his jaw is tight, the muscle along it flexing under the strain. I mouth, 'sorry.' He nods and opens his door.

Half a dozen squaddies have drawn up to my side of the car. I plant my feet so I can stand without hands to propel me up and, arms raised, climb out.

The squaddies are in full battle dress, aiming their SLRs at our heads. I run my eyes over each of them; they blink their surprise at the sight of a wee lassie, her hands raised. For five seconds we're locked in a tableau. Then one of them steps forwards, gesturing with his weapon.

'Hands on your head. Get on the ground.'

I lie in the road, grains of tarmac grazing my cheek. As soon as I'm down boots stampede over. Hands grab my arms, twisting them behind my back. I'm dragged off the floor and over to the nearest wall, thrown, face first, against it. A boot kicks my legs apart. They pat me down, rough hands pawing me; I remember Colm's tentative frisking the night I was Green Booked. A year ago today he was going about things with Aiden in East Tyrone.

My jacket is yanked off and tossed away. I hear the buttons click as it lands on the pavement. My right leg is hauled up, my boot unlaced and tossed too, then the left. The paving slabs are marble-cold through my socks. Someone turns me so I'm facing the road.

A crowd has gathered, wives with wee 'un on doorsteps, men hanging from windows; witnesses preventing us being shot in the street. I'm grateful for their protection but wish they weren't seeing what a balls up I've made of today.

Squaddies search the car, one looking underneath, two more crawling inside. A third opens the boot. He retrieves the rucksack.

'What's in this?' he yells to me.

I shrug and look for Danny, see him further up the road, also against the wall, also stripped of his boots and jacket.

'You, what's in this?' The squaddie points at Danny.

He copies my shrug. The private takes the bag to his captain who peers inside for one full second before striding to me. He hold the bag under my nose. Gunpowder fumes assault my nostrils.

'This yours?'

'No.'

'This?' He pulls out the lower half of the gun.

'No.'

'The car?'

'No.'

He goes to Danny, repeats the questions, gets the same answers. The bag is thrust onto a private and the order barked:

'Get the RUC out here.' He crosses back to me. 'Name?'

I don't reply.

'Name?'

I say nothing.

'You find her ID?' the captain asks the private who searched me.

'No, sir.'

'Jesus Christ.' He leans towards me. He had something garlicky for tea last night. 'What. Is. Your. Name?' The words are loud, well spaced, how Brits speak to foreigners. 'We'll find out at Castlereagh so just tell us now. It'll make things easier.'

'For you.'

'If you weren't hiding anything you'd tell us. We will find out,' he threatens.

I have no file, no paperwork in the north saying I was married to an O'Neill or that I even exist. The only way they'll find out is if someone tells them. Guilt crushes air from my lungs. If I won't say who I am they'll try beating it out of Danny. But our mission now is resistance, our weapon defiance. I have no choice.

'Good luck with that.'

He glares at me. I smile politely. He huffs over to Danny and reels off the questions. Danny doesn't reply either but for him it's token resistance; the peelers'll recognise him, match his prints. I look away.

Five squaddies surround me. One glances to his captain, sees him busy with Danny and grabs me round the throat, pressing me almost through the wall.

'You fucking shot him, didn't you, ya Fenian bitch?' His hand chokes words in my throat. 'I could fucking smell the gun.' His mouth twists into a snarl, his eyes are wide, wild.

I can't defend myself against his angry grief; it's our common ground.

The others have closed round us, shielding him as he throttles me. I shift my gaze, fixing on the houses across the road.

'Leave it, Gaz,' says another, tugging his mate's sleeve. 'She's not worth three days in the glasshouse. Anyway, her boyfriend's to blame.'

The pressure round my neck eases. Gaz drops back into line. I turn my head to check on Danny. The captain is strolling to the nearest Saracen; Danny is lost behind a scrum of soldiers. Dull thuds, punctuated by groans, rise from the melee. They think he's the sniper; I was driving, that's all. The scrum folds in on itself as they knock Danny over, land kicks, belt him with their rifles. I can't see properly but I know that's what's happening. I step forwards. A muzzle is jabbed in my side.

'Don't, hinny. I dinna want to have to shoot you, like,' says Gaz's mate in a Geordie accent that takes me back to somewhere I'd forgotten I'd ever been.

'He's done nothing. Leave him.'

Their wall becomes granite-hard.

I'm twelve. We're outside the Houses of Parliament. The UK has vetoed a UN General Assembly motion to expel South Africa over apartheid. My placard reads 'End UK Trade Deals With Racists'...

'Dad, I'm hungry. And cold.'

'I know, Kaylynn, but we've got to be here.'

'Why?'

'To show our government we won't put up with their mercenary, immoral trade dealings with fascist regimes guilty of crimes against humanity.'

'Mum, can't we go soon?'

'Love, you know we've got a duty to stand up to injustice, especially when it's our own politicians corrupting the system. It's sickening, Kaylynn, thinking we're trading with barbaric bigots to satisfy capitalist greed.'

'Why do they do that, Mum?'

'Power can be a potent poison, love.'

'Susan, they're sending in the police. Take my arm, Kaylynn, this might be a rough one.'

'Dad, I'm scared.'

'Don't be. Come on, we'll sing, show them we're not afraid. We shall overcome.'

'We shall overcome.'

'That's it, love. Louder. Make them hear how strong we are.'

'We shall overcome some day.'…

Singing was always their final salvo. I know doing it here, now, is reckless, something no self-respecting volunteer should do in this situation. But I have to. It's my fucking fault Danny's lifted, getting pulped with worse to come. I arm myself with words, start singing:

'Oh, Paddy dear, and did you hear, the news that's going round?

The shamrock is forbid by law to grow on Irish ground.

No more Saint Patrick's day we'll keep, his colour last be seen:

For there's a bloody law agin the wearing of the green!'

The soldiers exchange glances. I raise my voice for the next verse, hoping the rebel song will keep Danny's rebel spirit burning.

'Oh, I met with Napper Tandy, and he took me by the hand,

And he says, 'How's poor ould Ireland and how does she stand?

She's the most distressed country that ever I have seen:

For they're hanging men and women for the wearing of the green.'

Voices from the watching crowd chime in with the last four words; the song flounders, a swan trying to get airborne.

I fumble for the next verse:

'And… and…'

'And since the colour we must wear is England's cruel red,

Ould Ireland's sons will ne're forget the blood that they have shed.'

The rich tenor voice that gives me the lost line is Gaz's mate's. His eyes meet mine. Across the road the song swoops skyward:

'Then take the shamrock from your hat and cast it on the sod.

It'll take root and flourish still though under foot 'tis trod.'

Gaz's mate bends down, his lips brushing my ear.

'We know Ireland's history as well as you, hinny. We're not just thugs with guns. We're doing a job, that's all. It's not our fault, or yours.'

236

I glance at Danny. He's on his knees, spitting blood. Whose fucking fault is it?

'You cannae blame us for getting wound up, like, not when we've lost a mate,' he adds, following my gaze.

He's right. I can't, don't, blame them.

The singing soars for the final refrain:

'…We'll live and die still wearing of the green.'

Sirens shoot down the final notes. RUC Land Rovers squeal up, spilling peelers in riot gear. One goes to the army captain, who offers over my bag, explaining. The watching locals are silent, grim faces knowing what's to come.

We're cuffed and thrown, one into each van, to be driven to Castlereagh interrogation centre. I twist my head, looking for Danny who cranes to see me. One eye is swollen shut and his lip split but he manages to wink.

The interrogation room is small, dim and bare; a table, three chairs, no window. Sitting, hands cuffed in front of me, waiting, I run a finger round my neck, feeling for my locket but the chain was snapped off at the desk when they were printing and photographing me. I drop my hands, focus on recalling anti-interrogation techniques, wondering what I should paint. I decide on a massive landscape of Pearse's cottage rendered in thick oils, the Twelve Pins glowering in the distance, the lough dulled like old silver. Blank canvas prepped in my head, I mentally flick through the script, reminding myself of the acts and scenes in the play that will start, not with a rising curtain but an opening door.

The door bangs. Two Branch men enter. They, like most peelers, are locals, Prods. For them it's always personal. They want to break me. *When arrested a volunteer should expect the worst and be prepared for it.* They sit opposite. We're actors now, it's opening night and we're ready to headline in the drama of our own lives.

Cop 1: Name?

Me:

Cop 1: You know we'll find out.

Me:

Cop 2: Come on, love, tell us who you are and we'll have you home tucking the kiddies in bed tonight.

Me:

Cop 1: Tell us what you know and we'll sort this.

Me:

Cop 2: It was your boyfriend, wasn't it, did the shooting?

Me:

Cop 1: What were you doing at the Divis Flats?

Me: Visiting an old lady.

*(Cop 1 and Cop 2 exchange glances)*

Cop 1: Who?

Me: Mrs Murphy, number 347.

Cop 2: What were you doing?

Me: Taking her shopping.

Cop 1 *(sneering)*: Asked you to buy her an Armalite, did she?

Me:

Cop 2: Is the gun your boyfriend's.

Me: No.

Cop 2: Sure, it can't be yours?

Me: No.

Cop 1 *(banging on the table)*: Then who's is it?

Me: Dunno.

Cop 2: What about the car?

Me: Borrowed it.

Cop 2: From who?

Me:

Cop 1: We'll find out.

Me:

Cop 2: Are you a member of the IRA?

Me:

Cop 1: We'll find that out too.

Me *(shrugs)*:

Cop 2: You'll go away for a long time unless you help us. How will that be for you, your family? The kiddies? How many have you?

Me:

Cop 2: They'll be missing their mammy, won't they?

Me:

238

Cop 1 *(jumps up)*: Get this into your head, love: you are gonna talk to us. We'll make sure you do.

Me:

*(Cops 1 and 2 exit. Caoilainn stays in the chair at the table. Blackout)*

*(Lights up. Interrogation room. Caoilainn is in the chair at the table. Her appearance suggests she has been there several hours. Cop 2 enters with a plain clothes detective. They sit opposite her.)*

Cop 2: Are you ready to talk to us, love?

Caoilainn:

Detective: Let's go over today. You were asked to drive. That's all. You didn't know your boyfriend was going to shoot that poor wee soldier.

Caoilainn:

Detective: We know all about your boyfriend. He'll get twenty to life for murder. Help us and you'll not face the same.

Caoilainn:

Cop 2: Listen, love, you don't want my mate coming back. He's dead against you lot. There's no telling what he'll do.

Caoilainn:

Det: Help us help you.

Caoilainn:

*(Det and Cop 2 exchange glances.)*

Cop 2: Have one of these.

*(He puts cigarettes on the table. Caoilainn ignores them.)*

Det: Let's get these off you.

*(He removes Caoilainn's handcuffs.)*

Cop 2: Can we get you anything?

Caoilainn: A solicitor.

Cop 2: What about tea? Food? You must be hungry.

Caoilainn: Just the solicitor.

Det: Tell us who you are and we'll let your family know you're here.

Caoilainn:

Cop 2: You want to talk to us, so you do. I hate to think what'll happen if you don't.

Caoilainn:

Det *(to Cop 2)*: Put her in a cell. We'll get her boyfriend to spill his guts.

*(Det replaces handcuffs and drags Caoilainn from chair, shoves her onto Cop 2 who takes her arm and leads her from the room. Blackout.)*

*(Lights up. Caoilainn is in a cell, on a metal-framed bed with no mattress. Cell is completely bare apart from the bed. Lights are brilliantly blinding. Loud static like a radio tuned to a non-station can be heard. Someone bangs or kicks on the cell door. Blackout.)*

*(Lights up. Interrogation room. Caoilainn sits at the table. Cop 1 stands by the door. Detective enters, carrying a file. He sits beside Caoilainn.)*

Det: Your boyfriend's come to his senses. Told us everything for a deal. But I'm feeling sorry for you. Now's your chance to save yourself some jail time. *(He waves the file at her.)* Tell us everything and I'll not hand this to my governor. I'll give him your statement instead. You'll be the one with the deal.

Caoilainn: Is my solicitor here yet?

Det: Love, you've no need of a solicitor. This is the only way you'll get out while you're still young. You're what, nineteen? twenty? Help us and you'll only do a few years; still time to have a life, a family.

Caoilainn: What's my name?

Det *(laughs nervously)*: Have you forgotten?

Caoilainn: Have you found out?

*(Detective slams folder onto table, bangs his fist.)*

Det: Get her out of my fucking sight.

*(Cop 1 pulls Caoilainn up, bends to say something to her as he does. Caoilainn punches him. He yells. Policemen rush into the room. Caoilainn is swallowed up by them. Blackout.)*

*(Lights up. Cell. Lights still brilliantly blinding; white noise louder than before. Caoilainn lies on her back on the mattressless bed. One eye is shut by a purple bruise, her lip is swollen. Blood crusts her nostrils. She is awake. Voices shout through the door: slut, whore, bitch, cunt. She doesn't move. Blackout.)*

\*

*(Lights up. Cell. Caoilainn still on the bed. Lighting and noise as before. She stands, walks to the door and bangs on it. The peephole is opened; an eye appears. The door opens. A female RUC constable enters. )*

WPC: What is it?

Caoilainn: I need the loo.

*(WPC slams the door. Caoilainn waits. The WPC returns with a slop bucket which she throws down.)*

WPC: Here.

*(Caoilainn eyes the WPC, the bucket then the WPC.)*

WPC: Need the Pope's permission to piss, do ya?

*(Caoilainn drops her jeans and pants, squats over the bucket, pisses into it. The WPC watches. Caoilainn stands, pulling up her clothes, picks the bucket and flings the contents at the WPC. She screams. Three male offices charge into the cell. Blackout.)*

*(Lights up. Interrogation room. Caoilainn stands against the wall. Cop 1 stands in front of her. Cop 2 sits at the table, smoking.)*

Cop 1 *(shouts)*: Whore. Slut. Fenian fucker. I bet all the lads in the 'Ra've had a ride on you, haven't they? Pass you around, sticking their wee patriotic pricks up your cunt, don't they? Doing your bit for the Cause? Letting them fuck you front and back.

Caoilainn *(looking over Cop 1's shoulder at the wall)*:

Cop 1: Let's see what I'm missing, eh?

*(He strokes Caoilainn's cheek. Moves his hand down her neck and chest, squeezes her breasts. Begins unbuttoning her shirt.)*

Cop 1: Aye, you Taigs'll fuck anyone. That pure virgin stuff's shite, so it is. Anything for a ride.

*(Caoilainn's shirt is unbuttoned. Cop 1 slips a hand inside, fondling her breasts. He moves it down to her jeans, unfastens her flies and gropes inside.)*

Cop 1: Shall I see if you're wet? Bet ya are. Dying to have a go of a proper man, aren't you? Not them pathetic little shites yous've got in the Provos.

Caoilainn: *(looks directly into Cop 1's eyes.)*: Go on, so. Fuck me. And when I'm out of here I'll make sure all your peeler mates know you've had yourself a Taig. What'll they think then, when they know you've had your dick up a Fenian cunt?

*(Cop 1 snatches his hand back. Strikes Caoilainn in the face, twice, begins punching her stomach and chest. Cop 2 rushes over and pulls him off. Blackout.)*

*(Lights up. Interrogation room. Caoilainn and two different RUC officers sit round the table. The policemen smoke. Caoilainn is wearing only her bra and knickers. The bruises on her face are yellowing. Around her ribs and stomach are fresh purple ones.)*

Cop 3 *(offering cigarettes)*: Sure you wouldn't like one?

Caoilainn *(stares at the wall behind him)*:

Cop 3: A hard bitch, you are.

Cop 4: Let's see how hard.

*(He throws photographs onto the table. They show severed and bloodied limbs, torsos and heads. Caoilainn continues staring at the wall.)*

Cop 4 *(shouts)*: Look at them!

Caoilainn *(doesn't move)*:

*(Cop 4 comes round to Caoilainn, bends her over the photographs.)*

Cop 4: Fucking look at them. It's your fucking handiwork.

*(Caoilainn looks but doesn't react.)*

Cop 4: You're murderers, baby-killers, cowardly, brutal, vicious thugs that slaughter innocent people and pass it off as political.

Cop 3 *(gathering photos into a pile, leaving an armless torso uppermost)*: Look, love, I understand. Yous think you're fighting a war. You've been brainwashed since you were a wee 'un: Ireland's right to rise in arms. I admire the sentiment. My granddaddy was one of you, back when there was a war to fight. But those days are over. Don't you want peace for Ireland?

Caoilainn: Yes.

Cop 3: Then help us. Tell us what you know.

Caoilainn: What day is it?

Cop 4: If you're thinking of getting out soon, forget it. We've enough to charge you for the gun, killing that soldier. You're going away for the rest of your life for the murdering whore you are.

Caoilainn: So charge me and let me see my solicitor.

Cop 3: You're in no position to give orders, love.

*(Cops 3 and 4 exit, leaving the photos on the table. Caoilainn flicks through them. She cries. Blackout.)*

*(Lights up. Cell, bed removed. Caoilainn, now dressed, is curled up on the floor. Lights and noise as before. The door opens. Two officers rush in, grab her, push her against the wall, twist her arms behind her, handcuff her wrists and march her from the room. Blackout.)*

*(Lights up. Caoilainn is marched into a room with a mirror stretched across one wall. She is made to stand facing it, flanked by the two officers. One grabs her hair, yanks her head up. Pause for ten seconds.)*

Voiceover: OK. Take her back.

*(Caoilainn is dragged from the room by the officers. Blackout.)*

*(Lights up. Interrogation room. Caoilainn, bruises visible, sits at the table. Glass of water on the table. She raises it with cuffed hands, drinks. Her hands shake. Cop 2 and detective enter. Det carries a folder. Both sit. Caoilainn puts the glass down.)*

Det: Isn't this the thing? We've gone from no name to three. What is it we should call you; Kaylynn Ryan, Caoilainn Devoy or Caoilainn O'Neill?

Caoilainn *(raises head, stares)*:

Det: We've had you identified by a reliable source, someone who knows all about you. He's done us proud this time. Shall we talk about Hyde Park? Or would you rather start with a wee history lesson? Your granddaddy, the 1916 legend?

Caoilainn *(looks away)*:

Det: Aye, we know everything. Probably more than yourself.

Caoilainn: It's Caoilainn Devoy.

Det: Grand. Well, it's like this, Caoilainn, you're going down for the murder of that wee soldier, you and your Fenian brother-in-law. And with what our man's told us, we'll add conspiracy to cause explosions, possession of explosives, eleven other murders and we'll throw in membership of a proscribed organisation, shall we?

Caoilainn: Can I see my solicitor now?

Det: Wouldn't you like to know what else we've found out, first? Maybe something more recent, your ma and da, *(thumbs the file)* Charlie and Fiona?

Caoilainn: Murdered by yous lot.

Det: That what you've been told? Ach, I'm sorry for you, having nothing but lies to believe.

Caoilainn:

Det: But I'll tell you the truth, so I will. My wee favour to you, giving you something to think on in that eight-by-ten that's waiting for you. *(He lights cigarette, offering Caoilainn the pack.)* No? Suit yourself. So this is what we've learnt from our man. Your da kept up the family trade, IRA lifelong, so he was. 'Til they surrendered in '62. Then what's a man like him good for? He's been broken by the jail, given his life to the Cause and suddenly there's no Cause? Still, he's a pretty young wife, wee 'un coming soon. So he thinks on a fresh start for yous: America. But your ma, she's one for running about with a gun in her knicker leg, two more in her shopping basket. Won't hear of leaving, deserting the Cause. Your da knows she'll only go when there's nothing left of the 'Ra for her to mother. So he has a think, figures out a way he could mebbe do it. It's risky, mind; I reckon seeing you born's what decides him on it 'cos he starts talking soon after. Talking to people like me, telling us what we're wanting to hear. And don't we start finding weapons dumps, collaring men we've been after for years? Aye, Caoilainn, your da was a tout.

Caoilainn: The hell he was.

Det: Sure, you'll not want to believe it. It's true, though. And there's more. Doesn't your da go and make the biggest bollocks up of things? Tells us where there's a certain cache, gives us a date when there'll be certain fellas there we'd like locked up. Only he doesn't realise your ma's gonna be there too. There's a shoot out. Your poor, dutiful, stupid mammy gets herself killed. Eejits should've surrendered but yous prefer your heroes dead.

Caoilainn *(stares at him)*:

Det: Your da got her killed. Then what? All our man could tell us was that they found your daddy in the backyard, his brains making a mess of the begonias, his trusty gun beside him. Be nice to think it was his guilt killed him but mebbes his comrades found out what he'd done. What d'ya think your precious Army would've done if they had, Caoilainn? And now you'll spend the rest of your life in jail wondering why the fuck you're there for the Cause that made you an orphan.

*(Blackout.)*

# Castlereagh Interrogation Centre—
## 12<sup>th</sup> December, 1984

They put me in a fresh cell. It's quiet and the lighting is subdued. There's a bed, blankets and pillows. A WPC brings soggy toast and lukewarm tea. I force the food down, drain the cup too quickly and lie on the bed, grateful for the exhaustion that separates me from the pain in my body, and my head. Sleep comes. Ghosts hunt me through my dreams.

A clanking wakes me. The WPC is back.

'Your brief's here.'

She escorts me along a corridor, into a room. There's a window. Outside the sky is light. At a table sits a man, late twenties, in a crinkled navy suit, tie pulled slack and top button undone. He comes towards me, hand outstretched.

'Thank you, Constable,' he says.

The door closes with a soft click.

He takes my hand in both of his and presses it warmly.

'Mrs O'Neill, I'm Patrick Michael Duffy. I've been engaged to represent you.'

'By who?'

'Sinn Fein, Mrs O'Neill.'

'Don't call me that.'

'May I call you Caoilainn, so?'

His accent is gentle, university Irish with a hint of Limerick or Kerry. I cling to the two syllables that are all that's left of me. He steers me to a chair and retakes his seat.

'Your mother-in-law sent this.' He deposits a bag on the table. 'A change of clothes, cigarettes, chocolate.'

I notice there's an ashtray and a packet of Players on the table, a jug of water and two glasses. He pours water for us both. I take the cigarettes and light one with trembling fingers.

'Are you alright?' he asks, pushing the glass to me.

'Fine.'

'You haven't signed?'

'No.'

He nods. 'You're stronger than most.'

'I've had to be.' I've forgotten how to be anything else.

He smoothes his neat brown hair, running a trim nail down the ruler-straight side parting. 'I'm sure you have. Shall we talk about the charges?' He pulls a notepad from his briefcase.

'Is Danny alright?'

'He is. He didn't sign either.'

I feel like a puppet who's had her strings cut. I sag into the chair, exhaling smoke and relief.

'The charges?' he prompts.

'What's there to talk about, Mr Duffy?'

'Plenty.' He smiles, tightens his tie. 'And call me Patrick.' He rubs his shaved-smooth chin. Aftershave wafts across the table.

My hair is itchy with grease and my skin with dirt. I'm rank; sweat and blood. I fold my arms against my chest.

'They've a tout.'

'So it seems.' He scribbles something on the pad, tilts it towards me. It says, 'They are listening. Do you speak Irish?'

'Yes.'

'Grand.' He switches to Irish, speaking so softly I have to bend my head close to his. 'Any ideas who?'

I write on the paper 'Brian', circling the speech marks, hoping he'll understand.

He continues, in Irish, 'Someone you worked with?'

Conscious of uncleaned teeth, the sour-milk taste in my mouth, I nod.

'No doubts?'

'He's the only one who,' I figure out a coded way of explaining, 'went to the park but not the shop.'

Patrick nods. 'Don't worry. You didn't do what they're claiming. Their informant is mistaken.' He stares at me with steady grey eyes.

'It doesn't matter. The gun, the soldier...?'

Patrick grins. 'They're after charging you both with murder for that.'

'I'll confess. Danny didn't...'

'No!' He says the word sharply, in English, before returning to Irish. 'They're making a mistake, one we'll not be pointing out. There's a precedent: Rose McAllister, McAdorey

247

then she was. She and her son were both charged with possession of a single gun with intent to endanger life. The judge threw out her case; two people cannot both intend to endanger life with one weapon. And that being so neither can two people commit murder with one weapon.'

I shake my head. 'It's too risky. I can't let Danny...'

'If you confess they'll change Danny's charges to accessory. Sentences for that are nearly as long. You have to trust me, Caoilainn.'

'What does that mean?' I hiss.

'I don't want to give you false hope. There's a fight ahead but,' he smiles, 'we've a chance of winning.'

# London—14<sup>th</sup> December, 1984

## Blonde Bomber Accused of Slaughtering Eleven Woman Held Over Hyde Park Attack

Police in Northern Ireland have announced they are holding a woman over the 1982 IRA bomb attack on Hyde Park and Regent's Park.

Kay Lynne Ryan, (21) was arrested following the shooting of a British soldier in West Belfast earlier this month. Found in possession of a semi-automatic weapon, Miss Ryan was detained under the Prevention of Terrorism Act, pending investigation into the carnage in the royal parks.

The bombing killed eleven members from two regiments as well as causing the death of seven horses taking part in the changing of the guard ceremony. This is the first arrest in connection with the attack.

Miss Ryan, thought to have strong Republican connections, is known to have grown up in England and it is believed that she used a fraudulently obtained British passport to travel to London for the bombings.

Photographed by journalists as she was remanded to Armagh Women's Prison, Miss Ryan, a petite blonde, defiantly confronted reporters, gesturing to bruising on her face, understood to have been sustained when she resisted arrest. She refused to comment on the charges against her.

Addressing the Commons last night Leon Brittan, Home Secretary, confirmed he would seek the swiftest possible response from the Justice Department in this case. He said, 'The families of those who lost their lives in July 1982 have already waited too long for justice.' The trial is expected to begin early in the new year.

Dr Malcolm Devine, a criminal psychologist who provides mental assessments for the Home Office in terrorism cases said, 'I have no doubt Miss Ryan, and other girls like her, are duped into joining terror organisations, brainwashed by boyfriends. It is time that ruthless terror groups stopped hiding behind these girls who are as much victims as those injured in their attacks.'

In 1973 the arrest of sisters Dolours and Marian Price for the Old Bailey bombing shocked the world. They were sentenced to twenty years for their role in the attack. It is likely that Miss Ryan would serve a similar period if convicted.

# Armagh Jail—25th December, 1984

I'm on B wing, where remand prisoners are held: in solitary. Special Branch don't want me having any free association, even though that's part of the regime since the no-wash protest ended in '81. Patrick has petitioned prison officials but, desperate to crowbar out the confession that'll make their jobs easier, they won't budge. Neither will I. They're doing their duty. So am I.

Mairead Farrell, who's OC here, is the only Republican prisoner I've met. She's serving fourteen years for an attempting bombing on a Belfast hotel in 1976. Before that she was a medical student. She's been twice to my cell, explaining that I'm to communicate with the prison authorities only through her and checking on me. She's furious about my solitary, has seen the governor about it. He says it's not his ruling. She's worried I'll break and perches on my bed, tucking dark hair behind neat ears, a half-smile on her lips, her young face old. She chats, keeping me afloat. When she goes I sink down again. Poisonous thoughts course in my veins. I apply a tourniquet, stopping them reaching my brain, killing me. Lying on the bed I paint the out-of-reach ceiling; cliffs and mountains, loughs and seascapes, wee white cottages, friendly faces: anything peaceful. I crave gloopy oils, stiff brushes, finger-blacking charcoal. They won't even give me a fucking pencil.

Barb, the screw in charge of me, opens the cell.

'You've a visitor, lucky you,' she grunts.

I follow her along the empty wing. Everyone else is in the dining room, forcing down the drab Christmas fare.

She takes me to an interview room. Patrick is by the window, watching sleet swirl lethargically. He comes to me; Barb leaves.

'How are you?'

'Fine. How's Danny?'

'He's OK. Nora and Frank were up a couple of days ago. Said he's settling in, the lads are looking after him. I brought these.' He produces two packs of cigarettes. 'I've asked Nora to sort out some clothes for you, for the trial.'

I sink into a chair.

He withdraws some papers. 'We need to talk about your case. We'll be pleading 'not guilty', naturally.'

I nod.

'We've a date for it: January 18ᵗʰ.'

'That soon?'

He grimaces. 'I've tried stalling but dear old Baron Brittan is baying for your blood. However, they're going to try you on all charges here.'

'They're not extraditing me to England?'

He smiles and shakes his head. 'There's a row brewing over people arrested in the Six Counties being sent to mainland courts. It's complicated, political; some in the legal fraternity are arguing that if this is one united kingdom people should stand trial where they are detained. Having extradition orders between two parts of what is claimed as the same country is contradictory.'

I start shivering. Patrick takes his coat from his chair and drapes it round my shoulders before sitting next to me.

'Do you want your Christmas present?' He nods to the coat.

I slip a hand into the inside pocket and feel a hard paper knot which I transfer to my own pocket.

'But it could be to your advantage, being tried in a Diplock here where you'll only have the judge to contend with, especially given that they're sending one over from London to placate those who wanted you in an English dock facing an English jury.'

I snort. 'You think I've a better chance with an English judge?'

Patrick smiles. 'You might. His name's Haskell and he's a reputation for not suffering police incompetence.' He winks at me.

'You're sure about this business with the gun, this precedent?' I press again.

'Certain.'

'So Danny'll be alright?'

'Yes. It's only the one charge they have him on.'

'But I'll…'

'Be fine.' He squeezes my hand. 'Nollaig Shona.'

I roll the comm between the fingers of my other hand. Merry fucking Christmas.

I wait until the day screws have gone home to their fat children and lazy husbands, and the wing is locked down for the night before unfolding the comm. It's from Liam. I read the cramped writing three times, repetition making it real. I don't cry or cheer the news. I chew and swallow it, to keep the screws from finding it later.

# Newcastle, Co. Down—26th December, 1984

## IRA Shoot Informer
## Body Found on Cliff Path Near Minerstown

The body of a man has been found on a cliff path outside Minerstown. The man, identified as Brendan Gallagher, 35, had sustained two gunshot wounds to the back of the head. Police say he had been stripped and beaten before death. A note, left with the body, claimed he had been working as a British agent for the security services and warned against others becoming 'touts'.

A spokesman for the RUC said, 'We are investing the circumstances surrounding Mr Gallagher's death.'

No comment was made regarding the claim that Mr Gallagher was one of their informants.

The use of so-called 'supergrasses' to obtain convictions against those tried for political offences has been an area of controversy in recent years. In a 1984 report into the use of supergrasses former judge Lord Gifford denounced the system of accepting the statements of informants without any corroborating evidence, saying it was, 'not justice,' and, 'led to the telling of lies and the conviction of the innocent.'

# Belfast—18th January, 1985

Flashes pop as the Land Rover's doors open. A WPC helps me down, my manacled wrists denying me a handhold. I face the waiting press, expression neutral, no make-up, hair tied into a neat bun, the skirt and blouse Nora sent only slightly crumpled during the journey from Armagh. Questions are fired at me: Will you be entering a 'not guilty' plea? Is it true the IRA killed an informant in an attempt to derail your trial? Are you the Hyde Park bomber?

'You're famous, love,' a peeler mocks.

'Infamous, ya mean,' another replies. 'Sure, whatever happens, the Provos'll not want you after this, not when your face's been plastered over every front page between here and London.'

I'm rushed through the scrum into Crumlin Road courthouse.

Patrick joins me in a side room, watching as I'm uncuffed and the WPC steps back, guarding the door.

'Have you a cigarette? They wouldn't let me smoke in the van.'

He gives me one. 'I brought you something.' He reaches into his pocket, brings his hand out, my chain wrapped around his fingers, the locket and ring suspended from it.

I drag deeply. 'How'd you get that?'

'Asked.' He fastens it round my throat. 'Fixed the catch for you.'

The court is held 'in camera', howling media hounds barred. Armed police guard every door. I'm led to the dock. Patrick smiles at me from his defence desk. Across the aisle from him the prosecution shuffle papers, heads bowed, lips moving urgently. My legs tremble. Struggling to stand for the judge's entrance, I reach for the locket, rubbing my thumb into the familiar, comforting dent.

The judge, Lord Haskell, glides through a panelled door and takes his throne.

'Be seated.'

The charges are read: eleven counts of murder; two counts of conspiring to cause an explosion with the intent of endangering life; two counts of the possession of explosives with the intent of endangering life; one count, jointly with Daniel Seamus O'Neill, of murder; one count, jointly with the aforementioned Daniel Seamus O'Neill, of the possession of a prohibited firearm with the intent to endanger life; one count of membership of a proscribed organisation, specifically the Provisional Irish Republican Army.

I never knew Danny's middle name was Seamus.

'Miss Devoy, do you intend to enter a plea?' Lord Haskell peers at me over half-moon spectacles.

Patrick rises. 'Your Honour, I will be entering the plea on behalf of my client: not guilty in response to all charges.'

Haskell removes his glasses, rubs the loose flesh around his eyeballs. Sighs.

'Very well.'

Heat creeps up my neck. I should be speaking out against the oppression of Ireland by foreign troops, proclaiming the right of Oglaigh na hEireann to take up arms. But that would be received as an admission of guilt. The Army Council want me cleared of all charges. My hand gropes for the chain.

I tune out the opening statements; Patrick's I've heard before and the prosecution add nothing new. A clock punctuates the silences between the words. Haskell listens, hands clasped. Evidence is presented: the Armalite; ballistic reports on the bullet dug from the squaddie's brain; written statements from the BA boys who lifted me and Danny and the arresting RUC officers, who, for their own safety, don't testify in person. Patrick calls Mrs Murphy who will declare my innocence with old lady credibility. Haskell waves his hand.

'Unnecessary, Mr Duffy; I've read Mrs Murphy's statement.'

'Your Honour,' Patrick protests.

Ignoring Patrick, Haskell turns to the prosecution.

'Mr Whittingham.'

The barrister leading the attack rises.

'May I assume you contribute to the revenue of Her Majesty's treasury?'

'Your Honour?'

'And, presumably, like everyone who pays their taxes, you prefer not to see that money squandered.'

'Yes, Your Honour, but I don't see...'

'Then perhaps you will explain to the court why you have wasted an inordinate sum on this trial, pressing ludicrous charges?'

'May I approach the bench, Your Honour?' Whittingham whimpers.

'You may not. You may explain to me how it is two people can both kill, or even conspire to kill with a single weapon.'

There is uproar. The clerk calls for order.

'The joint charge of one count of murder and associated charge of possessing an illegal firearm are hereby dismissed,' Haskell intones.

'Your Honour, I request an adjournment,' Whittingham shrieks.

'Denied.'

Patrick winks at me. I inhale deeply.

Lunch is called.

I'm returned to the side room where Patrick joins me.

'See?' he says, grinning.

'Aye, but...'

'But nothing. Eat something.' He produces a lunchbox, decorated with Mr Men characters, and offers me a cheese sandwich. I gag on the first bite and make do with three cigarettes and a glass of water.

Court resumes at 2 P.M. Brendan's anonymous statement is read, detailing the Hyde Park operation, right down to me pressing the button. The term 'trigger-woman' is used three times by a red-faced Whittingham. Memories crowd me: the boom; the chaos; the woman, her leg bleeding; paramedics and policemen scrabbling for survivors; the fallen horses, gunshots ending their pain. The room recedes until I'm looking at it through the wrong end of a telescopic sight. It shrinks down to a tiny dot. Disappears.

Aiden is running toward me, calling and waving. I start running too. As I draw near I see the stains on his clothes, dark and glistening. He falls. Behind him Brendan stands, gun in hand. I'm pulled back. Someone calls my name, a faint two-syllable whisper: Kee-lun, Kee-lun.

I open my eyes. Patrick's blurred face hovers above mine. I struggle for focus.

'Are you OK?'

I'm cramped up on the floor of the dock. The WPC peers over Patrick's shoulder. He lifts me.

'Your Honour, my client is clearly distressed. A recess, please?'

'Granted. Fifteen minutes,' Haskell says, holding up a pre-empting hand against Whittingham's objections.

Patrick helps me into the side room, asks the WPC for water. My head spins. A sticky flush crawls over my skin. I think I'm going to go again; blood drains away.

'Put your head between your knees,' Patrick advises.

I do. It helps.

'Can I have a cigarette?'

'Not until you eat.' Patrick takes a Mars bar from his Mr Men lunchbox.

I nibble half of it and he hands over his fags.

Someone taps on the door. Patrick opens it. I knock ash from the cigarette with jittery fingers.

'Your Honour!'

I spin round. Haskell is in the doorway.

'I wanted to see if your client is fit to continue. May I?' He gestures into the room and Patrick admits him.

I stand but Haskell waves me down.

'Miss Devoy, I'm prepared to adjourn until tomorrow if you are unwell.'

'I'd rather get this over with, please.'

He studies me, perhaps wondering if my faint is a defence ploy.

'If you're certain. I too would like this concluded as expediently as possible. Five minutes, Mr Duffy.' He leaves.

We return to the courtroom. The prosecution glare at me. I glare back.

Haskell reopens the proceedings, asks about Regent's Park: is it claimed the defendant planted the bomb? No. Made it?

No. What was her supposed role then? Planning and reconnaissance. The supporting evidence for this accusation? None, Your Honour. The Regent's Park charges are dismissed in ten minutes.

Haskell returns to the Hyde Park charges which are three murders, conspiracy to bomb and possession of explosives. My heart stutters. Cold guilt swamps me. *You are a volunteer in the Irish Republican Army, the legal representatives of the Irish people, and morally justified in carrying out a campaign of resistance.* The phrase 'morally justified' fades too quickly. I call up Sands' funeral, Daideo's false teeth, Cathy's bloodied sweater: the warmth of Aiden's lips.

Haskell enquires about their witness; is he present to testify?

'We request our witness's identity be protected,' Whittingham replies.

'That does not answer the question.'

'M'Lord, if I may...?'

'You may not. Answer my question: are you able to produce your informant?'

'No, Your Worship.'

'Why not?'

'Our witness is recently deceased.'

'Deceased?'

I shiver. Haskell leans back, drumming his fingertips together.

'So on charges that compel me to award no lesser sentence than lifetime imprisonment, you expect me to convict on the word of a dead man?'

'Your Honour, our witness was an extremely trustworthy source for twelve months. His accounts have been corroborated on a number of occasions.'

'But not this one?'

'Your Honour?'

'You have no physical evidence, nor even a secondary statement?'

Whittingham glances at his papers. 'No, Your Worship.'

'Are you, Mr Whittingham, familiar with the 1984 report by Lord Gifford into,' he clears his throat, 'supergrasses?'

'Your Honour, I don't think there's need to refer to that document today.'

'That, Mr Whittingham, is for me to decide.' Haskell continues to tap his fingertips together. 'In view of the lack of supporting evidence the charges of murder, conspiracy to bomb and possession of explosives are hereby dismissed.'

Patrick leaps from his chair. 'Your Honour, I move this case be closed.'

'One moment, Mr Duffy. There remains the matter of your client's suspected membership of the Provisional IRA.'

Patrick grips the table with whitening fingers. 'If you contend that the testimony provided by the prosecution's informant is unreliable that must surely apply to every claim in the statement.'

'It must apply, Mr Duffy, to those claims I decide it applies to. On the lesser charge I am prepared to accept the witness account, to be considered alongside the corroborating evidence of your client's obvious Republican sympathies and associations which are suggestive of involvement with the Provisional IRA.'

'Corroborating evidence?' Patrick enquires.

'Her marriage to an acknowledged IRA member…'

'My client's personal relationships are not on trial,' Patrick interrupts.

'…Her support for the Republican Movement.' Haskell turns to me. 'Is it not your handiwork on the Sinn Fein building?'

Patrick replies for me. 'Painting a mural is not an offence.'

'Neither is singing…' Haskell ruffles through paperwork. '…'The Wearing of the Green' in itself but the cumulative weight of such factors dictate I grant the membership charge validity. This court will be adjourned until 10 A.M. I advise you use the adjournment to inform your client of the penalties for membership of a proscribed organisation and reminding her of the allowances made for guilty pleas.' A rap of his gavel concludes his advice.

Undone by love, art and a sing-a-long. Hindsight is 20/20 but I still don't see how I could have done anything differently.

The WPC calls two male officers to haul my lead-weighted body from the dock. I feel them moving me but am powerless to resist. I'm locked inside my own head, seeing and hearing but paralysed and mute. Images, sharp and bright, assault me as I'm bundled down steep stone steps and thrust through a door. Ahead a long gloomy corridor curves out of sight. The low arched roof is concrete grey. Pipes race along the wall to my left. Cloying heat wafts from them. I'm in the tunnel that runs five feet below Crumlin Road, separating, connecting, the courthouse and jail, where I'll spend the night. Synched between the male screws, I'm marched through the tunnel. Half way along smooth concrete gives way to mottled brickwork, Victorian like the jail it leads to, second home to Republicans for over a century.

Exhaustion trips me. The screws tighten their grip, stumbling me along.

'So much for the Provo's ice-hard queen,' one comments.

Tears scald my eyes. I blink them away, straighten up, fix on the steel door that's eighty yards and eight hundred years walk, and make the journey unaided.

Alone in my cell I surrender.

A key is clanked in the lock of the bare holding cell whose whiteness makes me jail-blind. I rub a sleeve over my cheeks, dampening the white cuffs, and gulp down sobs. My eyes feel raw. The door opens. I keep my face down, ashamed of myself for blubbing like a girl when I've fought so long, given up so much, for honorary membership to the 'men only' club of life.

A male voice says, 'I suppose yous'll want tea?'

'Thanks,' Patrick replies.

The door bangs shut. A hand touches my shoulder, stretching into an arm that encircles me. Fresh tears bubble over. Aftershave and fabric softener combine in my nostrils, a spicy, floral blend. He lets me sob myself dry. The peeler returns with tea that Patrick takes, blocking me from view as he does. The door bangs again. A steaming mug is pressed into my hands.

'We need words,' Patrick says gently.

'Aye.' I meet his gaze. 'Will they be listening?'

'Unlikely, but wise to be careful.'

I move up on the bunk, making room for him to sit close; there's nowhere else for him to perch and we need the discretion of whispers. In quiet Irish we talk.

'What'll happen to Danny?'

'Charges dropped. He should be released tomorrow.'

'I don't know how you did it.'

'Not me.' Patrick smiles. 'God, if you care to believe.'

'It's a miracle, alright.' I shake my head. 'One I don't deserve.'

'Someone's not agreeing with you on that.'

'I did it, Patrick. All the things they said and more.'

'In Ireland's name,' he reminds me.

I look away.

He switches back to English. 'About tomorrow: it's pretty clear Haskell will be lenient if you plead guilty.'

'How lenient?'

'Perhaps as little as six months.'

'If I don't?'

'Five years is the maximum.'

*All volunteers must realise that the threat of capture and of long jail sentences are a very real danger.*

'I might as well shoot myself as confess,' I insist.

'If you plead guilty you could be out and back to normal,' he emphasises 'normal', 'all the sooner.'

'But if there's a chance of not serving any time I have to take it.'

'You don't really believe that's likely?' Patrick challenges.

I don't. But I've already gone shit or bust. I won't fold now. I answer him with silence.

'You need to think about the future,' Patrick advises.


Sitting on the thin mattress, cell lit by the arcing beam of the security light outside, the past presses me with killing urgency. I cross-examine myself:

Why have I done what I've done, become what I am? Because I believe in the right to take up arms and free Ireland.

Now again, without the rhetoric? Because it was too important not to.

How can you be certain it isn't revenge motivating you? I can't... There've been times... but every action was military. That Brit was a sniper, an enemy soldier...

The civilians? Casualties of a war I didn't start.

That's a platitude. I did my best to protect them, given the nature of the engagement. I wish it wasn't this way; it's not my fault it is. I'm sorry for them.

What about your parents? Their choices are what killed them.

So you don't care about them at all? I didn't know them, how can I care?

What if someone ordered your daddy dead, pulled the trigger. Don't you need to know? What am I supposed to do about that here, now?

And Daideo? What about him?

Isn't this his fault? He tried to protect me. I made the decision to join: fight. He didn't want that. His war was over.

Is it over for you too? How can it be?

Will it ever be over? Yes, when there's peace. If...

At 7 A.M. the guard brings breakfast. I eat the cornflakes, drink the tea, am taken to the washrooms then wait for Patrick, my clothes straightened but still betraying the fact that I slept in them.

He arrives at 8.30.

'Did you sleep?'

'No.'

'Aye, shows.'

'Why'd you ask then?'

'To see if you'd lie.' He smiles. 'We don't have much time. I brought these. Hope they fit.' He hands me a Marks & Spencer bag containing a pair of grey slacks and a lilac blouse, still with the labels attached.

'When did you buy these?' I ask, changing out of my skirt.

Patrick, cheeks flushed, faces the wall. 'Last night. Have you decided what you're doing?'

'Yes. No deals. If they want to convict me they'll do it without my help.'

He sighs.

'You think I'm being an eejit?'

'It's your decision.'

'The wrong one?'

'It's not the decision, it's the consequences you've to concern yourself with,' he advises.

Consequences I've earned.

We stand for Lord Haskell. My legs are firm, my heartbeat steady.

'Mr Duffy, have you consulted with your client?'

'I have, M'Lord. My client has nothing to add.'

Haskell peers at me over his spectacles. 'You retain your 'not guilty' plea?'

'I do.'

He studies me a moment before addressing me:

'Then, having weighed the evidence presented to this court, I am compelled to find you guilty on the charge of membership of a proscribed organisation, specifically the Provisional IRA. I am further compelled by your intransigence in this court to sentence you to four years imprisonment, to serve a minimum of two under the present terms of fifty percent remission granted to prisoners in Northern Ireland. Do you wish to say anything, Miss Devoy?'

A Pearse quote pops into my head, 'Nationhood is not achieved otherwise than in arms... Ireland unarmed will attain just as much freedom as it is convenient for England to give her; Ireland armed will attain ultimately just as much freedom as she wants.'

But Haskell wouldn't understand. To those who've nothing to fight for, or against, war is stupid, reckless, immoral and futile; they wouldn't dream of starting it. To the rest of us war is brutal, horrible, desperate but necessary. We dream of ending it.

I say what I think Daideo would've probably said had it been him in the dock.

'Éire go bráth!'

Haskell removes his glasses and blinks at me.

'Would you like a translation?' I offer.

'I would not. I've had my fill of all things Irish.' He bangs his gavel on the desk.

Patrick and I are returned to our side room to wait for my prison escort. We sit in uncompromising silence. This isn't what he wanted, me rejecting the chance of a reduced sentence. But it wasn't his gamble to stake. I remove my chain and hold it out to him.

'Will you look after this for me?'

He takes it hesitantly. 'Aye, alright. Only if you'll promise me I'll be giving it back to you someday.'

'Promise.'

I'm taken directly to Armagh, onto A wing, and greeted by Mairead who's rearranged things so that I'm her cellmate. The routine of prison life begins.

Something A.M., you're told it's 7.30 but you've no watch. You hear the screws banging down the wing. They peer through spy holes, counting prisoners. You're checked off a list, packed and repacked every day.

The door is opened. You file out with your cellmate, greet comrades, go to the toilets to empty your piss pot, filled during the hours since lock-down. You wait for a free sink then splash cold water on your face. Only two days until your weekly shower.

You queue for breakfast; a quarter pint of milk, flask of tea and bowl of cornflakes. Food served, you return to your cell and pace your eating: too fast and you're left with more empty time; to slowly and you won't finish before the screws collect the slops. Then you'll be hungry long before lunch.

Breakfast finished and locked down again, the OC calls the roll. You listen at the door, answering 'aye' or, if you speak Irish, 'anseo*'. Then, if you have a book not read into your

---

* Here

264

memory, you flick some pages, storing characters and plot for when there's nothing to fill your mind.

10 A.M., so they say: the first exercise period. Sixteen of you are marched into the yard for ninety minutes, strolling in twos and threes, sharing news from home, cigarettes and sweets if you have any. If you're on the afternoon exercise you console yourself: your time is to come; theirs is over before lunch. You try to finish the letter you were writing.

12 o'clock. You're herded down to collect lunch: salad, limp and bruised; chips, black-burnt and greasy; if the chef is poorly, stale bread sandwiches made by the screws. You don't eat those; they spit in them. You try to eat without tasting the food that's a cold shadow of meals you once relished.

2 P.M. and your turn in the yard. It was sunny this morning but now it's raining. Screws shelter in the doorway, smoking king-sized cigarettes and touching up their glossy pink sneers. You huddle into yourself, teeth chattering. A comrade talks to you, trying to take you away from the high stone walls, overlooked by tiny barred windows. Tomorrow, if she's struggling, you'll do the same for her.

Four: teatime. It's lukewarm and sweet. Outside you didn't take sugar.

If it's Wednesday or Saturday you listen at the door, praying for feet to stop outside, delivering small comforts sent by loved ones; proper cigarettes (you hate roll-ups), new socks (yours are holey and your mammy was the one for darning), a magazine (never *Republican News*), letters. Sometimes the letters upset you; a girlfriend is engaged, another expecting her first. You'll be too old for that when you're released. Your cellmate gives you a dab of the hand cream she's been sent. If she's really worried she'll report to the OC who'll speak to you, even ask the governor for something to raise your spirits. You don't want to be a burden and pretend you're fine. Your problems are no greater than anyone else's.

7.30 P.M.: another day nearly survived. The wing is unlocked. You dart to collect supper, the only meal you gobble because you don't want to waste the free association period. You slip in and out of opened cells, visiting, pretending the wing is the back streets of home where you'd

265

slip like this into the houses of friends and neighbours. Someone has a good book they've finished. Does anyone want a trade? You accept, thumbing the tattered Mills and Boon as though it's a first edition by your favourite author. If the television has been repaired you'll gather with the others to watch something colourful. Anything that isn't the stale blue or sickly orange of the prison walls is welcomed.

Nine-thirty. Too early for bed but that's where you're sent. The screws chase you to your cells. You hear the final clang that marks the master locks being turned. They reckon there's no way of opening them until morning. You wonder what'd happen if a fire broke out. But then the rosary is called in Irish and the evening's entertainment begins. Three nights a week it's Irish lessons, words called from cell to cell, spellings, lenition, eclipsis. If you know more than your neighbours you teach them. Other nights it's bingo, a lecture on Irish history or political ideology, a quiz. And always some singing.

Midnight. You call, 'oíche mhaith dhuit*,' and lie on your bed, another few minutes chat with your cellmate if you haven't exhausted every possible topic or don't mind repeating yourself. Then you buzz for the lights to be switched off and darkness engulfs you. On your back between the scratchy blankets, you trace the searchlight's scything sweep across your ceiling. Outside a helicopter circles, the rapid whoop-whoop looping in your head. You fall asleep to its refrain. Soon it will be that time they tell you is 7.30 A.M. But you have another day behind you. Too many more lengthen ahead like winter nights.

*All captured volunteers feel that they have failed.* It's true enough. I fucked up. Guilt prises a confession from me, about how I let emotions override judgement: about Aiden. Mairead sits on the bunk beside me, holds my hand and makes a confession of her own. She was wearing platform shoes the day they bombed the Conway. In them she couldn't run fast enough to get away.♥ She says how stupid she felt and how lucky; one of

---

* good night

♥ Death of a Terrorist, 1989 24.58

the lads with her was killed fleeing the scene. It is what it's meant to be, she tells me. It doesn't help. Danny could've been banged up or, worse, banged out, because of me. I've let the Movement down, cost them a volunteer. But these are scenarios accounted for in the *Green Book*. What isn't accounted for is me.

On my first evening Mairead takes me round the wing, introducing me to A company, Armagh jail. I'm edgy, aware of our differences, listing them in my head as I shake hands, learn names.

My hippy childhood was unisex, monosex, polysex; the Ryans believed gendering was a socially constructed artifice designed to maintain power hierarchies. So I didn't have dolls, wear frocks, play tea parties and house. My toys were Lego, Plasticine, a tambourine; my clothes dungarees, t-shirts, jumpers, ponchos. I grew up with Buddhist mantras not Catholic catechisms. I empowered myself. Handbags are for carrying guns or detonators, not lipsticks and compacts. High heels and a skirt are a disguise. Apart from Briege, my friends are the lads. I think of myself as Vol. not Miss.

Now I'm one of 'the girls in Armagh'.

Always 'the girls' no matter what age, whether single, married or widowed, childless or mothers. Reduced to our lowest common denominator. But I'm the awkward remainder left when the fraction is multiplied out.

I don't tell Mairead this because I'm worried it'll sound as stupid out loud as it does in my head, especially when the others are fretting about elderly parents who mightn't live to see them released, fellas who mightn't wait around for them, children who won't remember them. But Mairead's smarter than I'll ever be about these things; she points me to the common land. We're all Republicans. We've all been ground through the mill by the Brits. We've all lost things we fought so hard for. We all hurt. We're all in here together. Our strength is in our comradeship: our sisterhood.

Mairead also explains the system, how to wriggle through the gaps in it, reassuring me that things aren't so bad since they ended the no-wash and hunger strikes. I try to be relieved that I'm not having to paint the cell walls brown but a spiteful voice in my head says I'm not suffering enough. It takes time, Mairead admits, to adjust. I shouldn't be afraid of asking for help. But she can't help me with everything.

The past has run up behind me. I have to turn and fight it.

My first visiting day rolls round. Nora and Danny come. He hugs me fiercely.

'I'm sorry,' he whispers.

'Jesus, whatever are you sorry for?' I demand, punching his arm. 'This is my own daft fault.' It's easier to be strong in front of them.

Nora dishes out cigarettes and talks of Briege, who is big with baby already. I ask questions, hoping I sound cheerful.

When they leave, Danny slips a comm into my hand. I transfer it to my knickers, smuggling it past the screws who, as long as we behave, don't watch too closely.

It's from Liam, spurring me to keep strong, survive my sentence. He doesn't say what'll happen afterwards.

'Sure, you'll be alright,' Mairead says. 'I'm going straight back, so I am. They'll want you to as well, if you're up for it.' She focuses her brown eyes on me.

I can't answer her.

'But let's get you through this first,' she adds.

We lie on our narrow beds, springs poking through thin mattresses. We talk in whispers, two kids having a sleepover. Mairead tells me her story. She got involved after growing up in Belfast, getting a political education on the streets, watching soldiers intimidate and harass Irish Nationalists with indiscriminate enjoyment. Her granddaddy also fought the Black and Tans so, like me, she was Republican before she was born. She understands what's brought me here. And she's been in Armagh since she was nineteen because of it: nine years, a third of her life. I think of what I've done in that almost decade and want to cry for her but she doesn't regret a minute. She passes me a book her mother sent, George Bernard Shaw's collected works. By the glow of a match I turn to the essay 'Maximums for Revolutionists' and read the quotation she underlined, 'the reasonable man adapts himself to the world; the unreasonable one persists in trying to adapt the world to himself. Therefore, all progress depends on the unreasonable man.' Or woman.

'In here's just a smaller version of out there.' She gestures to the tiny window high up the cell wall. 'You've to learn when to be reasonable. Save something for when you get out.'

The past has been a fiction; I have two years to work out how to deal with the fact. I settle down to reality because it's what needs doing.

Patrick requests a visit. Thinking there's been some legal development I agree.

He's at a table in the visiting room when I'm shown in.

'Has something happened?' I demand, brushing off his greeting.

'No, I just wanted to see how you are. I've brought you some things.' He lifts a sketchpad and an array of pencils onto the table. 'Nora tells me you draw.'

'Oh.' I slide the pad over and stroke the stiff, creamy pages.

'There's this, too.' He dangles my chain.

I take it, rub the back of the locket with my thumb as we talk.

When the hour is up he asks if he can come again. I agree. The locket is warm now from my hold. I could keep it, wear it. We are allowed. But I need something waiting for me on the outside. The chain, ring and locket are slipped back into Patrick's pocket as we part.

One Wednesday a letter arrives, envelop bearing an official crest and addressed to Kaylynn Ryan. 'Devoy' and my prison number have been scrawled across it.

Dear Miss Ryan,
It has come to our attention that your status as a British citizen is the result of a fraudulent claim to British nationality. As a result your United Kingdom passport is hereby revoked with immediate effect. Any attempts to travel on this document will result in your detention under the Immigration Act.

Should you wish to appeal...

I use up a precious match burning words telling me who I'm not. One of the screws smells smoke stronger than a cigarette, barges into the cell, accuses me of torching the wing. She calls me a crazy Fenian bitch and hollers for the male screws who loiter upstairs, permanently agitating for agro. Five of them clatter into the cell, grab me and wrestle me to the ground. Savaged by them, I turn savage in self-defence. They beat me down. My wrists are restrained, my ankles gripped and I'm hoisted over their heads, carried to the governor's office like a trophy carcass bagged on some big game hunt.

Mairead is there, discussing plans for the upcoming Easter Rising commemorations. Two female screws drag her from the room as the male ones throw me to the floor. I pick myself up, get kicked back down then hauled up by my ponytail.

The screw, Pam, explains, in hysterical tones, how she caught me fire-starting. The male screws justify my injuries, a bloody lip, black eye and broken tooth, with unexaggerated accounts of my violent resistance. The odds, five hulking shit houses against one wee girl, are ignored. I don't acknowledge the governor's authority and demand my OC be present. Mairead is brought back in. Shaking with rage that she fights to suppress with her invincible eight stone strength, she asks to speak with me alone. The governor refuses. The unburnt part of the letter is retrieved and examined. Mairead pleads the emotional stress of the moment. I get thirty days in the punishment unit; solitary, twenty-four hour lock-up, reduced rations, no parcels and threatened with the loss of my remission. I call the governor a Thatcherite lackey, get slapped by one of the male screws, ten more days on the boards and lose three months remission.

I'm tossed into a punishment cell, bare apart from a metal bed soldered to the floor and a thin mattress, no blankets or pillows. A screw hurls a Bible in.

'There's company for you, fucking papist,' she snarls, banging out.

I fling it at the door, denouncing her religious accusation; it explodes, showering paper leaves over the floor.

Lying on the bed, my temper cooling, I notice a chunk of the concrete wall is loose. I prise it free, turning the wedge in my fingers. One edge is sharp. I scratch into the flaking paintwork, scoring a satisfying line.

By the time the forty days are up I've decorated an entire wall with scenes from the *Táin*, stickmen and women peopling the cell, attacking hordes spilling over distance hills. They are my people, past, present and future. I've no home but Ireland.

The governor come to inspect. I expect forty more days for my vandalism.

'Do you consider yourself an artist?'

I'm not supposed to reply but give a curt nod.

'Put her back on the wing.'

In my cell, alongside the sketchpad and pencils Patrick brought, I find a small paint set, hard watercolour nuggets.

'Think he feels bad about what they did to you,' Mairead says. 'How's your tooth?'

'Killing me.'

'Do you want the doctor?'

'That butcher? I'd be as well getting it out via another smack in the mouth from a screw.'

She laughs.

'What'll I do with these?' I point at the paints.

She shrugs. 'Might as well use them.'

'That's OK?'

'It's hardly collusion. Plus, this place'd be the better for a wee bit of art.'

I start drawing and painting that night.

'You can say no,' Mairead advises.

I stare at the visiting request. The Ryans want to see me.

'It's OK. There's something I'm needing to say to them anyway.'

She nods, lifts the paper from my hand. 'I'll tell Chief Rat.'

*

They stand as I enter. It's a wonder we recognise each other after five years and a dozen lifetimes. It's easiest for me; they're still wearing corduroy and cheesecloth, beads and bandanas. She snatches his arm, clutching it. He stares blankly, his face greyed by prison lighting and, maybe, something else? I hesitate but a screw prods me from behind.

'You're blocking the doorway.'

I sit. They stay standing. He pulls her chair up and eases her down. I clasp my hands in front of me, resting them on the table, inspecting my broken nails.

She speaks first. 'Kaylynn.'

I don't correct the pronunciation.

'We've come a long way,' he states.

I raise my eyes to his. 'What do you want me to say?'

She gulps down a sob. 'Nothing, love.' She glances at him. 'We just wanted to see you, know you were alright. Whatever you've done you're still our daughter.'

'I'm not though.'

He stands. 'This is a waste of time. Susan, let's go.'

'No.' She yelps the word like a frightened animal and stretches a trembling hand to me. 'Is there anything you need?'

It's the Winter of Discontent. I'm sixteen, sitting on the cold tarmac outside a car factory in Humberside, sketching with frozen fingers the wind-rippled sea of banners and placards. In the foreground are a middle-aged couple wrapped up in second-hand winter coats and right-on rage. I don't include myself in the drawing because my apathy upsets the composition. Crisis, what crisis?...

'Wilson's not fit to run a tea party, never mind the Labour Party. Whenever people like him manoeuvre themselves into positions of power, they forget their responsibility to wield it for good.'

'But he's done some good, John, liberalised the country.'

'Come on, Suse! He's sold out socialism. Power perverts principle, that's always their problem.'...

For two days I sat in that road, freezing my arse off, trying to draw with frost-burnt fingers.

'Yes, I need to know why you lied to me all those years.'

'We promised your grandfather,' she bleats.

'We were protecting you,' he adds, sitting down.

'Yous were protecting yourselves.' I set my eyes on him. 'I know what happened to my ma and da.'

They avoid eye-contact.

'The peelers told me. Thought they'd break me with it.'

She crumbles into fresh tears. He blinks twice.

'We didn't want you making the wrong decision,' he says.

'Then you lost; I won.' I wave at our surroundings. 'This is what I chose, my cause. Don't come here if you can't accept that. Judging my choices won't change yours.' I scrape my chair back. 'Haven't you got a march to get to?' I stand. Two screws step towards us. 'We're done,' I say. I'm led to the door. On the threshold, I turn, give the raised fist salute to the people who taught me the gesture and shout, 'Tiocfaidh ár lá.' The visiting room erupts with defiant repetition of my call. I'm bundled back to my cell.

# London—25<sup>th</sup> June, 1985

## Thirteen Held Over Provo's Latest Terror Campaign
## One Suspect Accused of Brighton Bombing

Police have today confirmed they have arrested thirteen suspected IRA members in connection with a plot to blow up British seaside resorts at the height of the summer.

Following a lead, police discovered a viable explosive device in the prestigious London hotel, the Rubens. A controlled explosion was also carried out on a suspect package in a Brighton hotel and a hotel in Hull was evacuated. Both incidents were later found to be false alarms. Police are engaged in a nationwide hunt for further bombs.

The suspects, held under the Prevention of Terrorism Act, include Patrick Magee, also accused of the 1984 attack on the Grand Hotel in Brighton. Magee, 33, and an unknown female accomplice are believed to have carried out the bombing which killed five people and left others with life-changing injuries. Police continue to question Mr Magee about the Brighton attack and this latest terrorist campaign.

# Armagh Jail—30ᵗʰ June, 1985

Mairead enters the association room.

'Caoilainn, have you a minute?'

I follow her to our cell where she pushes the door to.

'This came for you.' She passes me a comm, still tightly folded.

I read it.

'Should I be worried?' she asks.

'It wouldn't help if you were.'

She slips out. I swallow the comm, wait to digest the news that churns in my stomach. Waiting is all I'm good for now.

The next day Patrick comes. I'm taken to an interview room. The screw locks us in.

'What's this?' I ask.

'I was told to visit you. Something's happened. What?'

'It's nothing.'

'They wouldn't have sent me if that was true so tell me.'

'Magee. Brighton.'

'I see.'

'He won't give me up.'

'I hope for your sake that's true,' Patrick sighs.

I'm sat on a stove, the gas full-blast beneath me. Fear, for Pat, what they're putting him through to get to me, torments me. I pace the cell, artwork abandoned. Mairead watches. She wants to help. Tries to reach me. I recoil, because it's my default setting. Frustrations boil up: over. Mairead warns me to get my head straight if I don't want to set things off in here; the screws have noticed my agitation. I cover sheets of paper with violent black scribbles, wearing down three HBs. It helps a bit. Days become weeks. I use up ten more pencils. And force myself to ask for her help. Mairead talks me down, up, over and through. Heat fades. Pat gets thirty-five years for Brighton and the planned summer campaign; I calmly ask for my brief.

'Tell him I'm grateful for what he's done. And sorry he's had to do it.'

Patrick and I speak in Irish whispers.

'What do you mean?'

'He's taken time that I should be sharing.' I squeeze Patrick's hand, helping myself to comfort.

'Isn't that what you do for each other, sacrifice yourselves?'

I snatch my hand back. He's still pissed off that I wouldn't plea-bargain my own sentence down.

'For a Republican brief you don't understand us, do you?'

'I understand you're determined to martyr yourself.'

I leap from my chair.

'I'm determined to do what's needed. Don't accuse me of having a martyr complex. Christ, you think I want this? Don't I wish none of this was necessary, that things were different?'

'They could be different.'

'How?'

We teeter a moment then he grabs me. His lips graze my cheek, his breath is hot and urgent on my skin. I only have to turn my head and we'll be kissing.

I shove him off. 'Fuck sake, Patrick.'

We glare at each other. He's hurt, confused, angry. I'm afraid: terrified. Because I'm sure now that I'm as much in love with him as he is with me.

'Maybe you'd best get yourself a new solicitor.'

He bangs on the door for out. It opens and he's gone.


When Jen is released Mairead asks me to be second in command.

'Pick someone else.'

She laughs. 'Who? Why?'

'Mags or Eileen. Because they'll be better at it than me.'

'If I thought that I'd not be asking you,' Mairead says.

'Then your thinking's wrong.'

'It's you that's wrong,' Mairead replies. 'You can do this. You're just needing to prove it to yourself.' She squeezes my shoulder. 'Sure, I know there's been more for you to adjust to here than locked doors but you're doing grand so far. This'll be good for everyone.'

She's after dissolving those last few grains of distrust lurking in me about myself as friend, not comrade.

'Put it to a vote,' I say. 'If it comes back 'aye' then I'll do it.'
'I already have. It did.'

Over the next few months Mairead starts deputising to me, having me go with her, then alone, to negotiate with Chief Rat. She's right about the responsibility being good for me. It teaches me to be reasonable without being weak, understanding without being judgemental. And it gives me a focus besides the stabbing in my chest that comes with picturing Patrick's face, something which I can't stop doing.

Nora brings Briege and the little one to visit. Saoirse stretches out in her mammy's arms, star-fish hands grasping at clothes, hair, nothing. Her gummy pink mouth reminds me of Daideo's. I feel sorry for her, named for something she'll probably never get to live out.

'Will you hold her?' Briege asks, offering me the bundle.

I glance around the visiting room; no one else has brought a baby today.

'It's not allowed. In case we're passing comms that way.'

'Well, she'll still be wee enough for a cuddle when you get out,' Briege sighs.

Nora glares at me. She's made a career of prison visiting.

'Changed the rules have they?'

I shrug. 'How's himself?'

Briege smiles. 'Grand, loves being a daddy, can't get enough of her.'

'Danny?'

'Fine,' Nora says. 'Nearly finished his apprenticeship. He's looking for work.'

It's as much as she can say; I hope there'll be more in the comm hidden in my shoe. I force out the next name.

'Frank?'

'Knees bother him some but he's alright,' Nora admits.

Life is going on without me, as though I'm dead.

Will I be able to rise again, like the Provisional's own phoenix, from the ashes of myself?

I have to believe the answer is yes.

# Armagh Jail—23<sup>rd</sup> September, 1986

Today is hard for two reasons: it would have been my fourth wedding anniversary and Mairead is being released, leaving me as OC over the thirty-two women that form IRA A company in Armagh.

I argued against the decision, I've less than six months myself; we should be preparing for a longer war. In the end there was a unanimous vote. I conceded on condition that Geraldine, who's doing ten for weapons possession and conspiring to do the usual, be second in command. She's got a patient strength that'll see everyone through once I'm gone too.

'Have you got everything?' I look around our cell.

'Think so.' Mairead shrugs on her parka; industrial blue with a traffic-cone orange lining, size man's medium that drowns her tiny frame. 'Jesus, I'll be glad to get into a coat that fits.' She rummages in her bag. 'These are for you.' She produces a spray of the purple flowers that grow in the cracks of the yard wall. 'For you and Aiden, I mean. Four is fruit or flowers. It's the best I could manage. I'll take him some lilies when I get to Belfast.'

'You don't have to.'

'Aye, I do.' She hugs me.

'Be careful out there,' I tell her.

'Don't worry about me, I've plenty waiting to help. It's yous I'm worried about. I wish I wasn't leaving you to this.'

There's talk of us being moved to the shiny new jail at Maghaberry. The uncertainty is unnerving.

'Don't be silly, you've done more than your whack. We'll be fine.'

'I hope so,' she says, chewing on her lip and blinking back tears. She leans into me and whispers, 'Remember, your mind's your strongest weapon. That's how we can always counteract whatever they do because they can't control our minds and they can't get inside them and that's their failure.'

I smile at her. 'Aye.'

We hug again. A screw interrupts.

'Bus is waiting, Mairead. Caoilainn, the governor said have you time for a meeting later?'

'Tell him I'll see him after tea.'

Mairead nods at me and is gone.

Time is running short. I have to decide what I'm going to do when I get out, about the future and the past.

# Armagh Jail—29ᵗʰ September, 1986

A scrap of paper is shoved under my cell door after lock-down, informing me we're being moved from Armagh tomorrow. Cheating bastards've done it this way so we can't organise resistance. We organise it anyway, shouting messages in Irish through the walls, me bawling from one end of the wing and Geraldine from the other.

In the morning they move us in pairs, singly if they think we're really dangerous. Our bellowed plans are scattered to the wind as each woman is handcuffed and surrounded by brick-shit house men in riot gear with trained attack dogs straining flimsy leashes.

They come for me last. I was keeping a listening watch, counting the doors banging, crossing names off a mental list as each voice shouted, 'Slán agat*, Caoilainn!' So I know when the door swings back that I'm the last.

I'm sitting on my bed, waiting: ready.

'I thought yous were leaving me here.'

Pam, who made head screw six months ago, steps into my cell. The dogs snarl and slaver to be at me. Male screws blacken the doorway and the corridor.

'Wouldn't I love to do that,' she sneers. 'Stand up.' She jangles a set of cuffs like they're a treat.

I don't move.

She smirks. 'I was hoping you'd be difficult. You'll be bucking up your ideas at the new place.'

She stands aside. Four male screws done up like Imperial Storm Troopers stamp in: swamp me. I make myself a dead weight. They drag me out, trail me down the stairs and hoik me into a meat wagon.

I snatch a last glance at Armagh Jail through the tinted van windows; a stately red-brick mansion with barred windows retreats into my past. Looking outside-in homesickness churns my stomach.

---

* Goodbye (to the person staying behind)

# Mourne House, Maghaberry Jail—
## 30th September, 1986

I'm in a holding cell, the walls so freshly painted it reeks of acrylic and turps, smells that make me long for canvasses and brushes. Apart from the fumes there's nothing else in the cell. I don't know how long I've been here. The only time-marker is the screaming, a banshee clock wailing at regular intervals. Each cry is closer than the last. When it's in here with me it'll be me screaming. I pace the room's diagonal, not thinking about what it is they're doing to us to make us scream like that. They want me to think. They want me afraid. I have to be stronger than them. I have to be strong enough for all of us.

I sit cross-legged on the floor, facing a pure white wall, pristine and primed for painting. Onto it I start to sketch, then colour Mairead's cheery face, her wavy brown hair, her encouraging smile. My eyes start to sting and water; I don't blink, daren't break the spell that keeps my brain painting, not thinking.

'Your mind's your strongest weapon.'

A draught on my neck blows me back into the cell. I glance over my shoulder. An unfamiliar female screw is in the doorway, holding a clipboard. Her shoes are shiny. She was cutting the tags off her uniform this morning. She barks my name and prison number then, without looking up, says:

'Undress.'

I get to my feet.

'What?'

She raises her eyes. 'Take off your clothes. All of them.'

My brain dumps debris. I sift through it for sense. The bollockses have changed the regs without letting on.

'If you're after making us wear prison uniforms yous can fuck right off.'

She flutters mascara-clumped eyelashes. 'It's just a wee search.'

I hold up my arms. She shakes her head.

'A thorough search.' She rakes my body with greedy eyes. 'It's how we do things here.'

They did strip-searches at Armagh sometimes, if they thought we were getting it too easy, smuggling more contraband in than they could ignore, but they were infrequent, one-offs, at least during my time. I never copped for one. I look around the bright, clean, modern cell. We've regressed. Are being sucked back to that period after the no-wash protests when strip-searches were constant and invasive. I understand the screams and why the cell is bare: ammunition-free.

'I want to see the governor.'

'After we search you.'

'I'm OC of these women, we've a right to…'

'You've a right to nothing,' she spits. 'You're not in charge here.' She flicks a tongue over glossy lips. She's a viper, eyeing me up, imagining how I'll taste. 'Now get your clothes off.'

'I'll help you the day Paisley blesses himself in front of the Pope.'

She bangs on the cell door. It bounces open. Four more screws in riot gear stomp in. I can see through their unisex visors that, on their days off, they're women. In the corridor behind them male screws form a line the ends of which stretch out of sight. Herself of the Clipboard stands aside. The others come at me, try to grab me. I smack one in the neck. Get kicked. Pain divides me. I pull myself together and lash out. They whack me and whack me, wrestle me to the ground. I batter their armoured bodies. My wrists are restrained. One sits on me. Air rushes from my chest. I'm hauled off the floor, thrown against the wall and pressed against newly painted plaster, wrists raked up to my shoulder blades. Hands clamp my ankles, dragging my feet from under me, tugging off my plimsolls and socks. My bare toes are crushed by boots that grind my feet into the tiled floor. I buck and struggle. Something hard, a baton, cracks across my shoulders. In the seconds of airless agony gloved fingers fumble with my jeans, unfastening, yanking. The rough fabric of their protective gauntlets scrapes down the inside of my thighs. Cold clings to my skin. My knickers are ripped off. Exposed, I have the sudden urge to pee. I turn my head, look through the doorway at the men gawping in, enjoying the peep-show. I pick one, lock my eyes into his: stare. After three long seconds he drops his gaze. I grasp the tiny triumph and fight harder, letting go of a warm stream of piss. One of the women shrieks in my ear. The two bracing me against the wall jump away. For all the time I'm pissing on the floor of their shiny new jail I'm winning. Then my bladder is empty. I'm clubbed to the ground, sat on, my arms stretched out like I'm going on the rack and my sweatshirt and vest pulled over my head. Underneath the small of my back a rapidly cooling puddle collects. The four female screws take a corner each and spread-eagle me. Herself of the Clipboard comes closer, leers over me and paws at me with her eyes. She squats between my legs to inspect. A face, Asian and avuncular, flashes at me. I block it, imagine instead blasting a loud, stinky fart at her. Visualising the sound, the smell and her prissy reaction drives laughter up from my gut. I howl. She frowns at me. She thinks I'm crazy. Maybe I am. I can't stop laughing. She stands. Edges away. Nods to the others who, in a synchronised movement, release me. I stay on the floor, the laughter ebbing gently.

'Get dressed,' she orders.

Moving slowly enough to not be ambushed by pain, I stand, confronting all of them with my nakedness.

'No.'

She gapes at me.

'You took them off, now yous can put them back on.' I know they won't move me naked and they can't leave me in the holding cell. I scan the faces of the women who've brutalised me. They dodge my gaze.

'Get dressed,' she repeats and waves her crew from the room.

The door clangs. I sit on the floor, my backside chilling, and wait.

The mind is a powerful weapon but it's also a fickle one. In those cold hours of stalemate it turns on me, aiming the barrel at my heart. I wrestle with it, straining to keep myself from pulling the trigger, dodging the excruciating humiliation designed to break me, telling myself it doesn't matter if the whole world and his dog sees up my cunt, nothing does, as long as we don't let them win. I'm married to the Cause. With this body I thee honour. Periodically the spy-hole opens; an eye blinks at me. I don't blink back. I have to be strong enough for all of us.

The door opens. Three female screws enter. Herself of the Clipboard isn't one of them. Changed out of their battledress they are ordinary: breakable. The youngest of them, she's about my age, gathers my clothes off the floor and comes to me while the others watch. I pity her; she's their whipping-girl. I bet she wasn't even one of the strip-mob. This is probably her first day and they can make her do this because she's as much their victim as I am. I stand, raise my arms. When she kneels, offers me my knickers, I step into them. But that's all the help I can give her because she made a choice just like I did.

It's teatime before I see the governor. He blanks the bruises on my face, informs me in a monotone that strip-searches are part of the regime. We'll have to endure them before and after visits, court appearances, hospital trips, and randomly whenever there's a suspected security breach. It's for the safety of inmates and staff.

On the wing later, seeing the swollen lips, black eyes, it's clear I wasn't the only one who fought. But it's harder to tell which, if any of us, won. There's anger, fear, shame: tears. I pep-talk them. The screws are afraid of our strength, desperate to break us. We're political prisoners. They're trying to reduce us to the frailest common factor, using our gender against us. It's about power, like rape. Terry admits that's what she feels has been done to her. Geraldine wraps comforting arms around her. Others nod their shared anguish. I repeat Mairead's 'mind-weapon' speech. We vow not to let them get in our heads. I don't believe it's a promise we can keep and swear privately to do something about it.

I get a visitation order to Mairead. She arranges the visit. I'm stripped, examined and knocked about before they take me in to her. I have to dress myself because if I don't I won't get to see her. This is a time for me to be reasonable.

She leaps up as soon as I'm through the door. Stiletto heels clack towards me. There's a flurry of colour and a cloud of fragrance as she hugs me.

'Jesus, look at the state of you,' she groans.

'Never mind me, look at yourself.'

Her long hair has been bobbed and permed. Large hoops dangle from her earlobes. Her smile is cherry-red and her clothes green, white and purple; a swirling print top and co-ordinated skirt.

'You look grand.'

'Thanks, but what about you?' She inspects my throbbing cheek.

I tell her about the searches. She frowns, grips my hands.

'We don't move forward without moving back first,' she sighs.

'The worst thing is I don't know how I'm to get comms through if they're turning us inside-out before visits.'

'We'll find a way,' she assures me. 'How's everyone coping?'

'OK. Some better than others. I don't know what to do for them.'

'We'll make a fuss, get media coverage, maybe get some women's groups on our side for once. I'll get the press office onto it.'

'That won't help with what's in their heads,' I say.

'I know.' She squeezes my hand. 'I remember feeling so unclean the first time. You have to keep them going.'

I nod. Promise I will.

'There might be some legal action we can bring, a discrimination case. I'll speak to Patrick.'

I haven't seen him in over a year. I've replayed the tape of our almost-kiss in my head so many times the film is grainy and worn. And I still don't know how I wanted it to end. 'No.'

'He'd want to help.'

'I can't have him coming here. I need to focus on this. Find someone else.'

'Ach, Caoilainn, you're too hard on yourself,' Mairead scolds.

'Don't we have to be?'

She lowers her voice. 'Sure, when we're fighting. But not when we're loving.'

I don't know if I have enough strength left to do both. I don't know if I can do the second at all anymore.

I acquire a boyfriend, Gerry, assigned by GHQ. We write letters about innocent things; art, books, movies, music, that go through the official censor. We blossom a romance on paper that justifies him visiting me, us kissing. Mouth-to-mouth is the only way to get comms in or out. I practice in the cell at night, swallowing hard paper lumps and regurgitating them, a mother bird feeding her chicks. We move things along as quickly as we dare. His first visit is planned. I feel sick at the thought of kissing a man I've never met, having his tongue in my mouth, tasting him. The night before I dream about Aiden; wake up thinking of Patrick.

Freshly stripped, dressed by my own shaking fingers, I stumble into the visiting room. Gerry greets me. He's older than I expected, hair thinning. He looks like an accountant, because he fucking is, picked from the network 'cos he's not known nor on any lists. He's not Aiden. Or Patrick. I go to him.

'It's grand to see you,' he says, hands circling my waist, lips closing over mine. His tongue slips in. I try to avoid making contact with it while wiggling the comm to him and taking the one he passes over. He keeps his mouth clamped to mine even after we've made the switch. I tug myself free.

For forty-five minutes we chat mindlessly. When the bell finally rings and he moves to kiss me goodbye I present my cheek.

Back in the cell I cough up the comm then brush my teeth, rinse my mouth: spit the taste of him. I'll be seeing him once or twice a month until I'm released. I peel apart the wad of paper and hope its news is worth the gagging heave of my stomach. I don't know what's worse: having to kiss him or not being able to kiss the man I'm in love with.

The comm's from Mairead. They've revived the 'Stop Strip-searches' campaign. A journalist is coming to interview me. We'll shame them into stopping before they shame us into submitting.

I recognise him easily, even though it's been years since he grilled me about my choices on a blustery Monaghan hillside. We're in a private room normally reserved for legal visits but, because he's a big voice in mainstream media now, writing for the *Irish Times* and the British *Guardian*, we're being granted privileges; the prison authorities need a favourable report on Maghaberry, bought by thirty million British tax pounds. And that's only a fraction of the cost of their old-fashioned belief in empire.

'So you've come round to my way of fighting,' he starts, tapping his pad with his pen.

'I fight with whatever's to hand.'

'Including your own body?' He nods at the patchwork of scabs on my knuckles, age-able by colour.

'If that's what's needed.'

'And is it?'

'Are you married? Have you daughters?'

'I am. And one,' he replies.

'Imagine it's them telling you what it's like to have the clothes ripped off your back then decide for yourself what's needed.'

I spare him nothing. He scribbles furious shorthand, eyes welded to the lined sheets that fill up with indignities and brutalities.

'Well?' I've finished now.

He braves eye-contact. 'I'll do what I can.'

Which is probably fuck all. I shake my head.

'You've a lot of support over this,' he says, 'especially from women's groups.'

'Where've they been 'til now? Hiding behind Mother Ireland? If they'd supported the Republican Movement from the start we'd not be in here, being treated worse than animals: worse than the men in the Blocks.'

'You want their support but on your terms,' he accuses.

'I want them to stop pissing about with petty inequalities and start fighting the big ones.'

He claps his notebook shut. 'You were a hard young woman five years ago; you're harder still today. How will you be five years from now?'

'That depends on what they do to me between times,' I say, 'because everything I am is what I've had to be to survive. Not that you'd understand.'

'Because I'm a man?'

'Because you're not a volunteer. This is only a good story for you because we're women; you can play the gender card, write up the outrage of us being treated this way.'

He blushes. 'How would you have me write this up?'

'We're prisoners of war. They're violating the Geneva Convention.'

'But the searches are harder for you,' he presses. It's what he needs to believe. It's what everyone wants to believe. It's why they do it. We resist by not believing.

'Everything is harder for us. That's why we're better at fighting it.'

I don't know how he writes up the story; we're not allowed newspapers. The strip-searches continue. I get a legal visit, not Patrick, and start the process of putting in a formal complaint. I go first because I want to see what they'll do to me before I let anyone else try it. The governor dawdles with the paperwork; I'm only three months from release and he's hoping to avoid confrontation. Geraldine and I chew over a no-work protest, weighing the likely benefits against the danger of it escalating into no-wash, going all the way to hunger strike. I have to snog Gerry half a dozen times, choking as his slippery tongue probes my mouth, to communicate with the Army Council about our situation. They think the new policy of 'pragmatic engagement' with the authorities is a safer play. They press the solicitor who's not Patrick, getting him, in turn, to press the governor who names a date for officially reviewing my complaint. Not-Patrick finds a sub-section, small print policy code stating that, pending the outcome of a complaint hearing, the issue under review must, wherever possible, be resolved temporarily in favour of the complainant. Strip-searches on me are suspended. Twenty-one more complaints are lodged that week. I suspect it'll be a brief reprieve but enough to let us regroup. And it means I don't need to swap any more spit with Gerry.

Geraldine and I use the lull to prepare for my release. She's taking over as OC. I'm happy I'm leaving them with her capable, compassionate strength.

The panel reviewing my complaint meets in February. They uphold the strip-search powers but limit usage to high-security alerts, restricting the conditions under which we can be flayed of our clothes and our humanity. That night we celebrate on the wing, dancing and singing, sharing chocolates and cigarettes. I know it's a partial victory but we take everything we can.

The long winter nights draw out. The snowdrift routine of prison life that has been settled on me for over two years melts slowly. I wonder what will be exposed when the last flakes have gone. There's a past to confront, a new life to fashion from the remnants of the old. It's the beginning and the end: midnight on a clock face.

# Outside Maghaberry Jail—18<sup>th</sup> March, 1987

Squalls scud across the grey sky, blowing in, dumping loads then blowing off to rearm. The metal gates are opened for me. I step out, walk forwards, turn, look back. Search lights crane their necks above foaming barbed wire that tops mesh fencing that tops concrete walls that hide squat grey buildings with Belfast doors that lock in my comrades: my friends.

In jail you lose 'freedom to' but you're given 'freedom from'. You don't have to face whatever you left outside. I glance up to the trees, over the fields and start walking down the slick black drive, towards the car park where Nora and Danny are waiting in a borrowed silver Rover. When I get there I see a second car, a black Mercedes, shiny with rain.

The Merc's driver-side door opens. Patrick emerges. It's been twenty months since I saw him. Pain and joy circle me as he walks towards me.

'What are you doing here?'

'Returning this.'

My chain dangles from his fingers. Afraid of what I'll do if I'm close enough to touch him, I daren't take it. He lets it slip to the ground then turns away.

He came back for me. I can't let him go again. 'I'm glad you came.'

He stops but doesn't face me.

'I'm sorry. You were trying to help. You did help.'

'Good to know.' He twists round, steps forward, reaches for my hand; I retreat.

'Nora's over there.' I nod.

He glances across, back to me, drops his hand. 'Caoilainn… I… will you take this?' He passes me a slip of paper with his number scrawled on it. 'Call me if…'

'I get arrested again?' I smile at him.

'I'd rather you called for other reasons.' He returns my smile.

'Thanks.' I want to say I will, soon, but that wouldn't be fair to him. 'I've things need sorting first but…'

'I'll wait. Here' He retrieves the chain from the tarmac.

'Keep it. It's a reason.'

'Alright.' It disappears into his coat pocket. He goes to his car and I to Nora and Danny. As he drives away I know I can do what needs doing.

There are hugs and kisses but no celebrating. On the journey to Belfast Nora tells me Briege miscarried her second baby, at thirty weeks, forced to endure a stillbirth. Will I go and see them? I promise I will without knowing if I'll be able to.

Belfast is unchanged, ghettos nudging suburbia. Pockets of resistance flame in the dull afternoon; freshly repainted graffiti reminds us that from the ashes the 'Ra arose. The phoenix is large with glory. We slide by it, small and pale.

Frank greets us at the door, hobbling on two sticks. He hugs me, a sob rippling through him. When he steps back his eyes are bright with tears.

Danny and I sit on either end of the sofa. Frank bustles, pouring drinks, offering me a cushion, a teacake, another cigarette. Finally Nora drags him away, leaving Danny to fill me in on two years in Provoland. Ciaran's survived but Rory's in the Crum, on an explosives charge, waiting for a court date. Liam's cut back on operations because they've had a major tout problem; Brendan was one of many. There have been executions. Danny's eyes roam the room; he lights one cigarette off another, hands shaking. I don't ask questions; the answers are clear enough. The rest of the time he's been keeping clean in Belfast, doing the occasional job in Derry or Newry, places he's not so known. The crack in his voice, the shadows under his eyes, the grey tinge to his skin, show he's been as much a prisoner as me, serving his sentence in the larger jail that is the north.

Tea is hearty but my prison-shrunk stomach can't cope with Nora's stew. I pick at it under her frowning eyes as Frank and Danny natter, their excitement pitching towards hysteria. The crescendo comes when Frank tells me there's a party for me at the Felons tonight. I'm now entitled to full membership and the committee are waiting to welcome me.

Callum comes home at seven, having eaten at a friend's. I've not seen him since the night Briege announced her first pregnancy. He's tall and thin, shoulders stooped. Wire-rimmed glasses, the lenses grubby, sit high on his nose. Seeing me he pulls up short in the doorway.

'Callum, how're ya?' I stand.

'Fine.' He backs out.

'Everything alright?' Danny shouts after him.

'I'm away to do my homework,' is the disembodied reply.

Danny shakes his head. 'If he says ten words to us it's a good day. All he does is come in from school and go up to his books.'

'Has your ma not seen anyone about him?'

'Aye. Docs were for giving him pills but what good's that gonna do?'

'Have you tried talking to him?'

'And say what?'

'Don't you remember what I said to you, when you were ready to blow?'

Danny grins. 'I try not to.'

'How old's he now?'

'Seventeen coming up.'

'Someone needs to have words with him before he gets into bother.'

'Knock yourself out.'

I tap on the closed bedroom door. 'Callum?'

'I'm busy.'

'I'll be quick.'

When he doesn't answer I go in. He's cross-legged on the bed, books scattered about, scribbling on graph paper, calculator beside him. He doesn't look up.

'What do you want?'

'To see how you are.'

'I've said.'

I perch on the bed. 'What're you studying?'

'Maths.'

'That your favourite?'

'Yeah.'

'Why?'

Anger blazes behind fingerprint-smeared lenses. 'Numbers follow rules, they're predictable, explainable.'

'Not like people?'

He stabs some numbers into his calculator.

'That what you want to do, be a mathematician?'

He flicks a page in his textbook.

'Good man, yourself.'

He scribbles $x^0 = 1$ $x^{1/2} = \sqrt{x}$ $x^{1/n} = \sqrt[n]{}$.

'So you'll be away to university.'

He draws a thick line through his work.

'I'll let you get on.' I rise. Am at the door when he finally speaks again.

'Can you study in jail?'

'You can, but it's not the best place for it.'

He chews his pencil.

I sit beside him. 'Are you thinking that's where you'll end up?'

'Isn't that what happens to all volunteers?'

'Is this what you've been hiding up here from? Danny says they hardly see you. Are you worrying they're after you joining?'

He nods. One tear splashes onto his notepad, blurring $x^2 - \frac{1}{4} =$.

'You daft bugger.' I grab him into a sisterly embrace. 'Nobody's wanting you to do that.'

'But you did, and Danny and…' Dampness seeps through my shirt, soaking my shoulder.

*Before any potential volunteer decides to join the Irish Republican Army he should understand fully the issues involved. He should not join the Army because of emotionalism.*

I hold him at arm's length, fixing him in place with a heavy look.

'Callum, you don't choose to join; it chooses you. It's a burning inside, a hole you have to fill, a…' I cast about for something he might understand, '…an equation you've got to solve. And you can't make yourself feel that way.'

'But Mammy…'

'Would be smacking your arse if she knew you were thinking you've to join to please us.'

He sniffs. 'Really?'

'Aye. And how proud will we be at your graduation, watching you in cap and gown?'

'But what about the Cause?'

'You can be our Michael Collins.' Callum gapes at me. 'Aye, he was finance minister in the Dail. But you need qualifications for that, so crack on.' I point to his homework. 'And promise me you'll not do anything that your heart's not in.'

'Promise.'

'Grand.'

I want Callum to be the one whose laughter is our revenge.

At eight o'clock we set off for the Felons in a taxi. Frank brags to the driver that I'm fresh out of the jail. Next to me, Danny tenses. I keep my eyes on passing houses, my mind blinkered to passing thoughts.

Patsy is on the door, older and fatter but jolly as ever. He hands me my membership card. It reads: Caoilainn O'Neill nee Devoy.

'I wasn't sure what name you'd be wanting. Frank said... will that be alright?'

I glance at Frank who beams. 'Aye, fine.'

Above the bar a welcome banner is strung. Frank displays me like a trophy: his daughter-in-law, the IRA volunteer. There aren't many of us can openly call ourselves that because so few get done for membership; the peelers prefer bigger charges that are easier to prove and harder to serve out.

I'm greeted by people I don't know. Drinks are bought for me, my fingers crushed in handshakes that work my wrist loose. I scan the crowd, see Liam and worm over to him.

'Jesus, how are you?' he asks, hugging me.

'Grand. Have you a minute? I need a favour.'

He frowns but leads me into the back room. 'What's up?'

'Can you get me a gun?'

'Steady on, you've only been out a day,' he laughs.

'I've something to take care of.'

'I don't think...'

'I wouldn't ask if it wasn't important.'

'It's against regs.'

'I know but I've been stewing on this for two fucking years, longer even. If I don't deal with it tonight I'll never get it behind me. Please.'

He pouts. 'Alright.'

Ten minutes later he slips me a handgun. I tuck it into my waistband.

'I'll need it back in the morning.'

'Fine.'

'I hope you know what you're about,' he cautions.

'I do.'

We're at the Felons until gone midnight. I tip my drinks down the toilet or abandon them on the bar as I circulate among well-wishers. The gun warms up against my spine.

Back at the house Nora chases Callum to bed and follows a few minutes later. Danny goes half an hour after; he has work in the morning. Frank offers me one final tipple. I accept and we sit in the living room.

'Wasn't that a great night?' he asks.

'Aye.'

'It's grand having you out. Still, you could've had it worse.'

I see him for what he is, a spent old man, and wonder if that's what my da was like at the end, if one day I'll be depleted too.

'I could.'

'So you'll be reporting back, will you?'

'Is that what you're wanting me to do?'

'It's up to you,' he replies, sipping his whiskey.

'Is it?'

He shuffles in his chair, sets down his glass with a shaking hand. 'Why wouldn't it be?'

'Sure, Frank, two years is a shorter stretch than most. But it gave me enough time to think, about you, what you did, why you did it, what I'm going to do about it: you.' I level the gun at him in a steady two-handed grip that is as involuntary as inhale/exhale, even after two years of breath-holding.

His eyelids flutter. His mouth twitches. He leans forward, hands raised.

'Caoilainn, what're you doing?'

'Giving you chance to confess. Did you pass sentence? Pull the trigger? Both?'

He deflates, slowly then suddenly, as though a tiny hole is now a massive rip and all that's been keeping him afloat is escaping. He flops against the cushions with a fumph. 'I… it was… he…' Sobs explode. His shoulders judder, chest expanding and contracting in rapid jerks.

'Jesus, Frank, be man enough to tell me.' I cross to his chair and rest the muzzle against his temple.

He nods. 'It was me.' The words are torn from his throat. Fear, guilt and despair fall with his tears. 'I had no choice and, by Christ, not a day's passed when I haven't thought on that night, on both nights. I've tried, so I have, to make it right.'

'I know, Frank. That's why you brought me back. I understand. But you shot my daddy.'

His face sets cement-hard with Republican honour. 'He was a tout. We had to.' *The Army must defend the war of liberation by punishing collaborators and informers.* 'If he'd kept his mouth shut your ma wouldn't…' Hot tears dissolve the mask he's worn for twenty-five years.

I pull the gun from his temple, sit on the sofa with it aimed loosely at him.

'Tell me what happened, Frank: the fucking truth.'

He nods eagerly. 'We'd been given the order to dump arms. Your mammy was taking me and some lads to a cache. She was high ranking Cumann na mBan, in charge of her own section and overseeing several weapons stores. We'd not been there ten minutes when a load of Free State bollockses showed up. Me and the lads, we'd prices on our heads; if we'd been lifted we'd have ended up jailed. Your ma said she'd give us chance to get away because she'd likely be let off anything they'd charge her with. The Gardai didn't go for jailing women much then and she argued it was more important we got clear.'

'So you left her?'

'I didn't want to, Caoilainn, but there wasn't time to reason with her. She was a strong woman, your ma, and there wasn't a thing she'd not do for the Movement.' He ruffles his hair. 'We were half a field over when I heard the shots. They reckoned she came out firing.'

'You think that's true?'

He raises watery eyes. 'Knowing Fi, aye, it's the sorta thing she'd do.' He shrugs. 'You'd be the same.'

Would I? Probably, if it was needed.

Frank continues, 'Afterwards Charlie was broken. Just sat in his chair, drunk most times, muttering it was his fault. Folks thought he blamed himself for not talking Fi into getting yous away to America. But it niggled me. We'd had too many lads lifted, dumps raided. I asked around, put things together.'

'So you shot him?'

Frank shudders. 'I went to talk to him. He confessed. It was a relief, I think.'

'You were doing him a favour?'

'I did us all a favour. There would've been a court-martial: an execution. People would've known. Your granddaddy would've been shamed forever, his own son a traitor. Instead it looked like Charlie killed himself over the heartache. Most believed that, turned deaf ears to the rumours; it was easier to mourn a grief-stricken widower who couldn't go on than admit one of our own had gone against us.'

'Did Daideo know the truth?'

He starts to shake his head. I raise the gun, sharpening my aim. He swaps to nodding.

'He'd had you out in your pram. Got back right after I'd... I told him; he'd half guessed already from your da's drunken ramblings and been quare* fretting over what to do. He thanked me.'

'Because you saved him a job.'

'Aye,' Frank sighs, 'but it's not what you're thinking. Sure, Pat was a rock-hard Republican and that would've been reason enough but you were the first, the only, thing more important to him than Ireland. There's nothing he wouldn't have sacrificed to protect you. Your da doing what he did, hurting you like that, Pat couldn't've let it alone. If I hadn't, he would've. At least I saved your granddaddy that, Caoilainn.'

---

* queer—Irish slang for very/really

He crumbles into a blubbering shambles of washed-out manhood, snot dribbling from his nose and spit from his mouth.

I slump against the cushions, rest the gun on my lap and mentally examine myself, a car crash victim checking for injuries. There are no bleeding wounds or broken bones, no pain because what happened didn't happen to me. It's not even that I was thrown clear of the wreckage; I wasn't even in the car.

Standing in the future I have a 360° view of the past. It lets me see the tragedy of what happened isn't in the deaths, the fatal flaws, the star-sketched circumstances. It's in the catharsis that comes from the catastrophic ending. What happened was tragic and wasteful but necessary and right. It gave me a clean page to write my story on.

I glance at the old man opposite. He gulps down tears.

'I'm so sorry, Caoilainn. I wish to Christ it could've been different.'

'But it wasn't.'

'Don't think too badly of your da. He was a good volunteer, just not a strong one. And your mammy was as brave and bold as they come. I hope you're understanding now, why your granddaddy sent you to England.' Frank wipes his face. 'What now?'

I slip the gun away. 'We've just to get on living with our choices, Frank.'

In the morning I return the gun to Liam.

'Alright?'

'Fine.'

He nods. 'What next?'

'Dublin, for a while. I need to be away from here.'

'Fair enough. You want a lift?'

I finger a scrap of paper in my pocket. 'Got one.'

As city bleeds into country the past lifts from me. Patrick chats about the weather, colleagues, music; he's a massive Led Zeppelin fan. I realise how little I know him and ask questions. My ignorance disappears with the miles and when we park outside Daideo's house the blanks are filled.

'Oh Jesus, Caoilainn,' he says, killing the engine.

The front door is boarded with graffiti-daubed plywood: IRA out.

'I'd no idea,' he moans.

I climb from the car and sweep the road, looking for clues that were washed away months, years, ago.

With a crowbar, we prise the boards off and get in. Pinned to the living room door is a search warrant, signed by the Chief Constable of the Dublin Gardai. At the request of the RUC, they have conducted a search. Furniture is overturned, carpets and floorboards lifted, crockery smashed. I pick my way through the rubble, detached from the carnage; these are things, they can be replaced. I'm fine. Until I get to the bedroom, find Daideo's two schoolboy paintings, the canvasses slashed.

'Fucking bastards. I'll kill them.'

'You won't,' Patrick warns, seizing me. 'Standing Order number eight...'

'Fuck SO 8. I'll...'

He crushes me to his chest. I wrestle him, anger steaming off me. He keeps hold, even when I thump him and long after I've cried myself dry.

He helps me do practical things; getting the power switched on; lighting the fire, cleaning up: things I've forgotten I have to do for myself. It's evening before the place is liveable. Patrick suggests a takeaway.

'What do you fancy?'

'Whatever.'

'There must be something you've been longing for.'

There is, but it isn't food.

'Fish and chips?' Patrick suggests.

I nod and he goes to the nearest chippie. The front door closes, not with a clang but with a click. I'm alone: free.

I wander from room to room, opening and shutting doors and windows. I stand on the front step, go out to the back garden, climb into the loft. I boil the kettle, flush the toilet, light the gas stove. I lie on the bed in Daideo's room, stretching into the corners. I listen to nothing. I turn inwards, searching for cracks, find none. I think maybe I'm OK. after all. Then Patrick returns.

We eat sat on the disembowelled sofa, its stuffing spewing over us. It reminds me of another sofa in another wrecked house, another night with another man. I drink too much for someone who hasn't had any for two years. Emboldened by Bushmills and panicked by loneliness, I try to kiss Patrick. He folds me down calmly.

'Not like this.'

He puts me to bed. In the morning I find him on the gutted couch, half-buried in its innards like a slaughtered monster's last meal.

Patrick stays a week, sleeping on the sofa until I force him to take Daideo's bed. On his final night we go to a quiet pub where we sip wine and slurp leek and potato soup. Earlier he took me to the bank, helping me reinvest what's left of Daideo's money so I've enough to live off. He also sorted me a car, an old banger that he paid for, arguing the sense of putting it through his law firm's accounts as a tax dodge. I didn't protest because I need a car, he needs to leave me self-sufficient and I need to let him help me. Although I do stop him taking me shopping; if I can't manage that I might as well give up now.

'You sure you'll be OK?'

'Yes.'

'I could stay another…'

'You've got work. I'll be fine. I need to do this on my own, Patrick.'

He nods. 'I should be giving you this.'

My chain appears on the table between us. I fasten it around my neck, the locket and ring resting against my jumper.

'You won't put the ring on?'

I shake my head. 'I need to leave it behind.'

'All of it?'

'That's a big question.'

'Sorry, none of my business.' He stirs his soup.

'I'll let you know when I've the answer.' I lace my fingers through his.

March grinds into April. The empty hours nag at me. I need something to do, a routine, a 'nine-to-five'. It's what I'm used to. I find out where to go to get one but while I'm still dithering about doing it Spy Wednesday sneaks up on me. I barricade myself in the house for the next ten days, drawing the curtains and unplugging the telly before the Easter Rising commemorations besiege me. I don't even pin a lily to my lapel.

A fortnight later the Easter bombardment is over and I'm done dithering. The job centre is a modern building, glass fronted and topped with a gaudy sign. Inside I present myself to a man in polyester slacks who smoothes down his comb-over. We sit at a plastic table. He produces a form, notes details; name, age, address. After that it's more complicated. What qualifications have I? None. Skills? Experience? I can strip an Armalite in under a minute, bull's-eye a target at a hundred yards, live a covert double existence: fight the enemy. I say I can draw. He probes; technical drawing? I show him my pad, filled with imagined life while my real one was suspended.

He sighs. 'What have you been doing for the last few years, Miss Devoy?'

'I've been away.'

'Where?'

'Armagh.'

'Doing what.'

'Not much.'

'You must have done something,' he says, tapping his biro.

'I was in the jail.'

The pen falls from his fingers.

'Jail? For what?'

'Two years.'

'I mean the offence, Miss Devoy.'

'Membership of a proscribed organisation.'

His lips compress into a thin line. 'I don't think we can help you.' He slips my form in his bottom drawer.

'That's right. As long as things are cushy down here in the Free State why would you?' I stand, knocking over my chair. 'Here you are in your safe wee world, not giving a toss about what's happening in the Six Counties, tight-lipped when children get shot with rubber bullets, blind-eyed when innocent people are punished over your unfinished business. You make me fucking sick.'

A uniform comes towards me, an older fella, probably retired Garda. I could have him on his backside in five seconds.

I leave of my own accord, before we both get hurt.


There's a knock on the door. A young girl is on the step.

'You're to be in the corner phone box in ten minutes,' she recites.

'What for?'

She shrugs and skips off. I collect my cigarettes and wander up the road, waiting in the box, smoking and defending it from potential users. The phone jangles on time. I snatch at the receiver.

'Hello?'

'We're needing words. Go to St Stephen's Green. Wait under the Traitor's Gate.'


I lean against cool stone, the pond behind me. I forbid myself to turn, afraid of not seeing three ghosts, a wee girl and boy with an older man, feeding the ducks. Instead I crane my neck. Above me, on the underside of the Fusilier's Arch that forms the Grafton Street entrance to the Green are the names of 212 men, Irish traitors who defended England's empire in the Boer War. Are you guilty if you don't know it's wrong? Is believing it's right worse? I scan the names. There's no O'Neill, no Devoy. There is a Ryan.

'Caoilainn? I thought it was you,' says a woman I've never met. 'Shall we grab a coffee?'

'Aye.'

We walk to her car. She drops the small talk and we head north to Clontarf in silence.

She parks by a row of shops; post office, butcher, baker, grocer, newsagent.

'In there.' She nods towards the newsagents. 'You're expected.'

A bell above the door announces my arrival. A middle aged man glances up from the racing form. He jerks his thumb to a doorway.

'Upstairs, second left.'

I find a small kitchen. Kevin is at the stove, the kettle whistling.

'Tea?' he asks.

'No, thanks.'

He puts two cups and the pot on the table.

'Away in. Close the door. Sit down.'

I shut the door but don't sit.

'What's up?'

'I just want a wee chat.'

'About what?'

He pours tea, pushes a mug towards me. 'You.' He nudges a chair out with his foot. 'Sit down, for Christ sake.'

I drop into the chair and light a cigarette.

'We were expecting you to check in.'

'I've been busy.'

'Ah, sure.' Pause. 'Didn't see you Easter weekend.'

'I didn't go.'

He raises his eyebrows. 'Why's that?'

'Have you got me here just for that, for missing…?'

He bangs a fist onto the table. The mugs jump up; tea slops out.

'You're here to explain what the hell you were about in the job centre.'

I could make excuses, say I needed to see what I've lost. I don't; I've lost nothing. Because I gave everything up. He continues:

'We'll have no trouble down here.'

'That's why you let the Gardai wreck my house, is it?'

He fetches a cloth from the sink, mops the spilled tea.

'I'm sorry for that but there was nothing we could do. We know what you've been through, Jesus, most of us've had the same and worse but...'

'Worse than finding out from the peelers your da was a tout? Did yous know?'

He searches the room for an answer. 'There was talk, things we thought best not repeated.'

'I should've been told.'

'It wasn't anything to do with us. We've enough problems with today's touts; we don't need to be bothering with yesterday's as well.' He changes the subject. 'If we hadn't got to Brendan you'd still be inside.'

'And if I'd broken you'd still have him leaking stuff to every G-man in the Six.'

'Fair play, you held out better than most but that doesn't give you the right to carry on like you did the other day. Until you're telling me otherwise you're a volunteer and expected to act like one. That means not getting gobby about it in public,' he warns, voice rising.

'Is that what this is? You want to know what I'll be doing now I'm out?'

'I do, aye.' He sits down.

'What are my choices?'

'You can't operate like you used to, you'll be on every list from here to shagging London. You'd be best off in public, doing something for Sinn Fein, like Mairead.'

'I'll not be a pin-up for politicians. I'm worth more than that. So's she.'

'Jesus, Caoilainn, that's not in doubt. You're both grand volunteers. But there are other tactics in play now. Mairead understands that. You could do a lot for the Movement; political rallies, campaigning against injustice: be the next Bernadette Devlin.'

'What for? When the enemy're making up the rules the game's not fair.'

Kevin sighs. 'Fine, but we've to be practical now you're a known Republican: a convicted one.'

'You said choices?' I press, stubbing my cigarette out on the edge of the table.

'Have you considered leaving?'

'The IRA or Ireland?'

'Either. Both. I'm just saying if you've had enough that's fine. We'll not ask more of you than you've already given.'

'What else?'

Kevin swirls the teapot and tops up our mugs. 'I suppose… but it wouldn't be my preference… I'd have to clear it with the Council.'

'What?'

'You could operate somewhere rural, remote, as long as you kept out of sight. But it'd be a hard life. You'd be cooped up most days, waiting for the next mission.'

*Life in an underground army is extremely harsh and hard, cruel and disillusioning at times.*

'I've plenty of practice at that.'

'Maybes too much. I can't even say they'd clear you for it but it's your only option if you want to be active again. We'd not put you in Belfast or Derry and not England, for sure.' He studies me, eyes narrowed like he's trying to bring me into focus. 'Go away, do some thinking, but head down while you do, or it'll not be a friendly chat next time. I don't give second warnings.'

'One's enough. Sorry.'


I stumble home on foot, two hours jostled and overwhelmed on crowded streets, exposed and anxious on empty ones, trying to find a way forward, round: through.

I'm too close to the details to see the whole picture. I need the perspective of distance to view the choices, work out which one it's to be.

On the doormat is a letter from Briege, inviting me to visit. I don't want to but I can't stay in Dublin; there's no room for me here.

# Galway City—27ᵗʰ April, 1987

Their house is in the Salthill district. I get ravelled up in the city's one-way system, finally untangling myself, driving over Wolfe Tone Bridge, at 10.30 P.M. Their street, Grattan Terrace, is 1950s-built compact starter homes. I park across the road from the baby-boy blue house rented by Mr and Mrs O'Neill, and debate leaving. An upstairs window is lit. A man's silhouette passes back and forth, a bundle clutched to his chest. Pain knots my stomach.

Fifteen minutes and two cigarettes later I ring the bell. Briege opens the door. Toddler-tantrum screams teem out into the tranquil night.

'Caoilainn, is everything alright?'

'You said I could come.'

'Aye, course. We just weren't expecting you. Away in.'

'Who is it?' Connor shouts down.

'Come see,' Briege taunts.

He appears on the landing, Saoirse struggling with tomcat fury in his arms, and descends, not seeing me until he's got four steps down. He grins.

'Look, Saoirse.' He turns her around.

I've only seen her that once, when she was a newborn-blob. Now, two years later, she's a little person, auburn hair in plaits, a green nightie, odd socks clinging to her kicking feet. Her red face is screwed into a wail but hearing the unexpected instruction she opens her eyes. They are blue: Aiden's eyes. She stops shrieking, ogles me. Connor brings her down.

'Thank Christ,' he says. 'She's been yelling murder all evening. Who's this, Saoirse?' His voice is gentle, coaxing.

She shakes her plaits.

'It's Auntie Caoilainn.'

I flush at the title, remembering Patrick's hand in mine.

She repeats my name. It comes out 'Kee-un'

Connor laughs. 'She's having trouble with her 'ls'.'

A memory, of another time, hearing my name said in an alien way, surfaces. I draw back from it and force a smile. Saoirse hides her face against Connor's shoulder.

'Now are you gonna be a good wee girl and go to sleep so Auntie Caoilainn doesn't think you're naughty?' he asks her. The plaits nod. 'I'll be down in a minute,' he tells us, carrying the suddenly shy demon to bed.

Briege takes me to the kitchen, makes tea.

'How are you?' she asks.

'Never mind me, what about you?'

Her face is pale, the freckles stark against white. Her clothes are drab, grey and beige, baggy. A fold of loose flesh wobbles around her midriff as she moves, the remains of her baby weight for a baby that isn't. Even her sunlit hair is dull, scraped back and lustreless. She's been bleached by light too bright.

'Oh, you know.' The kettle slips from her hand and clatters into the sink.

I go over and put my arms around her, something I couldn't have done two years ago. She sniffles against me briefly then pulls away, snatching kitchen roll and rubbing her cheeks with it.

'Sorry. I've been better lately but sometimes...'

'It's me should be apologising for not coming sooner. For being such a bloody...'

'Don't,' she scolds. 'You've enough problems without adding mine.'

Connor comes in, loops an arm around Briege's waist, smiling down at her.

'She's settled.'

'Thanks, love.'

Where she's withered he's rejuvenated, becoming colourful: purposeful. Time has rewound, letting him reclaim some of the sacrificed Kesh years.

Seeing the teapot he jokes, 'Is the whiskey off?' and reaches down a bottle.

We sit cosy in the living room among the dolls and teddies, on their faded plum three piece. China dogs adorn the mantelpiece and family photos the walls; their wedding, their folks, Saoirse as a baby, a school picture of Danny, another of Callum and, lurking in plain sight, a blurry snap of Aiden and me, on our wedding day. I drop my gaze.

Connor pours drinks. 'Sláinte*.'

They toast my freedom, I their family. Conversation turns to Saoirse, what a cute wee madam she is. Briege tells me how, having seen her darning socks, Saoirse presented a slice of bread with an air-pocket hole, proclaiming, 'Hole bread, mammy mend.' She's into everything, curious as a kitten, a charming imp.

'But she's a good heart to her,' Connor adds. 'When Briege came home from hospital she rushed over with a massive hug and a wee posy of flowers.'

'That she tore her dress picking,' Briege reminds him.

'Ah, she's a love,' Connor says, 'and we'll have more like her, so we will.'

The doctors have told them there's no reason why they won't have more wee 'uns. These things happen sometimes; maybe a worry on your mind, a stressful lifestyle: God's will. It was a boy they lost.

Briege turns the talk from babies to work. She's been busy these two years, mostly training camps. She's an explosives expert now, teaching the boys to build safer bombs. She'll be back at it when she's ready but there's no pressure from GHQ.

Connor asks what'll I do now? I give him the only answer I have: I don't know, and the subject changes again.

Connor and I swap funny jail stories, like Mairead and me spiking the screws' tea urn with laxatives scammed off the prison quack then watching them all running for the loos, cursing the chef. Briege recounts outraged and outrageous reactions she's had from cock-a-hoop volunteers wrong-footed by an accomplished female bomber giving them lessons, saying how she's verbally slapped them down. We laugh at the madness of it all.

Connor makes up the spare room for me and we turn in. I lie awake, the photo of Aiden and me gnawing at my heart. After a restless hour I creep downstairs and lift the picture from the wall. We're just a happy smiling couple, his arm around me, my head on his shoulder. I sit with it on my lap,

---

* Cheers

reviewing. Was there a moment missed? Could I have saved us?

The door creaks. Saoirse stands in her bare feet, auburn kinks spilling over her shoulders, a teddy bear snuggled to her chest. I rub tears away. She comes over, offering me the bear. It, her, everything from now and then, buries me alive. I cry fat hot tears. She climbs up beside me, throwing an arm around my neck, stroking my hair.

'Anois, anois*.' She croons the magic word that makes things all better.

'Saoirse, what're you doing up?' Connor is in the doorway.

'It's my fault. I disturbed her,' I apologise.

He takes her from me. 'Go to bed, a chailín bhig♥.' He points her at the door and she wanders out, leaving her teddy with me. Connor notices the photograph.

'I didn't think...'

I dry my eyes again, reach for a cigarette, letting my hand brush ted's fur on the way. 'It's OK. She's got his eyes, have you noticed?'

'Aye.' He lifts the photograph. 'It's hard, so it is. But we've got to keep going.'

'Why? We can't win, Connor. Jesus. How much more do we have to lose?'

'I've been where you are. Prison's hardest when you're out but it gets easier.'

'I'm not sure I deserve it easier.' I force myself to meet his gaze. 'If I'd made different choices Aiden might still be here.'

He frowns. 'What d'ya mean?'

'The abortion. Maybe if I hadn't... we could've stopped then, got out before...'

'You think yous would've done that, really?'

'Maybe.'

'It's fine saying this now but you did what was right then.'

'Did I?'

He squeezes my hands. 'Ask yourself this: are you regretting doing it or just feeling guilty for not regretting it?'

---

* there, there

♥ little one

I stay ten days with Connor and Briege, helping around the house, playing with Saoirse, doing the shopping, walking round the bay. But I can't play 'let's pretend' forever and I can't decide anything while I am. I need to think on my choices, made and to make, but I'm still not far enough away to bring things into focus. I get in the car and drive for Rosmuc.

A clean Connemara dawn greets me at Gort Mór. I stop the car on the main road, a spot with a view of Pearse's cottage. Stillness fills me; no voices yelling, no doors clanging, no shots cracking. The cottage is so bright and clean, a whitewashed monument to the past. I don't know which memory has drawn me here; the one of Daideo and Pearse, sitting around the fire, or the one of me and Aiden, kissing on the doorstep. I abandon the car and walk up the lane, birdsong soothing me.

The cottage is time preserved in stone and thatch. I peer through the windows, trail fingers over the cool whitewash, grip the door handle. But I'm locked out, just like last time. I sit on the step, smoking and letting the sun rise behind me, sprinkling the dark lough with flecks of orange. The cigarette burns down. I lean against the door, close my eyes and paint the fantasy in my head; smoke curling from the chimney, an old couple sipping tea by the cottage, the Twelve Pins smiling benevolently down on them.

A cast shadow wakes me. My eyes snap open.

'A Thiarna Dia*!'

A man stands over me, dressed in work clothes, a bunch of keys in one hand, a bucket in the other.

I jump up.

'You startled me,' he gasps. 'Who are you? What are you doing here?'

'I'm just… I came to see the cottage. Tá mé buartha♠.'

My Irish reply is rewarded with a smile and more Irish, 'It's not too many visitors we're having here. Where are you from?'

---

* Goodness gracious

♠ I'm sorry

310

'Baile Átha Cliath♥.'

'It's a fair way from home, you are.'

'I am.' I gesture to the cottage. 'I just came to look.'

'You're knowing then, what this place is?'

'Teach an Phiarsaigh♠.'

His smile broadens. 'It is.' He straightens up, pride knocking ten years off his fifty. 'I'm Michael, the caretaker.' He jangles the keys. 'Would you like a look inside?'

'I would, go raibh maith agat♦.'

He unlocks the door and strides in. I hesitate. Beyond that doorway are places I've dreamed of going. I step through, breath held.

The main room is plain, bare, with a large central hearth and three doors; right, left and ahead. The floor is grey stone, the walls white. He beckons to me, shows me round, which takes five minutes because the cottage is three rooms plus a pantry, and explains the cottage's history, starting in the middle with how the Tans burnt it in '21. In Pearse's bedroom he talks of the Rossa funeral oration that made an infamous rebel of a bashful schoolmaster and I wonder if that was the time Daideo was here. In the main room he describes how Pearse and his guests would have told stories around the fire. In the second bedroom he mentions Willie Pearse, the artist.

'There was a room in the thatch too.' He gestures overhead. 'Probably for the St Enda's boys he brought here in the holidays. But we've not got the access up there anymore.'

I stare at the ceiling, certain that was Finn's room.

'Is there something you're looking for?' Michael asks.

There is but I won't find it here. The cottage is time rewound; the future is time unwound.

'No, thank you. I'll let you get on.'

Outside the sun is warm and the sky blue. I stare across the valley at the Ireland Pearse fought and died for, green and unspoiled. Some of the lads in Milltown never even saw it.

---

♥ Dublin

♠ Pearse's cottage

♦ thanks

Their Ireland was slummy grey housing estates, homes wrecked by squaddies.

*A member of the IRA is such by his own choice, his convictions being the only factor which compels him to volunteer, his objectives freedom for his people.*

Freedom: Saoirse.

In the end choosing is easy. Telling Patrick won't be.

# Dublin—10ᵗʰ May, 1987

I return from Galway to find a soggy British red-top nailed to my front door. The headline screams 'SAS 8-IRA 0' and there are eight passport snaps of young men, each crossed through with a thick X.

I look round, wondering which of my spineless neighbours to blame. Curtain-drawn windows stare back at me, unanswering.

Inside I make tea and read news I've heard a dozen times since it broke yesterday, the printed words more final than the radio's ephemeral voice. At least this time they were killed in action; the Loughgall RUC station, picture on page 2, is destroyed. We have eight new hero-martyrs to join the H-Block lads, Terence McSwiney and the 1916ers. *The battle honours won, the blood-stained trail of sacrifice.* Jim and his boys will get their colour parties. It's the Republican legacy: we died trying.

War is the only situation where everything and nothing are both fair enough.

I contact GHQ.


A lad I don't know admits me, pats me down then takes me to the dining room. Kevin is at the table. Another stranger is beside him, late thirties, medium build, swarthy complexion, a greying moustache under a bulbous nose and heavy brows above dark eyes.

I stare at him.

Kevin grunts, 'Brendan Hughes, Operations Officer.'

Hughes offers me a hand and I stumble back seven years to the first hunger strike, realising who he is: Darkie Hughes. 'Have a seat.' His voice is soft but with a northern accent.

I sit. Kevin lights a cigarette, smoke billowing from his nostrils.

'Have you decided, so?'

'East Tyrone.'

Kevin snorts smoke. Hughes knits his brows.

'Are they not short of volunteers there just now?'

'After filling Big Jim's boots, are you?' Kevin barks.

'No, but I can be useful there.'

'You can be shot by the SAS there,' he replies. 'You're wasting our time. Go home.'

'Fine.' I take an Easter lily pin from my pocket and drop it on the table. 'Any idea where I can find the INLA?'

Kevin fingers the pin. 'You won't consider another way?'

*We have no recourse to any other means.*

'There isn't another way.'

'What about the political offensive?'

'Brits out first,' I say.

Pressure builds. I wait for the blast.

'It's your funeral.' Kevin flicks the pin back to me and bangs out.

Brendan drums his fingertips on the table. 'You're dead on: you can be useful in Tyrone. But you can't be reckless. Convince me you're not.' He stills his hands on the polished mahogany.

I mirror his calm pose. 'I've been doing this since I was nineteen. It's my life. If I can't be an active volunteer I might as well be dead.'

'Is that what you're after?'

'No. I'm after doing my duty: freeing and uniting Ireland.'

'We're all after that, so we are.' He reaches for his cigarettes. 'You're cleared for the Tyrone brigade.'

'Don't I need Council approval?'

'Granted.' He nods once then shrugs. 'Your record as a volunteer speaks for itself and the Council're aware of your views on the armed struggle.'

'Is that a problem?'

'Not to me. I'm a soldier, I believe in fighting for freedom. With Gaddafi's gear we're set for a major push but things in the Six Counties need a massive shake up first. I'm seeing it happens. We're after trusted volunteers. You were a cell leader in England?'

'Yes.'

'Up for it again?'

'Hadn't you better OK. that with the Tyrone OC?'

'Done.' Brendan grins. 'He's a friend of yours: Liam. We're moving him over as of yesterday. Belfast's fucked, riddled with touts; he's wasted in the city. I've also got you a couple of former comrades, Tommy and Joe. Yous can form a bombing cell. I'm still thinking who else to put out there.'

'What about Mairead?'

Brendan shakes his head. 'Too dangerous now she's the smiling face of Republicanism.'

'I didn't realise she was.'

'Sure, been giving interviews, speaking at the Ard Fheis, working with Sinn Fein,' Brendan explains.

'And she's happy with that?'

'If it's how she can best serve, aye. We've to play to our strengths. That's Mairead's right now.' He clears his throat. Continues, 'All operations get cleared by me, through Liam. Apart from that no one's to know about you. I'll not have another shagging Loughgall.'

'You don't believe the SAS were lucky?'

'I do not. We're looking into it. I'll see you have volunteers you can trust but outside the cell...' He shakes his head. 'You need to be covert. Jesus, you need to be bloody invisible.'

'How?'

'Hide in plain sight. Make your life an open book, a boring one no one'll want to read. Can you manage that?'

'Yes. What about...?' I jerked my head at the door.

'Don't fret on it. Get your cover sorted. Let me know when you're ready. No rush, we need things to settle up there.' He shakes my hand again. 'Be seeing you. Take it easy, now.'

I ring Patrick's office.

'Can you come down this weekend? I've that answer for you.' There's a long pause. I think we've been cut off. 'Patrick?'

'I'll be down Friday night.'

On Friday morning I go to a hairdresser across town, ask her to cut and dye my long blonde hair.

'Sure, it's a drastic change you're making,' she comments. She holds the scissors, blades open, and takes a lock of hair between her fingers. 'You'll not regret this, will you?'

'I won't.'

An hour later my old hair is coiled on the floor. My new reflection is ready for action.

On the way home I find a fancy dress shop and buy a blonde wig to disguise my disguise until I need it.

Patrick's Mercedes drives into the street at teatime. He must've left work early. I greet him at the door. Seeing my short dark hair he presses fingers into his eye sockets for a second, as though to reset faulty vision.

'Caoilainn, what've you done?'

'My duty.' I pull him off the step and close the door.

'So you're going back? I thought we were…'

'There's no other way for me. I've spent the last two months looking. It doesn't exist.'

'Maybe you've looked in the wrong places.'

He darts forwards. I don't realise what's happening until his mouth is on mine, warm and firm. Hands pull me in. I fight free, drawing back, clenching my fist.

He catches my wrist. 'That's your answer to everything, is it?'

'What do you expect? I'm a volunteer, fucking soldier. If I was one of the boys you'd not be after me to quit.'

'If you were one of the boys I wouldn't be in love with you. I thought you felt the same.'

'It doesn't matter if I do, I can't, won't, give in. It's too important.'

'We agree on that but there are other ways.'

'Like leaving it to the politicians, trusting those self-serving shites to play fair? Don't be naïve, Patrick.'

'What happened to 'a ballot box in one hand and an Armalite in the other'?'

'You need both hands to fire an Armalite. This is who I am.'

'Who you think you have to be,' he corrects.

'Either way, if you can't accept it you need to leave.' I march into the kitchen, light a cigarette and listen for the front door slamming, his car revving away.

His shoes tap across the lino behind me. I turn. He steps towards me, puts out a cautious hand and brushes my hair.

316

'I can't leave you anymore than you can leave the Movement.' He weaves his fingers through mine.

'Let me tell you the score first.'

While I talk Patrick cooks, scurrying from counter to cooker, chopping and slicing, mixing and frying until two plates of corned beef hash appear. I tell him about the job centre incident, visiting Briege and Connor, Rosmuc, Hughes' words about the upcoming offensive and all the reasons why I can't not be a volunteer. Patrick listens and chews but doesn't comment. I flag the obvious conflict: a lawyer, even a Republican one, and a terrorist. I want the word to shake him but he pours more tea with a steady hand. I outline the future: Tyrone; hiding in the open, risking capture, dangers he's no business facing. Grease hardens into shiny globules on our plates. I warn him this could last for years. The ashtray fills up with dog-ends. He tells me he's also battened down for the long war. I ask if he's prepared for visiting me in jail, shouldering my coffin. He holds my hands and answers with his eyes. The evening spectrum passes through orange, red, violet, indigo, dying blackly. I tell him there'll be no family life for him, no children, a future calculated in hours, days at best. He says he doesn't want children, that days, even hours, are better than nothing. I don't know if I believe him. And I'm out of arguments.

'The prosecution rests, does it?' he asks as I light my last cigarette. 'And now for the defence.'

'Patrick, it's late…'

'I'll be brief. I love you.' He gets up from the table.

'Is that it?'

'If it was anything else I would've left hours ago.' He smiles, 'That speech wasn't you talking me into leaving; it was you talking yourself into letting me stay. Wake me if you don't get through to yourself.' He heads into Daideo's bedroom, where he slept last time he was here, closing the door behind him.

Thoughts toss on my mind's tide. Fingers twitching, I search the drawers for more cigarettes, find a small notepad and a stumpy pencil. I sit in Daideo's armchair, rolling the HB between my fingers, stroking the pad. Guided by memory and imagination, the pencil moves over the paper, shaping a face, the features familiar yet alien; eyes, nose, mouth, chin, angled up, looking at something not yet there. Details emerge; light in the irises, a smile on the lips, a flush to the cheeks. The pencil fashions a second face, above the first but turned down towards it, eyelids lowered, mouth returning the smile. I focus on each line, sweeping them across the page, filling the space, not allowing myself to view the whole, recognise the emerging couple. The pencil won't be refused; I don't stop until both faces are finished. The composition matches the wedding photograph of Aiden and me but the faces are mine and Patrick's.

Is this what I want?

Well, you drew us.

So you could tell me.

How are we to know what's in your head?

Isn't that where you've come from?

Head, heart, is there a difference?

There should be.

People change, fall apart: reassemble themselves.

I throw the drawing into the empty grate and go to wake Patrick.

As I open the door the soft sound of his breathing and smell of his aftershave drift over. I step inside, light following me, falling onto his face as the door swings back. He stirs, a restless hand brushing the glare from his eyes. He sees me and props himself up.

'I'm going?' he asks.

I perch on the bed, lean over and kiss him.


The next day Patrick suggests we walk in St Stephen's Green, take tea in the Shelbourne.

'OK. but you can't laugh.'

'At what?' he asks.

I produce the blonde wig.

'Why cut your hair and get that?'

'I'm in disguise.'

'As who, yourself?'

'Aye.'

I explain as we stroll around the duck pond. The wig is hot and itchy, smells funny. I'm glad when we get home and I can take it off.

Patrick cooks again. Studying the rhythm of his knife, the deft sweep of a cloth he swishes over countertops, I realise how feral I've become. When the plates are cleared and cleaned we curl up on the sofa. The wig sits in Daideo's armchair like the Addams Family's cat. Patrick nods to it.

'This plan, hiding in plain sight, how're you going to do it?'

'Rent a place up there under a different name.'

'Any objections to that name being Duffy?'

I jerk forward. He holds up a hand.

'Don't panic. I'm not proposing. But I've an idea if you'll listen.'

He suggests he rents somewhere in his name. I'll live there as Mrs Duffy. He'll visit on weekends, my Belfast lawyer husband. During the week I can be a housewife. It's not so far from the truth, except the housewife bit, and it means we get a part-time life. It could work.

'But I'll have to clear it with the OC and if there's an active operation you'll have to stay away. I won't have you in that situation. I mean it, Patrick.'

'Fine.' He grins. 'Wouldn't be much good as your solicitor if I got myself arrested.'


I meet Liam in a lay-by near Three Mile House, where, a lifetime ago, we trekked through the Monaghan countryside on the last day of training. It's gone two in the morning and blackness presses us hard.

'It's good to see you again,' he says, hugging me.

'How're ya?'

'Getting my head around the move.'

'Things a mess?'

'Chaos. Everyone's pointing fingers.' He shakes his head. 'Darkie took two lads off last week. Doubt we'll see them again.'

'Jesus.'

'Aye, it's part of the Brits' game, making us think they've a load of touts so we'll rip ourselves apart.'

We get into his car.

'What's happening with Rory?' I ask.

'Trial starts next month. He'll get ten at least.'

'Christ.' I spark a cigarette.

'We're set, so?' Liam asks.

I outline Patrick's plan. Liam listens, interrogates: what does he know? enough; what will I be telling him? nothing specific; can we trust him? definitely; am I sure about this? yes; is he? yes.

'Sure, it's pretty big of him, doing all this.'

'Well, I am sleeping with him,' I reply.

'I was only saying.'

'Bollocks, Liam, you were fishing. If you've something to ask, do it.' I glare at him through the darkness. He doesn't flinch.

'Fine. How does this play out?'

'Romantically or militarily?'

'You've responsibilities to your unit. Involving an outsider's risky.'

'We use supporters all the time.'

'But we don't shag them. What if yous have a row? Split? Feelings impair your judgement.'

'You think because I'm a woman I'll…'

'I'd be saying the same to any volunteer so don't be arguing some women's lib bullshit. We know each other better than that.'

'Aye, sorry.'

He sighs. 'I'm worried you're making this too complicated.'

'I'm making this work, for everyone.'

He drums his fingers on the steering wheel. 'OK., but any problems and I need to know,' he says, 'before, not after.'

'Fair enough.' I quell the relief rinsing me by getting practical. 'What about the rest of the unit? Hughes said he was sending Tommy and Joe.'

'They arrived last week. Seem decent.'

'They are. Who else?'

'I brought Ciaran outta Belfast myself. He'll be with you.' Liam fumbles for a cigarette, avoiding eye contact. 'And Danny. The Brits are all over him in town, he can't even fart but they know about it.' He produces his lighter. 'And they're not the only ones with eyes on him.'

'Loyalists?'

'Hmm. Someone shot up his mammy's house last week. There wasn't anyone in but... it's safer for him deep in 'Ra country.' Cigarette gripped between his teeth, he mumbles, 'If it's a problem I'll put him in another unit.'

'No. He can live with me and Patrick.' In the flicker of Liam's lighter I see him raise an eyebrow. 'Sure, he's my wee brother,' I say. Liam shakes his head but he's grinning. 'Isn't the best lie the one that's closest to the truth?'

'It is.'

We talk on, finalising details. Liam suggests Ballygawley as a base. It's 80% Nationalist plus Jim's lads did over the RUC station a couple of years ago so there's a sense in the village that they've had their troubles, like growing pains. Also it's only three miles, across the fields, to Monaghan, a retreat I hope we won't need, and twelve miles from Dungannon, where Tommy and Joe have a flat rented. They'll set the plumbing/electrical business running again. Ciaran'll be in Coalisland, working a few shifts in a pub and lodging in a boarding house. That's further from Ballygawley but Liam'll sort him a car so that shouldn't be a problem. All I have to do is find a house, move in and become Mrs Caoilainn Duffy.

Patrick and I are married by Aiden's old forger friend who knocks up a marriage certificate for Mr and Mrs Duffy plus driving licence and passport for Mrs Duffy, a young woman with short dark hair and a Mona Lisa smile.

Studying the new name, I'm almost convinced I can have everything.

Patrick parks outside the estate agent in Dungannon. We've an appointment in five minutes. She claims she's found the perfect place for us; a two bed, cottage-style property, a mile north of the village, on a hillside overlooking Ballygawley and with spectacular views of the countryside.

'Before we go in I've something for you,' Patrick says. He hands me a jewellery box.

Inside is a plain gold band. Blood rushes to my cheeks, my mouth dries up and my heart stutters.

'I thought maybe you'd rather not wear the one you've got,' he mumbles.

'Thanks.' I slip it on my finger and twist it round, cold metal constricting my skin.

'Does it not fit?'

'It's fine. Thank you,' I say again.

I worry at the ring the whole time we're in the estate agents, making my finger raw from screwing and unscrewing it. It doesn't help that she keeps calling me Mrs Duffy even though I say Caoilainn's fine. But the house is right and Patrick signs the lease. I have a week to get used to the name and the ring.

The days count down. I keep busy with logistics: selling my car; planning the trip north without it; packing; spreading a rumour round the neighbourhood that I'm emigrating; sham-clearing the house and planting a stolen 'For Sale' sign in the garden. It should be easy, ending one life and starting another. I've done it before, more than once. I think of the homes I've had and the people I shared them with. But there is no precedent for this.

I leave with the morning commuters, walking to the bus stop wearing the wig, shouldering my rucksack like a student backpacker. At lunchtime I arrive in Belfast. In the bus station toilets I bin the wig and go to meet Patrick. His car loaded, the keys to our new house in his pocket, we set off. Four hours later Mr and Mrs Patrick Duffy are buying groceries and introducing themselves to the Ballygawley locals.

The weekend is our honeymoon, even though, according to the fake marriage certificate, we've been together five years. We sleep late, wake up together, make love, ramble the hills, drink in the village pub, eat the dinner Patrick cooks in our kitchen and fall back into bed. It's two days of bliss. On Monday morning he leaves early for a bail hearing. I wait for the telecoms bloke to connect the phone. He's late. I'm bored.

I make the bed, mop the kitchen floor, peg laundry on the line and realise I'll be insane by teatime if I don't find something else to do. Once the phone is sorted I wander into the village, buy a plain A4 pad, pencils, all HB because they don't stock any other type, a rubber and a packet of child's crayons. Sitting in the garden, overlooking the village, I sketch the valley. Tomorrow I'll catch the bus into Dungannon, buy paints, pastels and canvasses.

After tea, and before I start a still life of dishcloths, bleach bottles, brushes, rubber gloves and a feather duster to be titled 'The Housewife's Arsenal' I call Brendan, letting him know I've made it north. I ask him to check on the house for me. Daideo wanted to leave me the security of my own home, and, although it hasn't been home for too long, I don't want to totally abandon it, just in case. Brendan promises to get the lads to pop round off-times. Next I ring Liam, giving him the number in case he needs to contact me and directions so he can find me. He says he'll visit soon; Danny will be here next week, after he's been through decontamination so the Brits lose sight of him.

'You told Patrick he's joining yous?'

'Yes,' I lie.

Liam arrives after dark.

'Wouldn't want the locals seeing us, thinking we're having an affair,' he jokes.

'Not the first time we've been there,' I say, remembering Nora's suspicions during my first Belfast Christmas.

He takes the full tour, all five minutes of it, and craics on about my modest mansion.

'Sure, you'd not get this on a volunteer's allowance. Must be grand being a kept woman,' he teases.

'Jealous, are you? Because I've heard they're making leaps-and-bounds progress with sex change surgery these days,' I reply, grinning widely and passing him a beer. 'Mind, you'd have to pretty yourself up a bit.'

We start laughing, the banter restoring our balance.

'Before I forget, Hughes sent this.' He hands me an envelope. 'One of the Dublin boys found it on your doormat.'

It's type-addressed to Kaylynn Devoy, no stamp or post mark. Inside is a single sheet of paper. Glued to it is a yellowed copy of my 1984 mug-shot, clipped from a newspaper. A bold cross is scored over the image. Beneath, scrawled in red lettering, are the words 'your day will come'.

'It's from a fan,' I say, holding it out to Liam.

He scans it, expression grim. 'Fuck. You had any more like this?'

I tell him about the Loughgall newspaper clipping.

Liam shakes his head. 'You should've said something.'

'It's just one of the bloody neighbours.'

Liam sighs. 'Maybe. Could be Loyalists. I'd best let Hughes know.' He chucks it into the bin. We smoke in silence for a few minutes. 'Away outside. I've brought you something.'

Mist circles the cottage. We cut through it to the car. Liam pops the boot lid and pulls out an Armalite.

'Thought you'd like some practise.' He hands me the rifle, a handgun and two magazines for each. 'God bless Gaddafi. You need a refresher on these?'

I take up the Armalite, load and unload it, safety on/off, am about to take it apart when Liam stops me.

'Aye, daft question. Sorry,' he says, 'but watch yourself. Best if you go over the border, find somewhere you'll not be disturbed.'

'OK.'

'Grand. Well, I'll be heading off. You've my number if you've a problem.'

'Thanks.'

We hug and he drives away, fog devouring his car.

At dawn I take both guns, the Armalite disassembled in my rucksack and the 9mm tucked into my waistband, and hike into Monaghan. Finding a wooded grove far from any settlements, I reassemble and load the rifle. Aiming at a distant tree, I force myself to picture a face, young, the eyes straining, camouflage paint smeared around them, one squinting down a telescopic sight trained on Mrs Murphy's bedroom window. *It is not an easy thing to take up a gun and go out to kill some person.* I fire. The crack of the weapon tears through me. I miss, curse, adjust my aim and try again. It takes a dozen shots before I score a hit but I don't stop until both magazines are empty, my shoulder throbbing and my ears blistered by the rifle's retort. The handgun is gentler and by lunchtime I'm heading back, reassured.

Friday brings Patrick.

'I've missed you,' he says, pulling me into his arms, crushing my sore shoulder against his chest.

I flinch.

'Are you hurt?'

'It's nothing.' I step back.

'Let me see,' he insists.

The bruise is purple, yellowing around the edges.

'Where'd you get that?' He strokes the multicolour pain.

'Target practice.'

'You've a gun here?'

'Under the bed. Two, actually. Liam brought them but don't worry, they'll be back in the cache on Monday. We'll only keep weapons here if there's a need.'

Patrick sighs.

'You knew this was happening.'

'Aye, but, so soon?'

'We need a word.' I lead him to the table, make tea and offer him cake. He smiles when he sees it. 'Don't get excited, I bought it in the village.'

He pushes the plate away. 'Go on.'

'My brother's coming on Tuesday.'

'What brother?'

'Danny. He's going to stay here, with us. He'll bunk in the spare room and find himself a wee job, mechanic if he can.'

Patrick drums his fingers on the table. 'Does he know about us?'

'I'll talk to him when he arrives.'

'Liam says you've had threats.'

Brendan and I are in the snug of a country pub in Donegal, heads bent together, talking in voices too low to be overheard by the old codgers playing dominos two tables over.

'I'm not exactly popular with my neighbours,' I say.

He shakes his head. 'Are you sure it's them?'

'You're thinking it's Loyalists?'

'Maybe.' He gulps at his pint. 'They're on about sending me to the States, fundraising.'

The non-sequitur forces me to ask.

'Aren't you meant to be heading up operations, getting us on the offensive?'

'Seems not everyone's got the stomach for that.' Ash drops from the end of his quivering cigarette.

'What's that mean?'

'I'm starting to think… maybes some in the leadership are fighting a different war just now.'

Dread stiffens me. He can't fucking mean… I don't get to finish the thought.

'It's power they're fighting for. Political power. If they can win themselves a say-so in Northern Ireland I reckon they'll happily forget about a united Ireland.'

His words are monstrous, terrifying, fucking outrageous. He must be wrong. Or mad. Or drunk. It's not true. They'd never betray the Cause: us.

I'm seven, eight, ten, twelve, sixteen…

'Too powerful for our good.'

'We won't be bullied by self-serving bureaucrats.'

'They screw you over for their own ends.'

'Power can be a potent poison, love.'

'Power perverts principle, that's always their problem.'…

Hughes continues:

'Someone's pushing hard, from within, talking of putting up our guns: negotiating.'

'They're after running down the armed struggle?'

'Why else pack me off when we're readying for the big push?'

'Maybe it's tactical,' I suggest, trying to silence childhood lessons about power's corrupting potential.

He shakes his head. 'It's other things, too: Loughgall.'

The word ices me. 'You still think there was a tout.'

'I do.'

'You know who?'

'I've an idea. He can't be touched.'

'But you're on the Council, surely…'

Brendan shakes his head. I cower from pressing him to explain.

'I'm thinking the mission was sabotaged to get rid of Jim and his lads because they'd never agree to swap their bombs for ballots,' he says. 'There're powerful men straddling both sides of the line, using their influence to weaken us so's we'll have no choice but to support peace talks.' He taps his empty pint glass on the table. 'Those who won't move to a political solution will be forced over or forced out.'

He heads to the bar for a refill. I stumble, trip, fall into an unseen abyss.

# Ballygawley, Co. Tyrone—12<sup>th</sup> July, 1987

Danny and I stand in the lane, taking turns with the binoculars, spying on the Orange Order parading through Ballygawley.

Even without 10x magnification the orange slash, ripped up and down the village's L-shaped main road, goads us from our serene vantage point.

'Look at the shites,' Danny mutters.

'It's just willy-waving,' I reply. 'Them kidding on they're the ones in charge. I'm getting fried out here, let's go.' I head for the cottage's shady garden.

We shelter under the apple tree. The oppressive whomp-whomp of Lambeg drums drifts up from the valley. I close my eyes and draw down the sounds; flutes and whistles, the machine gun rattle of snares, cheering, singing.

'How can you listen to that racket?' Danny demands.

'If you let it bother you they win.'

There's a scrabbling then a clatter as he pitches a rock at the garden wall.

'When're we gonna do something? I might as well've stayed in Belfast.'

'We'll have a meeting soon.'

'Tonight?'

'No. Patrick's coming down.'

Another rock cracks the wall.

'Are yous getting married?'

'No.'

'Why not?'

'I don't want to.'

'Why not?'

'Christ, how old're you, two?'

He routes through the shaggy grass for another rock. I stamp a hand over his.

'Pack it in.'

'I'm just trying to work out what the fuck you're doing,' he snaps, pulling his hand away.

'Having a life. Half a one, anyway.'

'I thought we were your life.' He glares at me.

I don't know if he means the IRA or the O'Neills and I'm afraid to ask. I know he's grassed to Nora about me shacking up with Patrick.

'I still miss him, you know. But we've got to go on living, otherwise they,' I wave my hand in the direction of the village, 'win again. Here.' I offer him a cigarette, hoping for a peace pipe effect.

He lights up, puffing thick smoke into the heat-heavy air.

'Promise you won't disappear,' he says, eyes on the horizon.

His family is fractured, crumbling. He needs scaffolding.

'Catch yourself on, of course I won't. Stop worrying. You want a choc-ice? There are some in the freezer.'

'Aye, thanks.'


I take Danny to a motor auction. We buy a late 1960s Norton Navigator 350cc. It's a wreck but Danny's sure he can fix it. After nearly breaking my ankle on the kick-start we get it going and I ride back to Ballygawley, Danny tailing me in the car Liam got us, in case the bike conks out.

It doesn't. We wheel it into the garage. In the morning we'll start stripping and tuning it.


Patrick and I lie in bed. Heat from his body cocoons me. It's Saturday night. We spent the day hill walking, picnicked by a lough. We're so convincing as pseudo-us, hyper-us, we're beginning to believe it ourselves.

I check the clock. It's after eleven. Danny's not home from the pub yet.

'Caoilainn, are you awake?'

'He should be in by now.'

'He's fine.' Patrick's hand creeps up my bare back. 'Are you planning something?'

'What makes you think that?'

'The bike.'

'I just miss riding, plus it'll keep Danny busy.'

'I know when you've something on your mind.'

'Then you should know not to ask.'

'Please, be careful.' He reaches for my hand, twirls the plain wedding band.

'You're the one married to a trained guerrilla,' I reply.

'But I'm not, though. I mean it, be careful.'

'I will.'


Patrick leaves earlier than usual on Sunday, returning to Belfast to check everything's ready for Rory's trial which starts tomorrow. An hour later Ciaran, Tommy and Joe arrive, Ciaran parking his old green Hillman in the garage next to my Navigator, now tuned beyond the standard 80mph. They're boisterous, kids geed up for excitement: soldiers ramped up for action. I usher them inside. Danny pours tea and opens custard creams. I sit at the table.

'Are we on for something?' Tommy asks.

I slide a sheet of paper across to him.

Tommy glances at it, passes it to his brother and it goes round to Ciaran and Danny before coming back to me. It's a map of Fivemiletown, a route traced in pencil, Xs marked and 10.53 P.M. written up.

'It's a BA foot patrol,' I explain.

'What's the plan?' Joe asks.

'A bomb, medium sized, Semtex, remote control. We dig it into the verge here.' I tap an X. 'Practically zero risk for civilians; aren't any houses near and it's on the return route to the barracks. There's a spot here.' I tap another X. 'A hill, few trees for cover, so we can see who's in the area before we detonate. Snipers here and here in case.'

The lads nod.

'Where're we gonna make the bomb?' Tommy asks.

'Disused barn outside Garvaghy. How long will it take you?'

Tommy rubs his eyes. 'Dunno. Does it have to be Semtex?'

'It's what we've got in the cache, otherwise we'll be faffing around with fertiliser and I'd rather not wait; they might change the patrol route.'

'It's just, I've not used that stuff yet.'

'Couldn't Briege help?' Danny suggests.

'Maybe. I'll ask.'

'Grand,' Tommy says. 'She can train me up.'

'When's this on?' Ciaran asks.

'Soon.'

We agree Tommy will do the detonation with Joe waiting in the van so they can get away. Ciaran and Danny will take the sniping posts and I'll set the bomb.

'What about weapons?' Danny asks.

'Armalites for you and Ciaran. I'd rather we,' I glance at Tommy and Joe, 'didn't carry anything; safer if yous are stopped afterwards. You can pretend you're on an emergency callout and there'll not be anything to say you're lying.'

'Fair enough,' Tommy says.

Danny shakes his head. 'Aye, but what about if you're stopped carrying the bomb? You should have a gun. It'd give you half a chance of getting away. You could always chuck it after if you don't want to risk being stopped with it.'

'Sure, we'd never have someone planting a bomb without a weapon as backup,' Ciaran agrees.

'Fine, I'll take a handgun. Anything else?'

There isn't. Ciaran, Tommy and Joe leave. Danny starts dinner, bangers and mash. I ring Briege, who offers to come on Tuesday night. Talking in code she says Semtex bombs are her speciality now and promises it'll only take her a day, meaning we can do the job Thursday night, by when she'll be at home putting Saoirse to bed. I contact Liam, arranging to have bomb-making materials and weapons at the barn on Wednesday.

Danny shouts through from the kitchen: do I want beans? I say yes and wonder if, in the canteen of the Fivemiletown barracks, the squaddies are getting a similar choice. They'll be setting out on tonight's patrol in an hour's time. Four evenings from now they'll be doing the same but some of them won't be returning for cocoa or whatever they have to unwind after tramping through enemy territory for three hours, faces painted and weapons cocked. They'll be the latest war stats.

On Tuesday Danny collects Briege from the station in Monaghan. Tea that night, stew cooked by Danny, reminds me of evenings with the London cell; we tell jokes and laugh, drinking Guinness and getting merry. I notice Briege only sipping hers, refusing more when Danny tries to top up her glass, blushing when he teases her about being on the wagon.

She glances to me. 'Actually, we're having another baby.'

'Jesus, why didn't you say? I wouldn't have asked you to help.'

'It's OK. I'm fine. I wanted to.'

'Well, thanks and good on you,' I say, hugging her tightly.

She smiles then steers the conversation back to the operation.

We sit up late, talking and drinking. Briege persuades Danny to sing, then surprises us by singing herself, in Irish, a lullaby, she tells us.

'It was all that would get Saoirse to sleep when she was teething,' Briege adds. 'Although Connor was for rubbing her gums with whiskey.'

'Aye, get her a taste for it while she's wee,' Danny jokes.

'I've a taste for it now, myself,' I say. 'Have we any?'

Danny finds a bottle, hands around glasses. Briege puts hers down without drinking.

'Don't if you'd rather not,' I say.

'I'm just being a bit careful,' she says, 'after last time.'

'I'll put the kettle on,' Danny offers.

'Ah, I'm sure one won't hurt,' she replies, 'and we should have a toast.'

'To what?' Danny asks.

'A successful operation?' she suggests.

'It's you we should be toasting,' I say. 'Comhghairdeas!* Sláinte!'

Briege blushes but raises her glass.

I'm glad I can be properly happy for her this time.

Next morning, a whiskey headache splitting my skull, I study my reflection in the bathroom mirror. I look younger, like four years have been wiped out. Taking the chain from around my neck I remove the wedding ring, tracing the Celtic scrolls with my fingernail before shutting it in the bathroom cabinet.

---

* Congratulations!

*

It's lunchtime before we head to the barn; Danny and I are still hung-over, Briege suffering with morning sickness. When we arrive Tommy's van is parked outside and also, Liam's car. He and Tommy are dragging on fags.

'Where've you been?' Tommy asks.

'Inspecting the inside of my loo bowl for cracks.'

'Big night?'

I shrug.

'You alright?'

'Fine. What're you doing here?' I ask Liam.

'A minor hitch,' he says, crushing his dog-end underfoot. 'We couldn't get to the cache last night: Brits on the loose. You're alright for the bomb, I've got what you need from another dump but I'll have to send to Fermanagh for the guns.'

'I'll go myself.'

'You know I can't let you have access to a cache in another brigade area. Don't fret, they'll be here tonight. You can collect them when you pick up Briege.'

'I'll wait, then go through to Ciaran as soon as the weapons arrive.'

Liam scans the surrounding countryside. 'No. Best you're not all here. You never know. Come back later.'

'I'll take Ciaran his on the way home,' Tommy offers.

'No unnecessary risks, Caoilainn,' Liam warns. 'That's an order.' He grins.

I agree with a nod and a smile.

But the line between unnecessary and essential risks is only as thin or thick as the Brits decide to draw it.

With nothing to do, Danny and I kick around the house. He tidies the kitchen and bakes tattie scones. I get my sketchpad and start a family portrait of Briege, Connor and Saoirse, leaving a space for Baby in Briege's arms. Waiting is the worst part of operations.

At 10 p.m I go to the car. It won't start. I call Danny who prods the engine.

'Starter motor's dead.'

'Can you sort it?'

'Aye, when I get another one.'

'Shite!' I don't want Briege left at the barn longer than necessary. There's no phone there so I can't ask Tommy to drive her back, plus, he's needing to go to Coalisland with Ciaran's rifle. 'Get me the spare skid-lid and my rucksack. I'll go for her on the bike.'

Danny grins. 'She'll not like that.'

'I'll ride like a nun,' I joke.

Twenty minutes later I arrive. Briege is waiting for me.

'What's this?' She points at the bike.

I explain about the car and ask if she's done the bomb.

'Easy. Tommy's taken it, and Ciarnan's Armalite. Yours are inside.'

We go into the barn. I strip the second Armalite, pack it in the rucksack and tuck the handgun into the back of my jeans.

'Good job I didn't wear a skirt,' Briege says, eyeing the bike.

'It's fine. Hold on here, feet there.' I point out the grab rail and foot pegs. 'Lean with me in the corners.'

'Jesus,' she mutters, cramming auburn curls into the open-faced helmet which squishes up her cheeks so she looks like a greedy hamster.

She fumbles with the helmet's buckle. I kick the bike over and feel the suspension bounce as she clambers up behind me. We bump down the lane, the headlight marking a jittery path through the darkness. Briege sits stiffly behind me and I fifty-pence the turn onto the A5 because she counters the bike's lean but the rest of the road is pretty straight and we'll be safe home soon enough.

As we approach Ballymackilroy I slow for a hairpin. We wobble round it. White light blares out half a mile up the road, illuminating an RUC checkpoint and two peelers, standing by their Newry ice-cream van, ready to stop oncoming motorists.

'Fuck.' I slow the Navigator further, dropping into second. 'They weren't here when I came through before.'

Briege presses up against me. I feel a draught on the small of my back and icy fingers against my skin as she takes out the gun.

'What're you doing?' I hiss.

'Don't stop,' she instructs.

'They'll shoot us.'

'And what'll they do when they find we've two guns?' she demands. 'Put your foot down or whatever it is you do on this thing.'

I want to reason with her but the checkpoint is rushing towards us despite me dropping my speed to a crawl. One of the peelers gestures for me to stop. I nod, slow to walking pace and pull the bike into a wide arc towards him. Thinking I'm complying, he drops his arm.

I snap my visor down. Briege's knees pincer me, bracing. I release the throttle for a second, shifting my hand forward for a grip that'll let me wind on the power. The bike lurches, threatening to stall. The peeler steps to the side, pointing for me to park up. I nod again, start tightening the turn, straighten out with a jerk of the bars, kick down into first gear and snap the throttle fully open. The Norton's engine rages. Three shots crack out. I flick the bike's lights off, throwing us into cloaking darkness. In the rear view mirror I see the rozzer crumple to the tarmac. The bike skitters about as Briege twists to fire again. More gunshots bark. I feel a jolt. The bike slithers. I wrestle to keep us upright. Lose. The bike's backend washes out. Laws of time and motion implode. Glass-clear thoughts pierce my brain; we've been hit, the bike's going, the peeler is still shooting, don't get trapped under the bike: jump now!

I leap off, skimming the road on my side, friction burning my arm as my leather jacket grates to nothing on the tarmac. I'm still skating as I try to stand, stumbling awkwardly, feet flailing as though on ice. A hedge catches me. Ripping off my helmet, I spin round. The bike is further up, rear wheel sticking out of the hedge. Briege is pinned under it. In a crouching run I dash to her. She holds up the gun.

'We've got to get out of here,' I pant. 'I'll lift the bike up…'

A swarm of bullets bites the air around us.

'Just go, Caoilainn,' she gasps.

I put my hands out, patting inside her coat. Warm wetness oozes through my fingers. She moans.

'Jesus, no.'

A voice hollers, 'Put down your weapons and come towards us slowly.'

I glance down the street. Illuminated by their own floodlights I can see the dead peeler in the road, flying on bloody wings. The second is a bulging shadow crouch by the meat wagon. I grab the gun and fire twice. The shadow dives behind the van. Thoughts charge through my head, express train carriages whipping by: he'll be on the radio now; the nearest RUC station is Dungannon, twenty minutes for reinforcements from there; they could send an off-duty bollocks from Ballygawley or Garvaghy; I've ten minutes at most.

'Back in a jiff,' I tell Briege, fumbling around the edge of the helmet to stroke her cheek. 'Don't leave.' I feel her smile.

I creep along the hedge on the van's nearside, gun drawn. Peering round I see him huddled against the vehicle the way a child hugs its mother's skirts. I remember Callum cowering like that the night Cathy was shot. The peeler turns, blinks at me, starts to stand, splintering the memory. The glaring searchlight exposes his baby's face; fresh pink skin, plump and downy. His hands fly up in a gesture of surrender. Both of them are empty.

'Please, don't shoot. I…' he nods towards the road, '… dropped it. I'm unarmed.'

So was Aiden.

'Yous are the ones who wanted big boy rules. That means no take backs.'

I pull the trigger. He falls forwards. It's war. I'm not sorry.

Aiming for the floodlight I fire twice more, popping it like a balloon.

I sprint to Briege. She's still conscious but her eyes don't focus on mine and her replies are a mumbled jumble of Irish and English. She says Saoirse's name three times. I tug off her helmet, lift the bike with adrenalin-fuelled superhero strength and shove it away. It falls with a clanging, crunching that bounds up the road. Staining the pale fabric of her coat are two inky patches, one on her right shoulder, the other on her left hip.

'Need a hand, love?'

I jump up, gun aimed and cocked, confronting the voice that belongs to a man, fifties or older, standing in the street in his dressing gown.

'Steady, there.'

'Who the hell are you?'

'Terry Boyce, from over the way.' He points to the only house on the road, lights on, door open. 'Soon as I saw those buggers setting up quarter of an hour ago I knew I'd best watch for trouble. It's alright; I'm with yous.'

'You don't know who I'm with and for all I know you could be chief constable of the RU sodding C.'

'Anybody out here with a gun and no uniform's a Republican,' he tells me, 'and either you trust me or your friend'll bleed to death.'

'You a doctor?'

'No, but there's one in Monaghan I can call for you. You can take my car.' He points to a hatchback parked nearby. 'I'll get the keys.' He jogs to the house.

I crouch by Briege, pinch her earlobe. Her eyelids flutter and her lips move but the words are silent. I think she's praying.

'Here.' Boyce tosses me a key-ring, drops to his knees and starts ripping open first aid dressings.

I put the gun away and we staunch the blood, strapping Briege's side and shoulder with gauze and bandages. Boyce carries her to the car, a knight with a princess. He lays her on the back seat.

'This is the doctor's address. I'll call ahead for you.' He crumples a scrap of paper into my hand.

'I can trust him?'

'Aye. Now get going. I'll wait a bit then call the peelers. It'll look off if I don't.'

'What about...' I glance at the dropped Norton, our chucked helmets.

337

'Don't worry, just get her seen to.' He opens the driver's door for me. 'Jesus, didn't I never think I'd see two wee lassies gunning down peelers.' He smiles. 'You'll be village legends after this.'

Don't you have to be dead to be a legend?

I race down the A5, turn off for the cottage, clatter through the door and yell to Danny, 'Grab some towels. Get outside,' then dart to the car and climb in the back.

Briege is conscious again, shivering. Her face is blanched, her lips bluing. She fixes glazed eyes on me.

'I'm sorry.' Her voice is a thin whisper. 'Tell Connor and Saoirse I'm sorry.'

I blink away burning tears. 'We're getting you to a doctor. You'll be fine.'

'Jesus, what happened?'

Danny is behind me. I scramble out of the car.

'Get in. Keep pressure on her wounds. Keep her awake. We need to get to Monaghan.'

Danny clambers in. I start the engine.

A few minutes later bilingual place names signal we're over the border. I stamp on the accelerator, pushing the car to eighty and ninety, bouncing over potholes, railing around bends, headlights pinging off trees, wing mirrors brushing hedgerows. Danny talks to Briege but her replies are whimpers, Connor's and Saoirse's names, then nothing.

'Is she awake?' I demand.

'I... can't...'

'Don't let her go, Danny.'

'How?' he screeches.

'Sing.'

'What?'

'Fucking sing.'

We arrive in Monaghan to the first verse of 'The Queen of Connemara': 'When the black floor of the ocean and the white foam rush together, high she rides, in her pride, like a seagull through the gale.'

I strain to read the creased-up paper under the flash of streetlights. There are bloody smears on it but I make out the road name and house number.

'We need Hill Street. Can you tell what these directions say?' I pass the paper to Danny.

'Try a left up here.'

I go the wrong way down a one way street, take other left instinctively and come to a t-junction.

'Here,' Danny shouts.

I swing left again, onto Hill Street and bump the car onto the pavement.

The house disgorges a white haired man, his shirt buttoned up wrong.

I jump out. 'Terry Boyce sent me, I've…'

'He called, get in, quick.' He retreats inside.

Danny carries Briege into the house. The doctor leads us to the kitchen. The table is cleared and spread with a blue sheet. Medical instruments are lined up on the counter.

'Put him there.' He indicated the table, faces us, sees Briege and recoils.

'What's wrong?' I ask.

'Terry said you'd an injured volunteer,' he stammers.

'We do.' I nod at Briege, prostrate on the table.

He shakes his head. 'Is this your idea of feminism, getting yourselves shot?'

I choke down a reply about it being better than being beaten and raped by a husband you can't divorce and having a baby every year from sixteen 'til you hit the bloody change and say, 'Are you going to help?'

With a coal-faced expression he holds out a pair of scissors. 'Cut her clothes off.'

Danny's cheeks flush. I snatch the scissors. Danny faces the wall. The doctor tips liquid from a small brown bottle onto a gauze pad and holds it over Briege's nose and mouth.

'What's that?' I demand.

'Chloroform. Unless you'd rather have her coming round during surgery?' he retorts. He lifts the pad from her face, scrubs his hands then confronts the makeshift operating table. His examining eyes fall on the small mound of Briege's stomach.

He glares at me. 'How far along is she?'

'I don't know. A few months?'

He rounds on Danny. 'Yours?'

'My brother's.'

'And where's he?'

I shove the question aside with one of my own. 'Will she lose it?'

'If she goes into shock...' He shakes his head. 'You've no right risking an innocent life. The Republican Cause is one thing but this is over the line.'

'The line's where the Brits drew it,' I say, folding my arms.

He shakes his head again, examines Briege's two wounds. Suffocating tension and fear coil around me as I wait for his diagnosis.

'Seems you've God with you tonight. Both bullets've gone through muscle tissue.'

He sweeps a hand over Briege and I see it's not her shoulder but the top of her arm that's been sliced by the bullet; the bloody mess on her hip made by a jagged tear through her side.

'If there were organs damaged I'd not be able to save her. But she could still bleed to death, succumb to infection.'

He wants to frighten me, punished me. Is this what we deserve? *The Irish Republican Army's right to engage in warfare is based on the right to resist foreign aggression, tyranny and oppression.*

'I can stop the bleeding, sterilise the wounds, close up. Then we'll have to hope for the best. Both of you, wash your hands, you'll have to help.'

I go to the sink. Danny doesn't move.

'Christ sake, Danny, what's it you're wanting to save, her modesty or her life?' I yank him to the sink, hold his trembling hands under the taps and we start scrubbing.

'Right. You.' The doctor gestures to Danny. 'Pressure here, like this.' He presses on Briege's upper arm, hands close to her breast. Danny hesitates then does it. 'You, help me here.' The doctor beckons to me with his scalpel.

I clear my mind with a deep breath. He pins back the tear's ragged edges with long pincers, indicates that I'm to take them. I slip my fingers through the scissor-style handles and hold firmly. Blood, pooled in the wound, splashes at my feet. The muscle, slit by the bullet, looks like freshly trimmed steak.

The doctor squirts fluid from a squeezy bottle into the gap made by the parted flesh. He peers inside.

'Mother Mary, it's a miracle her bowel isn't perforated.' He points, forcing me to look.

A raw dimpled sausage quivers like blancmange. He stuffs gauze pads into the wound, pressing until they are blotted bloody then dumping them to the floor, tuts and repeats the process. Checks again and curses.

'It's bleeding badly. I'll have to use ligatures.'

He plunges two small clamps into Briege, sops up more of the red liquid that is flooding the wound and nods before selecting a needle, thread and scissors from the counter. A sliver of silver flashes up and down as he sews, knotting each stitch with a deft twist of fingers and needle. Done, he dabs the gash dry again and swills more fluid over it. Then he reaches for a small bladed knife, takes one of the pairs of pincers from me, releasing the flap of flesh, and cuts away the tattered edge, neatening. The trimmings drop to my feet with a splat and splash in the bloody puddles, spattering my boots. I gag, glance away, find myself looking at Danny's white, trembling face and force a reassuring smile on him. The doctor takes the last pincer from my grip. I step back while he slices off the other side then nips the two folds together with a clamp.

'Can you sew?' he asks me.

'No.'

He shakes his head. 'Didn't your mammy teach you anything useful? Watch, then you can close up while I see to the shoulder. Like this.' He inserts a tidy stitch. 'Do one.' He pushes the needle and thread onto me.

I copy his precise cross-stitch with a scruffier one of my own.

'It'll not be neat but it'll do.' He moves around to Danny's side and begins on the shoulder while I clumsily sew up Briege's side, fingers shaking as I jab the needle through her skin.

An hour later Briege, deathly white, sweating and shivering, held together with flimsy thread, lies on the living room sofa, drifting into a consciousness of pain and confusion. We

341

smother her with blankets. She twitches and groans. The doctor pumps antibiotics into a vein. A smear of her blood is slashed over Danny's forehead. My hands are sticky with it.

'Clean yourselves up then see to my kitchen,' the doctor orders.

'What about the baby?' I ask.

He just shrugs. 'God willing.'

As the dawn sun scorches the city we load a limp, drowsy Briege into the car and drive, half-dead with exhaustion, to Galway because I want her at home with Connor and Saoirse. She lost the baby in the early hours.

# County Tyrone—25th July, 1987

## Bomb Wipes Out BA Patrol
## IRA Strike Back in Republican Heartland

At approximately 11 p.m. on Thursday an explosion near the Fivemiletown army barracks killed five members of the Parachute Regiment and wounded four others, some seriously.

The bomb, packed with 20 lbs of the highly effective plastic explosive, Semtex, went off at the roadside as the patrol was returning to base. Residents reported hearing a loud bang followed by shooting. The RUC confirmed that three soldiers sustained bullet wounds. No civilians were harmed in the attack and there was no damage to surrounding properties.

This was the second incident in the area in twenty-four hours. On Wednesday Republicans attacked a police checkpoint in Ballymackilroy, killing two RUC officers. Local man, Mr Terry Boyce, 59, heard shots around midnight. He said, 'We're sick of the RUC stop and search policies. I hope this makes them think twice about harassing the public for no reason. This is a Republican area; if security forces don't know that by now they'll learn the hard way.'

There is speculation that both attacks are part of the IRA's response to the murder of eight Republicans at Loughgall in May. Addressing mourners at the funeral of the Loughgall martyrs, Gerry Adams, Sinn Fein president, said the execution of the eight man ASU would be, 'a bloody milestone in the struggle for freedom, justice and peace.' With these operations the IRA have underlined their commitment to that struggle and demonstrated their ability to engage the enemy in a war of attrition.

# Dublin—18<sup>th</sup> August, 1987

I cross the Liffey near the Four Courts. Mairead is waiting on a bench, under a tree, overlooking the river, her back to Justice, Mercy and Wisdom. The building's massive dome and Grecian columns throw their statuesque shadows on her. She spots me among the foot traffic and waves. Wearing a red skirt and geometric-print blouse, her matching handbag over her arm and glossy curls dancing on her shoulders, she's just another young woman, enjoying a precious day of Dublin sunshine. I wonder if I look so ordinary.

She hugs me. Her body is soft and warm, prison's hard edges rounded out.

'Caoilainn, it's grand to see you again.'

'And you. You look even better than last time.' Her face is tanned, fuller and her eyes glow. Her lipstick is the same crimson as her skirt. Seeing her smile, hearing the jangle of her bracelets, smelling the floral aroma of her perfume, you'd never guess she spent ten years in jail, four of them in shit-daubed squalor.

'Sure, freedom's a real beauty treatment,' she laughs. 'Do you want a coffee?'

My stomach contracts. 'Let's just sit.' I wave to the bench.

'How's she doing?' Mairead asks.

'Healing. But she miscarried.'

Mairead crosses herself. 'Poor Briege, it's terrible for them.' She grips my hand. A tear drips from my chin. 'At least the mission was successful,' she adds in a whisper.

I drag my palm over my face and sniff back the waterworks. 'I was for calling it off, staying with her, but she wouldn't have it. Jesus, though, when we had to drop her off and drive straight back…' The words choke me.

'Christ, Caoilainn, this wasn't your fault.'

'Not sure Connor agrees. How'll he ever forgive me for getting his wife shot and baby killed?'

'You mustn't carry this with you. It's hard when there's a pull between family duty and Army duty,' Mairead acknowledges. 'We've all felt it, fought with it. My da was sick over me going on hunger strike but I couldn't put that before the struggle. It's the life.'

*Commitment to the Republican Movement is the firm belief that its struggle is morally justified.*

'I know.'

'So what about you?'

'I'm fine.'

'You look worse than when I came visiting,' she says, nudging me back into Maghaberry's callous corridors. 'You know you can talk to me.'

I light a cigarette and offer her one, which she takes. 'Is that why you wanted to see me, to check if I'm breaking down?'

'Are you?'

I meet her glittering eyes. I owe her the honesty of comradeship, the trust of friendship. 'I was close, maybe even there, for a few frightening days but I'm OK. now.'

'Really?' She raises her eyebrows.

'Just OK.,' I admit, 'but that's better than I was.'

She smiles. 'Fine, but if you need to talk…'

'I know. Thanks. I will.' I squeeze her hand, suddenly overpoweringly thankful for her friendship, the spoils of a war that has taken so much. I change the subject. 'So you're happy working for Sinn Fein?'

'I'm helping where I can,' she assures me, 'but don't worry, my orders are from GHQ these days.'

'A promotion?'

She blushes. 'Hardly.'

'Assigned to GHQ, sounds like one to me,' I reply.

'They're just using people in the right places.'

'Take it you've met Darkie.'

'Aye, that was strange, shaking his hand, knowing we were on the same hunger strike seven years ago. He's…' Her long pause is uncharacteristic; Mairead's too articulate to be stuck for words. She alters course. 'Has he said anything to you?'

'He has and from the fact that you're asking me about it I'm guessing he has to you, too.'

She purses her lips as though refusing some foul-tasting medicine.

'And?' I press.

'I don't know, Caoilainn. Working for Sinn Fein, I've seen the good they're doing. It's a way forward that might mean we've not to bury another comrade, another friend.' She returns my squeeze. 'Maybe we've done enough now to be able to talk peace, make peace.'

'What if we haven't?'

'Haven't we a responsibility to find out?'

I think of Briege, how fragile, broken, she looked when I took what was left of her home.

'Yes. But what if Brendan's right about it being a sell out?'

'Do you really think the leadership would do that to us?' she asks.

Ingrained cynicism, a childhood scar, prevents me from being certain of the answer. The ground beneath me tilts; I'm slipping.

Lunchtime traffic congeals around us. I tell Mairead about the meeting with Kevin. Examined under a suspicious spotlight it could be read as him giving me up for dog meat. I mention the newspaper on my Dublin door, the recent letter. It could be the UFF but it could be something much worse. Panic patters my heart. Mairead rationalises; if the big men were after selling out the military campaign for political power they'd be more decisive about it than just sending threatening letters. But if Brendan's right about Loughgall they have been decisive. Now maybe they're regretting it, taking a subtler approach. If… Maybe… Mairead keeps talking, coaching me against Brendan's paranoia. We're all in this together, she reminds me, including the leadership, united for a united Ireland. I remind her that just because you're paranoid doesn't mean they aren't after you. But I say nothing about Loughgall because I don't want her thinking I'm irrational, even though part of me thinks that myself.

A young man in a baggy suit perches on the end of our bench, lunchbox on his knee. Mairead asks about Patrick. I blush but tell her.

'Good on yous. I always knew you loved him.'

'But where's it going?'

'If I'd the power to tell you that all our problems'd be solved,' she laughs.

The clerk finishes his sarnie and leaves. We return to our previous topic; she cogently argues the sense of her campaigning for Sinn Féin. But she didn't do ten years in Armagh without believing in the right to take up arms. Trying to cross a vast ocean in a deflating dingy, our only option is to keep paddling, hoping we won't sink. Rationally, logically, I convince myself she's right. Illogically, emotionally, I fret about Danny, Ciaran, Tommy and Joe. If what Brendan suspects is correct, they're in danger, along with any volunteer who won't lay down his or her arms without a final, fatal salvo. I should at least tell Liam. He's got the whole Tyrone Brigade to shield from the blast. But can I even trust him? The answer dissolves into the Liffey's murky waters.

It's late afternoon. The sun has circled us, blinding us now. Mairead gives me a number where I can contact her. We hug again and it's like our prison parting but this time, although we're both at liberty, it doesn't feel like either of us is free: safe.

I wander the city, sticking to public places, lingering near garda cars, oppressed by panic, raging at myself for not being able to fight it off. *The enemy is all those opposed to our short or long-term objectives. We must realise that not all our enemies are so clearly identifiable as armed Brits or RUC.*

As day fades I find a bar, mocked up with harps and Celtic symbols, for those who like their Ireland traditional and Troubles-free. But the Troubles are Ireland's tradition. I get a Guinness and sit where I can see the front door, fire exit, bar and most of the room. Through a cloud of cigarette smoke I watch but there are no faces I recognise and no one pays me any attention. The pint lasts until after dark. I set off for home.

Collar of my jacket turned up and cap pulled low, I stroll, glancing aimlessly, studying carefully. Nobody slouches in parked cars or skulks in darkened doorways. I loop around the block, vault the fence of the house behind mine and drop into my own garden like a burglar.

The house smells foisty, rotten. Dust coats the surfaces; cobwebs hang from the coving. The chill of emptiness pervades every room. Silence booms through the stillness. The first thing I do is check the post piled on the doormat. It's all junk mail. I try to be relieved. Gathering a few clothes, I hunt for a bag and remember Daideo's rucksack. Standing on a chair, I lift the loft hatch and drag down the rigid leather satchel. His bits of life are still inside. I stuff my clothes on top and buckle the flap, tracing the etched PWF insignia with a finger. Then I sit in the lounge, waiting for something I might have already missed.

# Ballygawley, Co. Tyrone—28th August, 1987

I'm back ten days before I visit Ciaran, Tommy and Joe, giving them the same story I've told Danny; we're going to be quiet for a while. If there's a problem, let me know, otherwise I don't want to hear from yous. They don't protest; Briege's sideswipe with death has them rattled.

I should've seen them sooner but I needed to think, away from Dublin and its portents of ruin. Ten days of thinking and the only clear thing is that it's pro and anti-treaty again, watching for who falls which side of the line that divides physical force from political posturing. I wish I knew how Daideo handled this in his day. Bits of me are breaking off, blowing away in the wind, leaves from a dying tree. If our own politicos destroy us before we've finished the fight what's it all been for? If we fight on when there's no need we're the murderers people have long accused us of being.

Patrick asks what's wrong. I convince him everything's fine; he's glad of the lull. We make the most of it, him coming down week nights as well as weekends, rush hour traffic all he has to battle for now.

The first week of September Danny, Patrick and I are in the garden, bathed in an Indian sunset, swilling cold beers and having the craic. The sky displays its plumage; the land slewed at our feet is green and lush. I long to capture this one perfect moment in delicately washed watercolours. Isn't this what we've fought for?

A V of geese flap left to right, silhouetted against the rose-gold heavens.

'Would you look at that,' Danny says. 'Sure, it's a grand life, flying free like that.'

'It is,' Patrick agrees. 'Going where life's trouble-free.'

'Troubles-free,' I correct.

The geese disappear over the horizon. The distant drone of a car nears, loudens. Tyres crunch on gravel.

'Is that visitors?' Patrick asks, twisting in his deckchair.

'I'll go.' I slip into the kitchen, blinking down the cool darkness and stumbling through to the hall.

Liam is coming in the front door as I emerge from the kitchen.

'Hello. What're you doing here?'

'I'm wanting a word with you.' He strides into the front room and stands, back to the fireplace, waiting on me. 'Patrick here?'

'Aye, and Danny. Outside.'

'Close the door.'

I do it. 'What's up?'

'I'm wondering why you've stood your unit down.'

'After what happened with Briege we were needing a break.'

'You should've talked to me first.'

'Sorry.'

He stares at me, grey eyes piercing. 'What's wrong?'

'Nothing.'

'Have you had more threats?'

I can't tell him the answer is 'don't know'. 'There've not been any more letters, no.'

'Something else, so?'

The floor cracks, a chasm opening up in front of me. Panicked by the drop, I inch away from the edge. 'No.'

'Do I need to stand you down, find another cell leader, another volunteer?'

'I'm fine. Just give us time to regroup.'

He sighs. 'O.K., but we've things in the offing. I'll have to know where you are soon.'

Fuck sake, come on, this is Liam. Tell him.

I can't.

Trust him.

I daren't.

'I'll be where I've always been, doing what needs to be done.'

He shakes his head. 'Come on, Caoilainn, I know you too well to be fobbed off with neat wee platitudes. Whatever it is you can tell me.'

His voice is soft with concern. I see myself crumbling, leaning against him, imagine the feel of hot tears filling my eyes, hear myself spluttering jumbled doubts, picture him hugging me better. I drag myself out of the tempting vision, forbidding myself to break. I can't risk it. If he's on the opposite side…

'Jesus, Caoilainn, don't you trust me?'

Isn't that what he'd say to make me betray myself?

'Don't be daft.'

'So bloody well tell me what's going on.' His voice comes off soothing, sharpens up. 'Christ, I'm not just your OC, we're friends. If you've a problem let me help.'

What if he's the problem? What if I'm the problem? What if the problem is the fucking problem? Acid corrodes me, paranoia eating through my bones, dissolving me. I push him away with the last of my strength.

'I just need to work things out in my head, Liam. You can't help with that. No one can. I'm sorry but that's it right now.'

He rubs his eyes. Tiredness? Irritation?

'OK. Let me know when you've done that.'

He puts a hand on my shoulder. I shrug it off. He winces. The pain of my rejection rebounds on me. I stiffen.

'Fine. I will. Is that all?'

He shakes his head, a 'what've I done?' pleading in his eyes.

I see him to the door. He trudges down the path, stoop-shouldered and head-bowed. I close the door before he reaches his car to stop myself calling him back. How many more doors are going to close before this is over?

In bed that night a stuttering movie, six years of memories, plays on a screen in my head: the boom and chatter of bombs and guns; the smell of cordite; the bodies, twisted and torn. Actions and reactions rise from the ground, ghostly spectres. I stand on a hilltop, overlooking the land of my past. Viewed from a distance it drenches me in a sublime terror that has lurked, unfelt and unseen, for as long as I let myself see only a sliver at a time. As single details it was manageable but taken as a whole it's too much for one person to have done: my Sistine Chapel. It's not a nightmare I can wake from.

I get up. Sit in the lounge in 3 A.M. chill, picking at an intricately knotted argument. Each time I pull a thread it comes away loose and the knot stays tangled. Are things better now than when I joined? No. And they won't be as long as the BA are patrolling the streets, the SAS leaping up from hedgerows, the DUP wielding their political swords. Do I believe we should be giving up the fight now? Maybe. *Tactics are dictated by the existing conditions*. But what the fuck are those conditions?

I regret nothing. There are things I wish had been different. But they weren't: aren't. I can only follow the directions given to me. If they're wrong I'll get lost.

I am where I am. It is what it is. I can only try to survive whatever's coming and hope the end is worth the effort.

I creep back to bed and crawl under the covers, huddling into Patrick's warmth.


Life becomes abnormally normal. I revert to a domestic existence I'd forgotten I could live. Danny finds a job with a local garage, repairing tractors mostly but better than nothing. Joe, Tommy and Ciaran go about their lives, visiting sometimes but for social reasons. Liam stays away, things between us strained, stretched beyond the point of elastic recoil. Patrick maintains the punishing commute from Belfast. Sometimes he works from the cottage. I finally collect the Norton from Terry Boyce's shed where it's been hidden since July. It's not rideable so Danny recovers it in the works van. Evenings when Patrick is pinned in Belfast we tinker with it together. I fill the rest of the space painting and drawing, regularly driving to Dungannon for materials then sitting on lonely hillsides, painting flowers, wee cottages, sheep-dotted pastures, sunsets and rises, my artistic palette only able to tolerate bland flavours after my Army diet of too little art and too much angst.

One day, while I'm buying stewing steak, Mr Quinn notices my paint-spattered hands, asks if himself and I are redecorating. I say I'm an artist, pictures. Am I now, he asks, and would I be selling them? I've not considered that but say I'll bring one down next time; if he likes it he can have it for whatever he thinks fair.

A week later I take two small canvasses, a lilac sunset and a landscape of the Tyrone moors. He buys the pair for a fiver and hangs them behind the bloodstained counter. People see them, admire them. A few locals place orders. Mr Quinn suggests I do more, offers to display them in his shop. I start making pocket money from my brushstrokes, mostly off wealthy wandering tourists. It's not the grand career Daideo wanted for me. It's not even the art I thought I'd be painting. It's so twee, so saccharine, not the conceptual art I used to do; something else I've lost: anarchic creativity. But, finally, at twenty-five, I'm doing something that can't get me arrested or killed.

The bike is fixed; I tour the countryside on bright autumn days, a sketch pad and pencils in my rucksack, parking at scenic lookouts to cast the view in pale grey lines that I fill with colour later. If I get home first I cook but there are more nights when Patrick or Danny have my tea ready, drying up in the range. They tease me over my slipshod housewifery; I return with quips about their feminine domesticity.

I think we could go on like this forever, pretending the war is over, the victory ours.

# Enniskillen, Co. Fermanagh—
# 9th November, 1987

## Bomb Blast Murders Eleven
## Remembrance Day Service
## Desecrated by IRA

A huge bomb, believe to be the work of the IRA, has exploded during Remembrance Sunday commemorations at the cenotaph in Enniskillen, killing eleven people.

Among those murdered were three married couples, a retired policeman and a nurse. Another 63 have being injured, nine seriously. Thirteen children are among those being treated following the blast which demonstrated Republicans' callous attitude towards innocent civilians.

It is thought the bomb was hidden in a nearby hall which collapsed during the explosion, hurling debris onto the crowd gathered to pay their respects to those who gave their lives defending Ulster during two world wars. Victims were buried under several feet of rubble, hampering the attempts of rescue workers.

Prime Minister Margaret Thatcher called the bombing, 'utterly barbaric,' and said it was, 'a blot on mankind.' Head of the Church of Ireland, Archbishop Robin Eames, who was attending the service said, 'I wish the bombers could have seen what I've seen.' The Queen sent heartfelt condolences to the survivors.

Enniskillen's history of support for Britain's international conflicts, along with its proximity to the Irish Republic, make it an easy target for IRA terrorists who probably fled to safety across the border.

No organisation has claimed responsibility for the carnage but an RUC spokesman said there was no doubt the IRA were behind the massacre and appealed for help to bring the murderers to justice.


Monday dawns bright and frosty. I wave Patrick off and stroll into the village for provisions and deliveries, three more oil paintings wrapped in brown paper and slung over my shoulder. Later I'll ride to Lough Erne; I've an order for a landscape.

In the butcher's Mr Quinn greets me with:

'Wouldn't you never think they'd do something the like of this?' His jowly face is creased into a grimace.

'Who do what?'

'The Provos,' he spits. 'It's wee 'uns and ould folks, nothing to do with anything.'

Fear swells in my stomach.

'Haven't you heard?'

'I've not had the radio on this morning.'

'They've let off a bomb at Enniskillen, at the war memorial.'

My stomach revolts. I rush outside and puke on the pavement, rice crispies floating in a murky pool of tea and bile. He comes to see if I'm OK. I wave him away and sprint home.

Danny is still in bed. I bang into his darkened room and shake him.

'Get up.'

His eyes flutter. He brushes me off with a limp hand.

'Fuck sake, wake up.' I rip back the covers.

The cold blast jerks him awake. He sits forward with a snap.

'Are we being attacked?'

'Get dressed. We're going to Fermanagh.'

'What for? Jesus, Caoilainn it's…' He fumbles for the clock and groans at the earliness of the day.

'Get dressed.' I bang out again.

Five minutes later he emerges from the house. I have the Norton ready and my helmet on. I hold the spare to Danny. He scowls at the rain-laden sky.

'Can't we take the car?'

I kick the bike into life. 'Get on.' He climbs up behind me.

I tear down the A4, taking the sweeping corners cranked over, our knees almost grazing the tarmac, blasting by cars and riding headlong into oncoming traffic, dodging and weaving through the morning commute. Horns blare and trees blur. Danny clings to me. I don't slow down. And it's buildings blurring, industrial units, shops, houses, a church; my horn blaring as I blast dilly-dalliers aside. I jump two red lights and rail into a side road, abandoning the bike on double yellows.

Danny leaps off, shaking and gasping, fingers white, frozen into the grip that was the only thing keeping him from bone-cracking impact with tarmac. He pulls his helmet off and fumbles for a cigarette. I light one and give it to him.

'Fuck, Caoilainn, you trying to kill us?'

'Come on.' I walk towards the epicentre, the stench of burnt death guiding me.

A flimsy police-tape barrier protects the desecrated memorial. The square is flooded with rubble. Uniformed men guard forensic examiners in white coveralls who kneel, finger-picking through the wreckage, to gather a rotting harvest. Brown stains patchwork the ground.

Instinctively Danny and I falter at the sight of peelers. I rationalise, we're not known here and my new hairdo has proved an effective disguise so far.

'We need to see this.' I tow him to the tape.

The nearest peeler wanders along.

'You can't come through,' he says, the shadow from his cap peak hiding his face, his feelings.

'We just want to see what the bastards have done,' I reply.

'You can do that, alright,' he says, stepping back.

Red poppies are swirled among the rubbish. Old death and new death mingle; a shoe, a wooden cross, a pair of glasses, a posy, a walking stick, a memorial card, a child's dummy. Danny reaches for my hand. His fingers are ice-cold, his grip crushing. We stand there, staring, imagining, knowing, memorising, hurting. *The enemy through our own fault is one we ourselves create through our collective conduct of the struggle.*

I turn away. Walk. Danny trails me. We get on the bike. Ride home.

We don't speak; words can't pull us from this sinkhole. At seven o'clock Patrick's car rumbles along the lane. Danny and I are slumped on the sofa, the air thick with smoke, dirty mugs littering the coffee table. The slamming car door wakes us from our private nightmares, throwing us into a shared one.

'You meant that, didn't you?' Danny says. ' 'What the bastards have done', you meant it.'

'I did, aye.'

*

I have no dreams about Enniskillen; my terrors visit during the day, consciousness denying me the escape of waking. Patrick begs me to talk; I can't. There's no way to legitimise or rationalise or justify. I pack Daideo's rucksack, spend four days tramping the hills, four nights dossing under hedges and in ditches, sleeping cold-soaked, waking covered in diamond frost. I walk due south, deep into Monaghan's empty quarter. I contemplate turning east, walking into the turbulent Irish Sea, letting the waves wash me out of my life. But all the tides only carry me back to Ireland. The time I needed to think, to watch and hope to float is up now. The box has been opened for me; to see the dead-or-alive truth I only have to look inside. On the fifth morning I hitch a lift into Carrickmacross and call Patrick who collects me. When I see him I don't know which of us has had it worst; his eyes are ringed with sleepless worry and three day's stubble grizzles his chin. He wipes mud from my face and kisses me. I hate myself for hurting him.

'Told you, you didn't deserve being lumbered with me,' I mutter into his crumpled shirt.

'Just promise you won't do this again.' His voice quivers with relief.

I say nothing.

His hands slide away from me. 'Caoilainn, please, this is enough. You have to walk away before there's no where left to walk to. You can't do anymore. It's another game now, the rules are changed.'

'Broken, you mean.'

I should call Liam but, the wound of our last meeting still raw, I can't. Our friendship has been maimed by the very war that made friends of us. If we're both standing on quicksand it's better I don't disturb the ground; that way there's a chance we won't both be sucked under. Instead I contact Brendan, rationalising it will be easier with him: just business.

# Ballygawley—18<sup>th</sup> November, 1987

Hughes and I sit at my kitchen table. Light from the window shows the pallor beneath his swarthy complexion. I don't know what's sickening him but I'm worried it's a contagious form of anxiety. He strokes his moustache and lights a cigarette, clearing phlegm from his throat before speaking in that unusual voice, soft tones and harsh accent.

'Where are you?'

'Depends on what you've got to tell me.'

'You've questions, sure, everyone's got questions,' he mutters.

'Only one: was it deliberate, part of this plot you're suspecting, a way of discrediting the armed struggle?'

He exhales twin funnels of smoke from his nostrils. 'I've no proof.' He settles dark eyes on me. 'Put it this way: I didn't clear it and I'm Head of Operations.'

I get up to boil the kettle, putting some space between us. More doubts, more circumstantials, that's all he has.

'So it could've been a mistake, inexperienced volunteers…?'

'Some bloody mistake,' he interrupts. 'Did you hear Bono calling us murderers on stage? Even Gaddafi's condemned us for this and it was his shagging Semtex.'

'Do you blame them? There's no justifying this, Brendan.'

'Maybes that's the point.' He knocks ash off his cigarette with a trembling finger. 'I don't know how deep this vein runs but if we tap it, it'll be our blood pouring out. You need to think on that.'

His words are bad dialogue from a Jack Higgins thriller. Reality is reduced to a spoof of the fiction that's too serious to be funny, too ridiculous to be credible.

I wet the tea and fetch it.

He blows across the surface of his mug. 'You haven't answered my question: where are you?'

'Where do you want me?'

He gulps the tea, wincing as it scalds his mouth, then produces a hipflask and tops up his mug. 'That's your choice.'

'You think I should get out? Will you take your own advice?'

He looks up, eyes unblinking. 'I will not. I've doubts, aye, but there's still a war to be fought as far as I'm concerned, more so now.'

'I thought the new strategy was political? Mairead was talking about negotiating: peace. If we can we've got to try, surely.'

'You think we're in any position to negotiate a fair peace deal after last week?' he demands. 'The only way I see us recovering from this is if we launch military attacks on legitimate targets, remind the Brits what they'll lose if they keep fighting us and force them to the table from a position of strength. Our goal should still be 'Brits out'.'

Should? I stare through the fog of cigarette smoke and uncertainties, longing for one clear answer, a switch that can only be flicked on or off.

He ducks my gaze. 'You've to consider our position now.'

'How can I when I don't know what it is?'

'What if I said there's a mission planned, a legitimate military target?' he asks, heavy brows raised.

Knowing my answer would be a breath-draining ramble of sinking, floating, drifting, swirling, bobbing-just-out-of-reach thoughts about whether I can/can't, should/shouldn't, will/won't I say nothing.

Brendan bumps me towards a reply. 'I'd like you involved. I trust you and this is a chance to show anyone with reservations about the military campaign that it has a role to play. We pull this off and we're demonstrating our ability to engage the enemy in a war they can't win meaning we can command a better peace deal later. It's leverage on all fronts.'

He's naïve if he really believes one big bang will solve the problems we've been fighting for centuries.

He's full of himself if he actually thinks he can, single-handed, win us the war and the peace.

He's a drunk, ruined by his years of struggle, left clinging to the old ways: engage the enemy; attack and counter-attack; die in battle.

He's a military genius, a tactician to rival Churchill, Napoleon, Genghis Khan, Michael Collins.

Fuck sake, which is it?

'You'll have to tell me what you're planning before I decide anything.'

'It's a bombing on a British overseas territory. You'll need an explosives expert: Tommy? Mairead'll be on it, too, and another couple of lads.'

'I thought she wasn't doing anything active.'

'We were after sending another girl but she thinks she's suspected so Mairead stepped up.'

'But Mairead's a known face. That's a massive risk.'

'When isn't it?' Brendan asks, adding, 'ach, we've plenty of counter-security measures in place.'

'It's far too dangerous for her,' I insist.

'There's no one else.'

'Did Mairead volunteer or was she put forward?'

'When she heard Siobhan had worries she volunteered.'

I wonder what, who, made Siobhan worry.

'So?' he asks.

If Mairead's in for it that means she thinks there's no other option; something has convinced her this is too important not to do it. If I'm looking for the safety of certainty that's where I find it: in Mairead. It's a simple answer because the question is not what am I fighting for but who.

'Fine. I'm in.'

'Grand.' Brendan grins. 'How's your Spanish?'

'Nonexistent.'

'Get a phrasebook. I'll be in touch.'

# Madrid, Spain—1<sup>st</sup> March, 1988

Tommy and I clear customs as a holidaying couple with nothing but beachwear and suntan lotion in our suitcases. Outside the arrivals door a young woman, dark hair flowing in glossy waves over tanned shoulders, holds up a sheet of white paper, stark against the glow of her browned hands. It reads: Mary Parkin + John Oakes. We introduce ourselves in guidebook Spanish:

'Hola. Me llamo Mary.'

She smiles, showing very white teeth, and offers a warm dry hand.

'I am Gloria,' she says in English. 'I have car. Come, please.'

She swishes to the exit, the pink and yellow print skirt swaying around her knees as she moves with the rhythm of a flamenco dancer, her sandals slapping out the beat.

'Jesus, she's a looker,' Tommy murmurs, admiring the smooth skin exposed by the halter-neck top, trailing his gaze down to her narrow waist and plump arse.

'Don't shit where you eat,' I hiss.

He grins. 'Aye, right.'

Gloria gets into a blue SEAT car. Tommy jostles me for the front passenger door, beating me to it. Hoping that Gloria's got more sense than him over intertwining business and pleasure, I make do with the back seat.

Heat blasts out as I get in. I wind the window down. Gloria starts the engine. We set off through Madrid's maze, Tommy valiantly attempting a chat-up, his mix of Spanish phrases and Ulster-English bamboozling Gloria's textbook language skills. I listen, amused, to his dogged patter, as the sunlit metropolis morphs into whitewashed villas, high-walled and flat-roofed, potted cacti abundant on verandas, palm trees lining the roads. Gloria steers with the palm of her hand, spinning the wheel with a casual flick, navigating roundabouts and junctions with Mediterranean flare, finally bumping off the main road and onto a gravelled path cutting through a citrus grove.

The SEAT curls up the track and through the opened gates of a villa. Gloria parks on the shady side of the building and I step out into the coolness of a Spanish hilltop. Below, Madrid sparkles in the sunshine, light winking off glass and steel, the city stretching, brash and vast, over the quilted green and brown countryside.

'What do you think of our safe house?' Gloria asks, waving a lithe arm at the columned entrance and arched windows of the sand coloured façade that fronts the ETA base that is our temporary hideout.

'Aye, grand,' Tommy grins. 'Bet there are plenty of bedrooms, eh?'

'Yes. Come, I show you,' Gloria declares, bounding up the terracotta steps to the veranda that encircles the house.

She takes us inside, introducing us to Alazne, a petite blonde whose chestnut skin makes her light hazel eyes and fair hair glow. Beneath her tanned features and the vibrant reds and greens of her dress, she is pale, sick from an old, still festering wound that makes her avoid our gaze and duck our questions, answering, when she must, in whispers. Gloria sends her for drinks and she skitters over the tiles like a kitten, claws scrabbling for grip.

'Do not mind Alazne. She has suffered at the hands of those Spanish pigs.' Gloria spits, a gob of phlegm splatting onto the stone floor with an obscene plop. 'They lock her up for days, no food or water. They beat her, rape her, to make her talk. Of course she breaks. Who wouldn't?'

Tommy glances at me. I look away.

'Now she blames herself for her two comrades, who were convicted by words pulled from her like teeth by those filthy bastards.' Gloria spits again, an actor avoiding the curse for naming Macbeth. 'She will not be active for ETA again but she must help. If you want food or drink she will make for you. Come, we sit until Felipe arrives with your merchandise.'

Felipe, when he comes that night, doesn't introduce himself and scowls when Gloria addresses him by name. He's accompanied by another lad, much younger. They arrive in a van and a black Fiat, both of which get parked behind the villa, hidden from traffic that doesn't pass anyway. Paranoia is clearly an internationally mutual terrorist trait. When we meet them Felipe shakes Tommy's hand.

'You have found everything good?' he asks.

'Aye, grand,' Tommy replies.

'You have the money?'

'Sure.' Tommy glances to me.

Gloria slaps Felipe's arm and douses him in furious Spanish. His face blackens and he strokes the dark curls that cling to his scalp. Gloria faces me.

'I tell him he is idiot. It is you he should speak to. You are in change, yes?'

'Yes,' I reply with a grin.

'He is sorry. Felipe, sorry?' she demands.

'Apologies, señorita. I did not know,' he mutters, scuffing at the parched ochre earth.

'Pah, men,' Gloria scoffs, giving him a second whack.

'I show you what we bring,' Felipe says hurriedly, clapping his hands at the young lad who leans against the Fiat, smoking.

The lad jumps to attention, darts to the van, flings open the doors and lifts down a crate.

'We have everything you ask,' Felipe declares.

The lad opens the case. Inside, packed in neat rows, are long creamy rolls, each labelled 'Goma-2 Eco: PELIGRO EXPLOSIVO'. I prod one. It's squishy.

'How volatile is this?' I ask.

Felipe shrugs.

'A big bang?' I smack my hands together.

'Very big. Is made for mining, they blow holes in our countryside with it.' He frowns. He means Basque country. 'Then we take and blow bigger ones in theirs.' His expression switches to a grin.

'Will you be OK. with this?' I ask Tommy.

'Sure, it's like Semtex. Jesus, though, there's a fair lot of it.' He points to the van, where two more crates await inspection.

'How much is there?' I ask.

'Sixty kilos,' Felipe replies.

Tommy whistles. I jab him with my elbow.

'Also guns.' Felipe nods to the lad who produces two handguns from under his leather jacket.

I shake my head.

'You no want?' Felipe asks.

'No. Thanks.'

Tommy mutters, 'Maybe we should… for Mairead and the boys, as backup.'

'Hughes said no.'

'But…'

'I don't like it either but it's an order.'

'Why you no take guns?' Gloria demands.

'Our boss says we don't need them and it's worse if we're caught armed. But thanks.' I smile at her and nod to Felipe.

Pouting, the lad tucks the guns under his jacket.

Tommy sighs as they disappear. 'Hughes better be right.'

About this, aye, about everything else I fucking hope not. But I can't deal with that until the mission's done and we're all safe home. 'Check everything; I'll settle up,' I tell Tommy. Facing Gloria, I gesture to the crates. 'This is OK.'

She smiles. 'How you say, grand?' She winks at Tommy.

For two nights Tommy and I work on the bomb. The Goma-2 resembles Plasticine; it regresses me to childhood. I ball it between my palms, squish it into cubes, shape it into flowers, hearts, wings, a bunny rabbit. Smirking, Tommy teases this'll be the prettiest bomb he's ever made; I stop playing and pack it into the canisters while he attaches fuse wire and makes the detonator, a radio controlled device similar to the Hyde Park one, small enough to fit into Mairead's handbag, carried as she watches the changing of the guard outside the Convent, the official residence of the Rock's governor. As we work Alazne supplies us with coffee, black and sweet, her eyes, frightened and yearning, locked on the wire coils and explosive sausages.

On the third day, while Tommy loads the boxes into the Fiat, she brings coffee, bread and a bowl of olive oil. She sets the tray on the step, stares for a moment then retreats. I call her name; she halts but doesn't turn so I go over.

'Thank you.' I nod to the food.

She twists her head, viewing me over her shoulder.

'You welcome,' she replies and moves to leave.

I catch her arm. 'They hurt you, la policía? Daño*?'

She drops her gaze. 'Sí.'

'Mí también♣.'

Her head snaps up, eyes wide. I squeeze her arm.

'You have to be strong, fuerte♦. Don't let them win. No los dejes ganar♠.'

'Thank you. I try,' she says, nodding.

'I'm done,' Tommy calls.

Alazne scuttles into the house.

'Fine, let's get some sleep. We've a long drive tomorrow.'

On Saturday morning, our cases sitting on the bomb, we say goodbye to Gloria and Alazne. Gloria shakes my hand.

'Bietan jarrai•,' she says.

'Tiocfaidh ár lá,' I reply.

Then she throws herself on Tommy, kissing him with Latino passion.

I look to Alazne, rolling my eyes and jabbing a mocking thumb at the canoodlers. She smiles and inches over.

'I be strong,' she says, each word cut sharp.

'It gets easier,' I say, hoping she understands.

She pecks me on both cheeks and hands over a parcel of bread and meat for the journey.

Tommy is still slobbering over Gloria. I get into the car, slamming the door. They jump apart. He sneaks a final snog, climbs into the passenger side and leans across me to wave and catch her flung kisses as we drive off.

'What the hell are you doing?' I demand.

'My bit for international relations,' he replies, grinning.

'Christ sake.'

---

* the police, hurt

♣ me too

♦ strong

♠ don't let them win

• keep up on both

The drive to Marbella, where we're meeting Mairead, is four hundred miles through Spain's arid interior. On the resort's outskirts, sheltering in a national park, we'll transfer the bomb to her hired car. As we cruise down the A-4, the sun roasting us inside the car, my stomach twists and churns. Sweat beads on my forehead and under my arms. My mouth dries up; the taste of soured milk coats my tongue.

We've done a quarter of the distance, the road a stretching black snake slithering across the scrubland, when I first feel it: a drifting, moving outside myself, sidestepping my body. I blink. The doubled yellow lines settle into singles again. My stomach lurches. My mouth fills up with saliva. My heart stops then restarts in double-time.

'You OK?' Tommy asks.

'Fine.'

'You've gone a wee bit pale, so you have.'

'I'm bloody fine,' I lie, dismissing the shivering as nerves.

Road signs count down in kilometres. My stomach knots around itself, coiling and flexing. Heat burns my cheeks but I shudder with a bone-deep cold. The road swings out of focus. A horn screams at us. I feel the car jerk, see Tommy's hand, knuckles white, gripping the steering wheel.

'Fuck sake, pull over,' he gasps.

I drag the car to the verge, swerving to a stop, open the door, step out and am immediately sick, splashing the coarse grass with the remnants of breakfast: pastries and coffee. I puke, my stomach clenching and heaving, turning inside out until there's nothing left. I sink to the grass.

'Caoilainn?'

I feel a hand on my neck, beneath hair still bobbed and brown.

'I'm OK. Give me a cigarette, will you.'

Tommy hands me one, lit. I take a puff and retch again.

'I'll drive,' he offers. 'Do you want a few minutes?'

'We can't be late.'

I let him help me up. We swap places and continue, waves of nausea swelling in my stomach, splashing into my throat. I keep the window down but the dry Spanish air is stagnant, flushing my face with dizzying heat, filling my nose with sickly fragrances: patchouli, thyme, jasmine. Tommy keeps glancing over but says nothing. I daren't eat the lunch Alazne made and make do with sipping water. We have to stop twice more for me to vomit the mouthfuls of clear liquid, turned cloudy by stomach acid that burns my chin as it dribbles down. We reach Marbella half an hour late.

'Is everything alright?' Mairead rushes across as I scramble from the car, heaving up bile.

'She's been like this the whole way,' Tommy explains.

I lean against the car, rinse my mouth with water.

'I'm fine.'

'You look terrible,' Mairead croons, her hand cool on my cheek. 'You're burning.'

'It's 40 degrees in the car,' I snap.

'Was it something you ate?' she presses.

'We've eaten the same,' Tommy says.

'I've said, I'm fine. Let's not hang about here.' I glance at the scrubby trees, their leaves blue-green shards that flicker in the evening breeze. The road is hidden by their spindly silver trunks but the thunder of traffic penetrates the grove threateningly.

With a sigh Mairead skips back to the hired Ford Fiesta; against nature's muted colours its red paint bellows a warning. Tommy opens the boot of our Fiat. I stand shakily, steadying my balance, then join them, helping to transfer the crates, the urge to gag caught in my throat.

When everything is loaded and Tommy's been over the detonation procedure with her, Mairead comes to where I'm lying in the cool grass, shadows lengthening across me. She crouches down.

'How're you feeling?'

I sit up. 'Better. Fine. Is everything ready?'

'Aye. We'll go into Gibraltar tomorrow, have a final recce and be ready for Tuesday.'

'The lads you've got, they're OK?'

'Dead on.'

'And you've not seen any trouble?'

'I haven't, and I've had a bloody good look,' she says.

'Keep looking.'

'I will.'

'You shouldn't be doing this,' I tell her. 'You're too well-known now.'

'Not out here,' she insists.

I hope she's right. 'I wish you'd had a timer. Then you'd be on your way home before…'

'I'll not be happy unless I trigger it myself, to be sure we've no civilian casualties.'

'We should've brought you guns,' I say. 'ETA had some for us.'

'There's no need. Sure, this is as easy as it comes.' She takes my elbow, helps me up.

I brush dry grass from my jeans. We hug and whisper lucky wishes to each other. She shakes Tommy's hand.

'See yous in Dublin in a few days,' she calls as she gets into the Fiesta, her brown curls flecked with gold in the sun's low-slung rays, life dancing in her eyes.

We wave her off as she steers out of the clearing. Our car radio plays 'Days' the new Kirsty McColl version.

Tommy and I wait, giving Mairead time to get most of the way back to Marbella before we drive in the opposite direction, heading for Jerez, the airport where we'll leave the Fiat to be collected later by an ETA comrade. From Jerez, it's hop to Madrid, skip to Amsterdam and, finally, jump to Dublin.

# London—7th March, 1988

## SAS Heroes Foil Deadly IRA Bomb Plot
## Three Terrorists Killed in Shoot-out
## on the Rock of Gibraltar

Three members of an IRA unit were killed yesterday afternoon in the British territory of Gibraltar. Caught planting a lethal 500 lb bomb, the terrorists, two men and a woman, were challenged by the SAS. In the shoot-out that followed all three were killed by soldiers.

Acting on intelligence from sources in Belfast and working with the Spanish authorities, the terrorists, named as Mairead Farrell (31), Daniel McCann (30) and Sean Savage (23), were shot when they refused to surrender to the SAS. Witness reports suggest McCann and Savage were in the act of drawing weapons when the SAS opened fire, preventing bloodshed on the sunny Gibraltar streets.

Following the gunfight, British military personal carried out a controlled explosion, making safe the suspect car. The MOD have confirmed that the explosives used suggest ETA involvement.

The incident took place on Sunday, at around 3.30 P.M. Gibraltar time as the IRA members were identified walking along Winston Churchill Avenue. Just prior to this one of them had been observed, by MI5 undercover agents, parking a white Renault 5 near the official residence of the British governor of Gibraltar. The Convent, the governor's seat, is close to the scene of the ceremonial changing of the guard which takes place every Tuesday. Intelligence sources confirmed this was the IRA's target. In 1982 the IRA carried out a similar attack in Hyde Park when a blast killed four soldiers and seven horses taking part in the changing of the guard in London.

Prime Minister, Margaret Thatcher praised the SAS for their bravery and skill in acting to take down three merciless terrorists without the loss of innocent lives.

# Dublin—8<sup>th</sup> March, 1988

## British Foreign Secretary Admits
## Gibraltar Three Were Unarmed
## SAS Shoot-to-Kill
## Claims Three More Republicans

In a statement to the House of Commons Sir Geoffrey Howe has admitted that the three Republicans gunned down in Gibraltar were unarmed. He told ministers that those killed, 'were found not to have been carrying arms.' He also confessed that no bomb was found in the Renault 5 car that had been parked in the locale of the changing of the guard.

Yesterday the IRA confirmed that three of its members, Mairead Farrell (31), Danny McCann (30) and Sean Savage (23) had been killed while on active service.

Eye-witnesses refute the SAS's claim that they issued a warning before opening fire on the ASU. Mr Derek Luise, who was at the nearby Shell petrol station when the shooting occurred, told reporters, 'There was no shouting, just shots, about five or eight, one after the other. There was blood everywhere.'

The families of those killed are calling for a public inquiry into why, despite several opportunities to do so, no attempt was made to detain Farrell, McCann and Savage, who had been under surveillance by Spanish and British security forces since their arrival in Spain on Friday.

The Irish Government, while acknowledging the need to tackle terrorism, has reacted to news of the shooting of three unarmed Republicans with unease, calling the events, 'gravely disturbing.'

A book of condolences will be opened outside the General Post Office on O'Connell Street tomorrow for those wishing to pay their respects to the latest victims of the SAS shoot-to-kill policy which has claimed the lives of more than fifty Republicans.

# Belfast—17th March, 1988

## Loyalist Gunman Murders Three at Republican Funeral

A Loyalist gunman has attacked mourners attending the funerals of the three IRA volunteers shot dead on Gibraltar ten days ago.

The lone assassin, named as Michael Stone, a member of the outlawed Ulster Freedom Fighters, opened fire with a handgun, killing three people and injuring a further fifty.

The first shots, fired as the three coffins were lowered into the ground, were initially mistaken for the IRA salute. As Stone continued to fire into the crowd Sinn Fein President, Gerry Adams, who was to give the graveside oration, used the loudhailer to warn mourners to take cover.

Stone then threw grenades into the crowd before being chased by unarmed young men who apprehended him as he attempted to escape on foot up the M1 motorway outside Milltown cemetery. He was arrested by the RUC who arrived on the scene minutes later.

Speaking after the attack, Mr Adams accused the security forces of collusion, saying that the reduced police presence at Milltown, negotiated by members of the Catholic Church in deference to the memory of those being laid to rest, had been known to only a few people in advance.

Those killed were two civilians, Thomas McElrean (20) and John Murray (26), both married men with young families, and Caoimhin MacBrádaigh, an IRA volunteer. Wounded mourners, several critically injured, were rushed to the Royal Victoria Hospital in private vehicles.

Tom King, Northern Ireland Secretary, condemned the attack and called for calm in the wake of the tragedy, warning against reprisals. The Loyalist paramilitary group, the Ulster Defence Association, under whose direction the UFF are believed to operate, denied sanctioning Stone's actions but stopped short of condemning him.

# London—20<sup>th</sup> March, 1988

## IRA Mob Executes Two British Corporals

Two off-duty British Army Corporals have been killed by the IRA after inadvertently driving into a Republican funeral cortege in West Belfast.

The murdered men, Corporal Derek Wood (24) and Corporal David Howes (23), were attacked after they became trapped in the procession making its way to Milltown cemetery for the funeral of Kevin Brady, the IRA man who died four days ago while attending another Republican funeral.

Howes and Wood were surrounded by a mob of angry, violent Republicans who smashed into their vehicle and dragged the soldiers away. Despite the intervention of local priest, Father Alex Reid, the soldiers were driven to waste ground, stripped, beaten and executed.

Northern Ireland Secretary Tom King condemned the killings and praised the soldiers for their, 'incredible restraint in using their loaded personal protection pistols only to fire a warning shot in the air.'

Images of the shocking attack were captured by journalists attending the funeral. The executions were also recorded on camera by a British Army helicopter surveillance team. Police are appealing for witnesses to assist in the hunt for the murderers.

# Belfast—20th March, 1988

## IRA Defend Republicans During Second Funeral Attack

The Provisional IRA has admitted responsibility for the deaths of two members of the SAS, executed after they launched an attack on the funeral of Vol. Caoimhin MacBrádaigh.

MacBrádaigh was shot dead four days ago by a Loyalist assassin while attending the burial of three comrades murdered by the SAS on Gibraltar. As his funeral cortege left Andersontown for the Republican plot at Milltown a VW Passat, driven by two plain-clothed members of the SAS, drove into the procession. The car's passenger fired shots into the crowd, causing terror among the mourners who feared a second attack by a UFF death squad.

Funeral stewards, on duty to prevent an attack similar to the outrage that occurred last week as Mairead Farrell, Sean Savage and Danny McCann were laid to rest, rushed to the scene, quickly overpowering the two soldiers and taking them away in a black taxi. They were subsequently shot by IRA members. Father Alex Reid of St Agnes Church was present to administer the last rites.

In its statement the IRA confirmed it had executed, 'two SAS members who launched an attack on the funeral cortege of our comrade.' It added that, unlike the three Republicans gunned down on the Rock, the men killed had been armed and only the swift reaction of funeral stewards prevented the deaths of innocent Catholic civilians.

# Monaghan—22nd March, 1988 (morning)

There's a voice, the stone-ring of an echo to it, the words densely filtered. I try drawing it down to me but it won't come. I stretch my limbs, putting my hands out, feeling cold clay under my fingers, my toes curling into gritty ground. The smell of soil, loamy and metallic, fills my nose and mouth with each tight breath. Darkness burns my eyes as I strain to see through absolute black. I'm lying in my own grave. The voice retreats; they're going to leave me here. I claw at the earth entombing me, feel it pattering down on my face like raindrops. The voice volumes up as I haul myself towards it. I make out my name. The blackness turns red, dawn light against closed eyes. The electric red becomes luminous orange, incandescent yellow: blinding white.

Patrick leans towards me.

'Welcome back, Caoilainn.'

My tongue is bloated. Words burn in my throat.

A bang resounds and a jolt charges up my arm: a remembered gunshot. I'm in bed in a white room. I sit, pushing a question through the flaming in my throat.

'Have I been shot?'

Patrick caresses my cheek. 'No, Caoilainn. You collapsed yesterday but you're fine.'

I feel over my body; head woolly, eyes gravelly, stomach clenching, hands throbbing. I lift them, flex stiff fingers, knuckles that are purple and puffy. They strain, tightness constricting movement. I plunge into hazy memories for an explanation that slips from my pain-charged grasp.

A doctor enters. 'Mrs Duffy, you're awake.' He scans the chart hanging at the bed's foot.

'What am I doing here?'

'You don't remember?' He glances at Patrick. 'That's not uncommon in cases of nervous collapse, a result of shock, brought on by stress and the exhaustion and dehydration you were suffering. How long have you been vomiting?'

Acid pools on my tongue, a Spanish motorway swings out of focus. Tommy yells for me to pull over.

'Since yesterday,' I say.

'A fortnight that I know of,' Patrick corrects.

A fucking fortnight? I gape at him.

The doctor replaces the chart, studies me. 'Twenty-four hours on fluids have you back to normal now.'

'Twenty-four hours?'

'I brought you here yesterday,' Patrick murmurs.

I search the view from the window. 'Where am I?'

'Monaghan,' Patrick replies.

'I want to go home.' The words are childish. I don't care. I want to fucking go home.

'I'd advise staying another night,' the doctor says, 'for observation. It's fortunate you didn't miscarry.'

'What?'

'Lose the baby,' he explains.

'Baby?'

'You didn't know you were pregnant?' he chides.

'I can't be. I'm on the pill.'

He tuts. 'Nature isn't so easily defied. If she insists on leaving you must ensure she rests, Mr Duffy.'

Fucking God-complex chauvinist. I start to get up. A sharp tug on my left arm stops me; a length of clear tubing, disappearing into a green vein, pulls taut.

'I will,' Patrick says.

The doctor strides out. Rage leeching away, I sink into the pillows, keep sinking, down through the bed, the floor and into the cool dark earth where I come to rest lying on my back, the world reduced to a thin shaft of light that I can close myself to. I shut my eyes.

They stopped being men when they were hauled from the car, becoming tumours to be ripped from Belfast's belly, monstrous and malignant, oozing the putrid puss of our eight hundred years war. Now they lie like fresh-picked scabs, bloodied and ragged around the edges. But they're not the cancer to be cut from our hearts; they're a symptom, not the cause, of our pain and rage and fear: they're victims of it as much as we ourselves.

Their naked bodies sprawl, raw-pastry pale, on the gravel-mottled ground. Limbs contort in agonising poses. Muscles pulse with pain. Their faces are the pulped flesh of rotten plums crushed underfoot. They whimper, lost kittens calling for the queen, and exhale breath rank with putrefying blood. Desolation vibrates the air; I feel the shivers against my cheeks. I can end their suffering.

Two moments collide, electrified wires touching, crossing, sparking: a horse, black and beautiful, eyes dark and pleading; a man, naked and bruised, lips trembling and pleading. I crouch, stroke, expect the silky texture of a coat, touch clammy, pimpled skin. I calm with sweeping caresses. In my other hand the gun's grip is warm. I rest the muzzle again the back of the skull. Fire once. The arm I soothe flops against my knee. I brush it aside and turn to the second man, brace for the second shot.

'Caoilainn, for Jesus sake, say something.' Patrick's shrill voice recalls me.

'The shot, it was me firing.'

The film in my head is paused on the image of two dead men. The frame twitches, held in place by an invisible thread. The thread snaps. The film rewinds; dead men stand, cars reverse, coffins rise from the ground, bullets return to barrels: Mairead skips backwards, turns and hugs me.

I throw off the bedcovers. A chill ripples across my bare legs.

'What are you doing?' Patrick demands as I strip the tape holding the drip in place.

'Going home.'

'The doctor said you should stay.'

I yank the tube from my arm. A scarlet jewel swells up. I obliterate it with my thumb and swing my legs off the bed.

'Where are my clothes?' I stand, the muscles in my thighs quivering under the sudden load. I sway.

Patrick grabs me, pushing me back onto the bed. He bends his face to mine.

'Caoilainn.' His eyes are bright with tears. 'It's my baby too.'

'I just want to go home, Patrick. Please.'

He rests his forehead against mine. 'Fine.'

# Ballygawley—22nd March, 1988 (evening)

While I was shooting two men, ending their lives, inside me a new one was humming, growing. Mine weren't the only bullets but they were the first, the fatal, ones.

We don't talk on the drive home. At the cottage Patrick offers his hand but I pull myself up, using the car door for support, and stagger, unaided, inside.

The house is damp with the cloy of decay. A vaseful of decomposing lilies putrefies the air. I stumble into the lounge and drop onto the sofa.

'Do you want tea?'

My mouth is still dry, my tongue rough. 'Please.'

He clatters around the kitchen. The kettle whistles. He returns with two mugs, lights the fire and sits beside me.

'You remember,' he says.

'Yes.'

'I'm sorry, Caoilainn.'

'What the hell are you sorry for?'

'I just meant... Mairead... I know how close you were.'

Mairead. She shouldn't have been on that mission. It was a fucking mistake. I'll never know whose. Grief and anger grip me, crush me. Muscles tense, lungs stutter, fists clench. I feel myself petrifying from the inside out.

Patrick sighs. 'I love you. I'll take care of you. We're in this together.' His words set off a seismic shudder that threatens to crack my stony core. I hold myself rigid.

'You're in nothing and the only thing I'm in's a fucking mess.'

'Don't say that.' He lays a hand on my knee. 'It's a chance for something good to happen.'

'Were you at MacBrádaigh's funeral?'

Patrick drops his gaze.

'So you know.' I hold up my bruised knuckles. 'How can there be anything good for me?'

'It's not for us to decide.' He takes my hands, wrapping them tenderly in his.

'Bollocks it isn't. I chose this life, the consequences are mine alone.'

'No!' He crunches my hands, telegraphing pain up my arms. 'You chose to fight but you didn't start the war. And you can't end it, either. But you can survive it.'

'How?'

'Marry me.'

'No.'

I send Patrick away; I can't see anything cowering behind him. As his Mercedes skitters over the gravel his shoulders hunch and shake. He lifts a hand from the wheel, rubs his face. Watching him hurts, pain I deserve. Three phone calls and I've cut myself off, telling Danny to stay in Belfast, getting Liam to keep the unit away, asking Brendan to hold the Army at a distance. They think it's grief; I don't correct them.

A storm blows into the valley, drumming the slates into submission, draping the cottage in a rain-grey shroud. I curl up at the window, watching droplets racing each other down the pane, falling into a growing puddle on the windowsill that drowns them. For as long as the storm lasts there are always more raindrops willing to race for the victory line that destroys them as soon as they reach it.

By morning the sky has cleared, the storm exhausted by its own anger, and I've endured: survived. I sit outside in the dappled dawn, marshalling thoughts that skirmish to overpower me. I rank them, call roll:

Patrick loves me.

This would make him happy.

I want him to be happy.

I love him.

I've fought for so long, no surrendering.

The fight is unfinishable.

I've already surrendered to it.

There's been too much death, too little life.

This is my penance.

And my revenge.

It's not a no-choice choice; it's a free-choice one.

*

# Dublin—3rd April, 1988 (Easter Sunday)

Patrick checks us into the hotel. I take his car to the safe house where Brendan is waiting for me.

In a bright clean living room, surrounded by polish-fresh furniture and watched over by the Virgin Mary, we drink tea.

'How are you?' he asks.

'Fine.' Nausea tugs at my stomach.

He offers me a cigarette.

'No, thanks.'

'You'll be there tomorrow?'

'I will.'

'Grand.'

I sip the tea, swallowing before the taste can settle on my tongue, gagging me.

'It's been an awful few weeks, so it has,' he says.

'Was Gibraltar a set up?'

He taps ash into a saucer. 'It's possible.'

'We've a collaborator?'

'Maybe.'

'But you won't say who you're suspecting?'

'I won't.' He frowns at me. 'Collusion's a serious charge to lay.'

'It's a serious betrayal,' I reply. 'Treason.'

'You want to watch who you're saying that to,' he cautious. 'You don't want to light that fuse and have the bomb go off under you.'

I reach for my cigarettes, sliding the packet between my fingers but resisting drawing one out.

'Take me off active service.'

'Don't knee-jerk. There're plenty who still believe in military action. We're not done yet.'

'I am, for a while, anyway.'

He pinches the bridge of his nose. 'Ah, how long?'

'About nine months.'

He coughs; tea dribbles down his chin. He wipes at it. I light the cigarette that's been tormenting me, take a deep drag and revel in the nicotine buzz.

'Jesus, really?'

'Aye.'

'But you'll come back?'

'Depends on what I'll be coming back to: for.'

'Fair enough. Well, good on you.'

He sees me to the door, shaking my hand. 'If you ever need help with anything you know where to reach me,' he says.

'Thanks.'


The crowd in O'Connell Street is a blend of tourists and locals. Milling among them, hiding in plain sight, are Oglaigh na hEireann members, congregated in Dublin for the Easter Commemorations. A few faces I recognise; others recognise me and I know them by their stares.

We stand near the GPO steps as Haughey, the incumbent Taoiseach, reads the Proclamation. I imagine Daideo, sixteen, fair and full of fight, standing there alongside Pearse, his long war just beginning. I take Patrick's hand and tow him through the throng to the site where Nelson used to leer down on the Dublin peasantry. Today nothing marks the spot except my own faded memory.

'What are we looking at?' Patrick asks as I sweep the bare ground with my eyes, crane my neck to the blank sky and trace a running star of light that plumes into an orange cloud.

'The past,' I reply. 'Not much to it, is there?' I tug his arm and we walk on.


After eating in an Italian bistro we wander the city, stopping when my stomach revolts against tomato pasta, ejecting my dinner into the nearest gutter.

'Are you OK?' Patrick asks, rubbing my back.

'Fine. It'll pass soon.'

We reach the Garden of Remembrance and wander over twilit lawns, darkening to Connemara green in the failing light. Behind them the Rotunda Hospital rises proudly. From a high window a face, shadowed by the glow of florescent lighting, peers down on us.

'That's where he was, after the Rising.' I point to the window.

'Your granddaddy?'

'Aye. Wonder what he'd make of this.'

Patrick loops his arm around my waist. 'I'm sure he'd be glad to know you're safe.'

We circle the garden twice then head for Parnell Square, Sinn Fein HQ.

'Sure you won't let me come in with you?' Patrick asks for the third time.

'No.'

'What are you going to say?'

'I don't know. Maybe nothing. Maybe everything.'

'Is that a good idea?'

'Don't worry.'

'How can I not?' he asks.

'It'll be grand, Patrick.'

'I'll wait up.'

He kisses me and we part at the door, him lingering to watch me cross the threshold.

The back room is filled with Republicans, some constitutionalists, others physical force men and women and a few who, I suspect, straddle the line. I sit towards the back, marking faces I know and wondering which of them I might not really know at all. Hughes is there. He nods at me, takes a seat nearer the front. A minute later Kevin joins him. Martin appears and sits across the way. The Sinn Fein leadership file out and line up behind the long table, Gerry Adams in the centre, flanked by his advisors. The meeting is called to order and opened with a minute's silence in honour of the 1916 dead and more recently fallen comrades. I think of Mairead. 'Thank you for the days, those endless days, those...' I'll always wonder, never know, why she was taken.

The speeches commence, grand rhetoric, calling for resistance, promising hope, inspiring courage: familiar rallying cries. Puny words, sounds that die as they're born.

The floor is opened to questions. Arms spring up. Someone asks about election prospects. Someone else raises the party's welfare policy. A female voice enquires about the role of women in the party. Slick political ripostes regress me.

I'm fifteen, clutching a placard I painted myself and chanting a slogan put into my mouth...

I'm eleven, sitting on a wooden floor in a packed town hall with a view of afros, afghans, cornrows and headscarves...

I'm six, squeezing a hand covered with henna tattoos and following bell-bottom jeans through a sea of people...

I'm four, feeding the ducks in the park with my grandfather...

'When the power of love overcomes the love of power there will be peace.'

'The government is the problem, we can be the solution.'

'Nothing about us without us.'

'If things aren't fair, fight to make them fair.'

The elastic yo-yoing me to and fro snaps. I'm dropped into now.

The woman who tabled the female agenda is still holding the floor. She's stood up. I don't recognise her. She's asking about our children's future. What future? What fucking future? She's satisfied with platitudes. I seethe silently. Someone redirects her question, asking about the current situation, future strategies.

'Our position is clear. It will never, ever change. The war against British rule must continue until freedom is achieved,' Adams says, his baritone rolling heavy over the audience.

I stand. Adams' eyes fall on me. He smiles and gestures for me to speak.

I swallow the urge to puke. 'Aye but what kind of freedom? Freedom from what, to do what?'

There is a very loud, dumb silence.

I'll never get the answer I need here because the only person I'm certain understands the question is the person asking it. And it's taken her twenty-six fucking years just to get that far.

This is how it ends; not with the banging of a gun but with the popping of a bubble.

I head for the way out. Audibly purposeful footsteps trail me. I squash down panic and force myself to walk, not run.

In the street I turn to face my pursuers: Brendan and Kevin. I don't untense.

'What was that about?' Kevin demands.

'We're either doomed to repeat the past or obliged to break with it,' I tell him, 'Dead one way, damned the other. Let me know when you've fucking decided which it's to be. I'll be waiting: ready.'

I pat Brendan's arm then stroll back to the hotel where Patrick waits for me.

# Ballygawley—15<sup>th</sup> April, 1988

Tommy, Joe and Ciaran are gutted when I tell them I'm taking leave but they understand, wish me well. Connor and Briege are chuffed. While Briege is offering me Saoirse's baby things I hear Connor in the background telling her she'll have a wee cousin to play with. I choke on the burning in my throat. She should have sisters or brothers, not a pretend cousin related only by a severed strand of the past. Danny's grand about it too, my worries that he'd consider it a betrayal of Aiden dissolving as soon as he smiles and hugs me. He comes with me to tell Frank and Nora. Their exclaimed congratulations are too bright; I can hear the faint resonance of Nora's grief for Aiden in her words and Frank's remorse for me in his. I hold his gaze; he shuffles off to make tea.

I stay long enough to see Callum in from college. He clears the bed of textbooks, calculations and formulas so we can sit. At seventeen and a half he's old and young enough to blush when I tell him. He manages a muttered, 'good on yous,' but doesn't look me in the eye until I switch to asking about his studies. He's a place at Queen's come autumn, if he gets the grades. By the erectness of his spine and the fierceness in his voice I know he believes he will. I believe it too. Callum is the reason I regret nothing.

There's only Liam to tell now. I can't stall any longer. My face is hot with shame at how I let our friendship collapse. I should never have doubted him but trapped in that maze of suspicions and fears I couldn't risk following anyone, or letting anyone follow me. Outside, looking back in, I feel bloody stupid. I was so panicked over an exit I couldn't find that I missed the one in fucking front of me. We've been friends so long. I don't know what we are now. My mistake, but not my fault. War is hardest on the survivors.

I pick up the phone, start dialling, fingers faltering over the simple task. It takes five attempts before I track Liam down, time I fill holding hypothetical conversations with him that heavy my anxiety about his reaction. Imagining him angry, disappointed, sad, I'm not sure which I dread most. Finally his real voice echoes down the line.

'Hello?'

'It's me.'

Pause. Then, 'How're you?'

'OK. You?'

'Fine.'

Silence. I wait for him to ask, realise he's waiting for me to say.

'I've something to tell you.'

'I know.'

'Oh.'

'Hughes rang.'

'Oh.'

Pause. Then, 'I'm happy for yous, you and Patrick.'

'Thanks.' Pause. Line, please? 'Sorry I didn't... I couldn't...'

'Sure, you've no need to apologise. I understand. You've had enough.'

'Haven't we all?'

'Aye.' Pause. Still pausing. Then, 'Keep in touch, let me know how you are, if you need anything.'

'I will. Thanks. Same goes.' Pause. 'Liam...' Pause. 'Be safe.'

'Always. And you.'

The phone clicks as he rings off. I hang up, deflated. That was easier than I deserved it to be. We'll not make a full recovery but there's still breath in us.

'Alright?' Patrick asks, looking up from his newspaper as I enter the living room.

I sink onto the sofa beside him. Everyone is happy for us: even me. 'Jesus, you know, I think I actually am.'

He chuckles, tosses the paper and curls around me.

'About bloody time.'

A mist rises, shading the world with an opaque wash, hazing details, fading colours. I live inside myself where poppy red blood flows, candy-floss pink cells multiply by dividing and life purrs with a steady, rumbling pulse. I become a closed system, needing nothing in, giving nothing out, a symbiotic circuit in which I feed off myself and myself feeds off me until we are ripe and contented.

Things happen around me but they are external: superfluous. I move through them in a meditative state of full awareness but relaxed detachment, revelling in the pleasure of watching myself from the inside out as I eat, walk, rest. This is the state I'm in when Patrick and I get married. The vows are repeated in my voice, I give my hand for the ring and know this is what I want without attachment to the idea of it crushing down on me.

I drift, my inflated belly breaking the water's tranquil surface, keeping me afloat.

# Ballygawley—14ᵗʰ October, 1988

The mist lifts. Colours deepen. Details are delineated. My son is born. As soon as he slid out of me, bloodied and screaming, I gave him his birthright: 'Fáilte go hÉirinn♥, Cian Enda Devoy-Duffy.'

Now he sleeps wrapped in a blanket knitted by Nora, dressed in a baby-grow sent by Briege and Connor, cuddling a teddy bought by Danny. But Cian Enda Devoy-Duffy is not their kin. The Fenian blood in his veins is mine, ancient and enduring, marked by Cian, echoed in Enda and underscored by Devoy.

The bedroom door opens. Patrick smiles in at us.

'Is he sleeping?'

'He is.' I'm sitting on the bed, peering through the bars of his cot at the wrinkled face, the eyes, now closed, that blinked, blue glittering, at me: Daideo's eyes.

'Are you OK?' Patrick murmurs, perching beside me.

'Oh, aye, grand, having just squeezed something the size of a watermelon out of a hole you couldn't hardly get a matchstick through,' I joke.

Patrick shudders and rubs my back.

'No, I'm fine. It takes more than that to break me,' I say with a grin.

'I don't think there's anything can break you,' Patrick replies.

I stretch forward, pulling my empty belly taut, to stroke the doughy cheek, brush the downy hair and scrape my thumb against the sharp fingernails smaller than a match-head. 'Let's hope we never find out.'

We watch Cian sleep.

'Are you happy?' Patrick asks.

'Are you?'

'I am.'

'That's two of us.'

'Go raibh maith agat.'

I laugh. 'What're you thanking me for?'

---

♥ Welcome to Ireland

Patrick gestures to the cot. 'I mean it. Go raibh maith agat. Tá mé i ngrá leat.'

'Tá fáilte romhat. Tá mé i ngrá leat fosta.' I lean against him, letting the weight off my spine and shoulders for an instant.

Patrick brushes my hair, blonde again, growing out of its Army crop. 'You did it, Caoilainn,' he says. 'You survived. Your war is over.'

Cian stirs, bringing a hand to his face, fingers curled into a peaceful fist. The fear that must have swarmed Daideo's heart when he looked on newborn me fills mine now, a codicil to his legacy. I understand why he sent me away.

I straighten up, a reassuringly familiar load pressing down through me.

My war isn't over: it's just been reborn.

# Belfast—4th May, 1989

## Hunt for Missing IRA Girl
## 'Blonde Bomber' Disappears
## in Republican Heartlands

Police are searching for clues in the disappearance of a prominent Republican woman who went missing from her Tyrone home sometime yesterday.

Caoilainn Duffy, nee Devoy, (27) was last seen on Tuesday when she returned to her remote cottage in Ballygawley after spending the weekend in Belfast with her husband, well-known Republican lawyer Patrick Duffy, and their eight month old son.

Mrs Duffy is described as; 5ft 5inches tall, slim build with fair shoulder length hair. She was last seen wearing jeans and a leather jacket, riding a Norton Navigator motorbike, registration BHZ 9144.

Police were alerted to Mrs Duffy's disappearance after she failed to return to Belfast on Wednesday morning as planned. Concerns were raised when the motorbike she was travelling on was found abandoned on the A5 near the border with the Irish Republic. A search of the Ballygawley cottage confirmed that she appeared not to have taken significant personal possessions with her. An RUC spokesman said they were investigating possible connections between Mrs Duffy's Republican activity and her disappearance but refused to comment on whether they suspected the involvement of Loyalist paramilitaries.

A friend of the family said they were worried for Mrs Duffy, adding, 'She's never gone off like this before. It's not like her. She's a loving mother and wouldn't just abandon her wee boy.'

In 1985 Mrs Duffy, then using the name Kaylynn Ryan, was convicted for IRA membership. She was also tried for the 1982 Hyde Park and Regent's Park bombings that killed eleven members of the Household Cavalry but the case against her collapsed when it was revealed that charges had been brought solely on the word of a 'supergrass'. She served two years in Armagh jail. There is speculation that she returned to active service with the IRA on her release and only left the Movement following the birth of her son.

Sinn Fein have confirmed they are aware of Mrs Duffy's disappearance and announced they are conducting their own investigation into the circumstances surrounding it. A

Republican spokesman said, 'In cases like this is it clear the RUC have little interest in doing their jobs,'

Police denied Mrs Duffy's past would have any bearing on their efforts to find her and asked Mrs Duffy or anyone who knows of her current whereabouts to contact them.

Inquiries into her disappearance are ongoing.

...our part
To murmur name upon name,
As a mother names her child
When sleep at last has come

*Easter 1916* by W. B. Yeats

## Killed by the Troubles

| | | |
|---|---|---|
| Fiona Finnighan | 3 September 1963 | Monaghan |
| Cathal Finnighan | 11 May 1964 | Monaghan |
| Fergus O'Neill | 18 January 1978 | Derry |
| William Stephenson | 31 December 1980 | Belfast |
| Patrick William Finnighan | 29 April 1981 | Dublin |
| Bobby Sands | 5 May 1981 | H-Block, Maze |
| Frances Hughes | 12 May 1981 | H-Block, Maze |
| Raymond McCreesh | 21 May 1981 | H-Block, Maze |
| Patsy O'Hara | 21 May 1981 | H-Block, Maze |
| Joe McDonnel | 18 July 1981 | H-Block, Maze |
| Martin Hurson | 13 July 1981 | H-Block, Maze |
| Kevin Lynch | 1 August 1981 | H-Block, Maze |
| Kieran Doherty | 2 August 1981 | H-Block, Maze |
| Thomas McIlwee | 8 August 1981 | H-Block, Maze |
| Mickey Devine | 20 August 1981 | H-Block, Maze |
| Richard Hanson | 3 October 1981 | Belfast |
| Cathy Keenan | 25 December 1981 | Belfast |
| Steven Carlton | 9 January 1982 | Belfast |
| Anthony Rapley | 25 March 1982 | Belfast |
| Nicholas Malakos | 25 March 1982 | Belfast |
| Daniel Holland | 25 March 1982 | Belfast |
| Anthony Daly | 20 July 1982 | London |
| Simon Tipper | 20 July 1982 | London |
| Jeffrey Young | 20 July 1982 | London |
| Roy Bright | 20 July 1982 | London |

| | | |
|---|---|---|
| Graham Barker | 20 July 1982 | London |
| Robert Livingstone | 20 July 1982 | London |
| John McKnight | 20 July 1982 | London |
| George Mesure | 20 July 1982 | London |
| Keith Powell | 20 July 1982 | London |
| Laurence Smith | 20 July 1982 | London |
| John Heritage | 20 July 1982 | London |
| Brian Campbel | 14 December 1983 | Coalisland |
| Colm McGirr | 4 December 1983 | Coalisland |
| Aiden O'Neill | 4 December 1983 | Coalisland |
| Noel Lane1 | 7 December 1983 | London |
| Jane Arbuthnot | 17 December 1983 | London |
| Philip Geddes | 17 December 1983 | London |
| Kenneth Salvsan | 17 December 1983 | London |
| Jasmine Cochrane-Patrick | 17 December 1983 | London |
| Stephen Dodd | 24 December 1983 | London |
| Anthony Berry1 | 2 October 1984 | Brighton |
| Eric Taylor | 12 October 1984 | Brighton |
| Roberta Wakeham1 | 2 October 1984 | Brighton |
| Jeanne Shattock | 12 October 1984 | Brighton |
| Muriel Machean | 13 November 1984 | Brighton |
| David Henderson | 4 December 1984 | Belfast |
| Brendan Gallagher | 26 December 1984 | Newcastle |
| Declan Arthurs | 8 May 1987 | Loughgall |
| Seamus Donnelly | 8 May 1987 | Loughgall |
| Michael Gormley | 8 May 1987 | Loughgall |
| Eugene Kelly | 8 May 1987 | Loughgall |
| Patrick Kelly | 8 May 1987 | Loughgall |
| James Lynagh | 8 May 1987 | Loughgall |
| Patrick McKearney | 8 May 1987 | Loughgall |
| Gerard O'Callaghan | 8 May 1987 | Loughgall |
| Anthony Hughes | 8 May 1987 | Loughgall |
| Rupert Wilkinson | 22 July 1987 | Ballymackilroy |
| Christopher Bates | 22 July 1987 | Ballymackilroy |
| Lee Weston | 23 July 1987 | Fivemiletown |